The Bitter Dawning

SARA FRASER

The Bitter Dawning

WARNER BOOKS

A *Warner* Book

Copyright © Roy Clews 1989

First published in Great Britain in 1989
by Futura
Published by Warner in 1994
This edition published in 1998

ISBN 0 7515 1302 4

Typeset in Baskerville by Fleet Graphics, Enfield, Middlesex

Printed in England by Clays Ltd, St Ives plc

Warner Books
A Division of
Little, Brown and Company (UK)
Brettenham House
Lancaster Place
London WC2E 7EN

Introduction

Ireland in the 1840s. A tragic land rent by famine and
rebellion. Grainne MacDermott, young and beautiful,
came back to her home-land to face hunger, suffering and
danger. She was also, in the midst of sorrow, to find
love . . .

Chapter One

The west of Ireland, February 1847

The winter dawn came with a grey harshness and in the market square of Clonakilty a woman, ravaged by hunger, stood with her dead baby in her arms. Around her shivered a mass of other ragged, skeletal women and men, some with skull-headed children whimpering at their knees. But only she cradled death to loving breasts.

Behind the crowd in the square the lights of the Clonakilty Hotel shone through tall windows, and smoke rose from its chimneys as those within prepared to welcome the travellers that daylight would bring to their doors. The starving crowd turned its attention towards the awakening hotel, staring at its bow-windows and lifting wasted hands in silent supplication whenever a bustling figure was glimpsed behind the fine net curtains. The woman did not turn with the crowd, however. She remained motionless, her sunken eyes fixed on a bend in the road around which the night Mail Coach moving from Cork to Skibereen would make its appearance.

It came with a slippery clatter of hooves and iron-bound wheels over frosted ruts, the breath from the horses' panting lungs wreathing their sweating muzzles and clinging in tiny beads to the clipped manes. The red-faced, well-muffled coachman hauled on the leaders' reins to slow them, and with him on top of the swaying coach the three dark green uniformed troopers of the Royal Irish Constabulary roused from their drowsy, cold boredom and checked the priming of their carbine guns. They were there to protect the valuable mails from wretches made desperate by hunger.

'Whooaaa, whooaaa! Pull up! Pull up, dammye!' the coachman's whisky-hoarse voice cursed his team, and his long whip cracked sharply in the freezing air to warn off any boldly importunate beggars. The coach lurched and juddered to a standstill, jerking both of its inside passengers into a chilled, stiff wakefulness.

James Mahoney cursed his painful bones under his breath; he was a middle-aged man, fashionably clad in a fur-collared blue paletot, velvet waistcoat and tight plaid trousers, a large scarf-cravat around his neck. His long grey-flecked side-whiskers and curled black hair added to his dandified appearance, while his dark brown eyes and olive complexion suggested a Mediterranean ancestry. He stretched and yawned, then thrust aside the leather curtain covering the coach window.

'Dear God in Heaven!' he gasped aloud, eyes widening with horror as they registered the scene in the square.

The woman lifted her dead baby towards the coach, and through the dirt-mottled glass Mahoney saw her lips move and heard her cracked voice begging him for money with which to bury the pitiful little corpse.

His eyes flickered up and down, up and down, from the blue-white face of the dead infant to the grey-blue face of its tragic mother.

'A tanner, your Honour, for the love o' God, spare me a tanner to bury me babby. 'Tis not for meself I ask it, but for to bury me babby.'

Muffled by the glass the woman's cracked voice assailed the man's senses, smothering all else in his consciousness and his hands went to his pockets seeking for coins.

'No! Don't pass her any money here!'

Mahoney jerked round in surprise to stare at his fellow passenger. She was a poorly clad young woman, not much more than a girl in years, and in the cold grey light of dawn she was a vivid flame of beauty, with her long lustrous black hair tumbling about her shoulders, framing her pale face and lucent green eyes. His lips moved to frame protest, but before the words could be uttered his fellow-passenger lifted her own hand to display the coins she held in it.

'Don't worry, I intend that the poor soul shall have this to bury her child with. But if those others in the square see you give her something then they'll take it from her before you can blink. So please, go on into the hotel, and I'll follow. I'll make sure that the poor soul gets this money without anyone knowing of it.'

Still stupefied by the shock of what he was witnessing, the man allowed himself to be directed, and after a momentary hesitation obeyed this green-eyed girl.

The peat fire glowed hotly in the dining room grate, and on the table a breakfast platter of mutton chops and devilled kidneys gave off an inviting scent. James Mahoney took one bite of the tender meat then experienced a wave of nausea as he saw again in his mind's eye the blue-white face of the dead infant. He spat the half-chewed meat from his mouth and snatching up the steaming cup of coffee before him drank deeply.

The hotel keeper came through the door as his guest spat out the food, and his plump features frowned anxiously.

'Is it the meat that's bad, your Honour?'

Mahoney shook his head. 'No.' He paused, and then pointed to the window behind him which gave onto the square. 'I cannot eat for thinking of those poor devils out there.'

The hotel keeper smoothed his white apron with both hands and answered commiseratingly. 'Sure, and I understand your Honour's feelings, and they do you credit . . .' He shrugged his fat shoulders expressively, 'But what can be done, Sir? There are thousands of the poor craturs wandering the land. Sure it'll get worse before it gets better.'

The seated man indicated the food on the table, the new-baked bread, the heaped platter of meat, the rich yellow butter. 'I cannot eat this. Give it to the people in the square.'

Alarm registered among the puffy folds of the other's

9

face. 'Jasus, Joseph and Mary! 'Tis more than I dare do, Sir. There'd be a bloody riot. They'd be at each other like mad dogs to snatch a bite.'

James Mahoney realized instantly the truth of the man's words, and felt a sense of anger that yet again he had shown stupidity in suggesting what he had after what the young woman in the coach had told him. Thinking of her he wondered that she had not yet appeared in the hotel, and he asked, 'Where is the young lady who was a passenger with me?'

The fat features of the other registered puzzlement. 'The young lady, Sir?' Then recognition came. 'Ohhh, you'll be meaning the wee MacDermott girl, young Grainne. Her that was over in England 'til now. She's gone on her way, Sir. There was a fella with a horse and car happened to be here who lives up along by her family outside Skibereen. He's given her the lift.'

To his own surprise James Mahoney felt a faint sense of chagrin. Beauty was a rare thing, and he would have greatly enjoyed seeing and talking with her again. He made a gesture of dismissal with be-ringed fingers. 'No matter,' he murmured, 'No matter.'

Turning his chair about he sat for long moments staring through the net-curtained window at the victims of famine. Then, from a flat leather-covered case at his side he took black lead pencils and heavy-textured cartridge paper. His hands moved rapidly and he breathed in deep concentration as on the blank surface the likeness began to appear of a ragged-shawled woman with haunted eyes carrying a dead baby in her arms . . .

'Many thanks to you, Mr Maguire.' Grainne MacDermott lifted her small bundle of belongings from the seat of the jaunting-car.

The old man lifted his hand in acknowledgement and put his horse into motion. Grainne turned and walked along the rough track which led to the isolated cabin she called home. The wind had risen and its icy gusts penetrated the threadbare gown she wore, causing her to shiver and to draw her shawl closer about her head and shoulders. The stony track was harsh to her bare feet and for a brief instant she regretted the sale of the shoes she had worn during her time in England, then smiled wryly. 'There's people dying from hunger here, and I'm pining for shoes. Haven't I become the fair, fine lady!'

Dotted about the bleak undulating country surrounding her were mud-walled cabins, but from only a few of their chimneys was smoke rising. The vast majority stood desolate and abandoned. Sudden anxious doubts crowded upon her, causing her to hasten her steps. 'Dear God, let my Mammy be still here,' she prayed silently. 'Let her still be living.'

In sight of her own cabin she gusted a sigh of relief. Smoke was wafting from its chimney, and although it looked as tumbledown and semi-derelict as those she had passed on her way, the evidence of continued habitation were the two children listlessly rummaging in the weed-strewn potato patch. When they saw the approaching girl the children ran into the cabin calling for their mother, and Grainne's heart began to pound as from the door a woman came. At the sight of Grainne the woman's hands went to her mouth and for a moment or two she stood motionless, then with a cry she came hurrying with outstretched arms.

A sob tore from Grainne's throat and dropping her bundle she ran towards her mother. Laughing and crying simultaneously the two women hugged and kissed fiercely, incoherent babblings of words tumbling from their lips, and within Grainne's mind she cried her thanks to her Maker that He had brought her safely back to her home.

Gradually the two women's overwrought emotions calmed sufficiently for them to be able to look at each other with searching eyes, each secretly disturbed by what they found. Theresa MacDermott gently stroked her daughter's thin face.

'Holy Mother o' God, but ye're not a wee girl any longer now, but a full-grown woman. But you've little enough flesh on your bones, honey. What happened to your fine situation in England? I'd thought you'd be set for life with

11

Lady Dunsmore, and wasn't she going to have you trained as a housekeeper some day and all?'

Grainne smiled ironically. She had gone to England some four years previously, aged only fifteen, as a lady's maid in the service of Lady Dunsmore. 'Lady Dunsmore was kind enough, Mammy, but her menfolk thought that all the female servants were there to be used for their own pleasures.' She chuckled as she saw the shock of alarm in her mother's face, and patted the older woman's careworn cheek reassuringly. 'Now don't fret yourself, Mammy, I've not been ruined! I've not become a fallen woman. I never let any of them make free with me, nor any other man either, come to that.' Sparks of mischief danced in her green eyes as she said laughingly, 'Wasn't I brought up to be a good Catholic girl, Mammy? Do you think I'd put myself in a state of mortal sin by tumbling about in the bed with a man, and me not wed to him?' She could not repress a gurgle of laughter at her mother's shocked expression. 'Oh, I'm very worldly wise now, Mammy. England has taught me a lot about the wicked sinful ways of this world.

'Anyway, like I said, the family menfolk thought they could have their pleasure with any of the servant girls they'd a fancy for, but I crowned the eldest son with a warming pan when he tried to force me into his bed.'

The elder woman's jaw dropped in awed astonishment, and again Grainne's laughter gurgled uncontrollably.

'So out I was sent, from the house, and from Lady Dunsmore's service without a character reference to bless myself with. I tried to find other work, but times are sore hard over in England as well, and without a character reference it was impossible to find a situation, and it was either starve or go to the bad entirely. So, not wanting to end my days as a kept trollop or a street whore, I scraped together what money I could, and came back to home.'

'And me heart's full o' thanks that you have come home, my love,' her mother exclaimed fervently. 'But God in His Heaven knows, the times are cruel hard here just now. People are dying from the hunger.'

The sparkle in Grainne's eyes dulled, and she nodded

soberly. 'I know that, Mammy. I've seen some terrible sights on the road from Cork to here.' She examined her mother's face with concern, noting that the flesh around one eye was bruised and swollen. 'I see that Da is still treating you like a dog,' she stated bitterly.

A deep flush rose from the older woman's throat and crimsoned her face. Her gaze fell as if unable to meet her daughter's anger, and hesitantly she told her. 'There's a lot changed since you left, honey, and though it shames me I'll have to tell you the truth on it. Your Daddy's gone from here. When the hunger fell upon the land he just upped and went one morning.'

'What?' Grainne could hardly credit what she was hearing. 'You're telling me that he just up and left you and the kids to fend for yourselves?'

Her mother nodded miserably, and her faded eyes filled with tears. 'I was desperate, Grainne,' she whispered hoarsely, 'I'd no one to turn to, not even the priest, because old Father Gilmore's died since you left, and I couldn't go to Father Boyce, him and your Daddy being so opposed in the politicking.'

Sudden comprehension illuminated Grainne's mind and she broke into her mother's recital. 'You've taken up with another man, is that it, Mammy?'

Shamefacedly her mother nodded.

'Who?' Grainne wanted to know.

'With your Daddy's brother, Jim.'

'Holy Mother o' God!' Grainne ejaculated in disgust. 'What possessed you, Mammy? What possessed you to take up with that useless drunken scut?'

Her mother now displayed a smoulder of sullen resentment. 'You've no right to becall me, or him. You weren't here. You were over the water there with a full belly and a fire to warm yourself by. You've no right to sit in judgement on me.'

'I'm not judging you,' Grainne stated sadly, 'I'm just wishing that you'd found yourself a better man, that's all.' She pointed a finger at the older woman's swollen eye. 'He did that, I suppose.'

At first Theresa MacDermott made no reply, only stood with a sulky expression. Then she sniffed loudly. 'He'd the drink in him. When he's sober he's all right. And anyway, it was me own fault for nagging at him.'

Grainne's heart sank at hearing her mother's words. Although she loved the woman dearly, she knew that Theresa MacDermott was one of those women who needed a man, any man, and once she had found a man who would live with her, then she would endure insults and brutality from him for as long as he stayed with her. Grainne realized that, for the time being at least, she could only accept the present situation, but she essayed one last effort.

'But I'm home to help you now, Mammy. Between us we can manage without anyone else.'

Theresa MacDermott's weak features moulded into a stubborn mask. 'You'll have to try and get on with your Uncle Jim while you're here, Grainne.'

The girl accepted temporary defeat. 'All right Mammy, I'll try,' she told the older woman quietly. 'I've a few shillings left with me, so I'll not be a burden to you, at least.' She retrieved her fallen bundle, and arm in arm they made their way inside the cabin.

Chapter Two

Daniel Shonley was a descendant of Kings, his ancestors had walked the Halls of Tara as Princes of the Gael. At least, this is what the gentle, feckless, impoverished Squireen repeatedly told his dearly loved English wife, Charlotte, and his equally dearly loved children, Conrad aged twenty years, the twins Sean and Mairead aged fourteen, nine-year-old Martin, and even his baby daughter.

Now, the descendant of Kings worked like a brute beast in an effort to feed his family.

The raw streak of new road pushed into the bog. Along its length swarms of ragged men, women, even children wielded spades or swung heavy hammers to break boulders into small pieces of stone. The bitterly cold wind gusted hails of rain, and adults cursed and children whimpered as the icy moisture penetrated already sodden rags.

'Would you look at it, Pa!' Conrad Shonley spat in disgust. 'The Great Road to Nowhere!' He was tall, and despite months of hardship and want his lean body was still broad-shouldered and muscular.

Daniel Shonley let his long-helved hammer rest its iron head on the boulder in front of him. His face was thin and haggard, his blue eyes deep-sunk, and the bony frame of his emaciated torso could be clearly seen through the rents in his clothing. He coughed harsh and chokingly, and despite the cold his body was hot and feverish. 'By God, I'm not well this day, son,' he told the young man when he could speak without choking, 'certainly I'm not.'

Con Shonley fought down the rush of sympathy that

15

threatened momentarily to overwhelm him. He had long learned that to give in to emotion only weakened men's resolve to survive this bitter time. He looked beyond his father to where in a crowd of women and children, the twins, Sean and Mairead, were also exerting all their puny strength to carry baskets of broken stone to fill holes in the made-up roadway.

These particular roadworks were only a minute fraction of the vast government scheme controlled by the Board of Works to give employment to Ireland's starving hordes. Eight pence a day for men, four pence a day for a woman or child, and men, women and children walked up to six miles each way from their homes, and fought to get onto the works payrolls. But the wages were not sufficient to feed them properly. Food prices had soared, the market manipulated by speculators and the local money-lenders, the Gombeen Men. This latter breed fattened like loathsome carrion-eaters on the sufferings of their fellow countrymen.

Spitting on his hands, Con Shonley lifted the hammer above his head, and grunting with effort brought it smashing down upon the boulder, the impact jarring up the helve of the hammer through his arms and shoulders. Again he swung the hammer high, but this time arrested it above his head and stared intently down the road. A body of spade-carrying men led by a small priest wearing a shabby black cassock and a broad-brimmed, low-crowned hat, had come onto the site and were marching purposefully towards the rough wooden and turf shanty where the Chief Overseer of the Works had his office.

Daniel Shonley, noting his son's sudden interest, used his hand to shield his eyes from the driving rain, and stared in the same direction. 'Who is the priest, Con? My eyes aren't strong enough to see him clearly.'

The youth let the hammer fall. 'It's Father Boyce, Pa, from Leap.' He named a neighbouring village, nearer the coast than Skibereen.

Daniel Shonley groaned aloud. 'Then it's trouble come, sure enough.'

'If it's trouble for Kearney, then that makes me happy,'

16

Con remarked grimly. Kearney, the Chief Overseer and local Gombeen Man, was cordially hated by all the workforce except for those few he favoured at the expense of the rest. The youth glanced about him, and saw the assistant overseers and gangsmen leaving their workgangs and hurrying towards the shanty.

'I think I'll take a wee walk myself, Pa. See what's afoot.'

Before he had taken two steps he felt his father's hands clutch his arm.

'Keep away from it, you young fool!' Fear caused Daniel Shonley to speak harshly. 'You know well that wherever that damned priest shows his long nose, there's trouble follows like day upon night.'

Con paused, reluctant to exert his strength to free himself from the older man's weak grasp. 'Father Boyce only does what is right, Pa, and well you know it,' he argued hotly.

'The man's nothing but a damned rebel!' his father rejoined, equally hotly. 'He's a Young Irelander, one of Smith O'Brian's crew. He wants to bring about rebellion against the Queen.'

Conrad Shonley's quick temper flashed. 'And he's right to want to do so, Pa. What has England's bloody Queen ever done for Ireland, tell me that?'

His father released his grip and waved his arms in the air. 'Don't you dare to speak of Her Majesty in that tone, you young whelp!' he shouted angrily.

Con took advantage of his release and walked quickly away. 'We'll talk of it later, Pa,' he called over his shoulder.

Daniel went to go after his retreating son, but a fit of coughing rasped in his throat and he was forced to halt until it had eased. By then the tall figure of his son was too far away to pursue.

'What is it ye want here, Father Boyce?' Michael Kearney was a bull of a man, and his rusty hair hung low over his narrow brow.

17

The young priest's long nose had collected a dewdrop which hung from its reddened tip, threatening to fall as he jerked his head excitedly. 'These men want work, Mr Kearney.'

The big overseer shook his head, 'I've none to give them, Father, my rolls are full.'

'Arrah yes! Of that I've no doubt!' The priest's dewdrop elongated as he nodded vigorously, and his high-pitched voice rose to almost screeching level. 'Your rolls are full of those who don't need work. That's a fact!'

'Is it now?' Kearney's tone was sneeringly amused. 'Is it a fact, to be sure.'

'It is that,' the priest insisted. 'There are men lounging about here as assistant overseers, gangsmen and stewards who have food and money enough, aye, and property too. This work, as you well know, Mr Kearney, was intended for those who are truly destitute. Not for those whose only thought is to drink the rot-gut poteen that you sell in that shanty behind you. These men with me have all got tickets from the Relief Committee which entitle them to work here.'

A murmur of assent came from the ragged, emaciated men ranked to the rear of the small thin figure of the priest, who in his billowing cassock and over-sized hat resembled an ugly schoolboy rather than a Man of God.

By now most of the assistant overseers and gangsmen had reached the shanty, and aware of their well-fed robustness and their personal loyalty towards him, Kearney was unconcerned about any threat of violence from the human wrecks in front of him.

'Listen to me, you men,' he growled, 'your tickets are no good to ye here. So ye'd best be on your way.' He nodded towards the priest. 'And take this wee fella with you.'

'Oh no, Mr Kearney, we'll not be on our way.' Father Boyce's thin features were hardset and determined. 'It's work these lads have come here for, and it's work they'll have.'

By now Kearney was ready to take hold of this human gadfly and tear him limb from limb. But Catholic that he was, he held back by ingrained respect for the Cloth, plus the cautioning thought that should he lay violent hands on the man, then even his own cowed workforce might turn on him, such was the local admiration for the redoubtable Father Boyce.

'Now Father,' he forced himself to assume a placatory attitude, 'if I've no work for these men, then what can I do? I'm responsible for the government's money here. It's my liberty that's at stake if the Board o' Work inspectors should think that I'm trying to cheat them by taking on more men than are required.'

'And it is your immortal soul that is at stake, Kearney, for the sinful way you cheat and rob these poor people who already are working under you,' Boyce answered him contemptuously.

The Chief Overseer's heavy face darkened with a rush of fury. Abruptly he turned on his heel and shouted to the gangsmen and overseers, 'Put these bastards offa the site. If any won't go easy, then make them go hard.'

The brutal faces of his followers tautened and one or two smiled with eager anticipation, as swinging hammers and spades they moved menacingly forwards. The priest knew that those with him in their present weakened state were no match for Kearney's men. Reluctantly, before an open clash could flare, he turned away also, and with a gesture beckoned his party to follow. Dejectedly they trudged after his small hunched figure, heads bent against the gusting rain, hearts heavy with the knowledge that once more they were returning empty handed to starving wives and children.

Kearney laughed jeeringly and his bullyboys joined in, hurling insults at the defeated men as they left the site. Only one man by the shanty was not laughing: Conrad Shonley. With a disgusted glare at the raucous jeerers about him, he walked back to where his father watched anxiously for him. Without a word the black-haired youth spat on his hands, picked up his hammer, swung it high and brought it down with such force that the boulder shattered into a dozen pieces . . .

Chapter Three

A little distance from the small town of Skibereen stood Clover Hill House, the residence of J Macarthy Downing Esq. Here in the warmly comfortable drawing room, its polished furnishings glowing in the soft lamplight, a group of men sat talking quietly, waiting for a visitor to arrive. A knock sounded on the green-baize covered door, and the black-clad housekeeper came in and curtsied.

'It's the gentleman from London has come, Sir, the Mr Mahoney.'

Macarthy Downing, a tall soldierly man, rose to his feet. 'Do come in, my dear fellow, and welcome to you,' he greeted Mahoney warmly and immediately introduced him to the rest of the gathering. 'Doctor Donovan, Doctor Crowley, Reverend Doctor Traill of Schull village, Mr Richard Inglis of the Commissariat Department, Reverend Caulfield, Father Barry, Sub-Inspector Hardy of the police, Major Parker and Mr Grady of the Board of Works . . . '

Mahoney regarded each man closely at he met them.

'Your servant, Sir.'

'I'm honoured to meet you, Mr Mahoney.'

Macarthy Downing wasted no time once the introductions were completed. 'I've taken the liberty of explaining your purpose in coming to Skibereen, Mr Mahoney, and the fact that you and I have met previously in England.'

Mahoney nodded, and spoke to all present. 'Then you know, gentlemen, that I've been commissioned by the *Illustrated London News* to record what is happening here.

Primarily I am a graphic artist, but in this case I shall also act in the capacity of a reporter . . . Let me be brutally frank with you. In certain of London's influential circles there is much suspicion as to the true depth of distress and famine here in Ireland . . .'

Indignant exclamations greeted his statement, and Mahoney was quick to soothe ruffled feelings. 'Let me hasten to add, gentlemen, that on my coach journey from Cork to here, I have already witnessed such suffering among the people as to convince me that even the most horrifying accounts of the distress that have reached London, are only understating the tragedy. With your assistance I shall do all in my power to portray the truth.'

'The truth is hideous, Mr Mahoney, Sir.' The speaker was the Protestant Reverend Doctor Traill of Schull. 'Yesterday in Schull there were interred thirty-seven bodies, and I know of another seven lying dead. My parish is in truth a veritable Aceldama, a field of death . . . Hunger and disease are doing fearful work.'

The Catholic, Father Barry took up the story. 'I am just come in from an unfortunate woman whose dead child lay beside her for the last two days, and three other children barely gasping. It is horrible to relate, but while I was giving the woman the last sacrament a famished cat got upon the bed and was about to gnaw the carcase of the poor infant. The husband and another famishing child were drowning in tears on their knees.

'My curate told me he attended a man whose wife died of hunger last week, and on one side of him lay a girl dead three days, and on the other a child dead since the morning. It was a blessing that the poor man died himself . . .'

'The famine fever has come as well.' The careworn face of Doctor Donovan twisted in despair. 'Both the black and the yellow. By the time I am called to them the poor creatures are already raving and violent, and the flesh is rotting with gangrene.

'Other of my patients get the swelling, even though their bellies have long been empty. Their bodies expand to

21

almost double size. I can do nothing more than try to ease their dyings.'

'What of the government relief work?' Mahoney asked quietly.

It was the Commissariat Officer, Inglis, who answered. 'All we have here in the local food depots are scant supplies of Indian corn. It is unground, and as such, inedible. The Treasury Department continually directs we of the Commissariat to close the depots for good. They appear to believe that there is ample food already available.'

'Indeed there is food, Sir,' Major Parker intervened. 'Why on Saturday last there was a market held here in Skibereen at which there was an abundance of bread, meat and grain for sale. But the starving cannot buy it, they haven't got money, and the prices are so high that only the better provided-for classes of the populace can afford to eat a sufficiently nourishing diet. It's to our shame that the wages we pay on the Public Works are not enough to enable our workers there to eat adequately.'

'I've started two soup kitchens here in Skibereen,' Richard Inglis told Mahoney. 'But it is with money from private individuals that I obtain the necessary supplies, and that money is sorely limited. The Reverend Caulfield here feeds some seventy to eighty people daily from his own personal resources. But we can only minister to a minute part of the suffering masses.'

The catalogue of horror continued, each man present, Irish and English, adding to it with his own story. James Mahoney's feeling of despondent helplessness grew and grew as he listened. What use would his pictures and his reports be to these dying people? What use could anything or anyone be to them now? It was too late . . . Too late . . .

'It is never too late for a nation to gain its freedom! To strike off its fetters, and rise from its knees to face and defy its oppressors . . . ' The fervent words of Father Boyce struck an answering chord in Con Shonley's mind.

Outside the isolated cabin the wind howled, rain drummed down in torrents and clouds veiled the land with

22

a pitch gloom. Inside the turf walls a solitary rush-light flickered in the draughts and its weakly gleam fitfully illuminated the intense face of the priest, sitting on the sole article of furniture the mean dwelling possessed, a broken-backed chair. A fetid stench of unwashed flesh, stale breath and greasy wet rags made the air thick and turgid. But the close-packed men sitting, crouching, standing upon the earth floor were not aware of the air's foulness. Intent upon the priest, engrossed by his words, they listened in a silence broken only by smothered coughs and harsh breathing.

'Daniel O'Connell, you've heard much talk of him . . . The great liberator!' Boyce's tone was scathing. 'He promised that the forced and evil union of England and Ireland would be repealed, and repealed by peaceful means . . . Well now, O'Connell is away in Italy, a broken old man, dying they say . . . And the cursed Union still is intact! But . . . thank the good God, other Irish leaders have arisen. The leaders of Young Ireland; William Smith O'Brian, John Mitchel, Meagher of the Sword, Fintan Lalor and a host of others.

'They don't believe that England will ever agree to free us if we continue to preach peace. To beg humbly for our freedom . . . What does Fintan Lalor say?' Boyce questioned rhetorically, then gave the answer to his own question, 'Forever henceforth the owners of our soil must be Irish! This famine opens the way for revolution . . . Unmuzzle the wolf dog! There is one at this moment in every cabin throughout the land, nearly fit to be untied . . . and he will be savager by and by . . . '

Like dogs themselves his listeners snarled their appreciation.

From outside the cabin came the twice-repeated hootings of an owl. Instantly the priest held his fingers to his lips enjoining silence, and dowsed the light. In the blackness they waited tensely, hardly daring to breathe. There came the sound of approaching footsteps splashing through the waterlogged ground.

'Father Boyce?' a hoarse voice called low and urgently.

'Father, will ye come now? A poor man is dying at the cross-roads, he's in desperate need of a priest.'

'I'll come.' Boyce metamorphized from man of violence to bringer of comfort. 'I'll come directly now.'

With tinder, flint and steel the rush-light was relit, and Boyce could be seen fitting his over-sized hat upon his sparse-haired head. 'Wait until I'm clear, boys. Then go yourselves in ones and twos. And go careful, there'll be informers watching for ye without doubt.'

'They'll be bloody wet ones then, Father,' a man quipped and a ripple of laughter erupted.

The priest smiled briefly, and was gone.

Con Shonley walked alone through the blustery darkness, unheeding of the rain beating upon his bare head. His mind was full of the priest's words, and his heart thrilled to the idea of rebellion. So engrossed was he in his thoughts that he failed to see the three shadows bulking large against the sides of the narrow bog pathway he travelled on.

Suddenly a ray of light flashed out from a bullseye lantern, striking the youth's eyes to dazzle and blind.

'Hold fast,' a deep voice ordered, and the shadows surrounded him. Rough hands pinioned his arms, and fingers twined into his thick hair and brutally jerked his head back so that his face was bathed in the light.

'D'ye know him?' the deep voice demanded; and one of the men clucked his tongue against the roof of his mouth. 'Tsk, let me think now . . . Yes, Con Shonley's his name. Daniel Shonley's eldest. That Shoneen fella that lives up agin Muldoon's pool.'

'What are ye doing out on a night like this, boy?' the deep voice questioned.

Fear and shock had caused Con's wits temporarily to desert him, and he could only croak an unintelligible reply. The fingers in his hair tightened, causing sharp pain in his scalp, and his head was roughly shaken. 'Speak up, you young scut! What are you about?'

Rain lashed across Con's upturned face and ran in streams down his neck.

'Be damned to this, we'll take him back to the dry. Let the Inspector talk to him,' the deep-voiced man instructed, and Con's hair was released. With a man each side of him he was force-marched along the rough pathway. His eyes recovered their night vision and he was able to make out the shapes of peaked forage caps and caped greatcoats. His captors were policemen.

Sub-Inspector Augustus Hardy, his black riding cloak swathing him warmly, was pacing up and down the lantern-lit cabin where the three men brought their captive.

'Who have you there, Sergeant?' He stopped pacing.

The bulky Sergeant Macarthy saluted. 'A young 'un by name o' Shonley, Sir. Conrad Shonley. He was coming from the direction of Castletownsend.'

The Inspector's narrow face beneath the gleaming black peak of his cap was expressionless. 'He'll be Daniel Shonley's son?'

'Aye, Sir.'

The narrow face turned to Con. 'Well, boy?'

The youth had by now collected his wits. 'Well?' he rejoined, with more than a touch of arrogance. The next instant Macarthy's heavy fist crashed into his kidneys, sending him staggering across the room.

'Keep a civil tongue in your head, and answer with respect,' the bulky sergeant threatened.

The youth massaged his aching back with both hands, and tried desperately to appear unafraid. 'I've done nothing wrong,' he told the Sub-Inspector. 'Why should I be treated like this?'

'Answer civilly, and you will be treated with civility,' Hardy told him. 'Now tell me what you are doing abroad in weather like this, so late at night and more than four miles from your own home?'

At one end of the cabin was a half-loft, used by its inhabitants as a sleeping platform. Con glanced over the policeman's shoulder, and saw faces staring down at him from the half-loft. One face held his gaze. It was a young girl, black hair framing her thin face, huge green eyes

25

intent upon him. Even in his present state of angry fear Con was struck by her beauty.

'Come now, Shonley,' Hardy's voice was impatient, 'I am waiting to hear why you are abroad this night.'

The youth met the older man's gaze. 'I was looking for something to eat,' he said quietly.

A spasm of emotion showed clearly on Hardy's face, and with a shock of surprise the youth recognized that emotion as pity. The Inspector swung away and moved to stand staring down at the dead ashes on the flat-stoned hearth of the cabin.

'Let him go, Sergeant,' he ordered after a long silence.

'But Sir . . . ' the sergeant began to protest.

'Let him go,' his superior coldly reiterated.

'You heard the officer,' Macarthy took Con by the arm and led him to the door of the cabin, 'Get you back home, young Shonley. Your mammy is no doubt worrying after ye.' The big man's tone was not unfriendly.

Con retraced his steps to pick up the path which led homewards, the vision of the Police Inspector's face with its spasm of pity re-occurring in his mind. An Englishman with a soft heart? Could it be possible? Con's lips twisted in a wry smile. 'Am I not half an Englishman myself, and does not my English mother constantly demonstrate her loving heart . . . '

The rain stopped quite suddenly and the clouds rifted letting the moonlight through. The youth kept a careful watch as he walked for any other lurkers in the shadows. He knew that the authorities were edgy and nervous about the unsettled state of the country, which the famine had intensified until the perennial likelihood of revolution now seemed a certainty rather than a possibility. And so, instead of food, they send soldiers, he thought savagely. Before him was the pale streak of the road which led from Skibereen to Leap village, and as if in confirmation of his thoughts, a troop of hussars, caped and busbied, came trotting with a metallic jingle from the direction of Leap. Con crouched low until the last trooper had passed, and then scurried across the road and into the shelter of the rough ground beyond. He skirted the outskirts of the town, where only a few dull gleams of light betokened life, and came at last to his own home.

Quietly he lifted the latch and entered, standing for a while inside the door, letting his eyes grow accustomed to the deeper gloom within, then went down the entrance passage to the kitchen at the rear.

'So, you've come home at last!' his mother's soft voice sounded from the stool to one side of the smouldering turf fire on the hearth.

Con started slightly, then felt a rush of fond exasperation. 'Mother, you should be sleeping,' he scolded in whispers.

Charlotte Shonley frowned worriedly, and settled the sleeping baby more comfortably in her arms. 'Where have you been, Con, roaming with the Croppy Boys again?' she asked tartly.

Her son tried to answer lightly, 'There are no Croppy Boys in Ireland now, Mother. They're long dead and buried.' He closed the door fully and went to crouch by the hearth, holding his hands out to the fire's feeble warmth. In its faint glow he could see the reflected paleness of his mother's face and the whiteness of the apron she always wore, and felt a surge of love for this girlish-looking woman who had aged so little in appearance despite the hardships of her married life. She was painfully thin, but then, thin people were all too common in Ireland now. Yet still her fair hair was lustrous, and her blue eyes clear and lucent.

'Why do you hate the English so?' Charlotte Shonley's voice held puzzlement. 'You carry English blood in your veins.'

Con searched for words. 'I do not hate the English people, Mother. How could I, you are English and I love you dearly, and I am half English in blood . . . But I consider myself to be a citizen of Ireland, and Ireland to be my first nation. I want freedom from England's government, and until we drive England's soldiers and policemen into the sea, then we shall never have that freedom to rule ourselves. We must own our own soil, Mother. The Irish people must own it, not the landlords who suck our strength from us like a leech sucks blood. If we must fight to be free of such as them, then I am ready to fight.'

Tears glistened in the woman's eyes, and reaching out her hand she gently ruffled the thick damp hair of the young man crouching by her knees. 'How many have died here in this unhappy country for sake of that word, "freedom"?' Her voice trembled slightly. 'And how many more fine young men will come to their deaths because of it? I don't want you to be one of them, Con.'

He sighed heavily and leaned against her knee. 'Does it matter how we die, Mother? By famine, by disease, or by the sword and gallows? It seems to me that the people of Ireland are doomed already to early graves . . . ' He lapsed into silence, and the silence deepened and lasted as they stayed together by the hearthside.

Chapter Four

'Jim MacDermott, are you awake?' Sub-Inspector Hardy called sharply, and from the dark cavity of the half-loft above his head the thin face of the girl peeped down, her expression anxious as she held her forefinger against her lips beseeching his silence. Her mute appeal struck the policeman so forcibly that the irritability engendered in him by lack of sleep softened, and silently he beckoned her to join him.

With agile grace she descended the short ladder and stood facing him in the half-light of the dawn, her black hair tumbled about her shoulders and her full high breasts and rounded hips moulded by the shabby, ragged-edged gown she wore. She pointed to the door, and the Englishman understood and followed her outside into the cold dank air.

'My thanks to you, Sir.'

Her voice was pleasing to hear with its soft musical brogue and involuntarily the man smiled down at her and said jokingly, 'I could wish I had a daughter as protective of her father's slumbers as you are, my dear.'

She tossed her head and the green eyes mirrored a deep-felt contempt. 'Sure, it's not him I'm protecting, and he's not my father, only my uncle. But if he's roused from his sleep then he's a foul-tempered pig, and he takes that temper out on my mother, God help her.'

Augustus Hardy nodded sympathetically. 'I see. Tell me, what is your name?'

'Grainne. Grainne MacDermott.'

'And your father, where is he?'

She shrugged, and once more the green eyes filled with contempt. 'He's gone. When the hunger came he ran off and left his family to fend for themselves. I don't know if he's alive or dead, and truth to tell, I don't care either way.'

Hardy found himself disturbed by the evident depth of bitterness displayed by such a young woman, and impelled by a curiosity which was not solely of a professional nature, he went on, 'Then it's your uncle who now cares for your family, is it not?'

The girl's white teeth gleamed in a mirthless smile, and she almost spat the denial. 'Not him! Jim MacDermott is the same stamp as his brother, my father. Good only for swilling drink and beating women. We care for ourselves.'

The policeman experienced a genuine sense of sympathy, and could understand why this beautiful young woman carried bitterness in her heart. 'It must be very hard for you,' he murmured, 'particularly in these grievous times.'

She stared calculatingly at him, and then said slowly and with a hint of challenge in her tone, 'Well now, Sir, if you were to pay me a few shillings for having had the use of our cabin this last night, it might help to smooth our pathway through this day, at least.'

At this point the instincts of the professional policeman surged up to the surface and the sympathy in Hardy's eyes was overlaid by the predatory gleam of the hunter. 'Most certainly I'll pay for the shelter of your cabin, my dear,' he told her in a kindly tone, 'and what is more, I am prepared to put before you the opportunity to earn further sums of money.'

Instantly suspicion frowned in the thin face, and he hastened to add, 'I pray you, do not think that I intend to offer any insult towards your moral character, Grainne MacDermott. No indeed, what I offer you is the opportunity to act as a loyal subject of Her Majesty, and to be well rewarded for so acting.'

For a moment it seemed that the young face before him had been superseded by an older, harder mask. She gave an abrupt shake of her head. 'You would offer me the opportunity to become as low a creature as my uncle. That I'll never do,' she whispered harshly.

The policeman instantly recognized failure and mentally shrugged, then said aloud, 'Well, at least think on it. You know where I am to be found if you should change your mind.' He reached into his tunic pocket and brought out coins which he handed to her. 'There are three shillings, Grainne. That's a fair enough rent for the shelter of your roof, I think.'

He turned away to go to his horse tethered nearby, and had taken only three steps when the sound of her voice brought him to a halt.

'Mr Hardy, I thank you for this money; we are in sore need of it. But be plain on one matter. You'll only ever find one informer in this cabin, and him you already have working for you. But I don't care a damn for loyalty to the Queen, and I don't care a damn for any rebel nonsense or Croppy Boys either. I'm only concerned with doing what I can to help my own flesh and blood. What stupidities you men get up to in your childish games is of no importance to me, and I want no part of it. For me there are no English or Irish, no Queen's Men or Croppy Boys. There are only people, and some of them are good, and some are bad, no matter what side they may profess to be on.'

Without looking back at her, Hardy nodded his head curtly and walked on.

Grainne watched while the policeman mounted his horse and rode away. She had taken no offence from the man's veiled offer of payment for information about any subversive activities in the district. What she had told him was the literal truth. She really did not give a damn for any idealistic dreams of patriotism. For her, it was only important that people lived in peace with one another, and did their best to aid each other when in need. All she asked was to be left alone to live her own life.

'How much did the bloody Peeler give ye?' Jim MacDermott's drink-husky voice disturbed her reverie. He had come from the cabin to stand a little distance behind her, and she swung to stare at him with acute distaste.

A stoop-bodied, wizen-faced man in his forties, he stood a little over medium height. His long tangled hair was a greasy ginger-grey, and the broken veins covering his grimy, red-blotched face were a visible token of the habitual drunkard. Dressed only in a torn check shirt and knee-breeches, with a week-old stubble on his scrawny throat and chin, dirty bare feet splayed in the mud, and emitting a foul odour of breath and body, he was a repulsive spectacle, and Grainne could not help but be disgusted by her own mother for living intimately with him as she did.

'How much was it?' he growled, and held out a black-nailed hairy hand. His decayed teeth bared in a threatening snarl. 'Give it over, girl.'

Although secretly nervous of his violence, which during the week she had been at home she had witnessed several instances of, she forced herself to show no fear. 'Why should I?' she asked coolly. 'The Peeler gave me the money to buy food with.'

MacDermott's head was throbbing painfully from the effects of the poteen he had swilled the previous night, and his nerves were jangling. He took a pace towards her, his fists balled in threat. 'If ye know what's good for ye, you wee slut, ye'll give the money over right now. Or by God, I'll give ye something to cry about.'

Until this moment he had not previously offered any violence towards Grainne. Indeed, his overwhelming emotion concerning her had been a powerful lust to possess her shapely body, and so he had made great efforts to be pleasant to her. Grainne recognized the danger she now stood in of actual physical assault. The breath caught in her throat and she cried out, 'If you lift a hand to me, Jim MacDermott, I'll have that Peeler back here before you're a day older. I've had a long talk with him,' she bluffed from sheer instinct, 'and he's promised me that if anybody offers to harm me, then he'll lay them by the heels.'

She saw the doubt in the man's bloodshot eyes, and

levelled yet another menace at his head. 'And another thing, Uncle dear. I was hearing the talk in Skibereen yesterday. It seems that the boyos there are very anxious to find out who the informers are in these parts. They reckon that when they do find one, then he'll be found head downwards in a bog the first dark night that comes along.'

Actual alarm showed fleetingly in MacDermott's face, and for a few seconds he made no reply. Then, abruptly, his attitude altered, and a wheedling tone entered his voice. 'Sure now, wee girl. I didn't mean to spake so hard to ye. It's only that I'm in desperate need of a dram to settle me guts with. I'm not feeling at all well this morn. All I'm asking is the lend of a few pennies. Sure, your Mammy would give them to me and gladly. She knows well that I'm a man of me word, and that I'll pay back them pennies with interest. I've money to come tomorrow that's owing me, and that's a fact. I swear by God that it is. So be a good girl now, and give me the lend of a few pennies.'

Grainne knew that for the sake of her mother she could not provoke the man beyond endurance. So, she decided to meet him halfway. 'The Peeler gave me three shillings, Uncle.' She showed him the coins. 'I'll give you a shilling of it, and use the rest to buy some food for us all. Is that fair enough?'

The man forced a grin. 'Sure now, that's real Christian of you, my jewel. You've the good heart, and haven't I been telling your Mammy that same thing.'

He snatched the proffered coin from her fingers and without another word went shambling down the track away from the cabin.

Grainne felt near to tears as she watched him go. 'Dear God, help me to keep my family safe from him,' she prayed despondently. 'And give my Mammy the sense to send him away from here.'

Heavy-hearted, she went back inside to rouse her mother from sleep.

Chapter Five

With the dawn the Shonley family rose and prepared for their day. Into a small earthenware pot Charlotte Shonley measured out minute portions of the yellow-coloured gruel made from the Indian maize flour and a few oats. Her husband and elder children put on their ragged clothing and broken boots, and taking the pot of gruel with them left for the three mile walk to the roadworks. En route Daniel Shonley was continually forced to stop as fits of coughing racked his chest. Con stared at his father with worried eyes. He saw the flush of fever upon the hollow cheeks, and the heat of high body temperature bringing out a sheen of sweat on the wasted neck and chest.

'Go back home, Pa,' he begged. 'It'll be the death of you to work today.'

His father waited until the latest fit of coughing subsided, and he was able to gasp out, 'Don't talk like a noddle-pate, boy. I've never felt better. Besides, it's payday. I must be there to take my dues. You know well that the clerk will not allow you to collect them for me.'

As they neared the site of the new road more small groups of men, women and children were met with, all hurrying in the same direction, all with the same abject appearance. But today there was a degree of light-heartedness among most of them which was absent on other days. Payday meant literally, life. The money would buy a little food, and for a few days the food would give people increased strength, and with that increased strength came the hope that they would survive.

Reaching the site the Shonleys split up and went to their separate roll-calls. Daniel and Con with the gangs of hammer-men, Sean and Mairead with the women and children who carried the baskets of stone. Work commenced its desultory progress. The overseers and gangsmen did not hector and bully their workers, they knew that hunger-weakened bodies could only toil slowly, and so, as long as a man made an effort to complete his given task they let him be.

The morning dragged on slowly, and for once there was no wind and rain, the weather was still, and Con, anxious for his father, blessed the mild conditions.

On the next gang's section of road an elderly man suddenly staggered, let fall his hammer and toppled to the ground. His mates gathered about the fallen man, and one examined him closely, then cursed loudly, 'Dead as a bloody nail, and him owing me four pence! Bad cess to it! I'll never see that money agin.'

The death created only a fleeting interest on the site. Such happenings were commonplace on the Public Works, and many men, their starved bodies taxed beyond endurance, had fallen so and died during the famine. Apart from his creditor no one knew the man well, but talk had it that all his numerous family were dead of the fever.

'Mayhap it's a happy deliverance for the man.' Daniel Shonley crossed himself as the corpse was carried past to be laid at the side of the shanty until carted back to the town.

'Happy deliverance for him that's sure,' his creditor joked disgustedly. 'God knows how many fourpences the bastard owed. I reckon he only died to spite me.'

'Well, that'll teach you a lesson in future, Donoghue. Only lend money to healthy, well-fed, long-living people,' one of his workmates mocked, and laughter rang out at the creditor's expression of chagrin.

At midday a halt to work was called and the Shonleys gathered together. Daniel sat with his back resting against a filled basket of stone, and handed the pot of gruel to Con.

'Here son, share this with the twins, I want none of it,' he said wearily, then coughed until it seemed that his lungs would tear themselves into shreds. The attack left him sick and spent.

'Dammit, Pa, you'll do no more toil this day!' Con burst out.

The older man shook his head. 'I'm still the head of this family, boy. You'll not tell me what I should do, or should not do.'

The twins sat with solemn eyes fixed upon their father, who tried to smile reassuringly at them, until more coughs shook him.

'Eat your food,' Con urged them. 'Go on now, take it all, I'm not hungry.'

The children's large blue eyes lit up with undisguised pleasure, and by turns they greedily sucked the watery gruel into their under-nourished bodies. Con watched them eat, then looked at his father lying with eyes closed, breathing jerkily, and inwardly prayed that the hours might pass quickly and this day be done with.

The pay-clerk came to the site in mid-afternoon. He rode on a jaunting-car drawn by a donkey, and with him rode a mounted escort of six armed policemen. His arrival brought cheers from workgangs and smiles to drawn faces. The Chief Overseer, Kearney, also smiled and nodded to two of his assistants. 'Get the jars ready, and bring me my tick-book.'

They hurried to obey him. One going to open the small heavily padlocked outhouse built against the rear wall of the shanty which housed the big stone jars of poteen, the other bringing Kearney a thick dog-eared ledger from the battered table in the office.

The people laid aside their tools and baskets, and under the direction of their overseers came to form a queue outside the shanty door. Two of the escorts, a bearded sergeant and a constable stationed themselves behind the seated pay-clerk in the shanty. The corporal and three remaining constables patrolled the environs with loaded carbines in their hands. Their wariness was justified. Payrolls were tempting targets for starving men with nothing to lose but their lives.

As each worker's name was called and amount of days' pay due to them by their overseer, so they stepped inside the shanty.

'John Shea, four days at eight pence,' the overseer shouted.

'John Shea, four days at eight pence,' the pay-clerk repeated aloud as he made the notation in his ledger. Then from the leather bag between his feet he selected the pitifully few coins, and carelessly tossed them onto the table. Shea made his mark in the ledger as receipt, then took up his money.

Kearney waited outside the shanty door, his thick forefinger running up and down the list of names in his own ledger.

'Good man, Shea,' he smiled bluffly. 'That's a shilling and three pence you owe me. Nine pence I loaned ye, plus interest; and the price of the wee drop o' poteen ye took yesterday.'

Shea clutched his money in one work-soiled hand, and with the other hand rubbed the back of his neck nervously. 'Mr Kearney, sor, could you see your way clear to letting me pay half this week, and the rest next week. Only me missus is badly and I must get the medicine, d'ye see.'

Kearney pursed his liver-coloured lips and whistled tonelessly.

Shea's discoloured teeth gnawed at his own chapped lips.

'Ahh well now, Shea, never let it be said that I'm a man of hard heart,' Kearney told him at last, and Shea sighed heavily in relief.

Kearney grinned, savouring his power. 'I'll just take the interest on the loan this week, and the price of the poteen. Then we'll see how things go next week for the rest.'

'Thank you Mr Kearney, sor, a thousand thanks, and God bless the kind heart of ye!' Shea was effusive, and almost eagerly pushed coins into the Chief Overseer's outstretched hand.

Kearney winked at him. 'And don't be going away without a wee dram. I've some good stuff round the back there.'

Shea's face wore a sickly grin. 'Arrah yes, I'll take a dram now, for health's sake.' He made his reluctant way to the rear of the shanty, and Kearney's waiting assistant splashed a tot of the clear fiery-tasting liquid into a metal cup and held it out in welcome.

'Daniel Shonley, eight days at eight pence,' the clerk intoned, and threw the money on the table.

Daniel signed his name with a flourish and the clerk regarded the flowing signature with interest. 'You write like an educated man,' he remarked.

'Education counts for little in these times,' Daniel stated simply, and went outside.

Kearney regarded him with distaste. 'And how does Mr Temperance feel today?' he sneered, as Daniel coughed and visibly swayed.

'You should act the man, Shonley, and take a few drams. That 'ud heal that sore chest o' yours.'

Con Shonley heard the sneer as he came from the shanty with his own wages. Anger boiled up in him. 'We've better use for our money, than to spend it in lining your pockets, Kearney.'

The Overseer's bloodshot eyes hardened. 'It's Mr Kearney to the like o' ye, my young buck,' he growled, then reverted to a sneer. 'Arrah, but then, a fine Shoneen gentleman like yourself, with the blood of the English nobility running in your veins wouldn't have the stomach for a good Irish drink. It'ud be too strong for your dainty taste, I'll warrant.'

Daniel Shonley stared warningly at his eldest son, but the youth's temper was beyond recall.

'I'm as true an Irishman as yourself, Kearney, aye, and a better one. I don't rob and cheat my own people. I'm not Gombeen scum!' He spat the words into the Chief Overseer's face.

For a moment it seemed that the man would strike out, but then he forced a laugh and shouted to the assembled assistant overseers.

'None of these Shonleys are to work here agin. Strike them offa the rolls.'

'For the love of God, Mr Kearney, don't treat us so. The boy's young and hot-headed. He doesn't know what he's saying,' Daniel Shonley begged the man.

In fury Con turned on his father, 'Don't beg, Pa! Don't beg him!'

'Be quiet, boy! Would you have us all starve to death for sake of your loose mouth.' The elder Shonley was equally furious.

Another man left the shanty, and Kearney beckoned to him. 'Come here now, Murphy, my buck. Don't be sneaking away like a thief in the night . . . You owe me money.'

Daniel Shonley tugged at the Chief Overseer's sleeve. 'Please, Mr Kearney, Sir. Don't turn us off the works. We'll die of hunger if you do.'

'Then die!' Kearney shouted, and with a sweep of his heavy hand hurled the frail figure from him. Daniel Shonley stumbled and fell heavily, and the coins in his hand scattered across the muddy ground. Half-weeping he frantically scrabbled on hands and knees searching for them. Tormented beyond endurance at the sight of his much-loved father being treated so, Con flew at the big man striking out with both fists at the unshaven jowls. Kearney roared with fright and pain as the hard knuckles cut flesh to the bone, and his henchmen came at a run. The flat of a swinging spade bounced off the side of the youth's head, and he dropped to his knees, bright sparklets of blood spurting from the thick black hair. Mairead Shonley screamed high in terror and ran to her elder brother's side. The swinging spade took her in the ribs, and she fell across Con, her impact sending them both sprawling.

A howl of protest went up from the watching crowd, and Kearney had sense enough to call his men off before a full-scale riot broke out.

He bellowed at Daniel Shonley, 'Get away from here, and don't let me see hide nor hair of any of youse Shonleys on this site agin.'

With the help of the boy twin, Daniel lifted the dazed Con to his feet, and led him away from the shanty.

Mairead, weeping piteously and holding her side, limped after them.

By the time they reached home Con Shonley's dazed senses had cleared, and apart from the sore swelling of his cut head he was no worse for the fight. Mairead's ribs were badly bruised, but none broken, and even Daniel Shonley's cough had eased. He told his wife what had happened, and hiding her own dismay she smiled easily.

'Well at least we have some money for food, Daniel. Mayhap there is other work to be found. Sit and rest by the fire now, and be thankful that tomorrow you need not go out to toil in this dreadful weather.'

The man returned his wife's smile. 'By God!' he burst out. 'I don't think there to be another man in the whole of creation who has the good fortune to possess such a wife as I.'

Con Shonley's swarthy handsome features were sullen with angry shame. He bitterly cursed himself and his own temper for bringing this fresh trouble upon them all. His mother kissed his cheek. 'Come now, Con. Cannot you give me a smile. I'm proud to have such a son, who will fight like a true man to protect his family.'

The youth forced himself to smile at the thin pretty face looking so tenderly at him. Then he went outside and walked for hours over the pathways of the bog.

'Fight for my family?' He remembered his mother's words, and forced back tears. 'All I bring on my family is trouble . . . But mayhap I'll bring them joy someday . . . How?' A tiny voice whispered in his mind . . .

Chapter Six

On the fourth day following his arrival at Skibereen James Mahoney accompanied Doctors Donovan and Crowley into the town. The morning was dry despite the dark clouds blanketing the sky, and the wind blew chill from the northeast. The three men walked down the broad earth road flanked by its low stone walls; Mahoney's artist's eye was taken by the beauty of the high blue-green hills behind the town, from the close set buildings out of which rose the square tower of a church.

'You see that church there, Mr Mahoney?' Doctor Donovan pointed to the tower, 'that is the Bridgetown area. It's through there we shall go.'

It was a huddle of streets, and every house in them contained death. The doctors walked past the houses, ignoring the piteous appeals for help which came from the wretched people in their path.

'I've spent the last two days in Bridgetown.' Donovan's careworn features wore an expression of hopelessness. 'It's like trying to command the incoming tide to turn. There are houses here where the dead have lain for up to six days. No one of their immediate families can raise sufficient strength to remove them; and the neighbours are too afraid of the fever to go near those who die. We have to pay large sums to persuade anyone to raise courage enough to bury a fever victim.'

The three turned into Old Chapel Lane, a rising, deeply rutted dirt alley, with rows of thatched cabins and two-storeyed, tiny-windowed houses on both sides. Abandoned carts, some without wheels lay in the lane, and one wheel-

41

less cart was tipped over into the filth of a huge midden heap. Haggard be-shawled women squatted or sat in groups upon the ground, with their withered children beside them, and their menfolk, some with battered pot hats on their shaggy heads, others wearing the traditional caubeen and short blue cloak, stood talking or merely brooding. From a cabin higher up the lane four men in ragged black swallow-tailed coats and caubeens, came carrying a coffin on their shoulders, and several women lifted clasped hands in prayer as the crudely fashioned box passed them, followed by the grieving relatives of the dead person keening their grief to the uncaring sky.

Doctor Crowley, until then silent, spoke out. 'Here is the house we want.'

Slightly larger than its neighbours, with no doors or windows left in its walls, it presented a foreboding aspect, and Mahoney found himself breathing quickly and shallowly in apprehension of what might meet him within.

There were only four bare walls and the poles and thatch of its broken roof from which a drizzle of liquid soot fell upon the seething tangle of human bodies that covered the earth floor, lying in their own filth. The terrible stench mingling with a foetid fog rose from the wet rags that were the sufferers' clothing and only coverings.

For a few moments Donovan and Mahoney stood side by side in the doorhole. In the tangle of bodies red-rimmed eyes moved and mouths gaped, groaning, howling with pain, babbling deliriously, cursing and crying out to God and His Saints for succour. James Mahoney's stomach heaved as the smell flooded his lungs and he gagged uncontrollably, and was forced to step back into the lane, where curious onlookers had already gathered to watch these well-dressed visitors.

'I think it best that you remain here,' the doctor told Mahoney, not unkindly. 'Even my hardened senses are affected by such sights and smells.'

The artist's answer was muffled by the large handkerchief that he held crammed against his mouth. 'My apologies, Doctor Donovan, for this unseemly display of weakness, I shall be quite recovered in a moment or so.' He stepped forwards and forced himself to stand and look into the room. He glanced at the bags both doctors carried. 'How will you treat these poor souls?' he wanted to know.

Donovan shrugged, and smiled bitterly. 'I shall prescribe opium, Peruvian bark, Dovers powder and various stimulants . . . All will prove useless, and the vast majority of my patients will die.' He shrugged helplessly, 'But what else can I do? I must apply the methods that I have learned, I know no others . . . ' He made as if to enter the room, then paused for a moment. 'I must advise you, Mr Mahoney, not to stand close-pressed with any of the people hereabouts. The fevers are undoubtedly contagious. I would not wish your death upon my conscience . . . ' He smiled bitterly once more. 'In these times, discretion is ever the better part of valour.'

The artist walked some way down the lane, and then from his own flat leather case took his charcoal pencils and paper. He began to sketch the scene in the lane, but all the time he worked his own troubled thoughts chided him with the futility of what he did . . .

Charlotte Shonley hurried towards the town, a threadbare shawl drawn over her fair hair, her holed shoes bound in rags to protect her feet from the rocky tracks. Her long skirts impeded her and she let the shawl drop to her shoulders so that her hands were free to lift the dress away from her aching legs.

Reaching Doctor Donovan's house she hammered frantically at the door, until a lounger in the roadway told her that the man she searched for had gone earlier into the town. Her breath coming in short painful gasps, she thanked the lounger and hurried on. Hasty enquiries finally brought her to Old Chapel Lane, and even as she ran up its rutted slope she saw Doctor Donovan and his assistant, Crowley, walking slowly down towards her.

'Doctor Donovan, please can you come with me?' she panted desperately.

The man's tired eyes softened as he looked at the

43

distressed woman. Despite her hard life Charlotte Shonley had retained the accents and manners of her gentle upbringing, and was undoubtedly a lady.

'There now, Ma'am, compose yourself. Certainly I'll come with you. Do you continue here, Mr Crowley,' Donovan instructed the other man. Then again gave his attention to the woman, 'Lead on, Ma'am, if you please.'

'My thanks to you, Sir. It's my husband and my baby; I fear they are both dying.'

With an effort the weary medical man hastened his steps to keep up with the hurrying woman. James Mahoney was intent upon his sketching and did not notice the oncoming pair. As they passed him, Doctor Donovan called, 'I must go immediately to a new case, Mr Mahoney. I'll meet with you later, Sir, at Clover Hill House.'

The artist looked up and smiled. 'Very well, Sir. Until later.' Then he glimpsed the fair-haired woman, and was visibly startled. 'It cannot be,' he murmured unbelievingly. ''Pon my soul, it cannot be!'

The couple were already many yards distant from him as he turned to stare after them. He saw the woman's delicate profile as she turned the corner at the end of the lane, and his heart thudded as his memory bridged the gap of long years. For brief moments he was again a young man in London, in love with a fair-haired girl . . . Whom another man had already taken for wife . . .

Martin Shonley, aged nine years, stood by the window of the bare-boarded room staring out at the cold bleak land and grey skies. Behind him on a straw-stuffed mattress to one side of the meagre fire his father tossed restlessly, muttering at intervals in disjointed, senseless sentences, then coughing and choking, then rasping breath into failing lungs. By the man's side the baby lay silent.

It was for this reason that the child, Martin, kept his eyes fixed on the world outside. He was afraid of the baby now that it lay so still, its half-closed eyes staring unseeingly at the smoke-darkened ceiling. A peculiar rattle sounded long and hard in his father's throat, and after its long-drawn gurgling finish, the man also was silent and still.

Martin felt terror rising, and he clenched his small hands into nail-digging fists, and screwed up his eyes as scalding tears brimmed from them and fell down his cheeks. His mouth opened to emit a high-pitched whimper, 'Mamma, come back! Come back now, Mamma! Please come back now!'

'I fear we are come too late, Ma'am. You have my deepest sympathy in your tragic loss.' Doctor Donovan needed only a glance as he entered the furnitureless room.

All colour drained from Charlotte Shonley's face, and she staggered and would have fallen if the man had not held her. A moment or two passed, and then he told her gently, 'Go to your living child, Ma'am. He needs you more than your dead.'

The woman made her faltering way across to where Martin stood, back turned to her. At her touch he flung himself at her, burying his face in the folds of her skirt. Slowly she sank to the floor, and gathered his slight body into her arms. It was only then that she began to sob.

Donovan made a cursory examination of the dead man and baby. It was all too sadly familiar to him. Hunger destroyed the body's defences, and fever brought death. Their sole covering was an old cloak, and the doctor carefully arranged their limbs, closed their eyes and pulled the musty cloth over their heads. He went to Charlotte Shonley and touched her shoulder.

'Where are your elder children, Ma'am?'

The woman wiped her tears on her sleeve. 'They went to Schull village before dawn. We had heard that the depot there was to open for the sale of Indian corn. Con hoped to be able to buy some. We have not eaten since yesterday morning.'

Donovan hesitated, not wishing to leave the newly-bereaved woman alone with her dead, but mindful of those still living who needed his help so desperately. As if sensing his inner conflict Charlotte drew a long tremulous breath,

45

and told him, 'My thanks, Sir, for your concern, but you may leave me now. I shall be well enough until my children come back. My Daniel was never cruel or unkind in life, what possible harm could come to me waiting here with his poor body.' Fresh sobs shook her shoulders, and she cuddled Martin to her, seeking to draw comfort from his young living flesh.

'Do you wish a priest?' Donovan asked.

'Neither Daniel or myself troubled overmuch about religion, Sir. There will be time enough for a priest when I come to bury my loved ones.' Again soundless sobbing wrenched at her mouth, and with a final touch of comfort on the thin shoulder, Doctor Donovan left the house.

Schull village was directly south of grey, bare-sloped Mount Gabriel and its smaller consorts. Some cabins, a large two-storeyed house on gently rising ground, and a decrepit white-washed chapel with a stone cross above its gabled entrance comprised its centre point. The nearest cabin to the chapel had been commandeered by the Commissariat Department for use as a food depot. All that depot contained were a few sacks of Indian maize meal.

Con, Sean and Mairead Shonley waited among the crowd of five hundred, mainly women, outside the barred door of the cabin. A solitary, carbine-armed policeman stood sentinel in front of the door, his forage cap pulled low on his forehead, his chin pressed deep into the collar of his caped greatcoat. The hours passed, and the women shuffled their bare feet, and talked quietly among themselves in low dispirited voices. Periodically some of the bolder women would question the sentry, asking when the sale of maize-flour was to start. Sympathetically he would shrug his shoulders and shake his head.

Finally, midway through the noon, two men in civilian clothing, wearing top hats and paletot coats came pushing through the docile crowd.

'It's themselves come!'

'It's the Commissaries!'

'Thanks be to God,' the women told each other in relief.

The taller of the two men shouted at the crowd, his accent betraying his Dublin origin. 'Now youse women, form an orderly line, and we'll soon have this business done.'

'What's the ration?' a gaunt, grey-haired woman with a shoal of children clinging to her skirts wanted to know.

'A pound of meal per person, and half a pound per child. At two pence the pound.' The man's wind-reddened face contained defensive anger, which deepened as a howl of execration burst from a hundred throats.

'Jasus, Joseph and Mary, t'wouldn't feed a cat!'

'May the saints forgive ye, ye bloody miser!' individual voice shouted.

'Tis not my doing,' the Dubliner blustered. 'I don't fix the ration scale, not the prices either.'

Meanwhile his colleague had unbarred the cabin door and gone inside. He now re-appeared, dragging a sack of the sulphurous yellow meal, and suspended a hanging-scale from a hook in the lintel of the door.

'Right, now, let's be having youse,' the Dubliner ordered, and the women pressed forwards, their hands clutching their precious coins and the battered utensils in which to carry the meal.

Con and his brother and sister joined the line. Each carried a small cloth bag, and Con handed the other two some coins. Nearer to the cabin a young girl was standing alone in the queue, her long black hair being blown about her slender shoulders by the skittish wind. Con noticed her, and stared hard, knowing that he had seen her before but at first unable to place where. Then it came to him. She was the girl in the cabin the night the police had caught him. He felt a pleasurable anticipation, and resolved to try and speak to her if possible.

Slowly the dolling out of the mealie flour continued, and now a soft drizzle started to fall, adding to the misery of those who waited. Con kept his gaze upon the girl, willing her to turn and look at him. But she remained facing the cabin, her body erect and proud, making no attempt to shield her head from the falling rain. The youth experienced a growing and strong attraction as he drank in the girl's beauty. Although thin, her body beneath its scant worn clothing was shapely, her breasts high and full, her hips rounded and her slender calves beneath the ragged skirt led down to dainty ankles and feet. Con felt compassion as he looked at her bare feet, almost blue with cold and streaked with the mud of the road.

'By God, she carries herself like a princess,' he thought admiringly.

The girl took her portion of meal in a tin bowl and walked away, not looking behind her or to the sides, but only straight ahead. Con's disappointment was acute that he had not caught her eye, and he decided to hurry after her as soon as possible.

The Shonleys collected their own meagre rations and started out on the long walk back to Skibereen. More than fourteen miles of winding rutted road had to be covered, and now thunder rolled in from the jagged indented coastline, and streaks of lightning flashed from the blackening skies.

Con set a fast pace, and his brother and sister were hardpressed to keep up with him. Always the youth's eyes searched the road ahead in hopes of seeing the proud slender figure of the black-haired girl. The land was empty of life, no animal grazed, no bird flew, no man, woman or child was met with on the road, and the isolated wayside cabins they passed were empty tumbledown ruins. Two, four, six, seven miles were travelled through the rocky surrounds of Ballydehob, that village seeming deserted, the buildings of its curved sloping main street closed and silent. Still Con had not glimpsed the girl he sought. His wish to see her became an overwhelming need as he paced onwards, and he selfishly disregarded the complaints and pleas to rest that both the twins constantly reiterated.

They passed into a shallow valley along which the road twisted snakelike to avoid the dangerous pits of greensedged bog, and on a rise to one side Con saw a solitary cabin. The rain had become a heavy downpour and the thunder pounded the land as the heart of the storm swept nearer. A bolt of lightning crackled and Con heard a terrified scream. He came to an abrupt halt and listened hard, his eyes searching the slopes of the valley.

'Did you hear that, Con?' Mairead's delicate face was fearful.

'Shh, listen!' The youth gestured for silence.

The scream echoed again, and Con shouted, 'It's coming from that cabin.' He moved quickly, leaping from one clump of sedge-grass to another across the bog before him, and then breaking into a run when he reached higher, firmer ground. Again the scream shattered the air, and as he ran he shouted, 'I'm coming! I'm coming.'

The black-haired girl was slumped against the outside wall of the cabin, her hands covering her face, and once more she screamed hysterically. Con was baffled as he approached her; he could see nothing to cause her terror. Then a sickly stench enveloped him, and from inside the cabin's shadowed interior he heard snarls and growls.

'Don't be afraid,' he shouted to the girl. 'I'll help you.'

He looked through the doorway of the half-ruined building, and horror stunned his mind. Three mangy, stick-ribbed dogs were savaging a woman's rotting corpse.

'Dear God!' Con half-sobbed, and fell back from the doorway. 'Dear God preserve us!'

For a few moments the shock of the terrible sight drove all volition from him. Then he recovered himself sufficiently to wave back his oncoming brother and sister. 'No! Stay there, don't come nearer.'

He went to the black-haired girl. 'Come now, honey.' Gently he took her arms and started to lead her away from the cabin. 'Come now, I'll look after you. It's all over now. It's all over. You're safe with me.' His words were an unthinking litany.

His broken boot collided with the tin bowl the girl had carried her flour in. The yellow sandlike grains had been washed across the ground by the pouring rain, and all was lost. Con stared down at the yellow-streaked mud, and could have wept with pity for the girl beside him.

The minutes passed and the shock of terror that had so unnerved Grainne gradually receded and she grew calm once more. The handsome dark-haired young man, whom she had recognized at the grain depot as the one brought to her cabin by the police some nights previously, gently questioned her, and she replied to his questions, telling him her name and her antecedents, and of her return from England to find her father gone and her mother living with another man, her uncle.

'Do you miss your Pa?' Con asked, his eyes hungrily fixed on her beauty.

She smiled mirthlessly, white teeth shining against full lips. 'No, I do not. I hated him for the way he treated my mother.'

'So you'll be happy now, living with her and your uncle?'

Again the mirthless smile. 'No! My uncle serves my mother like my father did before him.' Attracted as powerfully as she was towards her rescuer, a perverse imp of mischief stirred in Grainne, and she could not resist testing the strength of her own appeal over the young man. 'And he tries to make free with me if he gets the chance.'

Con experienced a surge of jealous fury. 'What do you mean, make free?'

Grainne stole a glance at his troubled face, and felt a pleasing gratification. 'He likes me!' she told herself, and could not help but torment him further. 'Well, you know what I mean, don't you. Or have you been raised for the priesthood?'

Already half-infatuated by her beauty the young man's jealous anger intensified. 'By God, if he tries to make free with you again, then come to me, Con Shonley. I'll break his blaggard head for him.'

Inwardly Grainne hugged herself with delight. 'He really does like me! He really does!' she told herself gleefully, then said aloud, but unable to keep a note of satisfaction from her voice, 'Whisht now, it's only when me uncle has the drink in him that he tries to lay hands on me. And then there's no great harm done. He only touches me.'

'Where? Where does he touch you?' It was like the compulsion to poke at an aching tooth.

Glorying in her power to disturb him, Grainne's devil of mischief held her in thrall, and she laughed aloud. 'Why, where do you think?' She drew a deep breath to lift and thrust out her shapely breasts. 'Are you an idjit? Where do men always like to touch women?'

Involuntarily Con looked at the full firm swellings of her breasts, and down to where her long thighs swept to merge with her lower belly.

Grainne's green eyes narrowed slightly, and despite herself she found a faintly malicious pleasure in baiting this man with whom she was fast becoming infatuated in her turn. 'But why should it concern you, Con Shonley? I mean nothing to you. Aren't we strangers to each other?'

'No, we are not strangers to each other!' Con declared hotly. 'Not any more, we're not.'

Her laughter rang out full and free, gay with her delight, and she let him take her hand and lead her onwards, and the long miles became short for them as they prattled artlessly to each other, and hung on to each other's every word.

All too soon for both of them they came to the parting of their ways at the ruins of the Cistercian monastery of Abbey Strowry, its hummocky burial ground scarred by the heaps of fresh-dug soil, under which the famine dead lay naked in mass graves.

Con took the three half-full bags of mealie flour and divided the yellow powder into two full bags. 'Here Grainne, take this.' He gave her one of the bags.

Grainne took it, and for a moment her heart was too full for her to speak. She stared speculatively into his rapt face. 'Will I see you again, Con Shonley?' she asked gravely.

His heart swelled with joy. 'To be sure you will, Grainne MacDermott, and mayhap sooner than you think.'

Suddenly, in the midst of her own happiness, terrible doubt assailed Grainne. 'I must be mad,' she told herself. 'To think of loving this man in the time that is upon us now. What about my mother? What about the wee ones?

How can I think of them, and at the same time think of love with Con Shonley?' A frown creased lines upon her brow, and for a moment she looked far older than her years. 'No!' she decided with a heart-wrenching effort. 'I can't let this affair go further. No matter how much I might want to see him again, I must put my mother and the wee ones first.' When she spoke out it was as if someone other than herself was speaking through her lips. 'Don't tell anyone we've met, Con. And don't be coming to see me. My uncle would not be happy if you did that.'

The young man stared blankly at her, not understanding her sudden hostility. 'But didn't you just ask me if we'd meet again?' he protested.

'Did I now,' she forced herself to speak coldly, 'I'm the best judge of what I meant by my words, Con Shonley, and don't be forgetting that.'

She turned and ran, her black hair flying out behind her, and Con stood staring helplessly after her until the gloom and rain veiled her slender figure.

His thoughts a jumble of puzzlement, he led his brother and sister back to their home. When he reached it and saw what awaited him, his thoughts were quickly clarified. A bitter anguish of grief drove all other emotions from his mind . . .

Chapter Seven

It was Father Boyce who came from his own parish a week later to conduct the burial service for Daniel Shonley and his infant daughter, the local priest, Father Barry, being ill with fever. After the necessarily brief ceremony the priest took Con Shonley aside.

'You know well that I'm sorry for your trouble, Con,' he began, and the ever-present dewdrop quivered on the tip of his long red nose as he drew a deep breath, then continued hurriedly, 'but the dead are gone from this unhappy life, and 'tis the living that we must concern ourselves with.'

The youth had by now come to terms with his grief. He nodded. 'I know that, Father.'

'Good man, yourself!' Boyce's child-sized hand patted the broad shoulder to which the top of his head only came level. 'Now, Con, great happenings are afoot. As I told you before, in January last, the leaders of Young Ireland formed an organization known as the Irish Confederation. The idea being to form "Confederate Clubs" in every city, town and parish in this country, composed of true Irish patriots prepared to fight for their country's cause.'

The priest's fervent voice dropped to a whisper, and he became suddenly despondent. 'Unfortunately we're not having a deal of luck with it. What was meant to be a revolutionary campaign, is become just a talking shop.' His voice rose shrilly, 'Arrah yes! Isn't it always so, you'll be thinking. Isn't that what always happens here in Ireland? Our patriots would gladly die for their country when they've the bellyfull of drink taken. But when they're sober again, then it's a different kettle o' fish altogether.' He glared aggressively at the tall youth, his wide-set eyes burning beneath the wide brim of his over-large hat. Lifting his forefinger he poked Con hard on the chest. 'But I'm telling you, young Shonley, that I am not prepared to allow such windbags to discourage me. John Mitchel has written in *The Nation* only two weeks back, that he and his followers can endure this horrible scene no longer. They are resolved to cross the path of the British car of conquest, even though it should crush them to atoms!' Boyce nodded vigorously and grinned in utter satisfaction. 'There now, young Shonley, what d'ye think to that? Isn't it grand?'

Con stood silent, remembering how his beloved father had appeared lying in the shoddy coffin with his baby daughter beside him. Not even the release of death had smoothed the deep-etched lines of suffering from Daniel Shonley's face. The youth's anger fed upon this memory. 'I'll tell you now, Father Boyce,' he said slowly and deliberately, 'my father lies in his grave because of the wicked policies of the British Government. I want vengeance for him!'

'And you shall have your vengeance,' the priest assured him vehemently.

'How?'

'With pike and musket, my son,' Boyce whispered, 'with shot and shell and flames . . . I've a man coming to my parish within the week. A trained military man. He is going to instruct us in the arts of war . . . Will you join us?'

Without hesitation Con nodded. 'I will, and gladly.'

The little man's tense body visibly relaxed. 'Good man yourself. I'll be in touch.'

With that, he hurried away, his cassock billowing about his thin body, his long nose cocked high as if he scented something on the breeze.

Con watched him go, and excitement burgeoned rapidly. 'By God, I'll avenge you Pa, I swear it,' he muttered aloud. 'On your grave I swear it.'

Chapter Eight

Grainne stood slightly apart from the wretched crowd clustered at the gates of Clover Hill House. Mercifully the morning was dry and the pale sunlight gave a degree of warmth to the air. At the gates two uniformed constables were stationed to prevent desperately hungry people from entering the grounds and storming the house itself to demand food and money from the Relief Committee which was meeting within its tall walls.

Grainne herself was fighting an inner battle with her own fierce pride. Never in her life had she asked for charity, and now, although she accepted the stark necessity of doing so, still she found it hard to contemplate standing before strangers to plead for the pittance they might then allot to her.

After long hours of waiting she was beckoned forward and admitted through the spiked iron gates. A large room leading off the main entrance hall had been utilized for the Committee, and Grainne stood before the long table behind which were seated J Macarthy Downing Esq, Mr Richard Inglis of the Commissariat, the Reverend Caulfield and Mr Grady of the Board of Works. To one side of the room Sub-Inspector Hardy was seated on a tall-backed chair, as if he distanced himself deliberately from the Committee.

The men stared appreciatively at the girl, her beauty a welcome sight to eyes jaded with the spectacle of femininity made ugly and degraded by bitter deprivation. Aware of the speculative gleams in the eyes fixed upon her Grainne stood with heightened colour, acute embarrassment adding to her distaste at having to beg for charity.

It was Macarthy Downing who questioned her as to her identity and antecedents. When he heard that she had recently returned from England, he exclaimed audibly in surprise, and demanded, 'Then what in God's name possessed you to return here, girl? Did you not know that you would only become yet another burden to add to the burdens we are already labouring beneath?'

Grainne's fiery spirit reacted instantly, and she met the man's accusing stare with angry eyes. 'Where else should I have gone then?' she asked heatedly. 'This is my home, and I've a right to be here with my family, haven't I? Should I have stayed in England and either starved there, or have gone on the streets as a common whore like so many other poor girls are forced to do?'

'Keep a civil tongue in your head, girl,' the florid-faced Reverend Caulfield admonished her sternly.

Grainne turned on him. 'How can it be uncivil to answer a question honestly?' she demanded spiritedly.

The florid face darkened with pique and the clergyman riposted, 'If it comes to that, how do we know that you do belong here, girl? Do you have anyone of respectable position to vouch for your identity, and for the truth of what you tell us? You come here with hand outstretched for succour, yet you do not bring any evidence to support your story, or any proof of your respectability.'

Before she could reply help came for Grainne from an unexpected quarter.

'I can vouch for the truth of what the girl has told you, gentlemen,' Sub-Inspector Hardy spoke from his chair. 'She and her family are known to me. She is of good character, although rather too free with her tongue to her betters.'

Grainne's gaze swung to the policeman, and he frowned slightly at her, his eyes giving friendly warning that she should now hold her peace.

Realizing that if she were to get anything from the Committee, she had indeed best remain silent, Grainne subdued her pride and for the remainder of her interrogation answered with the due degree of civility.

At last, after long deliberation, the Committee granted Grainne a ticket entitling her to work on the Public Road scheme at four pence a day.

'You'll take this ticket to Mr Michael Kearney, girl,' Macarthy Downing instructed her. 'Mind you do as he bids, and go to your labour willingly. Do you know where the road-works are situated?'

Grainne nodded assent, and the man waved in dismissal.

'Then be off with you, girl.'

'Well now, aren't you the pretty thing.' Surrounded by his henchmen Michael Kearney lounged back against the outer wall of the wooden shanty. 'And you're Jim Mac-Dermott's wee niece come back from over the water, are yez?'

Grainne squirmed inwardly as the man's lustful stare roamed over her body, seeming to penetrate the thin cloth that covered her breasts and thighs.

He sucked his teeth noisily and was about to say something more when a gangsman shouted to him from further along the site. 'Mr Kearney? Mr Kearney, the Engineer's on his way.'

Kearney's narrow brow creased in a scowl. 'Bad cess to the bastard! Coming to poke his bloody nose into things agin. You lot get back to your gangs, and get the bastards slogging hard afore the bloody Engineer sees 'um doing fuck-all.'

They hastened to obey and he grinned at Grainne. 'Go you on up to the end there, girlie.' He pointed up the site. 'Find Tommy Murphy and tell him I've sent ye. You can work on the basket-carrying with his gang for the time being.'

'Thank you, Mr Kearney,' she murmured, and would have walked away, but he gestured her to remain.

'I doubt you'll be thanking me after you've tried the work, pretty thing. The rain and the wind makes it sore toil at times. But then, who knows,' he leered suggestively at her. 'Perhaps if you and me becomes good close friends, I might be able to put an easier, better paid job your way.

57

Michael Kearney knows how to look after them who looks after him, in a manner o' speaking.'

Grainne shook her head. 'I'm a good-living girl, Mr Kearney,' she said quietly, but very firmly. 'I'll be content to work at the basket-carrying with the other women.'

His leer faltered, and he jerked his head for her to go. 'We'll see, girlie, we'll see. A few weeks in the wet and cold might change your mind for yez.'

Grainne smiled coldly. 'I doubt that, Mr Kearney.'

Turning on her heels she walked proudly away, leaving Michael Kearney staring at her back and sucking disgruntledly at his teeth.

The darkness had long fallen when cold, hungry and weary, Grainne walked slowly up the track towards her cabin. As she neared its dark hummock she heard the voice of Jim MacDermott bellowing oaths, and then came the high-pitched screams of her mother, mingled with the terrified shrieking and wailing of the children. Grainne broke into a run and went slamming through the half-open door of the cabin. Inside in the guttering glow of the rush-light she saw her mother cowering like a beaten animal on her hands and knees, blood streaming from her nose and mouth, and a drunken Jim MacDermott standing over the woman, fists clenched, mouth gaping wide as he screeched a tirade of filth.

A terrible fury filled Grainne's being and she hurled herself at the man, screaming at him while her fists belaboured his head and body. Taken by surprise he stumbled sideways and tripped and fell sprawling heavily. Grainne stared wildly about her, seeking for a weapon, and saw the heavy cast-iron skillet by the side of the smouldering peat fire. Snatching it up she brandished it aloft as MacDermott tried to rise to his feet.

'Stay there, you bastard!' Grainne screamed at him. 'Stay there, or I'll break your bloody head for you. If you move I'll bloody kill you! I swear, I'll bloody kill you.'

Cowed by her ferocity and the unexpectedness of her

attack, the man remained motionless, his bleared eyes staring apprehensively up at her.

Groaning and sobbing her mother painfully struggled upright, and used her ragged apron to staunch the flow of blood from her nose and mouth. The children's shrieking cries redoubled in intensity as they saw their mother's bloodied face, and Grainne beseeched them desperately, 'Be quiet now, kids, be quiet. Your Mammy will be all right now. Everything will be all right now. Be quiet, for the love o' God, be quiet.'

She glared down at her uncle. 'Get you gone from here, you bastard.' She hurled the words into his dazed face. 'Get you gone from here right now, or by God above, I'll swing for you.' She stepped towards him shaking with fury, the heavy iron skillet swinging menacingly, and like some huge, ungainly crab he scrabbled across the dirt floor and out of the open door. As he went through that door Grainne darted to it, slammed it shut and barred it with the thick wooden stave that served as a lock. Then she let the skillet fall and went to her mother, easing the moaning sobbing, bleeding woman down onto the rough wooden bench that flanked the crudely fashioned table.

There was water in the earthenware bowl by the fireside and Grainne tore a strip from the bottom of her dress and dampened it in that water then deftly and gently began to cleanse her mother's wounds, crooning softly as she did so. 'There now, Mammy, hush now. Hush now, darling. He's gone. He won't hit you any more. You're safe from him now because I'm here. I'll look after you. Hush now, Mammy. Hush now . . . Hush . . . '

On the following night when she returned from work Grainne experienced a sickening shock to find Jim MacDermott seated before the fireside in the cabin.

'What's he doing here?' she demanded angrily, but her mother refused to answer, or to meet her accusing stare.

Grainne confronted her uncle. 'I told you to go from here, and to stay away from us!' Her voice was high-pitched and throbbing with barely controlled anger.

The man's decayed teeth glistened blackly in the fire-light. 'Sure now, ye don't have the understanding of how me and your Mammy feels towards each other,' he said, and mockery laced his tone. 'It's like this, you see, Grainne, my jewel. Your Mammy's my woman now, and I'm her man, and although we might have our little spats now and agin, well there's no harm really done, and it don't affect the fact that we're sworn to each other.' A harder note edged his voice as he spoke to the older woman. 'Tell her, Theresa. Tell her how it is with us.'

Still unable to meet her daughter's accusing eyes, Theresa MacDermott mumbled through her swollen lips. 'Jim is my man now, Grainne, and he comes first with me, before all you kids. If you don't like it, then you must lump it.'

A sickening sense of betrayal flooded through Grainne, so strong that it caused her stomach to physically heave. Unable to speak she went blindly outside and for long minutes stood in the damp blackness of the night trying to marshall her maelstrom of emotions. Eventually she was able to think somewhat rationally about the situation confronting her. 'I can only wait and pray for me Mammy to come to her senses, and to see what a worthless scut that man really is. If I leave her now then he'll destroy her, just as surely as the sun rises in the morning, the bastard will destroy her. I'll have to stay here. I'll have to stay and do my best to protect her from her own stupid self.'

Feeling utterly alone and friendless in the world Grainne slowly returned to the cabin, and forced herself to ignore Jim MacDermott's triumphant grin.

Chapter Nine

James Mahoney waited for a full two weeks to elapse following Daniel Shonley's funeral before he went to call upon the widow. Rising early, he performed his toilette with care. Brushing his hair and sidewhiskers until they shone, cleaning his teeth and gargling with rosewater until satisfied his breath was sweet. He examined his appearance closely in the mirror of his bedroom at Clover Hill House, then tilted his top hat at a jaunty angle, lifted his silver-knobbed cane, and headed for the Shonley home.

As he neared the lonely building he felt all the nervousness of a young boy going to meet his first love. How would she receive him? Would she be pleased? Displeased? Or merely indifferent?

A small boy opened the door to Mahoney's rap. The man smiled down at the solemn face lifted to him.

'Is your mother within, boy?'

Martin Shonley stared in wonder at the elegant figure before him, so tall, so well looking, so perfumed. It was some moments before he became aware of the man's repeated question.

'Is your mother within?'

He nodded, and ran shouting down the hallway, 'Mamma! Mamma, come quickly.'

A door at the end of the empty stone-flagged passage opened, and Mahoney caught his breath. It was Charlotte, looking in the shadows still the young girl he had met and loved so long ago. Puzzled and half-afraid she hurried to him.

'Yes, Sir, what is it you want?'

He smiled, and saw sudden recognition flood her clear blue eyes.

'Why, it is James! James Mahoney!'

'Indeed it is, Charlotte,' he confirmed, and stared greedily. Beneath the blue eyes were the dark bruises of sorrow and hardship, her body was painfully thin, and her once-soft white hands were reddened and roughened by physical labour, yet he found her beautiful. He took off his top hat and for a while they stood awkwardly facing each other across the doorway. He gestured, 'May I?'

Embarrassment flustered her, bringing a glow to her pale cheeks. 'Oh, forgive my ill manners. Please, do come in. It has been such a shock. Your appearing so suddenly after all these years.'

'Seventeen years, Charlotte,' he told her gravely, 'seventeen long years.'

He followed her along the passageway and into the kitchen at its end. The ever-present turf fire burned smokily, and Mahoney welcomed its warmth, his body trembling with nervousness.

The room was spotlessly clean, the only furnishings three upright wooden chairs, an ancient rickety table, and a few pots and pans, one of which hung on a chain above the fire, yellow-gruel simmering in its bottom.

Still flustered, the woman took her visitor's hat and cane and placed them on the table, then invited him to be seated opposite her by the hearth. 'I'm sorry, but I am not able to offer you tea, or other refreshments,' she began, and he lifted his hand to stop her apologies.

'Please, there is no need. I know how you are situated.' Quickly, his own nervousness causing him to rush his words, James Mahoney explained how he had come to be in the district, and how he had seen her in the town. 'I can only offer you my deepest condolences on your sad loss, Charlotte. Naught can soften your grief but the passage of time.'

Sadness entered his own voice, and she noticed it instantly.

'You have also lost someone dear to you, James?' The question was really a statement.

'Yes,' he told her, and glanced at the child, Martin, standing by his mother's knee. 'My dear wife died in child-birth some years past. The boy would have been about the age of your son, if he had lived.'

Even in her own sorrow, Charlotte Shonley could still be moved by the man's transparent sadness. 'I feel for you, James,' she told him softly. 'Do you have other children?'

Mahoney shook his head. 'No, we had not long been wed. It was our first child.' He saw the blue eyes glisten with tears, and went on hastily. 'But enough of that. It is all long past. I have not come here with the intention of increasing your burdens, but rather to enquire what I may do to lessen them.'

She looked at him quizzically, and he was sensitive enough to realize why. 'Please, my dear lady, do not think for one moment that I come like one of those well-meaning missionaries to offer you the consolation of prayer . . . Indeed no!' he added emphatically. 'I wish rather to help you in a practical manner.'

'You are very kind, James. But I manage well enough,' she answered quietly, her pride showing.

His expression mirrored his concern. ''Pon my soul! I state my case too bluntly, and offend you I fear. But believe me, my intentions are of the purest.' He leaned forward, his dark eyes serious and intent. 'Pray hear me out, Charlotte, and do not interrupt, even though I may unwittingly offend your sensibilities . . . When I knew you, all those years ago, I loved you. Tragically, for me, you were a wedded wife and mother and happy with a husband whom you loved. Slowly, I learned to accept without bitter-ness, the fact that you could never be mine. But always you remained in my heart. By a miracle I have found you once more. Sadly, you are grief-torn and in want, like so many other poor souls in this unhappy land . . . Please, let me help you. If not for your sake, then for the sake of your children . . . And not least, for my sake . . . I am a very lonely man. To know that you were my friend would bring me great joy, and would do much to brighten and give purpose to my dull and empty days.'

As she listened, Charlotte Shonley sensed the sincerity behind his words. When he ceased to talk and sat waiting for her reply, she smiled, and said gently, 'I also sorely need a friend, I do confess . . . And what better than an old friend who was once very dear to me.'

He chuckled in heartfelt relief. 'Then I shall be that friend, Charlotte; and shall prove a true one to both you, and your children.'

Chapter Ten

'On the twenty-fourth o' May
Before the break o' day,
We all got under arms and to Prosperous made
way . . . '

The old man's voice quavered violently, and thin
tendons stood out in his wattled throat as he sang.

'Steadily we marched,
Under Captain Farrel's orders.
It's in the town we halted and set it in a blaze.'

'Good for ye!' one of his audience, half-drunk, bawled
jeeringly.

The old man scowled at his interrupter, but went on
singing.

'Bullets they were flying,
Soldiers groaning dying,
Smoke to the skies arising, and Swayne expiring
therrrrre!'

He dragged out the final note of his song and ended,
gasping for breath.

Good natured cheering went up from the large crowd of
men surrounding him in the small valley, and one of them
handed a jug of poteen to the singer, who snatched at it
eagerly. He gulped the strong liquor and expelled air
noisily.

'Arrah, 'tis the real stuff this.' He glared rheumily at his neighbours and his toothless mouth twisted contemptuously. 'But ye're not the real stuff! Ye're not the men o' '98!' he declared, shaking his bald head. 'Ye'll not match them brave boys!'

'How can you say that?' a young red-haired man, his hands clutching a hooked and hatcheted pike challenged indignantly.

The old man spat into a tuft of grass. 'Because I was one o' them meself. Didn't I fight at Oulart Hill, and Enniscorthy, and wasn't I at Thomas Cloney's elbow when we stormed New Ross.'

Con Shonley listened with fascination. Here before him was one of the legendary 'Croppy Boys'. One of those who had fought in the great rebellion of 1798 when French soldiers came to aid the Protestant-led United Irishmen and the Catholic Defenders in their bid for freedom from England's rule. He moved nearer to the ancient speaker, and was about to question him further, when a sudden shout from one of the lookouts on top of the valley slope distracted him.

'Now boys, make ready. Here's Father Boyce coming.'

The tiny priest was in company with a man much taller than himself. A strong-bodied, large-headed, strutting man, with a face burned deep brown by hotter suns than could be felt in Ireland. He wore the caubeen, short blue cloak, knee-breeches, woollen stockings and stout leather boots of a prosperous peasant farmer, but his erect bearing was such that the clothes seemed like a military uniform. His eyes were grey, and now hard with contemptuous anger as they noted the cask of poteen, and the jugs passing among the men lounging on the grass of the valley.

Most of the men, except for those too engrossed with drinking, got to their feet and clustered about the priest and his companion. Father Boyce was red-faced with the exertion of his journey, but he had sufficient breath to castigate his followers for bringing drink with them.

'I'm shamed, so I am,' he declaimed in his high-pitched voice, his hands waving in the air. 'This isn't meant to be a drunken spree. I've brought Mr Rourke here to give you military instruction, and some of you are too drunk to know what day of the week it is. I swear by all that is sacred to me, that if the Peelers and soldiers saw ye now, they'd die from laughing, and that's the only way you worthless scoundrels will ever manage to kill any o' them, if you continue in this manner.'

The majority of the men looked shame-faced, some resentful, and a few uncaring of the priest's remonstrances. Although Con Shonley had not drunk any of the poteen himself, he felt a sense of guilty shame. His youthful idealism had pictured this first training period as being a meeting of grim-faced men, determined to drive the forces of the Government into the sea. He felt acute disappointment because most of the men around him appeared to be treating it as a skylark, and an opportunity to get drunk.

'Well, never mind it now, we'll just have to make the best of it, and mind ourselves in the future,' Boyce's shrill voice broke Con's train of thought. 'I'll give you over into Mr Rourke's charge,' the priest went on, 'and I think I'd best join the rest of ye in the files, for I've not the slightest notion of the drill meself.'

His rueful admission was greeted with laughter, and the mood of the men lightened once more.

'Right, now, I want you to form into two ranks in front of me.' Rourke's basic accent was that of County Cork, but was overlaid by sing-song inflexions of speech that Con Shonley couldn't identify.

The men shuffled into two ragged, wavering lines. Rourke strutted along the ranks, his hard eyes evaluating their content. Some men carried pikes, two or three had fowling pieces, but most only possessed long staves. Con himself carried a long stave, and when Rourke looked at him the young man tried to hold himself like a soldier. The man's lips twitched in a smile as he noticed Con, and he checked his stride to say, 'Good man, you've the notion of it anyway.'

The young man felt gratified pride course through him, and drew his flat stomach in even further.

In front of the ranks once more, Rourke halted, and

stood at rigid attention as he faced his audience. 'You men are here to learn something of the art of war.' His voice carried easily to every ear. 'It takes months to teach a man his drills, and more months to teach him how to make best use of his weapons . . . And then it takes a battle to make him a soldier.'

Even those men who were drunk listened hard to his words. Something in the timbre of his voice penetrated their dulled senses and held them absorbed.

'Some day, God willing, you'll be facing some of the finest soldiers in the world. The British Army. I've faced them afore on the battlefield, and make no mistake, they can fight like devils outta Hell. But that's as maybe. You've the one great advantage over them. They're fighting for a shilling a day. You'll be fighting for your freedom . . . '

'This is grand stuff,' Con told himself. 'This is as it should be.' He experienced a birthing of hero-worship for the erect, sun-bronzed man before him.

' . . . You must listen well, and work hard,' Rourke continued. 'I'll make you into soldiers if you do . . . That I can promise you . . . '

Until the dusk came Rourke instructed them in the basics of foot and marching drill. Keeping them hard at it without pause. When some of the men protested and wanted to rest, his deep voice pounded them unmercifully, until shamed before their fellows, they ceased protesting and endured in silence with the others.

Con Shonley gloried in the hard physical exercise. He believed that at last he was doing something positive for his country's cause. He was taking the first steps to become a soldier of liberty.

'There were about fifty there, Sergeant. I know most of them by sight and a lot by name.' Jim MacDermott kept his voice low and his mouth close to Police Sergeant Macarthy's hair-tufted ear. It was nearly midnight and inside the cabin the sergeant's lantern and the glow from the hearth created a pool of light in which the two men sat.

Outside the cabin the wind soughed mournfully, and clouds scudded across the moon, dappling the land with shifting shadows.

From the half-loft she was sharing with her sleeping mother and younger brothers and sisters, Grainne MacDermott watched her uncle and the policeman, and strained her hearing to catch their muted words.

The sergeant sucked on the stubby clay pipe in his mouth, then cursed softly and took it from between his nicotine-stained teeth. 'Devil take it, the bloody bacco must be damp. I can't get a decent smoke from it.'

MacDermott's drawn features betrayed the hunger for tobacco he was feeling as he stared at the dead pipe. 'Would ye have the bit to spare, Sergeant? I've not had a taste of it this day long?' he beseeched.

The burly sergeant pulled a leather pouch from his greatcoat pocket and handed it to the other man, saying as he did so, 'Tell me now, who is this fella, Rourke? D'ye know him?'

MacDermott didn't answer until he had stuffed the bowl of his own clay pipe with the dark, strong-smelling leaf. Then he shook his head. 'I do not. And nor does anyone else there know him, except for the priest, that is. The fella looks as if he's bin in foreign parts, and he's got the cut of an old soldier, that's for sure. He knows the drills all right. I heard one of the boys ask Father Boyce where your man was from, but the wee scut wouldn't give the answer.'

From his capacious greatcoat pocket the sergeant drew a scrap of paper and a piece of charcoal. 'Give me the names of those ye know,' he ordered.

MacDermott was using a glowing lump of peat to light his pipe. He drew smoke deep into his lungs, then coughed and spluttered. 'Jasus, that's lovely so it is.'

'Come on, man, give me the names.' Macarthy's broad face showed a hint of temper, and MacDermott was quick to comply.

'There was Father Boyce, the three Murphy brothers from Leap. Old Sean Cassidy, him as was a Croppy Boy . . . There was young Con Shonley . . . '

Up in the half-loft Grainne MacDermott vented a muted gasp. 'Con Shonley a rebel! The Peelers will surely take him some day.'

The depth of her own concern disturbed her so that she was not able to sleep again that night. But she struggled against what she perceived to be her own weak selfishness. 'It's my Mammy that needs me, not him,' she reiterated over and over again, drilling the words deep into her brain.

Sub-Inspector Hardy studied the list of names written on the scrap of paper. Opposite him on the other side of the desk in the cramped office of the Police Barracks at Skibereen, Sergeant Macarthy waited patiently. After ten minutes of unbroken silence the inspector put down the paper and looked across at his NCO.

'It's as we thought then, Sergeant. The only name new to us is this man, Rourke.'

'Aye, Sir,' Macarthy confirmed.

Hardy ran one hand through his close-cut thinning hair, then with the fingers of the same hand eased the tight, high silk-stock around his neck. He brought both hands together in front of him, fingers forming a steeple, leaned back in his chair, and spoke his musing aloud. 'We already know that the Young Ireland movement want to bring about rebellion. Mitchel and Meagher are quite openly stating that fact. The Government are not unduly alarmed at this point in time about that prospect. There are not enough arms or powder in would-be rebel hands to stage an uprising, and pikes are no match for cannon and musket . . . '

'Should we arrest some of these local men, Sir?' Macarthy wanted to know.

The inspector shook his head. 'No Sergeant, there is no need. Let them carry on with their silly games in the valley. We'll continue to maintain a close observation, and naturally I'll send a full report to Dublin.' He laughed shortly. 'At least we know where to net all our birds if the need should ever arise . . . But try to find out more about Rourke, he interests me . . . '

Chapter Eleven

The weeks slowly passed, and now under orders from the Treasury Department the Public Works began to close down. Thousands of people were dismissed from their employment losing the meagre pittance that had been their hold on life, and landlords increased the forced evictions of their pauper tenants. The peasantry, no longer able to survive in their own districts, took to the roads. Begging, stealing, starving, and always dying, the dispossessed thousands and tens of thousands flooded eastwards towards England, Scotland and Wales, and more thousands went westwards, in the coffin ships that would carry them to the New World of America and Canada. The Great Exodus had begun . . .

For the Shonleys at least, temporary survival was assured. Through the influence of James Mahoney the three eldest children were enabled to find work of sorts when it was available at the local Commissariat depots. Mahoney also ensured that sufficient extra food and money found its way to the Shonley home to raise up their dietary standard. For Con Shonley, Mahoney's help was a source of resentment. Particularly it damaged his self-esteem for he felt that it reflected on his own failure to provide for his family. Also it was galling to be forced into accepting the charity of a man, who while bearing an Irish name, was of English birth and loyalties.

This resentment festered until it came to a head one evening in late March. Con came home proudly carrying some eggs he had managed to buy from one of the more fortunate farmers. He walked into his mother's kitchen and presented them to her with a flourish, waiting with expectant pleasure for her pleased reaction. She merely placed them on a shelf, and went on tending a stew made from vegetables and meat that James Mahoney had sent to her that same afternoon.

Con sat at the table in the kitchen and sullenly watched his mother bustling about her domestic tasks. Her thin features had filled out a little, and during the last few days she had begun to smile again, even to hum tunes to herself. The youth fuelled his resentment of Mahoney by deliberately thinking of his dead father, and his sullen resentment became a rage.

Charlotte Shonley became aware of her eldest son's sour expression. 'What's the matter, Con? Why do you glare so? Is it because the food is not ready, I couldn't help it, the meat is taking longer to cook than I had expected . . . But never mind, it'll taste all the sweeter for waiting.'

'Will it now?' The youth, even though beginning to feel ashamed of his own surliness, could not help himself. 'It takes little enough to make you happy, Mother. I can see that.'

Her forehead creased in a frown of puzzlement. 'Why should I not feel some happiness?' she asked slowly. 'Have we not cause to feel happy with such a fine dinner almost ready?'

'A pity Pa is not here to share it!' Con blurted out. 'He'd enjoy that damned Englishman's charity, without doubt . . . I'm just wondering what payment the Englishman is receiving for his charity, that's all?'

For a moment, Charlotte Shonley paled, and her face reflected her disbelief that she had heard correctly. Then hot anger forced blood to her cheeks. 'What do you mean by that?' her voice throbbed with emotion.

Con wished with all his heart that he had bitten his tongue out before saying what he had. Then his own guilt forced him to bluster in attempt to avert his mother's recriminations. 'I meant only what I said. Pa would have enjoyed the meal.'

The woman came to stand over his bowed head and shoulders. 'No, I want to know what you implied by wondering what payment Mr Mahoney required?'

Bitterly repenting of his outburst, and lost for words, the youth could only shake his head. 'I implied nothing.'

'You are a mean-minded, despicable coward!'

Con stared in amazement as his mother hurled the words at him, never having seen her so angry in his life. Half-apprehensive he went to stand up, and her work-roughened hand cracked across his mouth with such venom that it cut his lips.

'Get from my sight! Go this instant, before I do you a mortal injury!' she screamed at him, the only colour in her face now two fiery patches on her cheeks. The next instant she moaned and slumped down, her hands covering her eyes, her body racked with weeping.

His throat thick with remorse, Con went to her and put his hand gently on her shoulder. At first she tried to push him away, but he held her firmly. 'I'm sorry, Mother, truly I'm sorry. I cannot think what drove me to say such a vile thing. Please forgive me.'

Still weeping she turned to him and choked out, 'What is happening to you, Con. Tell me what is happening to change you so? Tell me.'

Tears stung in his own eyes, and he could only reply, 'I cannot tell you, for I don't know myself . . .'

Chapter Twelve

It was the first day of April, and the hard grip of winter was still not completely broken. A storm of sleet and hail lashed the gardens of Clover Hill House, and James Mahoney's mood was as sombre as the dark skies. His commission for the *Illustrated London News* had long been completed, but he had stayed on in Skibereen, so that he could be near Charlotte Shonley. He had fully accepted the fact that he was again in love with her, and often wondered if during the past fourteen years, he had ever not been. The difficulty lay in persuading her to love him in return. Recently he had begun tentatively hinting at marriage. But she had chosen deliberately to evade any talk between them of a shared future.

Although Mahoney was comfortably situated financially, he was by no means a wealthy man, and could not continue to remain in Ireland indefinitely. His home in England, with his cook, maid-servant and man-servant had still to be maintained at considerable expense, and now that his payment from the periodical was gone, he was forced to live on capital. He must of necessity return to England and seek other commissions for his work.

Since meeting again with Charlotte Shonley, he had given his future much thought, and realized that without her to share it, it did not hold much attraction for him. But, he also realized that the time had come for a firm decision on his part. He must leave no doubt in the woman's mind as to the strength of his own feelings for her.

He decided to make a direct proposal of marriage. If her answer was negative, then Mahoney would return immediately to England . . . If her answer should be affirmative, James Mahoney smiled happily at the thought, then he would return immediately to England, with his new family beside him . . .

'Marriage?' Charlotte Shonley's delicate features reflected her uncertainty.

The man standing before her spoke urgently. 'Oh I know, my dear, that the earth has barely settled on your poor husband's grave. If I had time to observe the proprieties of society, I would not have been so boorish as to ask for your hand at this point. But we are not living in normal days, or among normal society. We are living in a period of calamity. Death stalks through this land like a reaper at harvest. To think of the dangers you face remaining here chills the blood in my veins. Who can tell what fresh afflictions may befall you and yours if you stay in this country. I offer you an honourable means of escape.' He paused, and his eyes shone with intense sincerity. 'You know that I love you, and have loved you ever since I first met you. Become my wife and with your children return home with me. You are an English woman Charlotte, your true home is not here in Ireland.'

'But my children are Irish, and this is their home,' she argued.

'Your children are very young, my dear. They can adapt themselves easily to change.' He thought of another compelling point to make. 'Surely it will be to their best advantage to live as gentlefolk in England, rather than to struggle to exist here. Doing work of the most menial. Suffering want and hardship. Risking bodily injury and disease every time they go forth from this house.'

The woman absorbed his impassioned words, and inwardly acknowledged the truth of them. The future, and what it might bring, terrified her. But she had deeply loved Daniel Shonley. He had been the first and only lover she had ever known. She knew with utter certainty that the emptiness his death had left in her heart could never be filled by any other man. Therefore how could it ever be fair and just to enter into marriage with another man, who, as a husband, had the right to demand her devotion and love.

She studied James Mahoney with troubled eyes. He was handsome, of that there was no doubt. He was kind and generous. He was a true gentleman, and she believed his protestations of the love he bore her to be sincere. Yet she also knew that for her he could never mean more than a companion she was deeply fond of.

But there was not just herself to consider. Her children needed the care and protection that only a father could give them . . .

She saw the face of her eldest son in her mind's eye. 'Con needs no one, I fear,' she told herself sadly. 'He has become hard, and unfeeling. But little Martin, and sweet Mairead and gentle Sean, they need protection and care . . .'

James Mahoney had the sense to remain quiet and leave the woman to come to her own decision without pressing her further. He went to stand gazing out of the window.

Martin Shonley was outside, playing some game known only to himself. James Mahoney watched the solemn-faced child gravely arranging stones in elaborate patterns, then equally gravely skipping around and over the whorls and arabesques he had created. The man smiled, and felt the stirrings of old sadness. 'How I wish my own son were playing like that.' He experienced a sudden swelling of fond compassion for the thin legs and arms, and realized that he could come to love this small boy as if he were really the son of his loins. After a while he became conscious of the warm presence of Charlotte Shonley at his shoulder. She remained there, also gazing out at the child. At last, unable to restrain himself any longer, James Mahoney asked softly, 'Well, my dear, what is it to be?'

She smiled tremulously. 'Are you really sure that you want to marry me, James? Are you sure that you have not mistaken pity for love?'

He turned his head and told her simply, 'I know what is in my heart, Charlotte. I am a man, not a boy. There is some pity there, of course . . . But love is the dominant emotion.'

'Very well, I will marry you, James, and will endeavour to my utmost to make you a good wife.'

With great tenderness he drew her to him, and held her close . . .

Some time later he asked, 'Do you wish me to tell Con, and the other children of our intentions? I fear it will come as a great shock to them.'

She smiled at his worried look. 'No, I think it best if I do that myself. You must come to know them slowly. They are naughty at times, as are all children, but basically good and loving.'

'I would not wish them to resent me. To think that I am trying to drive the memory of their father from your mind . . . That is a thing that I will never try to do . . . I swear to it.'

Not for the first time she experienced an impulse to kiss him. His nature was so truly good and gentle.

'They will not resent you, James, of this I'm sure. I shall tell Con myself, when he returns home . . . Go now, and leave me to my own thoughts.'

This time she did touch her lips to his before he left her.

'How can you? How can you betray Pa like this?' Con Shonley's mind was a maelstrom. Anger, revulsion, disbelief all swirling uncontrollably and mingling one with the other.

His mother, pale and nervous, but determined, spoke sharply. 'Do not talk like a fool, Con. I am not betraying your father, whom I loved more than you could ever know. But he is dead and buried, God rest his soul. It is the living I must consider. Your father would have wanted me to do the best I can for those of us who are left.'

'But to marry another man, to share his bed, to know his flesh? You disgust me!' The youth's swarthy features contorted with an expression near to hate.

Charlotte's breathing became ragged, and her breasts rose and fell sharply. Her face was haggard with distress, but her determination did not waver. 'If I disgust you, Con, then I am deeply sorry for it . . . But I tell you now, I am going to marry Mr Mahoney. He will be the head of this family. We shall go to England to live.'

'I will not!' he interrupted her rudely.

'That is for you to decide. You are no longer a child, although at times you seem one. You have the choice before you. You may come with us, and help us to make a new life in England, or you may remain here.' She softened, and beseeched him, 'Come with us, Con. James will help you to establish yourself in whatever field of activity you should choose. He is a kind and good man, if you were not so wilfully blind you would see that for yourself.'

Through a daze of misery the youth heard her, and his revulsion deepened. 'I see what I wish to see, and that is the truth . . . I understand well. You and that damned Englishman have planned this very carefully. You don't really want me to come with you. You want me to stay here. I remind you too readily of my poor father, do I not? If I stay here, then you can the more easily forget him. Forget the dreadful wrong that you are doing his memory.'

Charlotte's pain as the bitterly unjust accusations were hurled at her, was like a knife blade ripping into her body. Waves of acute nausea caused her stomach to heave, and she feared that she would physically vomit.

'Well, you can tell your new man to keep his money. I want none of it.' The youth was weeping tears of rage and anguish. 'You'll see me no more. You are dead to me now! I have no mother . . . She is dead!' He slammed through the doorway of the kitchen, and she heard his footsteps clatter down the passageway. The outer door crashed open, and he was gone.

'Oh Con!' Charlotte moaned his name. 'Con!'

Outside the house Con Shonley walked rapidly, head down, arms swinging, conscious only of the shock of this new bereavement.

'I'm alone in the world now,' he told himself fiercely. 'I have no family . . . I'm alone.' Unbidden, sorrowful remorse overlaid his anger, threatening to bring fresh tears to his eyes. But he fought the weakness down, and forced himself to concentrate on the memory of his father. Without being aware of it he was heading for the hidden valley where the drill sessions took place. After two hours of hard travelling he arrived there, and descended into its still peace.

Throwing himself onto the thick springy grass he lay face upwards, staring at the billowing clouds above him, uncaring of the sogginess of the ground beneath. Slowly his mood calmed, and he began to wonder what he should do. In the pocket of his trousers he carried four pennies, his entire worldly wealth. A spattering of rain fell, and the youth knew that he must find shelter before night brought its customary downfall. He sprang to his feet and ran lightly towards the distant village of Leap. Father Boyce would advise him on what he should do . . .

When he reached the hamlet he found the priest sitting in the small chapel there.

'So Con, you've left home and family, have you. The fledgling has spread his wings and flown from the nest.' The priest's bright eyes twinkled, removing any suggestion of sarcasm from the words. 'Arrah, why shouldn't ye leave home. Everyone must, be it sooner or later . . . But where should ye go now, and what should ye do, that's the point . . . I think you should pray to Our Lord for guidance.'

Con hid his disappointment. He wanted practical advice, not this exhortation to prayer. The youth stared at the big crucifix with its suffering Christ that faced him from the wall above the altar. The ivory-hued wooden features crowned with bloody thorns stared blankly back at him. Con wished with all his heart that he could be one of those who believed in the teachings of the Church. At least the believers drew comfort from the holy statues and the lighted candles, and their conviction that a benevolent Deity heard their prayers and answered their pleas.

He faced the tiny priest and admitted frankly, 'It would be no use me praying, Father. I haven't faith.'

Boyce chuckled. 'D'ye think that you're the only one that has doubts, Con Shonley. Indeed, there are times that I think my own faith is all a nonsense . . . Still, let that lie for now, I've no wish to preach at you. You must come to God in your own way and your own time. Only remember that He is always watching over you.'

The youth couldn't control his irritation. Was the priest's kindly God also watching over the thousands dying miserably each day in ditches and barren fields, he wondered? Boyce's voice cut into his thoughts.

'You've no money, I take it.'

Con shook his head. 'I've only four pence, Father.'

'Arrah, that'll be right, I don't doubt . . . Ye can stay here with me this night, at least. You can bed down in Mr Rourke's room. He has a big mattress. There's not a deal to eat, I'm afraid, but we'll make do, and water's plentiful, thanks to the good God. We can always fill our bellies with that blessed juice, can we not.'

The little man's light-hearted perkiness did nothing to lighten Con's own heaviness of heart, and he was disappointed with the priest's failure to guide him in what he should do.

'Good man, yourself, Con Shonley!' Boyce clapped the younger man on the shoulder. 'Now I must go away on some errands. You carry on into my cabin, there's a good fire there. You'll have Mr Rourke for company.'

The cabin was only a few yards from the chapel. It was slightly more luxurious than the cabins of the poor. It had stone-flagged floors, white-washed inner walls, plus several straw-seated sugan chairs and a well-scrubbed table. On a shelf fitted to one wall was a row of leather-bound books.

Rourke was sitting at the table reading one of them. He had cast aside his cloak and caubeen, and his bald scalp was as sun-bronzed as his face. He wore a clean blue calico shirt, black breeches, and was well washed and shaven. He smiled a welcome, and pulled a chair forward for Con to be seated on.

'How are you, boy?'

'I'm well thank you, Mr Rourke,' Con told him.

'Good, because I'm bored outta my mind.' The man's big head nodded vigorously. 'And that's the whole truth of it. There's nothing in this damned country but rain. Morning, noon and night, all it does here is rain.' He slammed the book shut and replaced it on the shelf, then strutted restlessly about the room.

Impelled by instinct, Con told him, 'I've left home, Mr Rourke.'

The man stopped his pacing, and nodded. 'A good thing too. You're a man now, and you have your own way to make in the world.'

Con eagerly grasped at this sentiment, because guilt was gnawing at him for the way he had behaved towards his mother.

'What will ye do now, young Shonley? Off to America, is it?'

Surprise caused the youth to fumble for words. 'America? No, I've no thought of that. I want to stay here.'

'To do what? Make your fortune?' Mockery tinged the deep voice.

'Why, to fight for my country,' Con answered boldly, 'to help set us free!'

Baring strong brown-stained teeth Rourke threw back his head and roared with laughter.

Resentment burgeoned in the youth. 'What is so amusing about that, may I ask you, Mr Rourke?'

The older man's laughter ceased abruptly, and he scowled. 'Don't you be giving me the hard looks and tone, boy,' he advised menacingly. 'You'll need to eat a deal more praties before ye can match Phelim Rourke for strength.'

The sudden metamorphosis from laughter to aggression sent a tremor of apprehension through the youth. 'I didn't mean to offend you, Mr Rourke.' He tried to appear cool and calm. 'But surely that is what you want also. To set our country free from England's tyranny.'

The hard grey eyes bored into Con's. 'Why should you think that, boy?' he growled.

Con drew a long deep breath in an attempt to steady his

81

racing heartbeat. 'Well, you are instructing we people hereabouts in the military arts, are you not?'

Rourke's manner again changed abruptly. 'That is true, young Shonley, that is true.' He sighed heavily, and came to sit by Con at the table. The grey eyes were troubled now, and almost diffidently he said, 'I'm going to tell you something, boy, and you must keep it locked in your head. It must remain a secret between you and me.' He paused interrogatively, and Con nodded. 'It will be kept so, Mr Rourke.'

'Good!' The man went on quietly, 'I'm not long back from India. You heard no doubt about the fighting between the British and the Sikhs that took place about a year or more past?'

'I did,' Con murmured.

Rourke's teeth bared in his peculiar half-smile, half-grimace. 'I was in that fighting, boy. Only I was on the side of the Sikhs. I was one of those Europeans who helped to train their heathen army. It's not important how I came to be doing such a thing . . . '

Con could guess how. The man before him was more than likely a deserter from either the Crown or East India Company armies. A renegade, who had joined other renegades to help make the Sikh army into the formidable force it had been.

'The British hammered us into the ground, although we fought hard and well,' the man was saying. 'The Sikhs broke, and the slaughter was terrible. Any European who was taken prisoner by the British soon had his neck stretched.' One brown hand crept up to fondle the thick muscular neck. 'Phelim Rourke had a powerful wish to keep his neck the same length as it is now. I got out from there quick, I'll tell ye, and managed to get back here. Well, 'twas no use escaping the hangman only to starve to death here, was it . . . Through an old friend I found that there was a little money to be earned giving military instruction to the Confederate Clubs . . . That's why I'm here, boy. Not for love of Mother Ireland, but to put some food into me belly.'

Con heard the story with mixed reactions. Like all

idealists he was contemptuous of mercenary motives. But, knowing hunger from personal experience, he could not bring himself to condemn the man before him.

Rourke smiled knowingly. 'I know what you're thinking, boy. I might not have any education to speak of, but I've a good head on me, and a deal of knowledge of this world.' He sat musing for a few seconds, and then, as if coming to a decision he pushed his broad face close to Con's, and grasped the youth's wrist in a tight grip.

'Hark to me, boy,' he urged vehemently. 'I doubt if there will ever be an uprising by these Young Irelanders and their friends. The poor devils in this country are too weak and sick to fight . . . And if there should be an uprising then they'll stand no chance of winning. They'll be slaughtered. Pikes and a few fowling pieces cannot do very much against cannon, and Brunswick rifles and percussion cap muskets. If you've any sense in your head, you'll forget all this nonsense about fighting for liberty, and you'll take a chance on finding your own liberty across the seas. Get to America, boy. It's a young country, there's fortunes to be made there. Get away from this cursed land . . . Ye'll only find a pauper's grave here . . . '

The hero-worship that Con had given this man withered and died as he listened to the impassioned words. The youth felt a sick emptiness of heart. It seemed that in a few short hours all the trusted supports of his being had proven themselves to be weak and rotten. His mother, the priest, and now Rourke, had all failed him. Con closed his eyes, and in this self-imposed darkness the secret voice in his mind spoke to him once more; 'You must be your own man, Con Shonley, and rely only on yourself.'

A strength of purpose he had never before known filled him. He released his wrist from Rourke's fingers. 'Then I must lie in that pauper's grave, Mr Rourke,' he rejoined quietly, 'for from this moment on, I'll go my own way, and I'll be my own man . . . '

When Father Boyce returned from his errands, Rourke was alone.

'Where's the boy?' Boyce wanted to know.

The other man shrugged his broad shoulders. 'God might know, but I don't. He said he was leaving, and he went.'

A frown of concern creased the priest's brows. 'The night's bitter cold, and there's more rain coming. I hope the young idjit has the sense to keep under shelter . . . '

The rain battered against the window of the kitchen. For perhaps the hundredth time that night Charlotte Shonley rose from her chair and wearily peered out into the darkness. She could see nothing, but could not help maintaining her fruitless vigil. Her tears had long since dried, and she had no more left in her to shed.

'If there is a God above, then protect my son,' she prayed silently. 'I beg you to protect my son . . . '

Barely a mile distant from the house, Con Shonley huddled in the ruins of an abandoned cabin. He was cold, wet and hungry. He needed money to survive, and he knew how he could earn that money, if he could only find courage enough. He steeled himself to endure the long hours of darkness that lay before him.

The image of Grainne MacDermott's dark beauty came into his mind, and he clung to that image, drawing strength and courage from it, picturing a future in which he and she would be united.

'Some day we will be.' The thought became ever stronger in his mind until it metamorphosed into conviction. 'Someday Grainne MacDermott and myself will be joined and share the rest of our lives together . . . Someday . . . Someday . . . Someday . . . '

Chapter Thirteen

Dr Philip Donovan regarded the youth standing in his dispensary with scarcely concealed impatience. 'I don't think you know what you are about, Shonley,' he snapped curtly, and continued to measure out dark drops of tincture of opium from the tiny bottle he held, into the larger flask of red wine placed on his littered desk.

'With respect, Sir, I do.'

The man shrugged his bowed shoulders. 'Aye, well I'll not argue the point with you. You have seen sufficient of what is happening here.' He looked over his raised arm and fixed the youth with a piercing stare. 'I was talking with your mother, and Mr Mahoney this morning. They are both very anxious about you.'

It was Con's turn to shrug. 'They've no need to be. I shall do well enough on my own.'

The doctor completed his task, and after replacing the tiny bottle on the bench, came and rested his hands on the youth's shoulders. His face was kindly and concerned. 'They leave on their journey to England tomorrow, young man. Your brothers and sister are happy to be going. Why do you not join them? They wish above all else that you would do so.'

Con ruthlessly smothered the will-weakening flood of emotion that rose up within him. He shook his head. 'They must go their way, and I go mine.'

A flash of annoyance crossed the doctor's faded eyes. 'Then you are a fool, boy, to abandon a loving family as you have done.'

Con's dark sombreness was unyielding. 'My family lies buried in the graveyard, Doctor Donovan.'

85

The man sighed, and dropped his hands. 'There is no foolishness to match that of youth,' he muttered, as if to himself. 'Mr Mahoney has asked me to pass this on to you.' He fumbled in his trouser pocket and drew out a small purse, heavy with gold coins. 'He wants you to use this to follow your mother to England. He has also asked me to assure you that his home is your home, whenever you wish to come to them.'

The youth refused even to look at the purse. 'I want none of his money,' he snapped stiffly.

'Then you are an ungrateful young whelp!' the doctor burst out angrily. 'People are dying for want of money to buy food, and you act like a surly blaggard in rejecting a gentleman's kindness as you do.' He hesitated as he saw the pain in the boy's face. 'Oh well, 'tis no concern of mine. I have more than enough to contend with.' He lapsed into silence.

Con seized the chance to come back to the reason for his visit. 'Doctor Donovan, you know you need men to clear the dead from the houses and bury them. Let me do it.'

The older man put his hand to his care-lined forehead, his fingers digging and rubbing in a fruitless attempt to ease the ache of bone-weariness. 'As I said previously, Shonley, you do not know what you are about. The men who do this foul task are the very dregs of society. They spend the generous amounts we pay them on drink and debauchery. They come to the work reeling drunk, and the reason for that is that they exist in a state of awful dread, not knowing when the fever may strike at them . . . Do you know how many of them die within days of commencing such work?' The last question was rhetorical. 'Almost all of them, Shonley. And the ones that live become like brute beasts, without any sense of decency, without respect for the dead, or for the living, or even for their God.' He shook his head. 'I could not permit you to do it. I knew your father too well. He was a gentleman, even though poor in material possessions.'

'But surely, Sir, since I must find work, or starve to

death, and this is the only work open to me, then it is better that I should do it here, where at least I can come to you for treatment should I fall ill.' Con saw that this new argument had some effect. 'Because if I must, then I will do this work elsewhere. Where I am unknown. I have no other choice.'

Donovan again held out Mahoney's purse. 'You have a choice, Shonley. You can accept this money in the spirit in which it was offered to you.'

'That I will never do.' The youth was adamant, and the older man knew that nothing would make him change his mind. He accepted defeat.

'Very well, Shonley. Go to Mulrooney's in Old Chapel Lane. It's there my burial men lodge. Tell them I sent you, and may God forgive me for doing so . . . But then, God knows only too well how desperate is my need of strong arms to bury my dead . . . '

It was the largest house in Old Chapel Lane, three storeys high if only narrow-widthed, once a tavern, now a lodging house cum shebeen. Con knew of the place by repute. Prior to the famine no respectable person would be seen entering its doors; it was patronized only by the wasters, ne'er-do-wells and criminal elements of the district. Mulrooney himself had long disappeared, now it was his wife, Bridget Mulrooney, who ruled the establishment. A tall, raw-boned woman of indeterminate age, she was as strong-bodied as any man, and could use her fists, teeth and feet in a brawl as savagely as any of her customers.

She grinned with jagged stumps of blackened teeth at the youth who had knocked on her door. 'Why would a handsome young fella like you come knocking here, I wonder? What would you be wanting?'

Con regarded her battered face topped by a mass of frizzy grey hair and an equally grey mobcap with a foreboding he was careful to keep from showing in his expression. 'The doctor sent me. Doctor Donovan,' he told her. 'I'm going to work with his burial men.'

The woman was momentarily shocked. 'Jesus, Joseph

and Mary, what in Heaven's name would make you want to do such a thing?' she demanded in her hoarse voice.

The youth smiled grimly, but made no answer.

'Ah well, needs must when the Devil drives, isn't that what they say?' Bridget Mulrooney beckoned him to enter. 'Come inside to the warm then, handsome. Ye'll catch your death o' cold standing there, and I'll be doing the same if I stay here gassing with you any longer.'

The long front room was low-beamed, gloomy and filthy. A vile smell compounded of sweat, urine, excreta and rancid food made the air a torment to breathe. Con felt his stomach turn, and the woman cocked her head, her shrewdness understanding only too well what was in the youth's mind. 'Ye'll be smelling worse than this in the work ye'll be doing, my handsome fella, be sure o' that.' Her tone was not angry, merely explanatory.

He tried to ignore the stench, and by breathing through his mouth found that he could avoid the worst effects of it. For a brief instant he thought wistfully of the clean pleasant smell of his home, but rejected that memory. 'I'll get used to it, Mrs Mulrooney,' he said quietly.

'To be sure ye will, my handsome. That's a certainty.'

There were benches and trestle tables lining the room, and some stools around the brick hearth, on which three men were sitting.

'Callaghan?' the woman spoke to one of them. 'Here's a young fella come to join yez.'

The man she addressed was short and stout, his greasy black hair hanging down over the shoulders of his old black swallow-tailed coat. He wore only a waistcoat over his bare chest and a woollen muffler around his neck. Beneath his waist a pair of soldier's blue trousers with a thin red stripe running down the outer legs ended at a pair of wooden clogs. The skin between the clogs and trouser bottoms was black with dried mud. He chuckled merrily, his toothless mouth forming an empty roundness as he examined the newcomer.

'By the right! But ye're a fine-looking young fella-me-lad.' His voice gurgled with enjoyment. 'I'll not be asking yer name though, son. Being in here ye might well die on us afore ye could spit it out.'

His shoulders heaved as he chuckled again. Con could not repress an answering smile, so infectious was the man's good humour.

'Have yez any rhino with ye, son? Money, I mean?'

Con nodded. 'I have four pence.'

Callaghan's bright blue eyes turned skywards as he whooped with laughter. 'Four pence, is it,' he gasped out as his paroxysm eased. 'By the right, then ye're a bloody nobleman, so ye are! A bloody Corinthian! Where's your carriage and pair, son? Did ye leave them outside in the lane there?' Again he whooped with laughter, and involuntarily Con laughed with him. 'Come, sit ye down, son, you must be starvin' with the cold.' The man pulled a stool closer to the turf fire.

Con accepted his invitation. For a while he stared into the glowing heart of the fire, conscious that the other was studying him.

'Would you look at them two, wouldn't they remind ye o' two corpses at a wake?' Callaghan snorted in mock disgust, as he drew Con's attention towards the two silent men sitting with them. They were derelicts, human wrecks, bodies wasted to near skeletons by hunger and hardship. Con would have spoken to them, but they both kept their deep-sunk eyes downwards and wouldn't meet his look.

'Ah well, there's no harm in them, for all their miserable faces,' Callaghan declared expansively, and shouted, 'Bridget Mulrooney, bring us a couple of tots of your firewater, will yez. I want to drink this young fella's health.' He winked at Con. 'And by Jase, ye'll be needing it, son.'

The woman appeared in the dark doorway that led into the rear rooms of the building. 'You owe me, Callaghan,' she told him bluntly. 'I'll need to see the colour of your money afore I'll be giving ye more drink.'

The man laughed uproariously. 'Isn't she the caution! Isn't she just! She's a darling woman, so she is. A darling woman.'

Con once again could not help chuckling in sympathy with him, and even Bridget Mulrooney's tough face lost some of its aggressiveness.

'Will four pence pay for a tot, Mrs Mulrooney?' Con asked politely.

'Indeed it will,' she answered, smiling at him.

'Then please give Mr Callaghan a tot of whatever it is he wants. I'll pay.'

'By the right! You're a gentleman born and bred, sor.' Callaghan's round face assumed an air of exaggerated awe, and he ordered the woman, 'Come now, Bridget Mulrooney, let's have some service here. You heard what this gentleman said.'

The woman frowned slightly. 'He seems to be a bigger fool than yourself, Callaghan. Ye'll make a fine pair, so ye will.'

'Indeed we shall, Bridget Mulrooney. As God is me judge, ye'll never spake a truer word.' Callaghan clapped both hands on his knees and laughed, and laughed, and laughed . . .

During the months that followed Con came to bless the unfailing laughter of Denis Callaghan. The work they did was nightmarish. The odour of death and corruption became impregnated into Con's senses. He became hardened to the horrific sights that daily met his eyes, and attempted to become equally hardened to the sufferings that those sights represented. But he could not prevent his own emotions from vicariously identifying with the tragic victims. Unlike Callaghan he kept his body and clothing meticulously clean, but like Callaghan he began to trust in the efficacy of raw liquor to safeguard him from the fevers they dwelt among.

The two other men with them both sickened and died. Others took their places, and in their turn also quickly sickened and died. But God, or the poteen, protected Con Shonley and Denis Callaghan. The youth ate well because of his generous pay, and his body gained strong muscular height and weight. He appeared to physically thrive on the dreadful work, but inwardly paid a terrible toll in youthful innocence.

The burial men were always shunned by the people around them, who were afraid of the infectious diseases that they knew the burial men dared each and every day; and the long black swallow-tailed coat that each burial man wore began to represent in Con's mind a symbol as fearsome and shameful as the mark borne by Cain.

He came to regard Callaghan as his dearest friend, and felt for him a love as strong as that he had possessed for his own brothers. Without Callaghan's laughter, Con knew that he would have been driven into insanity . . . And without his dream of a future to be shared with Grainne MacDermott he would have lost all hope . . .

Chapter Fourteen

April passed, and May, and the days of June. The weather was glorious, the crops of grain promised a bountiful harvest. The Dublin Season, always noted for its gaiety, lived up to its reputation. Its only interruption was the illness, followed by the death on May 16 1847, of Her Gracious Majesty's Deputy, Lord Bessborough, the Lord Lieutenant of Ireland. The day before Bessborough died, Daniel O'Connel, the great liberator, also died at Genoa, Italy, broken-hearted, his life's work all to no avail since the cause of 'Repeal of the Union' was moribund.

Supplies of Indian corn had poured, and were pouring into Irish ports in huge amounts, and its market price dropped, dropped and dropped again. Yet still the masses starved and died. The Public Works, including those around Skibereen had nearly all closed, and there were no wages with which to buy even the cheapest of foodstuffs.

The British Government passed the Soup Kitchen Act earlier in the spring, and each Poor Law Union throughout Ireland was made to set up distribution centres for soup. At first the pride of the peasantry rebelled against the humiliating mode of distribution, but pride was of necessity humbled. Humiliation, no matter how degrading, was preferable to miserable death, and those that could get it, ate the soup . . .

Michael Kearney, the Gombeen Man, lived alone, a mile from Skibereen on the road to the minute port of Baltimore. His house was two-storeyed, well built and slate-roofed as befitted a man of his position in the district.

An elderly aunt kept house for him, but these days the work was becoming too much for her to manage, and the hobbling between her own cabin and his house was a trial of strength for her. Kearney had recently come to the conclusion that he needed a young woman to care for him, and to share his bed.

Women were available in abundance. Desperate for food and shelter for their children there were many women who would prostitute themselves. But Kearney, although a man of indiscriminate sexual appetites, had tired of bodies worn with hunger and slackened by child-bearing. He wanted a firm, tender, virginal body for his pleasure, and one that would not demand payment each time he slaked his needs upon it. He accepted the fact that to obtain what he wanted would more than likely necessitate marriage, but then, all men should marry sooner or later in their lives.

Once he had come to this decision Kearney started to look about him for a suitable young woman. One took his eye and his fancy above all others... Grainne MacDermott, nineteen years old, and as fresh and beautiful as a spring dawn.

Now Michael Kearney made ready to call on the girl's uncle. He was well clad, a thick woollen shirt and a waistcoat topped by a blue swallow-tailed coat covered his bulky torso. Pulled down low on his rust-coloured hair was the tall narrow-brimmed felt hat known as the 'pot hat'. Corduroy breeches, ribbed woollen stockings and a pair of heavy boots completed the ensemble.

He drove his own jaunting-car drawn by a plump donkey, and beneath the seat was a stone jug of poteen and two fresh baked wheaten loaves. When he pulled up outside the MacDermott's tumbledown cabin a swarm of ragged, underfed, runny-nosed children came out to stare at him with wide eyes. Kearney got down from his seat and after tying the donkey to the remnants of a fence, he cracked his whip fiercely, and warned the children, 'If any o' youse touch this car, I'll have the skin from your backs.'

He swaggered into the cabin without knocking. Theresa MacDermott, Grainne's mother, stood nervously by the door, her face mottled with fresh swollen bruises where James MacDermott had punched her during a domestic dispute. The man was slouched on a rickety three-legged stool, warming himself by the peat fire. He glared up at the visitor, then realizing who it was, jumped to his feet.

'Now, Mr Kearney, this is an honour. What can I do for you?'

Already MacDermott's sharp wits had guessed at the reason for the Gombeen Man's visit. He had heard rumours that Kearney was interested in his eldest niece. The Gombeen Man's small eyes searched for the girl, but she was not inside the cabin.

'Please, Mr Kearney, won't ye sit down,' MacDermott invited, smiling fulsomely, then snarled at the woman. 'Bring that other stool to the fire here, ye damned knucklehead, are ye waiting for Judgement Day?'

She hastened to obey, and Kearney sat down, grunting with the effort. He settled himself comfortably, and unbuttoned his waistcoat to ease his large belly. 'Send your woman out to the car,' he instructed MacDermott. 'There's a jug o' good stuff, and some bread. We'll have a few drams while we talk.'

MacDermott was lavish with his thanks. Kearney waved them aside, and once the poteen jug had been broached and both men had drunk a mug full of the liquor, got down to business.

'I'm needing a house-keeper. The old aunt is too feeble to manage on her own now.'

'Oh I'm sorry to hear that. 'Tis a pity for her, and her such a good woman, God bless her.' The poteen was already going to MacDermott's head.

'I'm of a mind to do you a favour, MacDermott,' Kearney continued. 'I'm thinking of offering your niece the job of keeping house for me. It'll be one less mouth for ye to feed here.'

Their eyes met, and each man knew just what the other was thinking. James MacDermott had had his own plans for Grainne, and lately his hunger for her young body had been tormenting him almost beyond his control. But the

Gombeen Man was a powerful figure in the district, and MacDermott could see the advantages to be gained by having his niece in Kearney's bed. He took a lingering drink of the musty-tasting spirit, savouring its throat-tightening heat.

'By Jase, but this is good stuff right enough, Mr Kearney. A man could forget his troubles iffen he had a jug of this at his elbow o' nights,' he remarked meaningfully.

The Gombeen Man's liver-coloured lips parted in a satisfied smile. 'Well now, MacDermott, I always say that if a man has a good friend, then he must always try and look after that friend. Particularly in these terrible times that are on us . . . '

The woman stood listening, and felt a fearful loathing for the two men. She envisaged the Gombeen Man's gross body rutting upon her daughter's slenderness and shuddered. But she knew from bitter experience that any word of protest would bring an instant brutal retribution upon her. Her body and face throbbed agonizingly as a result of last night's merciless beating. She dare not risk another. 'My poor Grainne,' she wept inside her mind for her daughter, 'my poor wee girl!'

'If I was agreeable to letting Grainne work for you, Mr Kearney, what sort of a wage would you be thinking of paying her?' MacDermott enquired with a forced casualness.

The other man hid his growing irritation. He despised MacDermott for what he was, but even in these times the mores of the society they were part of must be paid lip-service.

'Well now, as to that, I've a very pleasant surprise for you, MacDermott.' The Gombeen Man winked, and took a swallow from the cracked drinking mug he held between his pudgy hands. 'It's in my mind, that if the girl is suitable for the job, and if we get on well together, then I might well be offering for her hand.'

MacDermott heard this with very mixed feelings. If Grainne was only Kearney's paramour, then he himself need not abandon hope of using her sexually. But if she became the man's wife, then he knew that there would be little chance of achieving that particular ambition. But, on the other hand, if she did become Mrs Kearney, who knew what largesse might come the way of her family. MacDermott drank deep, his mind racing.

Kearney's bloodshot eyes narrowed as he watched the play of expression on the other's features. Inwardly he was laughing with satisfaction. He knew that he had already gained his object. The girl would be coming back with him this night. Not to his bed. He accepted that even in these days a young girl's chastity must be seen to be respected. The peasantry had high standards of sexual morality, and the priests were always on the alert for any flouting of those standards. But Kearney was confident that once Grainne was living at his house, then it would only be a matter of time before she shared his bed.

'Well, are ye agreeable, MacDermott?' he said aloud.

The other man's decayed teeth glistened. 'Aye, I am.'

Kearney's heavy jowls quivered as he looked towards the silent woman. 'And you, Mrs MacDermott?'

'She's agreeable,' her man growled.

Kearney remained watching her, and her lips quivered, then with downcast eyes she nodded acceptance.

'That's settled then.' Kearney became expansive. 'We'll have another drink on it, to seal the bargain.' He refilled both mugs, splashing the colourless spirit carelessly, and drained his drink with evident pleasure. MacDermott's sly eyes never left the Gombeen Man's face. He waited with a tangible air of expectancy.

Kearney grinned at him. 'Naturally I'll be helping you to better yourself, MacDermott. I can't have my house-keeper's, and mayhap my future wife's family, living in want, can I now.'

MacDermott visibly relaxed, and his wizened features glowed with pleasure and poteen. 'You've the good heart, Mr Kearney. There's no man can deny that.'

Grainne MacDermott's bare feet made little sound upon the pathway and she entered the cabin without their hearing her approach. Her green eyes took in the scene, and her lips tightened.

'Here's herself come, just at the right time,' her uncle said gaily. 'You'll be going with Mr Kearney to his house, my jewel. You'll be keeping it for him. His poor aunt has become too feeble to manage by herself any longer, God save the poor owld soul.'

Kearney's tongue ran over his lips as he feasted his eyes on the girl. She remained standing in the doorway, tall and proud, a shawl covering her long black hair, her thread-bare knee-length dress only emphasizing the full rich curves of her breasts, hips and thighs. The man's breathing shortened as his imagination dwelt on what lay beneath the thin dark cloth.

'We'd best be getting ready to leave, Grainne,' he said, and his voice sounded hoarse to his ears, 'then I can explain you your duties, and show you over the house while we've still the daylight to see by . . .'

The girl stared ambiguously back at him. 'It's all been decided then, has it?' she questioned boldly.

Jim MacDermott scowled menacingly. 'Indeed it has, my jewel. You're a lucky girl being offered such a fine position in the house of a gentleman like Mr Kearney here.'

Grainne glanced at her mother, but all she could read on the bruised features was fear. Again the green eyes swung towards the Gombeen Man, and he tried to smile re-assuringly.

'Come now, Grainne, ye'll be paid, and eat well, and ye'll have the whole ordering of the house. 'T'will be as if you were mistress of your own place.'

'I hope I'm not meant to be mistress to its owner,' Grainne said levelly, and watched with satisfaction the flush of embarrassment reddening Kearney's jowls.

'As God is my judge, ye'll be as safe in my house as you would be in a nunnery,' he flustered.

'Hold your tongue, girl!' MacDermott shouted. 'What sort of a trollop will Mr Kearney think he's sheltering iffen you say such wicked things?'

'That's just what I'm trying to make plain,' the girl

answered spiritedly, 'that I'm not a trollop, but God-fearing and respectable.'

By now Kearney had recovered his aplomb. 'Of course you are, my dear . . . And that's a fact that's well known hereabouts. Wasn't it for that very reason that it was you I wanted for housekeeper. I'll not have it said by loose tongues that Michael Kearney shares his house with women of easy virtues.'

While he was speaking Grainne's eyes again moved to her mother, and she, conscious of Jim MacDermott's rising anger nodded beseechingly at her daughter. 'Go with him, Grainne. Go with Mr Kearney, there's a good girl. It'll save us all from starvation.'

Grainne's lips twisted in momentary anger, but then she realized what faced her mother if she herself refused the job.

'All right then, I'll get my things . . . ' She climbed up the ladder to the half-loft, and Kearney's mouth dried as the thin dress moulded to the perfect half-globes of her buttocks.

Grainne's possessions were pitifully few. A comb, a brush, another dress as ragged as the one she wore, and a cheap wooden rosary. For a moment or two she paused, expecting to feel a sadness because she would be leaving her family. But no sadness came. For months now, ever since Grainne had lost the work on the roads, her mother had treated her only as an unwelcome burden. Instead there suddenly burgeoned an increasing sense of excited anticipation for the new experiences she would soon be faced with. She descended the ladder and told the Gombeen Man, 'I'm ready, Mr Kearney.'

'Good.' He breathed a sigh of relieved satisfaction, and rose ponderously to his feet. 'Finish the jug, MacDermott,' he invited the other man, and winked. 'There'll be more from where that came from.'

MacDermott grinned beatifically.

'I'll be sending you some food tomorrow, Mrs Mac-Dermott,' Kearney told the woman, who was fighting to hold back her tears. Rarely for him, he felt a moment of compassion for this cowed, beaten woman. 'Now don't fret about your daughter. She'll be living easy and well, and you'll be able to come and see her if you want.'

'God bless ye for that, Mr Kearney.' Theresa MacDermott wrung her hands together, and burst into tears of anguish.

'Shut that bloody row!' Jim MacDermott bellowed, and moved as if to hit her.

Kearney sensed Grainne moving from behind him to defend her mother, and spoke sharply to the man. 'Sit ye down and drink! 'Tis only natural that your woman's having the wee sob.'

With bad grace MacDermott obeyed, and Kearney basked in Grainne's fleeting smile of gratitude. The girl kissed her mother's worn cheek. 'I'll be fine, Mammy, you wait and see. Hush now, no more tears.'

Then, as she went through the doorway after the Gombeen Man, she paused and glowered at her uncle. 'Don't you be lifting your hand to Mammy when we've gone, d'ye hear . . . Or I'll tell Mr Kearney, and have him deal with you.'

With a sudden shock, Jim MacDermott realized that he could well have created a rod for his own back. He had seen the way Kearney devoured the girl with his eyes.

'It's more than likely she could get him to deal with me,' MacDermott told himself ruefully, but outwardly pretended to sneer at the girl's threat, and concentrated his full attention on the well-filled jug of poteen.

Waving good-bye to her swarming brothers and sisters, Grainne went from her home sitting on the outward-facing seat on the body of the jaunting-car. In front of her Kearney hummed happily to himself, and for a change was light-handed with his whip.

Grainne settled herself comfortably, and her green eyes glowed as a thought came to her mind. 'Your man here is rich. He's got money aplenty. Perhaps enough of it could come my way to get me over to America. I could live like a lady there . . . ' Her perfect teeth gleamed whitely at the pleasing notion. ' . . . Yes indeed, America would suit me fine, so it would . . . ' Her fancy soared. 'But how much better it would suit me if Con Shonley were with me there.'

Time passed and Grainne settled to her new way of life, and found it pleasant enough. One Saturday there was a market in Skibereen and Grainne went to it to buy provisions for the week. Bacon and beef, bread and vegetables, candles, lamp-oil, soap, and a new petticoat for herself, ribbons for her raven-hued hair, and various other sundries.

She placed the heavy wicker-work basket on the boards of the jaunting-car, gave a half-penny to the ragged urchin who held the donkey's head, then mounted the driving seat and commenced her homeward journey.

The day was of rare beauty, and the girl let her fancy guide the trotting donkey. She followed the road along the right bank of the Ilen river, and past the ruins of the Cistercian Abbey of Strowry. Further along she halted the jaunting-car and sat gazing seawards. She could see the small castle of Kilcoe at the water's edge, and beyond it in the blue-green sea the tiny Mannin Islands, and beyond them the dark humps of Horse Island and Castle Island, and even further out the hazed outlines of the Calf Islands. She drew the sweet scent of green grass, brilliant yellow furze and rich blue escallonia deep into her lungs, and found herself wishing that she had a lover with her to share this beauty.

The girl sighed. The only man available to her was Michael Kearney. That he wanted her was sure, but despite his rough kindness to her, she could feel nothing for him but a detached tolerance. Until now, he had not made any strong sexual approaches to her. She knew however that his desire for her was becoming unbearable to him, and inevitably it would sooner or later drive him to a determined attempt to share her bed. She had insisted from the first on sleeping in the adjoining cabin with his ancient aunt, but lately he had begun to grumble about this, saying that it was inconvenient, and pressing her to sleep in the house.

Her green eyes became tinged with calculation. 'If I was to sleep with him, what would I gain?' She tried to weigh the question dispassionately. 'Only babies!' She laughed softly, and turned her thoughts to the hidden store of money she was amassing. She knew she had not near enough yet to get her to America, and frowned with a now-familiar frustration about how slowly her tiny hoard was increasing, because she still helped her mother from her own scant income. 'The mean bowsy's too tight with the housekeeping money. I can only lift pennies from it, when it's pounds I'm needing . . . Maybe if I let him make free with me, then I could get a lot of money out of him.' She considered, but then the thought of his gross, sweaty body bearing down on her nakedness, and his liver-coloured mouth crushing hers, sent a shiver of disgust through her. 'Jesus! I couldn't bear that!'

She mentally contrasted Kearney's grossness with the lithe muscularity of Con Shonley and that contrast brought a wry smile to her lips. 'It's like comparing a pig with a prince.' A sudden yearning filled her being. 'I'd love to see you again, Con Shonley,' she murmured softly. 'How much I'd love to see you again . . . '

After a while, for perhaps the thousandth time, Grainne wondered where Kearney hid his main store of money. She knew that he distrusted banks and that he kept it somewhere in his house or its environs, but exactly where was still a mystery to her. Whenever she was alone in the building she always searched, but had never gained any inkling of its location. 'At least I know where it's not,' she joked wryly, and then doubted even that fact. 'The crafty scut might well be changing it over to places I've already looked in . . . Ah well, time will tell, I suppose.'

She abandoned the puzzle, and started to turn the donkey back towards Skibereen. As she did so a group of men came into view from the direction of Ballydehob. She saw that they wore the black coats and woollen caubeens of burial men.

'Holy Mary, Mother of God, please don't let me catch a fever,' she requested fervently, because having recognized the tall young man walking in front of the group, Grainne intended to stay just where she was until they came up to her . . .

Con Shonley was hardly aware of the jaunting-car, or its occupant. The poteen that he and Denis Callaghan had drunk that day was still fuddling his mind, and now a dull ache was throbbing in his skull. They had been in Ballydehob to bury a family of seven, three of them only infants, and it had brought unwelcome memories to Con of his own infant sister's death. He kept his eyes on the ground as he strode out, trying to drive his memories from his thoughts.

'Hello, Con Shonley.'

The soft call brought the youth's head up sharply.

Grainne MacDermott smiled at him from the jaunting-car. 'Well, aren't you even going to wish me the time of day?' she demanded with feigned annoyance.

'I'll see you later,' Con told his companions, and went to within a few paces of the girl. 'Hello yourself.' His headache had miraculously eased, and he smiled at her with deeply-felt pleasure.

'I'll stand here,' he added, shamefully aware of the fear people had of close proximity with him.

'You'll do no such thing.' Grainne's own fear dissipated as she remembered this youth's kindness to her, and saw again what a fine handsome figure he cut. 'I'm not about to shout my conversation so that the whole world can hear it.'

Despite her urgings Con only advanced a little way nearer to her. He was too well aware that the danger of transmitting a fever was greatly increased when fresh from handling its victims. 'It's better that I stay here, Grainne,' he said quietly.

'Tell me, have you thought about me at all?' she flirted.

'Yes,' he answered truthfully, 'many times.'

The green eyes studied his face closely. 'You've changed, Con,' she observed gravely. 'When I last met you you were still only a boy. Now, you've the face of a man.'

102

Puzzlement etched her smooth brow. 'But it's been only a few months, Con?'

The youth knew that his features had hardened and matured, and he knew also the reason why. 'Months can have the effect of years sometimes, Grainne.' He was very serious. 'What I've done and seen these last months would age anyone.'

The girl found him frighteningly attractive. 'Dear God, if Michael Kearney was like you, I'd have jumped into his bed that first night,' she admitted silently, and her breath became tremulous.

The sun was already beginning to sink westwards, and Grainne knew that she must return to Kearney's house without delay.

'I've got to go now,' she said reluctantly, then patted the space beside her on the driving seat. 'Come, you can ride part of the way back with me.' She saw the indecision in his face, and went on, 'Don't be foolish, Con Shonley. I'm not one of those stupid people who fear to be near a burial man. If the fever wants you, it'll take you no matter where you hide, and if it doesn't want you, then you can walk through a houseful of it without harm.'

For the first time he relaxed, and allowed his emotions to flower free and found that the infatuation he had had for this girl still maintained its potency. 'I'll walk by your side, Grainne, I wouldn't wish to put you in any danger.'

'Why?' The question was immediate, and so was his answer.

'Because I think that I'm in love with you, girl.'

The simple declaration touched her deeply, and she flushed and smiled brilliantly at him, but made no answer. As he walked by her side, she told him all that had befallen her, and he returned her confidences, ever aware of the hold she was strengthening upon his affections. They reached the parting place, and Grainne asked, 'Will I see you again, Con Shonley?'

He chuckled ruefully. 'The last time you asked me that question, when I gave you the answer, you became angered with me.'

Her lips curved deliciously. 'I'll not be angered this time, Con Shonley, unless you answer no.'

He threw back his head and laughed with joy, before asking, 'How will I meet you?'

'Come to the Calvary.' She pointed at a wayside shrine some considerable distance ahead of them on the road. 'Come at dusk each night. Whenever I can, I'll meet you there,' she instructed him eagerly, and with an equal eagerness he agreed.

He was walking from her when she called after him, 'Wait a minute, Con.' She jumped from the jaunting-car and ran to him, her lovely face marred by anxiety.

His heart fell. 'What is it? What's wrong?'

She came to stand so close that he could feel her breath on his face as she looked up to him. 'Tell me, Con, d'ye still go to the valley and drill with the other men?'

His eyes hardened. 'How would you know about the drilling. It's meant to be a secret.'

Grainne couldn't help but laugh at him. 'Don't talk like an idjit,' she teased. 'When has there ever been a secret in Ireland that's not been known to half the population.' Her laughter ceased abruptly. 'Tell me though, d'ye still go?'

He nodded. 'Sometimes . . . But to be truthful, I haven't bothered for quite a while now. It seems a waste of time to be drilling with bits o' stick.' Another reason for not going, which he kept to himself, was his disillusion with Rourke and Father Boyce. 'But why do you ask me that?'

'Because the police know about it, and the names of those who go there,' she almost whispered. 'Don't ask me to tell you how I know that, because I can't, not now, anyway . . . But I'd hate for ye to be put in jail by the Peelers. I'd sooner you never went drilling.'

His face was sombre. 'The drilling might be needed one day, Grainne . . . ' With an effort he threw off his sombreness and smiled at her. 'I'll be at the Calvary at dusk tonight, try and come.'

She reached out and touched his cheek. 'I will.' With that she turned and ran back to the jaunting-car, and with a final wave sent the donkey trotting hard along the road.

Con watched until she had gone from sight, then went whistling on his way . . .

'That'll be your beau, will it?' Old Biddy Kearney could not walk well, but her eyes were as sharp as a hawk.

Grainne pulled the jaunting-car to a halt by the wayside shrine where the old woman had been kneeling at her devotions. The girl's smile was wary. 'What are you doing here, Aunt Biddy? Spying on me?'

The toothless mouth pursed and an indignant rebuttal spewed from it. 'Sure ye've the wicked heart in ye to accuse a good-living woman like meself of minding other's business for them.'

Groaning audibly the old crone scrambled painfully up beside Grainne, who sent the donkey on again.

'Holy Mary and all the Saints have mercy on me. I'm terrible sore-boned, so I am,' the old woman whined, then her bright black eyes flicked sideways searchingly. 'Did ye bring it?' she questioned eagerly.

Grainne's eyes glinted mischievously. 'Bring what?' she teased.

'Don't be coddin' me, ye young witch!' Biddy Kearney scolded.

Grainne laughed, her white teeth glistening in her sun-kissed face, and reached back to take a square, black-glassed bottle from the capacious basket behind her. 'Here.' She handed it to the greedily snatching hands of the crone.

'May God bless ye! Ye're a fine, good-hearted girl, so ye are.' After a quick swig of the brandy the bottle held, Old Biddy stowed it away in the inner layers of her dark-coloured bodice. Again her bright eyes flicked across the young face next to her. 'Was that tall fella a friend of yours?' she enquired casually.

'He was.' Grainne smiled.

The old woman's eyes narrowed, and with one claw-like hand she tapped Grainne's arm for emphasis as she spoke. 'Then heed me carefully, girl. Ye know well that me nephew has a powerful liking for ye. He'll not take kindly to the idea that ye have a young fella trailing after your skirts. Take heed Michael doesn't find out. He's the terrible bad one to cross.'

'Well now, Aunt Biddy,' Grainne answered lightly, 'he's not likely to find out, is he. For I shan't be telling him.'

The old woman felt the hard outlines of the bottle nestling against her withered dugs, and cackled gleefully. 'Nor me either, my sweet lamb. Not while ye're being so good to a poor friendless old soul like meself.'

They shared a knowing glance, lustrous green eyes meeting bright black eyes, and laughed together . . .

As dusk caused the stars to glimmer, Con waited by the wayside shrine. His skin tingled from the effects of cold water scrubbing, and the clothes he wore were still damp from washing. He felt a mixture of apprehension and pleasurable expectancy. Then his throat thickened, and he swallowed hard as Grainne came walking erect and proud towards him.

He sensed, rather than saw her smile in the gloom of the evening, and then her warm sweet breath came upon his face, and the soft moistness of her lips upon his mouth. He drew her deeper into the shadow of the shrine, and knew that he loved this green-eyed girl with all his being . . .

For a time they stood mouth to mouth, clasping each other close. Con's desire was fierce within him, but he fought to control his rampaging need for her, afraid that if he tried to assuage that need he would frighten or offend her. Innocent as he was of women's needs he did not understand the message she was giving him as she kissed and clung and moulded her body to his.

Virginal though she was, Grainne's sexual passions were strong, and instinctively sure that Con Shonley loved her as deeply as she loved him, she meant this night to consummate their love. Drawing her head back from his searching lips, she cupped his face between her hands and whispered huskily, 'Let's go further back from the road, honey. Someone might pass and see us here.'

Close-twined they moved beyond the shrine until they

reached a small dell, thickly carpeted with soft grass and moss and fragrant with the scents of wild herbs. Grainne pulled her shawl from her shoulders and spread it over the moss then sank down to her knees upon it, her head bowed so that her long hair hung like a veil before her face.

'Love me here, Con,' she whispered. 'Love me now.'

He knelt before her and slowly unfastened the bodice of her dress, his fingers trembling as he did so. Released from their covering, her full, shapely breasts were a glory to his eyes and with a sense of wondering adoration he gently fondled their warm velvetly firmness and pressed his lips to the dark aureoles of her nipples. Her breath came with a sobbing moan and she reached for him, pulling his clothing from his taut-muscled body and enfolding his erect manhood in her hands. Naked they lay side-by-side, touching, exploring, caressing, and then Con moved above his beloved girl and with an infinite tenderness brought her into womanhood, pouring his love and passion into her until they cried out in a mutual ecstasy and were spent . . .

Chapter Fifteen

Charles Edward Trevelyan, Permanent Head of Her Britannic Majesty's Treasury Department, was a man of rigid integrity and of ardent religious feelings. But he refused to let his Christian charity interfere with what he conceived to be his duty towards the State. It was his considered opinion that too much had been done by the Government for the distressed people of Ireland . . .

They had indeed grown worse instead of better as a result of government munificence, and now independent exertion must be tried instead of government action. After all, the summer of 1847 had been one of magnificent weather. The grain crops were superb, and although only a fraction of the usual potato acreage had been planted, in that fraction there were no signs of blight.

Irish Famine Relief under the Soup Kitchen Act must end by the last days of August 1847 at the very latest. All Commissariat Depots must be closed. Sole responsibility for the destitute in Ireland must now devolve upon the local Poor Law Commissioners and the Boards of Guardians in that unhappy land. Besides, Great Britain herself was in the throes of a vast financial crisis. The money to feed the hungry masses was not available any more in the coffers of the British Treasury . . .

By the second week in August the closing of the depots was completed, and Trevelyan, tired out by two years of hard and continuous work went to France with his family for a fortnight's holiday.

By October the new scheme had shown itself to be unworkable. One of its basic requirements, to avoid overwhelming floods of applicants, was that outdoor relief should be made almost impossible for able-bodied men to obtain. Therefore these able-bodied men could only obtain relief if they became inmates of the local workhouse. Room must be made in these grim havens by emptying from them the aged, the infirm, the widowed, the children, and allowing them an outdoor relief of cooked meals only. To their credit the majority of Boards of Guardians indignantly refused to implement this.

The collection of the levied Poor Rates on land and property occupiers also became almost impossible to implement. The landlords had moved first, taking the crops of their tenants for rent. Troops and police had to be called in to enforce the collection of the rates.

On those holdings valued at £4 and under, the landlord himself was liable for the rate. In many of these cases ruthless evictions of the smallholders by the landlords were resorted to, since empty holdings and ruined homesteads could not be rated . . . Shielded by law, the landlords called in police and troops to enforce these evictions . . .

It was a large, well-kept cabin. A small garden of flowers fronting its walls, and wild roses climbing up towards the eaves of the thatched roof. The single door was closed fast, and the small windows shuttered and barred.

Jonas Clarke, six feet high and burly, the agent of the landlord, Lord Carberry, hammered upon the door panels and bellowed, 'Come on outta that, John Tumelty! 'Tis no use you hiding behind the door.'

Clarke ceased hammering and listened carefully, but no sound came from within. A large body of men and women were massed some distance behind Clarke, their gaunt faces wolfish with resentment and hatred, but the presence of the intervening lines of mounted blue-jacketed Hussars, and dismounted carbine-carrying policemen inhibited the crowd's mood from violent expression.

Police Sub-Inspector Augustus Hardy's thin face was impassive as he paced up and down behind the line of his motionless men in company with Lieutenant O'Donoghue of the Eighth Royal Irish Hussars. The young cavalryman, elegant in blue and gold, puffed out his pink cheeks beneath his brown fur busby. Periodically he swung his scarlet-lined pelisse higher on his shoulder and rattled his sabre in its low-slung scabbard.

'I'm damned if I like this work, Hardy,' he scowled, and ran long nervous fingers across his luxuriant mustachios. He nodded at his troop of grim-faced soldiers. 'And my men don't like it either. Makes the blaggards surly and hard to handle.'

The English policeman was curt in tone. 'That is understandable, Lieutenant O'Donoghue, they are, after all, an Irish regiment. It is almost certain that many of them come from similar backgrounds to this poor devil, Tumelty . . . But, unhappily it is our duty to aid the eviction, and your men's duty to obey their orders.'

'And a damned foul duty it is, Sir!' the young officer spat out. 'I joined the army to fight Her Majesty's enemies, not to aid and abet low curs of bum-bailiffs!'

Clarke's great fist pounded the panels once more. 'Come on, Tumelty, let's be having yez. Or I'll have my men smash the place down with you inside it.'

A frightened, but defiant voice yelled from inside. 'The rent is paid, Clarke, and well you know it. Ye've no right to evict me.'

The agent pushed his pot hat back on his sweaty forehead, and his brutal features flushed with temper. ''Tis not the rent Lord Carberry's concerned about, 'tis the bloody rates, and ye've paid not a penny of those, have ye now . . . Now, are ye coming out, or do we come in and drag yez out by the neck?'

From behind the door shrill wails rang out, and a woman's voice piteously begged her children to hush and be quiet.

'Be damned to the rates!' the man yelled. 'It's not me that should pay them . . . And if it was I've got no money anyway. It's gone wi' me crops as rent to your man, Carberry.'

'And be damned to ye, as well!' Clarke roared, and stamped away from the cabin. He approached the two officers, who stopped pacing and faced him expectantly. The big man's manner was subserviently civil.

'I'll hope you'll see, sors, that I've done me best to get the man out peaceably.'

Hardy nodded, his eyes cold and contemptuous, but when he answered his tone was deliberately neutral. 'I have noted it, Mr Clarke. Do you not think it worth a little longer attempt at persuasion though?'

Clarke's large head swayed ponderously from side to side. 'Divil a bit o' good, sor, with all respect of course . . . I know this man, Tumelty. He's a hard-chaw, even if small-bodied. He'd not come out peaceable if the Angel Gabriel himself was to beg him to.' Again the large head swayed. 'No, sor, we'll have to put the ram to the door, I fear.'

Lieutenant O'Donoghue abruptly turned away. 'Then get on with it, blast you,' he muttered, his pink cheeks glowing with anger.

For a moment Clarke stared at the elegant slender back with a scarcely concealed sneer. Then touched his hand to his hat brim in a mock-military salute. 'At your orders, sor.' He grinned, and left the pair to go to his own men, who were grouped around a long heavy pole. They were the outcasts of the district, bully-boys and petty criminals, for no man who respected or had compassion for his fellow human beings could do their work.

'All right boys.' At Clarke's words the men lifted the wooden pole, muscles bunching beneath ragged clothes, mouths grunting with effort.

A rumbling growl came from the watching crowd and the policemen facing them gripped their carbines tighter, while the Hussars steadied their glossy-hided mounts.

The great pole crashed against the barred door and the panels cracked and bent inwards before the impact.

'God's curse on ye for this day's work, Clarke, and the rest of you devils!' a woman howled from the crowd, and a score of others vented execrations.

'Let me remind you that we are acting to the letter of the law,' Inspector Hardy shouted into the glowering faces in

111

front of him. 'If any of you should intervene, then you are breaking the law, and will be dealt with accordingly.'

Again the ram smashed into the door, white flakes and dust jetted from its surrounds, and from inside the cabin children shrieked in terror. The third smash sent the remnants of the panels flying inwards, and out through the dust a small wild-eyed man came charging, wielding a short-handled shovel. He shattered the arm of the nearest ram-holder with one blow, and the man screamed in agony. Even as Tumelty lifted the shovel again the other ram-holders were on him, punching, kicking, tearing . . . Tumelty threw back his head, his mouth a gaping black hole in his blood-reddened face, and roared his defiance to the skies. He was dragged clear and hurled bodily through the air. His flailing body thumped to the earth and the ram-holders' boots hammered into his flesh and bone until he was collapsed and still. Only the jerking of his stick-like ribs showing that he still lived.

'Clear the cabin, boys,' Clarke bellowed, and his men rushed through the ruined doorway, only to re-appear within moments lugging the pitiful household possessions with them, and throwing pots, stools, bedcoverings, cups, plates all across the dirt.

The woman and her children came out shrieking and wailing, she to throw herself on the bleeding body of her husband, her little ones to run aimlessly backwards and forwards, tears and terror blinding their eyes.

Already the ram was aloft again, battering the mud-brick walls of the cabin into ruin, and causing the roof to sag and collapse as support was knocked from beneath it.

'Draw sabres! Close up!' Lieutenant O'Donoghue had seen a surge of threatening movement developing in the furious crowd. Faced by the joint menace of loaded carbines and sharp steel blades, the movement subsided into impotent, seething rage . . .

In the middle of the mass, Con Shonley turned away and began to push through the press of bodies. He was filled with a sickening awareness of helplessness, and could no longer bear to stand and watch what was taking place. Eyes downcast he strode from the scene and was unaware of his follower until Father Boyce spoke.

'Arrah now, that was a dreadful performance, was it not, Con.'

The tall youth halted and swung about, his swarthy face displaying his own feelings only too clearly.

'But what could anyone do to prevent it?' Boyce questioned rhetorically, his hands spread wide in appeal. 'Sure isn't it happening all over the country . . . D'ye know that I was in Castlebar at the end of September. I saw there, men standing in droves in the streets, their reaping hooks in their hands, offering themselves for work at eight pence the day . . . And d'ye know what? May God be my judge! There was no one able to hire them.' The priest's long nose lifted high and his face assumed an expression of exaggerated amazement. 'Not one of the local landowners or farmers could afford to pay eight pence the day to get the crops in.' The amazed expression metamorphosed into scorn. 'They didn't want the crops in, that's the truth of it. The fat-bellied hounds want the labouring men dead and buried, so they can put children to work in their places for less wages.'

Con Shonley shrugged his broad shoulders beneath the black swallow-tail coat, not fully accepting the priest's accusations, but not wishing to dispute him openly. 'Well, Father, if there is no money available how can labourers be paid?' he said mildly.

The little man reacted sharply. 'Well, if there is no money to pay the men, then why not let the men get the harvest in anyway, and so save the crop so that they can eat it themselves?'

Con was forced to smile and give best. 'Yes, there is logic in that,' he admitted.

'And yourself, Con, you're looking very well, I'm happy to see . . . You and that rogue Callaghan, are regarded somewhat like a modern miracle, you know . . . I mean how you keep alive, the pair of ye. 'Tis a thing beyond earthly understanding . . . How many other burial men have died while you've been working at it?'

For a moment Con thought back, and felt a shock of acute surprise at the total. 'It must be near a score of them, Father.'

'Indeed now!' The priest stared quizzically up into the face above him. 'Do you ever pause to consider, Con, that perhaps God is saving you for a purpose?'

The younger man shook his head. 'In truth, Father, I don't know what useful purpose I could serve at this time be it for God, or for anyone else.'

A fanatical gleam sprang into the priest's eyes, and his voice grew fervid. 'I know a purpose, Con Shonley. You are young, and strong, and have courage to spare. God wants you and the other young wolf-hounds of Ireland to lead the fight against our oppressors.'

A resentment burgeoned in Con's mind. 'How?' he demanded bluntly, 'By drilling with bits of stick, and swigging poteen while doing so?'

The priest waved this aside. 'Never mind that now, Con . . . Did you know that Phelim Rourke is back?'

Con vented half-bemused laughter. 'I didn't even know that he'd gone, Father.'

The dewdrop trembled on the tip of the long nose beneath him. 'Arrah yes, your man's been gone right enough. But now he's back . . . And what is more, he's brought a few things with him.'

'Such as?' Con enquired politely.

'Such as muskets!' the priest whispered dramatically. 'And bayonets, and caps and powder and ball!'

Con felt a swelling excitement.

Father Boyce's shrewd gaze noted the youth's reaction, and he smiled contentedly. 'There now, Con Shonley, the drills you spoke of would be of interest to you now, I take it.'

'Indeed they would, Father,' the youth assured fervently. 'Dear God above, when I think of what happened here today, I could take up arms tomorrow.'

Boyce grinned delightedly. 'Arrah yes! That is what I wanted to hear from your lips, my friend.' He tapped a fingernail on the side of his nose. 'But there'll be no rising of the pikes tomorrow, Con, nor for a while yet. But things are going forwards, that I can swear on my immortal soul. Things are fast going forwards towards the day when Ireland's fetters shall be struck from her limbs by her own fine sons.' He drew a deep breath, his eyes shining at the vision he had created in his mind. 'Do you wish to come back now to the drills, Con? It'll be a different style of thing entirely, that I promise you.'

Con Shonley nodded his head, once only. 'I'm your man, Father Boyce.'

The priest crowed happily, and clapped his hand on the muscular shoulder above him. 'No, Con, ye're not my man . . . Ye're one of Ireland's fighting wolf-hounds . . .'

Chapter Sixteen

The next drill session Con went to was on an October night of full moon. It was not held in the valley however, but in the confines of Father Boyce's small chapel, its interior lit solely by the moonbeams streaming through its windows. There were only a score of men present, including Boyce, Rourke and Con himself.

The little priest winked wisely at Con's patent surprise. 'Arrah yes, my son, it's a shock to you, is it not. Still we're not altogether fools. We know well when we drill in the valley there are informers among us. But we still drill up there, with our bits o' sticks.' His eyes slyly twinkled at Con as he said that. 'But the reason is simple to understand. While the police think we've only sticks and a few pikes to drill with, they're happy just to let us do so. They know where they can find us then, and they see no threat to the Government. Pikes and sticks are no use against cannon . . . But here . . . ' He kicked the side of the wooden coffin that lay at his feet. 'In here we have muskets . . . They're a threat all right.' He paused, and studied the gathering closely. 'You men have been very carefully chosen. There are no informers among you, that I'm sure of, and you can be trusted to keep this a close secret. Say nothing of it to anyone, not wife, mother, child, father, brother, sister . . . No one! You will be the Grenadiers of our revolution. You will be the ones, and thousands like you all across our nation, who will set Erin free once more, and make her a nation once again.'

He signalled to Rourke, who came to the coffin and opened its lid. From the dark interior he lifted a long wood-brown,

116

steel-grey musket. Holding it up in his brawny arms, Rourke's strong stained teeth showed in a savage grin. 'This is the India-pattern long musket. Converted from flintlock to percussion. Commonly known as, Brown Bess.' His hard eyes swept the rapt faces of his listeners. 'She'll prove a true sweetheart to you, and I'll teach ye how to make her serve ye well.'

Some miles distant from the tiny chapel a house rang with rough laughter, jeers and disputes which became increasingly belligerent as drink slurred voices and heated tempers. Michael Kearney sat at the head of the long oak table in his parlour, his own senses half-fuddled, his shirt and waistcoat torn open to bare the thick red fur matting his chest. Along the table's length his cronies shouted and sang, disputed and laughed, took great gulps of raw poteen spirit from stone jugs and tore voraciously at hunks of yellow-fatted bacon and dark-wheaten bread. Above their heads three lanterns swung flaring and smoking from the beams of the ceiling, and their ever-shifting light heightened the animal-like brutality of the faces beneath.

In the kitchen to the rear of the building Grainne Mac-Dermott sat at the cooking range fire in company with Old Biddy.

> 'The Harp that once thro' Tara's Halls
> its soul of music shedddd . . . '

Despite his drunkenness the singer carried the tune well, his pure tenor echoing above the noise of the gathering and coming clearly to the women's ears.

> ' . . . Now hangs as mute on Tara's walls,
> as if that soul were fledddd . . . '

'Your man sings nicely,' Old Biddy nodded, and from beneath her black bodice drew out the square bottle of brandy. 'Will ye take the wee drop, my lamb?' she invited.

The young girl shook her head, and her long lustrous

hair fell about her shoulders. Old Biddy took a long swallow, her protruberant glottle jerking violently beneath the wrinkled wattles of her scrawny throat. Then she replaced the bottle in its hiding place, and regarded her companion questioningly.

'Ye look a picture o' beauty this night, my lamb. Are ye away to see your friend in a while?'

'No.' Grainne's eyes reflected the reddish glimmer of flames as she stared into the fire.

'And why not? It's rare the night ye've not met him these last weeks?'

'He had to go somewhere,' the girl answered absently, and the old woman was quick to seize on this.

'Arrah it's likely he'll be meeting some other lass, and giving her the sweet talk.'

Grainne smiled absently, and inwardly answered, 'No, old woman, Con is mine. I've only one rival, and she's not a real woman . . . ' A frown marred the smooth forehead as her troubled thoughts dwelt on this. 'If she were a real woman, I'd know how to fight against her . . . But how can I fight against the Shan Van Vocht?'

How could any woman of flesh and blood fight the insidious enslavement of men by the Old Woman of Irish Legend. The ancient Bitch Goddess who brought men to their premature and violent deaths as they strove to serve her . . .

' . . . breaks the night, its tale of ruin tells.
Thus freedom now so seldom wakes . . . '

The singer's voice throbbed into Grainne's consciousness and intruded upon her sombre thoughts. 'If we had money, then Con and me could go to America . . . We'd be happy there,' she told herself. 'Con would be safe from all this nonsense of rebellion, and I could sleep in his arms at night without care . . . '

'You seem unhappy, my lamb,' Old Biddy persisted, and again produced her bottle. 'Sure now, take a sip of this. It'll cheer your heart, so it will.' The old crone had become genuinely fond of Grainne and did not enjoy seeing her so pensive. The girl smiled and this time did accept a sip from the bottle. The pungent heat ran down her throat and spread through her chest, but did not immediately lighten her mood as she had hoped.

Bellowed curses and the smashing of crockery and wooden furniture denoted a fight in the parlour, and Grainne heard Kearney roaring at the combatants to stop brawling.

'Jesus Christ, but it makes a long night of it!' she grumbled angrily. 'Why can't we just take ourselves off to the cabin and get some sleep.'

'Holy Mary and all the Saints! We'd be murdered in our beds,' the old woman exclaimed nervously. 'At least we'd be murdered after them hard-chaws in there had had what they wanted from us.'

Grainne was forced to laugh at the vanity of the old crone, who was convinced that every man she met with wanted carnal knowledge of her shrivelled body.

'No, fair play to him, me nephew is quite right to make us keep here in the kitchen while them drunken blaggards are about the place. We can be safe here, d'ye see. Michael can watch over us, and guard us.'

'And who is to guard us from him,' Grainne thought, but aloud demurred, 'I can't think that those fellas in there would try to rape us, Aunt Biddy.'

The crone's toothless mouth opened and closed rapidly like a feeding fish. 'Well you're still innocent of the wickedness of this world iffen ye think that, my girl . . . But I know better! We'll stay here, as Michael wants us to.' With that she pulled out her bottle and took yet another wholly satisfying swig from it . . .

The hours wore by and Grainne only stirred to place fresh peat blocks on the fire. Old Biddy dozed off, her mouth open, her arms crossed over her hidden bottle. The noise from the parlour slowly lessened, and at last, all was still. Grainne lifted the lantern from its ceiling hook, and went to see what was happening.

As the parlour door creaked open a rush of over-heated

air enveloped the girl. Loud snoring and disjointed sleep-mutterings came from the men sprawled around the room and across the table, on which jugs lay on their sides, and remnants of bacon and bread were strewn.

Kearney was lolling in his chair, a jug of poteen before him. He had by now discarded both waistcoat and shirt and in the light of the lamps his gross body, where not matted by red hairs, was white and greasy with sweat. His heavily muscled arms stretched out to both sides of the stone jug, and when the door creaked open he stiffened them to push himself to his feet. Swaying, he pointed to the jug with one hand, and beckoned with the other.

'Come and take a drink with me, my little love.'

The girl shook her head. 'No thanks, Mr Kearney. I'm away to my bed now, I'll take Aunt Biddy with me.'

His jowls wobbled as his head rocked on his shoulders. With a conscious effort he steadied his stare on her. 'It's to bed ye're going, is it?' he slurred. 'And by Jaze, I bet you look lovely in it as well, wi' yer hair all across the pillow.' He grinned lopsidedly at her. 'Tell me now, my little love . . . D'ye like me at all?'

She hesitated, before replying guardedly, 'Well, you're a fair enough man to work for, Mr Kearney.'

He waved his arms ponderously before his face. 'Don't call me Mister . . . Call me, Michael,' he told her. 'I want us to be good friends, and maybe more.'

Grainne looked downwards and made no answer. Her breath caught in her throat as she heard him move, and his towering shadow fell across her skirts. 'I'll go then, Mr Kearney, and wish you goodnight.' She went to leave, but his fingers gripped the soft flesh of her upper arms, and he pulled her round to him.

'No. Don't go . . . I've something to tell ye.'

Lifting her chin she stared into his drink-mottled face. 'What is that?' she questioned, trying to fight down her increasing nervousness.

He grinned again, and a streak of saliva ran from the corner of his thick liver-coloured lips. 'I want to tell ye that I'm powerful fond of ye.'

His foul breath gusted against her nostrils, and involuntarily she jerked her head back. A wary look livened his dulled eyes, and he scowled. 'What's the matter with ye? Don't you want me to be fond?'

Aware of his uncertain temper, and afraid of its eruption, Grainne forced a smile. 'Well yes, Mr Kearney. I do want you to like me.'

The scowl vanished immediately, and a grin of satisfaction replaced it. 'That's good, my little love. That's good! Come now, light me to me bed, there's a good child.'

'Wouldn't you be better here with your friends?' Grainne's voice was now betraying her nervousness. 'Only, if they wake, and you're not here, they'll be worrying what's become of you.'

The man swung his head and spat in the direction of the nearest prostrate man. 'Worry about me? These? These aren't friends, girl!' he growled morosely. 'These are animals . . . Drunken worthless scum!' His eyes came back to her, and now all the drink-induced dullness had left them, and they shone with an evil joy. 'But these scum has helped make me a rich man!' he boasted. 'Yes . . . Me . . . Michael Kearney, a rich man.' He laughed into her face. 'Did ye not know that I was rich, my little love, aye?' He nodded his head. 'Well it's true, so it is . . . I am rich, and iffen you was to be a good girl, and do all that I wanted ye to, then you could well share in it with me.'

Grainne was torn by conflicting emotions. Repulsion, disgust, fear, battled for mastery against curiosity, and greed for the gold that could take her and Con Shonley over the seas to the new land beyond.

Kearney closely regarded the play of expression across her features, and told himself, 'I thought that the mention of the lovely yellow sovereigns would appeal to ye, ye wee bitch.' Aloud he asked her, 'Come now, light me upstairs to me bed.' He tried to push her before him, and as her body stiffened in resistance he cajoled, 'Don't be silly, girl, I'll not harm ye. Wouldn't ye like to see me money now? Wouldn't ye want to see the truth of what I'm saying with your own eyes?'

Burning curiosity won the mastery, and Grainne allowed herself to be led by his side up the broad stairs. He staggered slightly upon the first wooden steps, and gripped her arm tighter to steady himself, but made no other physical approach. At the bedroom door she hesitated again, but he urged her through.

'Come on, girl, it's just inside there, but I daren't bring it out with the doors open for fear them below might come up and catch a sight of it.'

The room was large and well-furnished. A great four-poster bed dominated the floor space, and sideboards and chests lined each wall. He took the lantern from her hand, and pushed her towards the bed.

'You stand over there, my love, while I do the necessary.'

Grainne's breathing was rapid and shallow, and already she was regretting the impulsions that had brought her to this room. 'I'd best go down,' she flustered, 'your Aunty's sleeping near the fire, she might fall and do herself an injury.'

This time Kearney's drunken temper showed itself. 'Ye'll stand there until I tell ye to move, you little bitch,' he snarled at her, and clenched his fist threateningly before her eyes. 'D'ye take me for a fool, girl, a bloody cod? Is that the way of it? I know ye've been looking for me money every chance ye've had.'

The sudden widening of her eyes in shock betrayed her guilt to him, and he laughed uproariously. Then he abruptly sobered, and warned, 'Now stand quiet, or ye'll feel the weight of me hand.' As he turned away from her he sneered. 'Try and look happy, my little love. Ye're after going to see what ye've been hoping to find ever since ye got here . . . '

Setting the lantern down on one of the chest lids, Kearney slumped heavily onto his knees in front of a great ornately carved mahogany sideboard. For a moment he swayed back, resting his huge buttocks on his heels, and Grainne stared with a nauseous disgust at the hairy white flesh which overhung his broad leather belt in thick wads of blubbery fat. He pulled out the bottom drawer filled with folded linen, and put it to one side. All the time he panted and grunted, then broke wind and a foul odour filled the room.

Bending low, forcing even thicker wads of fat back from his immense gut, he plunged both arms into the vacated space and fumbled in the concealed bottom of the sideboard. There came two sharp clicks and with another louder grunt, Kearney pulled his arms clear.

In his hands was a metal box, six inches square in dimension. It thumped heavily on the floorboards as he placed it down. A brass catch held the lid shut, and the man pressed it back with his thumb and snapped the lid open. He almost slavered with pleasure at what lay revealed. 'There now, would you look at them.' He sighed voluptuously. 'Aren't they the little beauties.'

Grainne, overcome by curiosity, moved closer and peeped over the fat hairy shoulder of the kneeling man. She gasped audibly. The box was crammed full with stacked rounds of gold sovereigns. Clutching the sideboard to assist him, Kearney clambered to his feet and stood at the girl's side, both of them entranced by the dull golden shimmerings given off by the coins in the lantern's guttering beams.

'And there's more than them to be seen . . . ' The man seemed to be talking to himself, so engrossed was he by the money. 'Lots more! Hidden where only meself knows, and every single one o' them belonging to me . . . '

The girl's thoughts took flight in wild imaginings. She saw herself dressed in splendid clothes, before a splendid house, seated in her own carriage behind a pair of matched blood-horses; and she saw Con Shonley with her. Only no longer dressed in ragged clothes, but like a fine gentleman, with a shiny top hat, and a fur-collared coat, velvet-braided trousers and soft leather boots. Her lips parted, and she sighed in dreamy longing.

Kearney's glance slid sideways as he heard the sigh, and his manhood began to swell with lust as he watched the rise and fall of her firm high breasts straining against the fabric of her dress.

'Wouldn't ye like to be having some o' those for yourself, Grainne?' he whispered.

Still rapt in her daydreams, she nodded silently.

The liver-lips suddenly dried, and the pustuled tongue slid between them to moisten their surfaces. 'Sure now, I'll show ye how to gain them,' he muttered thickly, and reached for her breasts.

She roused from her dream in sudden terror, as his hands clutched and kneaded at her tender flesh. He forced her against him and his mouth clamped down over her own. Her arms were trapped to her sides by his enfolding grasp, and as she frantically twisted and wriggled she felt his massive manhood crushing against her lower belly.

Slowly Kearney began to move towards the bed, half-dragging, half-carrying his slender burden, his senses smothered by his terrible hunger for her body. The softness of her wildly threshing thighs, and the firm breasts burning against his chest through their flimsy covering acting like a flaming goad to his ravening lust. Even as his mouth still sucked at her lips, guttural groans of need rumbled in his throat.

His knees cannoned into the sides of the bed and he fell forwards with her body beneath him. Rage mingled with his lust as she continued to struggle violently and frustrate him. Brutally he wrenched both her hands together above her head so that he could pin them there with one of his own. Then, with his freed hand he gripped her throat and squeezed hard, and all the time kept his mouth clamped to hers.

Grainne feared she was dying in a nightmare of crushing strangulation. Her lungs were a tearing agony, and her sight filled with blackness rent by flashes of dazzling light. Without knowing what she did her teeth bit hard on the pustuled tongue that stabbed into and violated her mouth.

'URRGGGH!' Kearney tore his head away and blood spattered from his mouth on the gusted breaths of his bellows of pain. In atavistic instinct Grainne exerted all her remaining strength in one mighty effort to break free of his body, and threw herself towards the bedroom door. She crashed it open and ran for the stairs. In her distress, and the darkness of the night, she missed her footing and fell headlong.

Her shrill scream was smashed into silence as her head struck the rough bricks of the lower walls, and she knew no more . . .

Chapter Seventeen

Doctor Donovan finished his bandaging and pinned the loose end, then stepped back from the side of the box bed, and studied his patient. Grainne lay white-faced and still, and only the faintest rise and fall of her chest gave evidence of life.

'She'll do well enough now, Mrs Kearney,' he told the old crone, and busied himself with repacking his instruments into their leather bag.

'Thanks be to God for that, Doctor.' Aunt Biddy wrung her claw-like hands in relief. 'I heard the poor lamb scream, and then the terrible thud when she hit, and when I saw her lying all bloody and crumpled at the foot of the stair I thought she was dead, and me heart stopped within me, so it did.'

The medical man smiled kindly. 'The girl is strong and healthy, Mrs Kearney, it'll need a deal more to kill her than a broken head . . . Here, take this.' He handed the woman a small bottle. 'It's laudanum. If she comes round let her drink a couple of drops of this mixed into a glass of wine or cordial. That will keep her sleeping, and allow time for her bodily humours to recover their equilibrium.' He completed his repacking of the bag, took up his top hat, and with a word of farewell left the cabin.

Old Biddy fumbled in her bodice and drew out her bottle. As she sipped from its neck, her bright eyes stared at the motionless girl. It was many hours past daybreak, and her nephew's cronies had long since left the house, nursing their aching heads and sick stomachs. Michael Kearney himself was locked in his bedroom, and the only answer that Old Biddy had been able to get in reply to her knocking on his door, was a mangled oath. He had refused to open the door even when Biddy begged him for help to move the unconscious girl from where she had fallen. Two or three of his drunken cronies had eventually gathered sufficient of their scattered wits to help the old woman carry Grainne to the cabin, and then one had gone in search of the doctor.

The girl had a deep cut above the hairline of her forehead, and a large bruised swelling around it, but Donovan was satisfied that no bone had been broken, and that after rest Grainne would be none the worse for her mishap.

The old woman smacked her thin lips, savouring the fruity after-taste of the brandy, and then muttered to herself, 'That bloody nephew o' mine tried to do this wee girl a mischief, of that there's no doubt. Bad cess to him, the drunken baste! Well, he'll not come near her again, not while there's a breath in my body to deny him. Filthy pig that he is!' With that resolve, Old Biddy squatted on a stool close to the bedhead, and settled herself to watch over her young friend.

Up in his bedroom Michael Kearney, bleary-eyed, unshaven and badly hungover, used a hand mirror to examine his injured tongue. The row of blue-edged punctures made by Grainne's sharp teeth were still oozing a bloody fluid, and the man winced at the pain his probing fingers caused when it touched the wounds.

'Hell's curse on the bloody bitch!' he swore, then recollection of how her body had moulded to his swept through Kearney's mind, and despite his pain he felt sexual excitement stir through him.

'By Jase, but she's ripe!' he told himself. 'I'll have another crack at her, or me name's not Michael Kearney . . . Only next time I'll take good care to keep me tongue from between her teeth . . . '

As Doctor Donovan's old mare ambled back towards Skibereen, his own thoughts dwelt on what had happened to the girl. 'That she fell, is beyond all doubt, but I wonder why she fell? Was that drunken blaggard Kearney frightening her? Or one of his dissolute friends?' The Doctor made a mental note that he would question the girl closely when he called back on the morrow to check her condition.

'Let the girl be, Michael, ye've done sufficient harm to her already.' Old Biddy stood in the cabin doorway and refused to move when Kearney came there the following morning.

'Now Aunty, don't talk silly,' the big man told her with rough jocularity. 'Sure I'd the drink taken, and all it was was a bit o' fun.'

'Fun, is that what you call it?' the ancient voice was cracked and screechy. 'The poor lamb has her head broke, and you call it fun!'

'That's what I said.' Kearney's jocular tone was tinged with irascibility. He reached into the pocket of his brown frock coat and pulled out a square bottle. 'Here,' he offered. 'I've brought ye a little something to keep the cold from your bones. 'Tis French brandy. The finest!'

Her wizened face puckered doubtfully. 'Why should ye bring that to me?'

'Sure aren't ye me aunty?' He forced a smile. 'Aren't ye the only breathing relative I have? Why wouldn't I be bringing ye a little present now and again?'

'Why indeed? Ye've never done it before!' she screeched triumphantly.

The man's scant patience was by now wearing thin. 'Well I've done it now, and if it's more like this ye'll be wanting, ye'd best stand back from the door and let me talk to the wee girl for a few minutes.' He saw that he was gaining, and wheedled. 'Come now, Aunty, a few minutes is neither here nor there. What harm can it do?'

The lure of the bottle overcame the old crone's scruples. 'Ahh well, I don't suppose the wee chat will do any harm.' She hobbled to one side and let him enter.

Grainne lay in her bed and stared at him, her green eyes huge in her pale face. Kearney stood some distance from

128

the bed, and without preamble, said, 'I'm sorry ye've hurt your head, but ye brought it on yourself with your own silliness . . . I'd the drink taken, and when you led me on, it went to me head.'

Grainne lifted her forefinger and pointed to the thick swathe of bandages around her skull. 'It went to my head as well, Mr Kearney.'

'I see that.' The man's small bloodshot eyes kept switching from her face to the shapely body outlined by the bed-coverings, and as always were loath to leave the firm breasts pulsing up and down. 'Have ye said anything to the doctor about what happened?' he wanted to know.

'How could I?' the girl answered spiritedly. 'Wasn't I senseless when he was here.' A calculating frown showed momentarily. 'But I'll have to tell him when he comes to see me today.'

A spasm of alarm crossed the man's mottled face. 'Now don't be so hasty, Grainne. Sure, there was nothing to it.'

The girl twisted the figurative knife. 'Nothing to it? To begin with I never led you on in any way . . . And I wouldn't call attempted rape, nothing!' she declaimed indignantly. Inwardly her natural fear of the man was lessening dramatically; and her agile mind could already foresee ways of utilizing what had occurred for her own advantage. 'I'll make the drunken animal pay,' she told herself with a grim determination, 'and I'll be doing it for my own future, and for Con's future.' Her train of thought was interrupted by the Gombeen Man's nervous blusterings.

'It was only a kiss or two. There's no harm in that.'

She counter-attacked immediately. 'It wouldn't have stopped at a kiss or two if I'd not managed to get free of you,' she accused him. 'And how about this?' She lifted her slightly cleft chin disclosing the mass of bruises on the soft skin of her throat. 'Didn't you nearly choke me to death? If I tell the doctor, then he'll bring the Peelers here, and you'll go to jail, Mr Kearney.'

The talk was going completely the opposite way to that the Gombeen Man had envisaged. This young innocent timid girl had turned out to be a fearless sharp-toothed vixen. For a moment Kearney's temper tried to dictate a course of raving, ranting threats, but his own acuteness forbade this. He feared now that without careful handling this girl would most certainly lay charges against him. Even if he was found not guilty, the dirt would stick and many of his lucrative sources of income would be closed to him. Even in these times a young girl's chastity was sacrosanct in the West of Ireland. He essayed a forebearing smile, but could only produce a sickly grimace. 'Now let's not get all upset, Grainne.' He tried to soothe her. 'Sure, haven't I said that I'm sorry.'

A sensation of joyous cruelty swept over the girl. She found that she was enjoying his discomfiture immensely. 'Sorry doesn't mend broken bones, does it? Sorry doesn't buy much either. You can't eat it, or wear it, or shelter under it, or use it for anything.'

He caught the implication behind her words, and with unvoiced curses accepted temporary defeat. 'I was thinking of giving you a few shillings to buy yourself something with,' he said with an outward meekness, and a terrible inward rage.

For the first time the girl's white teeth showed in a smile. But there was no kindness in that smile, only the cruel satisfaction of a predatory huntress. 'It'll need more than a few shillings to keep me quiet, Mr Kearney,' she stated coldly. 'Much more.'

'Be damned to ye then,' Kearney's caged gutter-devil broke free and snarled, 'Name your price, but iffen it's too high, then ye can go to Hell!'

Grainne's spirit soared in victory, but from some previously unguessed at source within her, she drew caution, and decided to let him wait for his answer. She moaned audibly, as if in pain.

'Ohhh my God, you must let me be now, Mr Kearney. My head is throbbing so sore that I can't think straight.'

His temper was now prodding him. 'Oh no! Oh no, we'll settle this matter now, ye damned hell-bitch. I'm not a man to wait on any whore's whims.'

130

A thudding of distant hoofbeats sounded faintly from outside the cabin and Grainne smiled secretly. Aloud she murmured, 'That'll be Doctor Donovan. D'you want to talk to him, Mr Kearney?'

The man's mottled complexion purpled with frustrated fury. 'Just be very careful what ye say to Donovan,' he growled. 'Because iffen ye say the wrong thing, there'll be none of the lovely yellow sovereigns that ye're so fond of will come your way.'

The huge green eyes were unafraid, and openly mocking. 'Come and talk to me later then, Mr Kearney. Maybe I'll be feeling better able to converse with you.'

The man blundered from the room, cursing sibilantly, but impotently.

Grainne called to the old crone, who had been listening at the window to all that had passed between the pair. 'Aunt Biddy, if that's the doctor coming, tell him that I've taken the laudanum and I'm fast asleep. Ask him will he come back tomorrow.'

The old woman stared with bright gleeful eyes at the young girl, and cackled admiringly, 'Aren't ye the cool one, my sweet lamb. Aren't ye just that!' Then went to do Grainne's bidding . . .

131

Chapter Eighteen

The party of mounted policemen trotted through an ice-cold rain hurled into their faces by the blustery night wind. At their head was Inspector Hardy, following the route to Skibereen by instinct, all his conscious thoughts directed towards what he had witnessed that day. A rate collection where the collectors had, under the protection of police guns, snatched even tools and threadbare clothing from the small-holders in lieu of payment in coin. The broken-hearted sobs of the women, the shrill wailing of the children and the hopeless pleas of the men still echoed in Hardy's ears, and he felt a sickness that was both spiritual and physical at such cruelty, lawful though it might be.

Far away to the east a spark of light erupted in the murk. Reluctantly the policeman turned his head, exposing the sides of his face and neck to the stinging needles of rain. He focused on the distant spark, which strengthened into a steady glow even as he studied it. Then another glow lit up in the south, as if in answer to the first, and Hardy cursed loudly.

Sergeant Macarthy whipped his horse into a brief canter to come alongside his superior. His face was a featureless blur in the darkness, and Hardy could only judge the man's mood by his tone.

'It could be that another one has been done, Sir.'

'Could I be imagining a certain satisaction in his voice?' Hardy wondered, but dismissed the thought. His NCO was a first-class policeman, and loyal to his Queen, and his superiors in the Constabulary. 'I'm becoming as panicky as those confounded political dolts in Dublin Castle,' the

Inspector chided himself. 'I'm starting to see rebels under every blade of grass.' To his sergeant he replied, 'We'll know soon enough, Macarthy,' and as the man reined in and fell back, Hardy gave his full attention to the two lights and the obscure land around him.

What he feared to see happened as a third spark blossomed and steadied further east than the first, if he judged his distance correctly. Hardy accepted this third repetition as confirmation of what he feared. Yet another landlord, or landlord's agent, had been assassinated that day.

Driven too far, the peasantry had recently reverted to Ireland's age-old answer to brutal repression. The killing of those they judged to be among their worst tormentors. During a space of only two months, seven landlords had been murdered. After each death celebratory bonfires had been ignited by the local people to mark what they regarded as a justified blow of vengeance. Mentally computing distance and area, Hardy tried to guess which landlord in the Clonakilty district had died this day. He abandoned the attempt quite quickly. There were too many potential victims to choose from.

'I don't doubt that we'll soon have some in our own district,' he reflected. 'There's been sufficient cruelty shown by certain of the proprietors to bring it about.'

The small cavalcade rode through Leap village. It could have been an abode of the dead; not a light shone, nor a dog barked.

'Well at least it's all quiet here,' Hardy thought relievedly, and allowed himself to look forward to a hot rum toddy, a dish of fried beefsteaks, and a warm bed . . .

From the window of the chapel Father Boyce watched the black shadows of the police move beyond his vision. He waited tensely for further minutes until satisfied that there were no stragglers, then jumped down from the bench he had been standing on and went towards the main entrance of the building.

'Arrah yes, it's safe enough now. Light the candle.'

Steel struck flint, sparks flew, tinder smouldered and a

candle was lit. A high-pitched whinny echoed out and the priest instructed excitedly, 'In the name o' God, quieten your horse. Put a hand to his muzzle before he wakes the village . . . They'll be thinking the Devil is in here.'

'I think he might be in me, Father, for what I've done this day.' The speaker was a small gaunt man, hardly taller than the priest. He was bareheaded, and had only a short cloak to cover his torn muddied shirt and breeches.

'We'll talk of that later,' the priest told him, and stared reflectively at the big black stallion the man was soothing with practised hands.

'The horse is a problem,' Boyce stated. 'It's too fine for the likes o' ye to be riding, Tumelty, no offence meant of course. But the soldiers and the Peelers will stop you and ask where you stole it from.'

The man's gapped teeth bit worriedly at his lower lip, and the grey stubble on his throat and face seemed to ripple in the pale light as his jaws moved. 'But what else could I do, but take your man's horse? I had to get away quickly, Father. If I'd stayed on foot the Peelers would have run me down in short order.'

'You're sure he's dead?' Boyce questioned.

This time the man's mishapen teeth bared in a rictus-like grimace of hatred. 'Arrah yes! Jonas Clarke is dead. Of that there's no doubt. I hit him with me stick until the whole side of his head was knocked in . . . '

'Don't tell me any more about that,' Boyce curtly ordered, cutting the gory description short. 'You've killed Lord Carberry's agent, that's enough for me to know.'

The man looked down at the candle on the floor, and rejoined sullenly, 'And I'm glad I did. No matter what else can happen to me . . . I'm glad.'

'You're also in a state of mortal sin.' The priest in Boyce came uppermost. 'And the sooner you give confession with proper repentance, the better it will be for your soul.'

Tumelty's eyes glared at Boyce, and tears of anger and grief fell from them. 'Repent, d'ye tell me, Father? Fine healthy children I had, and a good, loving wife, and that bastard Clarke evicted me, and for weeks hunted us out of

134

even the ditches we tried to find shelter in. You know well enough how miserably my dear ones died, God rest their souls. I couldn't even put a turf shelter above their poor heads as they lay dying . . . ' His face twisted in violent spasms, and he broke into loud, keening sobs.

'There now, man dear, try and think of your family as being happy in God's love. They know no more suffering now, where they have gone.' Boyce patted the shaking shoulders, feeling the hard knobby bones beneath his fingers.

After a time Tumelty managed to bring himself under control once more, and the priest went on talking, 'Arrah now, what are we going to do with you, I wonder . . . And with that great brute ye have there.'

As if knowing he was being referred to the stallion moved restlessly, its iron-shod hooves striking metallically upon the stone-flagged floor.

'Have ye any money?' Boyce asked. Tumelty shook his head.

'Hadn't your man, Clarke, got any money on him?'

Tumelty glared indignantly. 'Sure I was after killing him, not robbing him, Father . . . I'm no thief!'

The unconscious gallows-humour of the reply struck Boyce, and he was forced to hide an involuntary smile, silently begging forgiveness of his God for his unseemly mirth.

'Well . . . ' After a long silence the priest formulated a tentative plan. 'Ye'll have to remain here with me for a while, Tumelty. There's no doubt but that the Peelers will already suspect that 'twas you who killed Clarke.'

'They will that,' the man agreed quickly, 'for I made no secret of my intention.'

Boyce experienced a self-confusing mixture of respect and contempt for Tumelty as he heard this. Respect that the man had been so forthright as to what he intended doing, and contempt for his stupidity in being so open about his aims.

'So, we can safely assume that your description is already being circulated locally to the different barracks,

135

and that the Peelers will be watching for you. It's no use you trying to run for Cork or Limerick, or any of the smaller ports, they'll be expecting you to do that, and will pick you up in hours. They know well that you can't take to the mountains or bogs either, this weather would be the death of ye.'

As if in agreement the wind shook and rattled the casements of the chapel and the draughts caused the candle-flame to ebb and gutter.

'I can hide ye, but I've nowhere to hide this horse.' Boyce shook his head. 'And I'm no horseman, so I can't ride the animal away from here. If we just turn it loose they'll find it, and know that you're in this district . . . ' He pondered the problem for some moments, then nodded abruptly. 'I know who can ride it though, and get rid of it.' He turned his head to look at the other man. 'You stay here now, there's still a long night left ahead of us. I'm away to see someone. Put the candle out when I'm gone, bar the door and keep the horse still and quiet . . . '

The priest's exit was marked by the slam of the wind-pressed door, and Tumelty waited in the darkness, his throat dry with apprehension.

When Sub-Inspector Hardy reached the police barracks in Skibereen he was forced to dismiss all thoughts of a warm bed for that night. His superior, District-Inspector MacMahon, florid-faced and bulky bodied was waiting for him, in company with two senior officers of the Hussars.

'I'll be brief, Hardy,' MacMahon said in his harsh Ulster accent after the necessary introductions had been made. 'I've just come from Lord Carberry; it was his agent, Jonas Clarke, who was murdered this day. The noble Lord is extremely angry, and wants us to spare no effort to lay those responsible by the heels. I can tell you in confidence that Lord Carberry has much influence with the Government. It will go hard with us if we fail . . . However, I do not anticipate failure, and our friends of the army will be aiding us.'

Both mustachioed Hussars nodded in grave agreement.

'Do we have any information as to suspects, Sir?' Hardy requested.

The District-Inspector smiled grimly. 'Yes, thank God. It's almost certain that a man named John Tumelty is one of the fellows we need. Apparently he's been making open threats to kill Clarke for some time now. He was also seen riding Clarke's horse and heading in this general direction. Naturally there may have been others involved with him. Clarke was a very strong man, and it may have taken two or three men to batter him to death.

'We've already covered all the roads out of Clonakilty, but Tumelty could have slipped past our patrols by using some of the bog paths.' The grim smile returned to the florid face. 'One thing in our favour is this damned weather. Your man will be forced to find shelter and lay up there, or be practically certain of dying of exposure. Now whoever gives the scoundrel shelter, has also got to find a place big enough to hide the horse. That should narrow the prospective hideouts considerably.

'You'll begin a search of the neighbourhood at first light, and get whatever men you have available now out to cover roads and tracks. Major Curtis here will tell you where his patrols are operating . . . Here.' He handed a large piece of paper to Hardy. 'I've had the descriptions of Tumelty and the horse written down. Get your clerk to make fair copies and have them circulated immediately. Incidentally, Lord Carberry is offering a hundred pounds reward for the capture. That should give your men incentive enough, as well as bring all the informers hereabouts from out of their bogholes.' He paused to frown meaningfully at his underling. 'I'll remind you, Sub-Inspector, that your career in the Constabulary can be much helped, or equally much hindered depending on the result of this case. As I said before, Lord Carberry is a gentleman who wields great power and influence. He can cause heads to roll if he feels that those heads are not doing their utmost to further his interests.'

Hardy listened to the scarcely veiled threat with a calmly neutral expression. Inwardly he was deeply resentful. 'I'm

137

a good policeman,' he told himself, 'and I always enforce the law to the utmost of my ability. This arrogant oaf has no call to issue threats.' Aloud he said, 'Very good, Sir. If you will excuse me for a while, gentlemen, I'll be about starting the business.' With a slight bow he went from the room calling for Sergeant Macarthy.

Despite the lateness of the hour, Father Boyce saw lights and heard the strains of fiddle music coming from Mulrooney's as he struggled up the muddy ruts of Old Chapel Lane. He recognized the tune being played, and chanted to it under his breath.

> 'St Patrick taught the happy knack
> Of drinking of the whisky,
> 'Twas he that brewed the best of malt,
> And understood distillery . . . '

He reached the door and hammered on it loudly. It opened to disclose the battered features of Bridget Mulrooney. Boyce grinned at her, and sang out,

> ' . . . For his mother kept a shebeen shop,
> In the town of Inniskillen . . . '

The woman recognized the priest, and opened the door wider in invitation. 'Step in, Father, it's yourself is always welcome here. 'Tis them other sort, like that Father Matthew forever prating of Hell and Damnation, and down with the drink, that I can't abide.'

'There is no need to prate of what is unhappily all too easy to see around us these days, Mrs Mulrooney, and I see no harm at all in taking a few drams to cheer the heart,' Boyce answered, as he stepped across the threshold into the smoke and stench-filled room.

Clustered around the fireside at the far end were a group of wild-looking men and women tinkers, singing to the fiddler's tune and passing a big stone jug backwards and forwards between them. One glance at the flushed,

138

sweating faces and Boyce knew that it wasn't water the jug contained.

'Order now! Let's have some order, iffen you please.' Denis Callaghan was acting as chairman of the gathering. Perched on a three-legged stool, which was itself perched on the nearest trestle table to the fire, he waved his arms and his face shone scarlet from drink and shouting. 'Iffen I don't get order, I'll be taking a stick to your thick heads,' he warned jovially, then burst into laughter, and laughed so hard he nearly fell from his precarious seat.

The noise subsided a fraction, and Callaghan pointed to a shaggy-haired young woman, wearing only a skirt and a man's shirt through the rents of which her limbs and breasts could be glimpsed as she moved.

'I call upon Miss Maggie Nolan to oblige the company with her famous slip-jig,' Callaghan declaimed grandly, and stumbling to his feet essayed an equally grandiose bow. Only quick hands shoving him back prevented him tumbling headlong. The young woman curtsied gracefully, and stepped away from the crowd to a clear space.

The blind fiddler's milk-white eyes coupled with the long white hair that fell to his shoulders and his thin aesthetic features suggested the appearance of a medieval saint. But his words dispelled that illusion. 'May your bollocks rot, you bleedin' scum! Shut your bleedin' gobs and let me hear me key,' he screeched waveringly, and Callaghan's laughter pealed out above him.

'That's it, my jewel. You tell these ladies and gentlemen here how they should behave in polite society . . . Silence now, let the dog see the rabbit will ye . . . '

'In the merry month of May . . . ' the notes danced out from the strings, and Callaghan sang the words, ' . . . I left me home and started out to see the world . . . '

The young woman threw back her mop of hair, lifted her skirts to show well-muscled legs, and stepped off. Her bare feet skipped across the worn-smooth stones and her legs created a poem of rhythmic movement.

Father Boyce admiringly watched her, and watched also the noisy crowd grow silent and become absorbed in the dance. The little priest felt a lump rise in his throat . . . These were his beloved people. These wild, ragged, drunken wretches who could be held and moved emotionally by the ancient music and dance of their race. Waves of love for them welled up in the priest's heart, and he was forced to swallow hard and fight back the tears which came to his eyes.

The dance ended to the accompaniment of a storm of applause, in which the priest joined whole-heartedly. Callaghan saw him then, and his beaming face became suddenly wary. Moving with surprising steadiness considering the amount of poteen he had imbibed, the burial man stepped down from the table and came to where the priest was standing.

'Who is it ye're looking for, Father? Is it young Con?' The blue eyes were hard and accusing in their red rims.

'It is,' Boyce answered shortly. 'Where is he?'

Callaghan's head jerked upwards. 'He's asleep.'

'Take me to him,' the priest ordered.

For a moment Denis Callaghan remained with his hard stare fixed on the other man. Then he said, 'I don't think that ye're very good company for young Con, Father.'

Boyce smiled, and his glance swept over the noisy group by the fire. 'And you and your friends are good company for him, of that I've no doubt, Callaghan.'

His sarcasm left the other man unruffled. 'We are that, Father. At least he'll not get his neck stretched with us . . . And he's the fair chance of that happening if he keeps on mixing with you.'

'I don't think so,' Boyce answered levelly.

His accuser hawked and spat on the filthy floor. 'I know so, Father. Me old Grandad, who I never met, was hung in '98 for being a Croppy Boy. You and them Young Irelanders are on the same road that that old fella took. I'd not like to see Con travel down it with ye.'

The priest shook his head in rebuttal. 'He's a man, not a child. He'll make up his own mind about that . . . Now, will ye take me to him?'

Callaghan persisted, however. 'D'ye know he's courtin' that wee MacDermott girl. From what I gather, he'd like to wed her.'

'Just so.' Boyce smiled. 'And why should he not. She's a pretty girl, and as the blessed Paul said, 'tis better to marry than to burn.'

'Even if she's made a widow in short order?' Callaghan retorted instantly.

Boyce turned away. 'I'll find Con meself.'

'No, there's no need.' Callaghan restrained him with a touch on the cassock's sleeve. 'I'll show ye where he lies . . . But I just wanted to make my feelings plain.'

'And ye've done so,' Boyce told him equably. 'And while I do not agree with your views, nevertheless I respect the way that you state them so plainly.'

The burial man thrust his way through to the fire, and returned with a flaming rushlight. He led the priest out through the rear of the room and up the narrow rickety stairs. The air was cold, and impregnated with the clammy stench of poverty and decay. Below them the fiddle wailed out a lament, and the voices chorused the sadness of parting from home and loved ones to go across the seas into exile.

Callaghan chuckled throatily. 'By Jasus, there's plenty today who have cause to sing that.'

'Indeed there is,' Boyce answered, more to himself than to his companion, 'and there will always be plenty who have cause, until our country is set free.'

Callaghan's pink cheeks caught the glow of the rushlight as he turned and grinned sardonically. 'And when the old country is free, Father, who will be sitting in power in Dublin Castle then? Will it be the likes of us, I wonder?'

The priest remained silent, refusing to be drawn into further argument. They reached the end of the first flight, walked a few paces along the broken floorboards and mounted a further staircase. At the top of this one Boyce saw a ladder which was placed beneath a square opening in the ceiling.

'Here.' Callaghan handed the rushlight over. 'Go ye on

up. Me head is reeling from the drink, I'm like to fall iffen I go any higher. Con's sleeping up there.'

With that the priest was left alone, but for the rustle and squeaking of the mice behind the wainscoting.

He climbed the ladder and by the feeble light saw Con Shonley lying on his back on a low pallet. For a moment or two Boyce stood looking down at the sleeper. He found himself envying the taut muscled body, and the swarthy handsome features topped by thick clean black hair. 'By God, if I had been so blessed in my physical form as you, Con Shonley, I doubt that I would have taken the Cloth,' Boyce admitted privately, and thought wistfully of the girls he might have loved, and been loved by. Thrusting the tantalizing mental images from his mind, he sighed, and shook the young man's shoulder. Con Shonley came awake as gently as an innocent child. He blinked in the light, and narrowed his eyes to see the priest's face. 'Why Father? What do you here?'

Boyce quickly explained his reasons for coming, and finished, 'Will ye come with me now, Con, and get the horse away?'

The young man didn't hesitate. He threw his covering aside and scrambled into his clothes. Then the two of them made the creaking descent to the ground floor of the house. When the priest would have re-entered the front room, Con held him back.

'No, Father,' he whispered, 'we'll go out through the yard at the rear. It's best that no one should see us leaving together.'

'But Callaghan knows it's you I came to see,' Boyce argued.

'Denis is all right, I can trust him with my life. But some of the others I cannot,' Con said simply, and the priest allowed himself to be led.

Chapter Nineteen

'Thanks be to God, ye're back!' John Tumelty was hoarse with relief. 'I feared I'd been discovered.'

'Why?' Boyce was instantly alert.

'Some horse sodgers was through the village scarce an hour past, and didn't one o' them get down and try to come in here. 'Twas lucky I had the door barred, or he'd of found me, sure as God.'

Boyce's long nose tilted up, and its ever-present dew-drop trembled violently in his agitation. 'It's not taken long for the search to spread, has it.'

'It was me they was looking for then, d'ye think, Father?' Tumelty's fear could be plainly heard in his voice.

'Arrah yes, without doubt,' the priest muttered, then perked up. 'But don't fret, man dear, they'll not find ye . . . And Con here is going to get rid of this great brute.'

Con busied himself checking the saddle and harness of the horse and letting it become accustomed to the feel and scent of his hands and body.

'Where will ye take it?' Boyce wanted to know.

Con shook his head slightly. 'I think it better that you don't know, Father. Then, if I should be caught, you'll have less lies to tell.'

Boyce grinned impishly. 'Ye'd make a good Jesuit, Con. Ye have their type of mind.'

Once satisfied that the horse would handle easily, Con led it out into the blustery night. He had decided where he would ride. Due north along the banks of the Ilen, cutting across the main Cork to Bantry road, then through the hills between Bantry and Dunmanway and up into the wild country of the Shehy mountains. He would abandon the horse there and make his way back on foot. At a rough estimate it was a round trip of some forty miles. But there was no burial scheduled for the next day, and Con knew that if he could get back to Skibereen by the following night he would not be missed.

Sudden exaltation filled him, and he wished with all his heart that his beloved Grainne could see him riding this fine horse and bravely setting out on this perilous venture.

The stallion was a blood horse and travelled fast and strongly. Before the dawn came Con had crossed the main road and was into the hill country. The wind had dropped, the day was cold, and misty drizzle blanketed the land. The young man blessed the mist, it helped to hide him from curious eyes, and made him feel that he rode through an empty land in which only he had being. He felt fresh and alert and kept a careful lookout as he rode.

Sometime later he entered country that was unknown to him, and now continuously studied the eastern skies for the brightening in the dark mist which would indicate the sun, and confirm his direction. Unable to see any brightening, he began to doubt his accuracy, and was becoming afraid of circling back on himself, as the rough terrain continually forced him to deviate and change direction around obstacles formed by boulders and ditches and patches of wet bog.

At a small plantation of leafless, writhing-branched trees, Con drew rein and dismounted to rest. He loosened his mount's girth and lightly hobbled the forelegs, then freed it to crop the tough yellowed grasses that flourished at the treeline. He rubbed with both hands at his back and thigh muscles, which, unused to riding these days, had stiffened painfully. He stood, searching the enveloping mist for the sun, but still could not discern any lightness in the sombre overcast.

A faint human-sounding echo came to his ears, and cautiously he went in the direction he judged it originated from. The voice became louder and clearer. It was a man singing.

'Oh the French are on the say, says the Shan Van Vocht.
The French are on the say, says the Shan Van Vocht . . . '

Con's caution lessened as he heard the words. It was an unlikely air for a soldier or policeman to be singing in these times of threatening rebellion. He moved on further through the bare, moisture-dripping trunks of the trees.

' . . . Oh the French are in the bay, they'll be here without
delay
And the Orange will decay, says the Shan Van
Vocht . . . '

It was an old man in shirt sleeves and corduroy breeches, his thin grey hair lank on his freckled scalp, and his face a ruddy-brown from long years of outdoor toil. He was working in a peat bog, cutting the long wet blocks of black-brown fibre with a curved-bladed loy spade, and swinging their heavy weight over to the side-banks of the work trench with an effortless ease that belied his apparent years.

Con halted at the edge of the trees, half-hidden behind a thick elm trunk, and warily looked over the scene. Without appearing to notice him, the old man spoke.

'A soft day surely, thanks be to God!'

Con was surprised enough to reply unthinkingly, 'Thanks be to God, it is.'

The old man rested on the long handle and grinned up at Con. 'I heard ye coming a full ten perches away.'

Con's answering grin was rueful. 'I thought I was walking quietly.'

'As quietly as a regiment o' soldiers,' the old man chuckled. 'Are ye passing through here?'

Con nodded, and his caution was still assertive enough to make him guard his tongue. 'I was heading west, towards Dunmanway. But with this mist I'm not sure of my direction any longer.'

'Then that's the way ye'll be wanting.' With a bare, stringy-muscled arm the old man pointed directly over Con's shoulder.

'Fine. Many thanks. I'll bid you good day, and God bless your work.'

'And God bless your path,' the old man answered, and continued working as Con retraced his footsteps, happy that he now knew his compass points once more. His happiness would have been tempered had he seen the old man lay aside his low spade and move after him. Concealed by the trees he watched as Con re-tightened the horse's girth, took off the hobble and continued on his way due north.

The old man muttered to himself, and rubbed his stubbled chin as if debating some point. Then swung on his heels and walked purposefully away.

A very few minutes later he was at the house of the plantation owner, talking to a sergeant and four troopers of Hussars, who had been billeted there for some nights. The talk lasted only three minutes, and then with an air of urgency the soldiers were mounted and went cantering in the direction advised by the old man.

As the morning lengthened a breeze cleared the mist, and occasional rifts let the sun shine briefly through the higher layers of cloud. As the mist cleared Con caught glimpses of the cloud-topped Shehy Mountains and the tree-cloaked slopes of the Tomies hills ahead of him each time he crested rising ground on his path. Another five or six miles he estimated would be far enough for his purpose. He hit a wide well-trodden track leading north and followed it, relaxing his vigilance, and letting his thoughts wander.

'Hey, you?' The shout came as Con was passing between two large plantations of saplings. He glanced back over his shoulder, and his heart leapt in his chest . . . soldiers! They were coming fast, their hoofbeats thudding clearly in his ears. He cursed himself for letting his mind wander, and so missing any earlier sounds of horses. For a brief moment he considered making a run for it, then dismissed the thought. There was probably an ambush party of more soldiers ahead of him, and these five behind were acting as beaters to drive the quarry into the net. The plantations offered no possible escape route either. The saplings were too close-set to pass a horse and rider through at speed, or even slowly. Even as he was thinking this, his hands and knees were turning the horse and moving it back down the track to meet the oncoming men. The Hussars halted with a jingling of metal, and a panting, stamping flurry of excited horses. The sergeant came to Con's side. A taut-bodied whip of a man, whose lean face bore the scars of brawls and hard-living. His mustaches were full and luxuriant, and his light eyes keen and searching.

Con decided that the best form of defence was attack. 'What the devil d'you mean by bawling at me so?' he demanded indignantly.

The sergeant's gaze swept over Con's shabby clothing and broken boots, then examined the horse and saddlery. He grinned fiercely, and in that grin Con could see that his own assumed Anglicized Shoneen accent and indignation was not impressing the soldier.

'Well now, that's a fine horse ye're riding,' the sergeant's lilting voice was of the west of Ireland. 'Might I ask where ye got it?'

Con was forced to continue in the manner he had chosen to begin with. 'Why? Can't a man ride peaceably along his way any longer in this damned country, without having to answer to any Tom, Dick or Harry for it?'

The sergeant's grin never faltered. 'Whist't now, my young Shoneen, don't try to act the lace-curtain gentry with me. Just answer the question.'

While he was talking his four men were edging their mounts until they ringed Con, cutting off any possible exit. The young man felt an angry regret that he had not made a run for it instead of trying to bluff his way; and his mind jumped from idea to idea, searching for an escape from this situation. He glanced quickly at each of the Hussars in turn. They stared at him with lowering expressions, each man having the stamp of a veteran soldier, brutalized by the iron discipline they were subject to.

'There'll be no rebel-hearts among these boyos,' Con told himself, and to gain time in which to think, blustered aloud, 'Why the devil should I be stopped and questioned

147

in this manner, while I'm merely going about my business?'

The sergeant's grin was becoming strained, but he replied evenly. 'Because these are troubled times, and any stranger passing through our patrol area, well we like to know more about him, that's all. So it'll save your time and my patience, if you'll tell me who you are? Where you're from? And where you're heading now?'

Con could not help emitting a small sigh of relief. These soldiers didn't appear to know of Jonas Clarke's murder, or be searching for his horse. It seemed that he had been stopped by a routine patrol. Gaining confidence with this notion, Con decided to continue his bluff. 'I'm a horse-dealer, my name is Jack Monahan, and I'm on my way to Killarney to sell this stallion.'

The NCO nodded agreeably. 'I see . . . Where did ye buy him?'

'From Lord Carberry's stables at Clonakilty, some weeks past.'

'So it's Clonakilty ye've come from, is it?'

'No, I've come from Bandon.'

His questioner nodded again. 'I see . . . And it's to Killarney ye're heading?'

'It is.'

The fierce grin came again. 'Then why did ye ask the old fella ye met the way to Dunmanway? Sure, if ye came from Bandon, ye'd have already passed through Dunmanway on the coach road.'

Con heard that the old man had informed on him with a shock of fear. He hesitated, seeking a good explanation, before replying, 'These are troubled times, Sergeant, as you said. It doesn't pay to let anyone know your route, especially when you're riding a fine horse like this one. I'd not want to have him thieved from me by some Culchie highwayman, would I now?'

Unfortunately for Con, his plausible explanation had been overlaid in the sergeant's acute mind, by his hesitation before giving it. The NCO lifted his hand, and his men snatched their carbines from the bucket-slings

148

beneath their right hips and thighs. Four round black holes ready to vomit out death levelled at Con's head, and he swallowed nervously.

'Why the hell are you pointing guns at me?' he tried to bluster convincingly.

'Because I'm not happy about ye,' the sergeant grinned, then kneed his mount forwards so that he was within inches of Con. From the white canvas haversack he carried over his right shoulder he took a length of leather thong. 'Put your hands together behind ye, and look sharp about it.' His grin was now only a mask for enmity. 'One silly move from ye, and there'll be four lead balls looking for lodgings in your skull.'

Helpless to resist, Con obeyed, and the sergeant bound his captive's wrists together. He tugged at the bonds until satisfied that they would hold, and the pain of the thin straps cutting into his flesh caused Con's breath to hiss between his lips.

One of the troopers replaced his carbine in its sling bucket, and took the stallion's reins in his hand. At a single word of command from the sergeant, the party began to trot southwards, away from the cloud-shrouded mountains.

It was a long hard ride, and night had fallen when Con Shonley and his escort arrived at the town of Bandon. Founded by an Earl of Cork on the banks of the wide river from which it took its name, the town was traditionally a Protestant stronghold. Large ruinous sections of its once mighty walls still frowned upon the surrounding countryside, and Con remembered the legendary story of the inscription carved over its main gate; 'Turk, Jew or Atheist may enter here, but not a Papist.'

As if the sergeant could read his prisoner's thoughts, he remarked, 'I like what the Catholic wrote in answer to that inscription above the gates here,' and went on to quote; 'Who wrote this, wrote it well, the same is written on the gates of Hell.' The sergeant's grin widened into a laugh. 'That man must ha' been a quare one, mustn't he.'

Few people were about in the streets, and those that were

stared dourly at Con Shonley. No sympathy showed on their faces for his plight, in contrast to the prayers and blessings offered openly for his well-being by the country-folk they had passed on their journey.

The sergeant led them to a large barrack-building in the town and in its wide stable-bounded courtyard they dismounted for the first time in many weary miles. Con's legs were weak and trembling, his buttocks and inner thighs burned as if they had been flayed, and all feeling had left his badly swollen hands from the effects of the over-tight leather thongs lashed about his wrists. Soldiers in white canvas fatigue dress and pork-pie forage hats were busy about the yard but none spared him more than a casual glance. Bound prisoners were too common an occurrence here to attract interest.

With two men half-dragging Con, the party went up a short flight of stone steps into the main building. More Hussars and some policemen were lounging about the corridor and the rooms leading off it, and the air was thick and grey with the smoke from their short clay pipes. Like their comrades in the yard, they paid little attention to the incomers. In one of the rooms, furnished as an office, Con was placed in front of a desk at which a dark-green frock-coated District Inspector of Police was sitting writing in a ledger. The Hussar sergeant saluted smartly.

'Beg to report, Sir. My patrol arrested this man this morning on the track leading north from Mr Bedlin's estate towards Shehy Mountain. He was riding a horse that was too fine for the likes of him to be astride, and when questioned returned an unsatisfactory explanation of his business. Following standing orders I brought him here for further questioning.'

The broad florid face of District-Inspector MacMahon lifted slowly, and he regarded the young man before him with unconcealed boredom. 'What are ye, a horse-thief?' he enquired with a yawn.

Con made no reply, and the policeman grimaced. 'Oh, it's a hard-chaw ye are, is it . . . Well we like hard-chaws here. We turn 'em into a pap that a babby could suck with ease.' His florid face tilted towards the sergeant. 'Take this hard-chaw to the cells, and when he's learned to talk, bring him back.' The inspector took up his quill pen once more and recommenced writing. Then, abruptly, laid it aside as the escorts were taking Con out through the doorway. 'Hold fast! Bring that man back here.'

Stolidly the soldiers obeyed. The florid face was now animated.

'Keep him here while I go and look at that horse he was riding.'

In silence the men waited. Con's apprehension was now an acute fear, which he fought to master. He knew why the District-Inspector wanted to see the horse for himself. The young man's fears were fully justified when MacMahon came hurrying back and barged into the room to confront the prisoner.

'Now, my young scut, let's be hearing that tongue of yours move.' The policeman's large hands clenched and unclenched at his sides. 'That's the horse of a murdered man ye've got there. Where did ye get it?' One of the clenched fists came swinging from waist level and pounded Con's head to one side. 'Speak! C'mon now, let's hear it!'

The blow was painful and left Con's head ringing, but paradoxically drove out his fear by causing his hot temper to ignite. 'I found it wandering loose,' he replied hotly. 'It was running free, so I took it.'

'So, ye're a horse-thief, are ye? A self-confessed horse-thief?' the policeman shouted, his gaping mouth only inches from the younger man's features.

Con smelt foul breath and felt flecks of spittle striking his skin. 'No, not a thief! A finder! A horse-finder . . . Self-confessed!' he said defiantly.

The florid face purpled with either real or assumed anger. 'I think ye're more than a thief? I think ye're a damned murderer! 'Twas you and John Tumelty together who battered Jonas Clarke's head in, wasn't it.'

Con shook his own head in vigorous denial. 'I've battered no one, or nothing. I've never heard of the man you name.'

151

Once more the big fist pounded, and Con staggered, but was restrained by the Hussars at his sides. This time the ringing in his ears caused by the blow took longer to subside, and he heard only the final part of MacMahon's shouted question. ' . . . what time did ye do that? Was it afore or after?'

Con stared uncomprehendingly, and yet again the fist smashed into the side of his face. 'Dear Jesus,' he thought agonizingly, 'this man's knuckles must be made from iron.' Dazedly he felt himself pulled back out of the room and down a flight of stone steps. The corridor at the bottom was dark and ill-lit by a solitary hanging lantern. It was lined each side with narrow sheet-iron covered doors. Great metal padlocks and bolts securing them closed, and their sole opening a small hole set at eye-level.

One of the doors was opened. Con was pushed through it, and the heavy door clanged sonorously shut behind him. As he peered unseeingly into the pitch blackness, he heard the bolts rammed home, and the click of padlocks being snapped closed. The jingling of spurred boots died away, and all was silent.

Con's head and body were one mass of soreness and pain, and he was weak with fatigue and hunger. An intense depression overwhelmed him, and he sank to the damp cold floor, his shoulders propped against the rough stones of the wall. Then gave himself up to his misery . . .

Chapter Twenty

Grainne had taken off the bandage, and now she examined the stitches in the mirror, barely visible among the black roots of her hair. The swelling had subsided, and apart from a certain tightness and an odd twinge she felt no discomfort from the wound. She washed her body using a flannel and bowls of fresh spring water. Then brushed her long hair until it lay sleek and shining. She dressed herself in the clothes she had worn when first entering Kearney's service, and carrying her possessions in a bundled shawl she left the cabin and went to the house.

Michael Kearney was sitting at the parlour table, his puffy face sullen, and when the girl came into the room he glowered at her with virulent hatred. Grainne ignored his expression, she had no fear of this man now, only an absolute contempt.

'D'you have the money ready?' she asked without preamble.

'I have, blast ye for a wee whore!' he growled, fumbling in his coat pocket.

Her green eyes mirrored his hate. 'Whore I'm not, and never will be,' she retorted spiritedly. 'You would have turned me into one if you'd had your way, that I know . . . So I'll take my money and be gone from this house.'

Slowly and reluctantly the man took a handful of gold sovereigns from his pocket and began to count them into small piles on the table before him. The girl watched the count, her lips slightly parted and her pink-tipped tongue just showing through them.

' 47 . . . 48 . . . 49 . . . 50.' The man finished the count, and snarled. 'There, that's what ye asked for, and that's what ye've got. But ye'll not get a penny more outta me. No matter iffen ye shout about what happened to ye from every roof-top in the country.'

Grainne smiled tightly, and with quick darting movements of her hand, lifted the piles of coins and stored them in a small leather bag. She tightened its draw-strings and hung them around her neck, then allowed the small bag to slide down between her breasts and bodice. 'Don't worry about that, Mr Kearney,' she told him, her voice pregnant with loathing, 'this is all I'll ever trouble you for . . . And this is no more than you owe me.' Without another word she left him sitting glumly at the table.

Outside, the heavy clouds were threatening rain, but none was falling, and Grainne drew a deep breath and expelled it in a noisy sigh of relief and burgeoning satisfaction. Fifty sovereigns! Fifty British pounds cash! She could give her mother a tidy sum and still have enough for her and Con to get wed on. Enough to take them both to America; and enough so that they could land there with gold in their pockets.

'Holy Mary, thank you for your blessed mercies,' she prayed fervently. 'Thank you for helping me so.'

Half-skipping, half-running, Grainne hurried down the road towards the grey slate and red tiled roofs of Skibereen. 'I must tell Con straightaway,' she kept on repeating to herself, and her heart pounded with joy as she envisaged his happiness at her news.

'Grainne, me wee lamb, where are ye away to?' It was Old Biddy, kneeling at the wayside shrine making her devotions. A cloud of sadness darkened Grainne's mood. She had grown very fond of this old crone.

'I've done with working for your nephew, Aunty,' she said gently, and hugged the small frail figure to her young strength. 'I'm awful sorry to be leaving you though.'

The bright eyes beneath Grainne's chin brimmed with tears. 'And 'tis me heart that is breaking to see ye go, my sweet lamb. I'll miss ye terrible, so I will . . . Terrible!'

The young girl's own tears ran hotly on her cheeks. 'And

I'll miss you, Aunty, and I'll never forget you.' She kissed the withered cheeks, and then ran on, hearing the old woman calling blessings on her head.

By the time Grainne reached Skibereen, she had dried her tears, and once more was happily imagining Con's face when she would tell him that they could wed and set out for America as soon as he wished.

Although Grainne was very conscious of the wealth resting between her firm breasts, still she felt no apprehension about entering the slum of Old Chapel Lane. It was a very rare happening for a young girl to be accosted or insulted in these western provinces. Nevertheless, before she went into Mulrooney's she took care that her sovereigns were well concealed, and would not clink with her movements.

Of the previous night's revellers, only the blind fiddler, Maggie Nolan and Denis Callaghan remained. Nursing sick bellies and sore heads they crouched around the fire, unable to steady the trembling of their bodies. Bleary-eyed, Callaghan watched Grainne walk up to the hearth, and managed a feeble grin.

'Jase, but ye're as welcome as a summer's day, and as beautiful to behold, me dear,' he told her gallantly.

She mock-curtsied her thanks for the compliment. She liked this light-hearted friend of her beloved Con.

'Is it himself, ye're wanting to see?' Callaghan questioned. Then chuckled wryly and pointed to a vacant stool. 'For the love o' God, sit ye down at my level, pretty girl. It's making me head ache to lift it up to look at ye.'

'Is he here?' Grainne asked, as she settled herself between Maggie Nolan and the blind fiddler.

Callaghan shook his head. 'He'll be back later,' then clasped his skull with both hands and groaned in agony. 'Dear God, and all his angels. I thought for a moment there, that me bloody head was falling off.'

'You need the hair of the dog that bit you.' The girl smiled.

'Arrah, that's true enough,' Callaghan agreed, then added meaningfully, 'but I need the collar and the lead to

155

put on the dog and hold him, so I can get a taste of his hair.'

In the pocket of her skirt Grainne carried a few loose shillings. She handed them to Callaghan. 'Here, Denis, this will buy a few drinks for the company.'

'May the blessing of God the Father, God the Son, God the Holy Ghost, the Virgin Mary, John the Baptist, the Angel Gabriel and Denis Callaghan Esquire be on your beautiful head,' the burial man declaimed sonorously, beaming with joy. 'Bridget Mulrooney!' he bellowed, 'Mrs Bridget Mulrooney? Let's have some service here, if you plase.' Then he clapped his hands on his head again groaning loudly. 'Dear Jasus, that time I thought I'd lost this bloody useless thing entirely.'

Grainne's laughter pealed out at his droll manner, and she settled happily to wait for Con's return. Her happiness was marred by a deepening apprehension as the long hours wore on, and her wait became a vigil . . .

Chapter Twenty-One

It was some days before the news of Con's arrest and subsequent identification filtered back to his friends and acquaintances around Skibereen. It was a credit to Con's character that the vast majority of those who knew him refused to believe that he had had any complicity in the killing of Jonas Clarke. Unfortunately the only people who could confirm the young man's whereabouts at the approximate time of the murder were Bridget Mulrooney and Denis Callaghan, whose characters were non-existent in the eyes of their peers. In company with Grainne they went by hired jaunting-car to the barracks at Bandon, but were not allowed to see the prisoner or even send food and drink in to him. A bored police clerk took down Callaghan's and Bridget Mulrooney's depositions that Con was sleeping in his room during the period of the crime, and then they were summarily ejected from the barracks.

Denis Callaghan's jovial face was for once devoid of humour. 'They'll hang the lad, for sure,' he stated gloomily. 'Those bastards aren't interested in the truth. They only want to put the rope around someone's neck.'

Although the authorities would have indignantly denied such an aspersion, nevertheless there was some justification in what the man said. Lord Carberry was delighted than an arrest had been made. If the prisoner was now to be released, then the nobleman's sanguine choler would most certainly be directed against those who had been foolish enough to arrest an innocent man. So to protect themselves, and in the absence of John Tumelty, the police seemed determined to place the guilt for the murder of Jonas Clarke squarely on Con Shonley's head.

When the trio arrived back at Old Chapel Lane, Denis Callaghan walked alone to Leap village, without telling his friends where he went. Father Boyce was in his cabin.

'So, man dear, you've come to see me about Con Shonley, I don't doubt.' The priest was hatless, and his scanty hair stood up in unbrushed spikes on his smooth dead-white scalp.

'I have that,' Denis Callaghan's tone was as grim as his expression, for he blamed this man before him for what had happened to his young friend.

Boyce was subdued, lacking his usual jauntiness. 'Arrah yes, it's a sad problem we face here, I've heard all about what has happened. They think Con had a hand in killing your man, and they're going to bring him to trial for it.'

'Listen to me, Father, you must know who it was killed Clarke, as well as I know that it wasn't Con did it. But the Peelers won't believe me or Bridget when we tell them that Con was asleep at home. They don't want to believe it . . . I reckon it was that fella, Tumelty, on his own, who killed Clarke . . . and I reckon that you know well where Tumelty is right now.'

The tiny priest didn't flinch from answering, 'Yes, I know where he is, and I know that he killed Clarke.'

'Then go to the bloody Peelers and tell them that!' Callaghan ordered angrily.

This time Boyce's answer was hesitant. ' . . . Arrah yes . . . but . . . but it's not that simple.'

'And why not? Why bloody not?' his companion shouted.

Boyce held both hands up, palms outwards as if to deflect the wrath. 'Tumelty came to me seeking sanctuary,' he explained, and his face twisted with an actual pain of distress. 'I can't give him over to the Peelers. Not after granting him the sanctuary he sought, and hearing his confession. It would be a mortal sin against God's Holy Writ to do so.'

The other man's toothless mouth formed a round hole of aggrieved bafflement. 'Jasus Christ above! Isn't it a sin against God to let an innocent man's neck be stretched for something he hasn't done?' he spluttered furiously.

The priest tried to mollify him. 'Now don't upset yourself so, Mr Callaghan. We won't leave Con to be hung. I swear by all that I hold Holy, that we won't.'

'And how will ye stop it?' Callaghan wanted to know. 'By storming the bloody jail and rescuing him?'

The tiny head nodded vigorously. 'Just so, man dear. That is just what we will do if we have to.'

'Who are ''we''?' Callaghan jeered scathingly. 'Are ''we'' that kettle o' bloody daft Croppy Boys that runs around the mountain like idjits waving pikes and shouting that they're rebels? Is that who ''we'' are?'

Boyce made no immediate reply. Instead he turned to the table beneath the window, and fingered the leaves of a vast old Bible which lay open upon it. Then, as if coming to a momentous decision, he looked directly at Callaghan and nodded once more. 'Arrah yes, that's correct. The outbreak of rebellion is nearer than you suppose, Callaghan. The Young Irelanders are almost ready. We'll rescue Con, never worry about that.'

Callaghan laughed mockingly, then jeered, 'The Young Irelanders are all wind and piss, my little man. Ever since I was a wee boy I've heard men like you shouting their mouths off about the ''Great Rebellion'', and how it's nearly all prepared . . . And how they only need just a little more o' time, and a bit more money, and a few more pikes and guns . . . It's all wind and piss, so it is!'

'No!' the priest insisted quietly, yet doggedly. 'This time it is true.'

His hearer was not impressed. 'Well, true or false, I'll not hold my breath waiting for it. I'll go to the bloody Peelers right this minute, and tell them that you've got Tumelty hidden somewheres here about, and that you know he killed Clarke. So I'll say good-bye ye wee black crow, and be on me way.'

'Oh no ye won't, Callaghan!' Unnoticed by the others, Phelim Rourke had come to stand in the open doorway of the adjoining room. In his hands he held a loaded musket, and it was aimed at the burial man's heart. 'Ye'll go nowhere, my bucko, until Father Boyce says ye can.'

For a moment Denis Callaghan considered tackling the man. Then looked into the merciless grey eyes and felt his courage fail him. He saw his own death mirrored there.

Back at Mulrooney's, Grainne lay on her lover's pallet in the cold attic room and for a while her tears of distress fell freely. The image of Con's face as last she had seen it, laughing and gay in the moonlight, saturated her mind, and during these moments of time her love for him reached an intensity she had never known before.

The fear that he might hang, that the handsome laughing face might blacken and swell as he swung from a rope's end, sent waves of terrified agony shuddering through her body. Gradually her mood calmed and her tears ceased to flow as her inborn courage fought to dominate the terrors she was experiencing. At last, dry-eyed, she sat up on the pallet and blew her nose hard into her handkerchief.

'I'm not going to let them hang you, my love,' she muttered determinedly. 'I don't know yet how I'll prevent it . . . But prevent it, I will.'

Cheered by this resolve, she lay back on the pallet, green eyes narrowed, and set herself to think . . .

Chapter Twenty-Two

Sub-Inspector of Police, Augustus Hardy, was deep in thought as he pored over the report from the Cork Headquarters of the Royal Irish Constabulary. 'There had been strong, but as yet unconfirmed rumours,' the report stated, 'that considerable quantities of muskets were being smuggled into the country by elements hostile to Her Britannic Majesty's Government. A box of percussion caps to be used in converted flintlock muskets had been found hidden in a warehouse on the docks at Cobh. The caps were of French manufacture. A small quantity of cartridges and ball ammunition had been discovered with the caps, plus one musket with its stock broken.' Hardy re-read the last paragraph. 'The broken musket had been an India Long Pattern, converted from flintlock to percussion . . . '

The Englishman's narrow, almost bloodless lips pursed thoughtfully. He also had heard rumours of these modernized weapons circulating throughout the counties of Cork and Kerry, but as yet not one of his normally all-seeing informers had been able to actually see one of these muskets. The man leaned back in his chair and placing his hands' palms together in front of him, he steepled his long slender fingers and gently touched their tips to his lips.

'Boyce and Rourke! If guns of this type were in this district then it was a pound to a penny that those two had knowledge of the fact,' he thought.

Hardy was far from convinced that their rebellious activities consisted solely of the drill sessions that were held in the valleys and hills with pikes and staves. No modern guns had yet been produced there for the instruction of would-be rebel soldiers. So if such guns existed here, then they were being used in more secret locations. But where? And by whom?

Unlocking a drawer in his desk Hardy pulled from it a thin sheaf of papers. On them were written lists of names. Names supplied by informers of those men present at each drill.

Not quite knowing what it was he sought, the policeman began to scan the names, and compare one list with another. The same names cropped up again and again: Clancy, Muldoon, Johnson, Clarke, Macphee, Maclagen, Hourigan and many more. Hardy frowned, deep furrows etching the pale fine skin of his high forehead, then, suddenly, he knew what it was that he unconsciously sought . . . Which names, once frequent, now no longer occurred on the latest lists.

'Goddam me for a slow-witted oaf!' he cursed, and then eagerly sought afresh. Very soon he had a number of names he thought well worth further investigation. Prominent among them was Shonley. Conrad Shonley . . . The policeman was grimly satisfied. 'At least I know where that young man can be immediately found. He can serve as the starting point.'

Suiting action to thought, Hardy came to his feet shouting for his orderly.

The cell was icy cold and filthy puddles of water, urine and excrement covered its floor. Con Shonley, shackled at wrists and ankles, huddled in the corner nearest to the door, vainly hoping to draw warmth from the walls that were on the inner side of the building. There was no light of candle or lantern in the cell, but occasionally the night-clouds made ragged by wind would part sufficiently to allow a gleam of moonlight through the tiny barred casement set high into the outer wall.

As near as he could judge Con had now been incarcerated for a week, never leaving this seven feet by five feet tomb. At irregular intervals leather boots would stamp down the corridor, the door of the cell would crash open, and District Inspector MacMahon would enter. The questions and threats, the blows and kicks would seem to endure for eternities of physical pain and mental anguish.

'Where's John Tumelty? Who's hiding him? Who gave ye the horse? Where's John Tumelty? Where is he? Who's hiding him? Ye're going to hang, Shonley! Your neck's going to be stretched! Don't be a fool to yourself, man, tell us where he is. We'll pay you well for it. Do you really want to hang, you fool, because I promise you that you will. Tell us where Tumelty is. Tell us who's hiding him and save yourself . . . Where is Tumelty? Where is Tumelty? Where is Tumelty?'

'I DON'T KNOW! I DON'T KNOWWWW! I DON'T KNOWWWWWW!!!.

Con started violently, his entire body shaking, knowing that he was screaming the denials aloud to an empty cell, and wrenched by the terrifying fear that he was going mad. His breath rasped in his throat, his mouth quivered helplessly, and his heart pounded like a tortured animal against the high ribs of his chest.

'Dear God, give me courage . . . Don't let me go mad,' he groaned.

With a throat-choking dread he heard booted feet tramping down the corridor. 'Oh no. Not again . . . Not another kicking. I don't think I can stand much more . . . ' His thoughts scurried around his mind like frightened mice. 'No more beating, not yet! Please God, not yet!'

The boots halted, keys rattled, bolts slid in rusty sockets and the door crashed open. A flood of lantern light illuminated the cell, and a man's voice cursed softly, 'What in Hell's name is this?'

'Is what, Sir?' a second voice asked.

'This damned filth and water?'

'Sure, it's the weather, Sir. The rain leaks down through the roof joints. There's naught we can do about it 'til the roof is fresh slated.'

'Here, give me the glim, I'll shout when I need you.'

One pair of booted feet marched away, and in his corner Con kept his eyes closed, and his head turned away

163

from the door. Impelled by the irrational hope that should he appear to be asleep, his questioner would leave him be.

Augustus Hardy shook the young man's shoulder, and drew breath sharply when the bruised, grotesquely swollen features turned to him. Even in the icy, scent-deadening air the stench of Con Shonley's excrement-fouled body was a thick miasma, and hardened policeman though he was, Hardy felt bile sour his mouth.

'Well, Shonley, do you know me?' he demanded harshly, not allowing any of the pity he felt to betray itself in his expression or tone.

The battered head, fresh and stale blood caked in black streaks upon it, nodded painfully.

'Are you prepared to answer my questions concerning Tumelty?' Hardy went on.

Con summoned remnants of courage. He swallowed, and from an arid throat croaked, 'No, I am not. I know nothing.'

The policeman decided to change tactics. 'You're a brave man, Shonley; and I admire you for it.' He moved his narrow head, and the polished black peak of his forage cap bounced back slivers of lantern light. Sighing regretfully, he continued, 'What a pity John Tumelty has not your courage. He would have made a worthy comrade if he had.'

Con's dulled mind suspected a trap, but he decided to go a little way along the policeman's route. If only to keep back the moment when fists, boots and clubs would smash him into agony once again.

'I don't know John Tumelty,' he said, forcing the words thickly through his ballooned lips. 'Why do you speak of him?'

The Inspector forced an appreciative laugh. 'Yes, you are certainly brave, but do not think me foolish, Shonley. I know that Tumelty was once your friend . . . I say once, deliberately. For now he's turned Queen's Evidence, and he blames you for the murder of Jonas Clarke. You will most certainly hang, while Tumelty goes free. Think on it.

He'll go free, and you will hang and become an anatomist's carving joint . . . I'll leave you to dwell on it for a while. Then we'll talk again.'

Keeping a sympathetic smile on his face, Hardy left Con Shonley to the damp, the cold, the darkness.

Walking down the corridor the policeman experienced a long-familiar sense of self-disgust. 'At times I feel soiled by my work,' he admitted gloomily, but then was honest enough to accept that normally he enjoyed being a policeman, and believed in the essential justice of what he did. 'After all, without we policemen to control the human wolves, what would happen to the weak and defenceless among us. We are their sole guardians.'

In the barrack office District Inspector MacMahon was waiting with a pewter jug of steaming hot rum toddy. 'Come Hardy, take some of this,' he invited expansively, 'it'll wipe the taste of that damned cell from your mouth.'

Hardy accepted the thick glass of liquor, and drained it appreciatively. 'I wish it would wipe the sight of that man's head from my mind's eye,' he remarked.

The other's florid face was stern. 'Do not waste your sympathies on the likes of him, Hardy. He is a killer. My sympathy is for the victim, and the victim's family.'

Hardy moved to placate his superior. 'Of course, you're quite correct, Sir. But I must confess, I don't like seeing even murderers treated with such a degree of harshness.'

'No more do I,' the big man told him, 'but how else can we extract the truth from villainous ruffians. They show no mercy, and neither can we afford to show it to them. Otherwise the country would be at the mercy of blaggards . . .'

There was a mutual pause, during which they refilled their glasses and sipped slowly. Then MacMahon spoke; 'D'ye think Shonley knows where these damned muskets are hidden?'

Hardy nodded. 'I am only going on instinct at this time, but yes, I am sure of it.'

'Just as I am sure that he knows where your man, Tumelty, is hiding,' the District Inspector rejoined expressively. 'The trouble is, Shonley has proven to be a genuine hard-chaw. I'm feared that he'll die at our hands before telling us what we want to know.'

His colleague could only concur regretfully with that statement.

The darkness of the cell was equalled by the darkness of Con Shonley's thoughts. With each passing hour the conviction that he would hang pressed more heavily upon him. Time and again during his imprisonment he had felt the impulsion to try and save himself by informing the police of John Tumelty's whereabouts. Yet each time he opened his mouth to speak of what he knew, some inner conscience restrained him. Con castigated himself for a fool. The man Tumelty meant nothing to him, and had no claim on his loyalties. Tumelty was a self-confessed murderer, and now it appeared was sufficiently cowardly to allow an innocent man to be hung in his stead. Yet, against all logic, still the belief persisted in Con Shonley's mind, that he would not be hung. Somehow he would be saved from that. Somehow he would be rescued . . . But he knew that his will to resist and endure was fast becoming eroded.

'Dear God, let me be rescued quickly,' he prayed with heartfelt longing. 'I'm near to breaking! Save me. Lord, save me please!'

Hardy drained his glass and replaced it upon the desk.

'I'll have another word with Shonley,' he said, and then was struck by a sudden idea. 'With your permission, Sir, I'll take what is left of the toddy with me.'

His superior stared in surprise, and seemed inclined at first to indignant refusal, but then nodded. 'Very well, Hardy. You can but try new tactics. All I've managed to achieve for my pains are badly bruised knuckles. Perhaps the toddy may extract information where the fist has failed . . .'

Con blinked at the glass held before him, and his need for what it contained throbbed through his body. There was warmth there, and a sweetness to drive the fetid taste from his mouth; and in his weakened, half-starved condition there could also be achieved a temporary lifting of his spirits and an infusion of courage. Even knowing as he did that a high price would be expected of him in return for the spicy liquor, yet he accepted what was offered with an unconcealed gratitude.

The alcohol bit painfuly into the raw cuts on his lips and inside his mouth, but Con welcomed the rich taste and the heat exploding through his chest and stomach. Hardy poured out more toddy from the pewter jug, and Con sucked it into his body with unashamed greed. The Englishman's thin face was sombre in the lantern's steady glow, and his eyes were shadowed hollows in a surround of pale flesh.

'I do not enjoy seeing Daniel Shonley's son brought to such an unhappy pass,' he stated quietly, 'and to speak truthfully to you, I do not believe that you had any hand in Jonas Clarke's murder.'

Con stared up at him, searching for visual proof that the man was sincere in what he said. The hot drink had eased his throat so that when he now replied, his voice was a hoarse whisper rather than a barely unintelligible croak. 'If that is so, Mr Hardy, then why do you keep me here, chained like a wild beast in my own filth?'

'It is not I who keeps you chained here, Con Shonley, but yourself,' the policeman's tone was sympathetic. 'You have only to tell us the truth, and you will go free on that instant.' Again he refilled the glass and guided it towards the young man's mouth. 'I know that you are a man of honour. Daniel Shonley's son could not be otherwise,' Hardy continued very seriously, 'but you are allowing that honour to be soiled by letting unprincipled rogues use it for their own base ends . . . We are on opposing sides, you and I, Con Shonley. You are a self-declared rebel, I am a loyal subject of Her Majesty, Queen Victoria. Yet I can respect even rebels when they have courage to act openly, and fight in open battle like men of honour.'

Con sipped his fresh drink, and smiled mirthlessly. 'The rebels who acted openly, and fought like men of honour in open battle in '98, were treated like so many mad dogs by the loyal subjects of the British King. They were flogged, pitch-capped, hung and slaughtered without respect, justice or mercy.'

The policeman grimaced wryly. 'Touché, young Shonley. I accept there is a degree of truth in what you say. But equally, you must remember that atrocity begets atrocity, and both sides were guilty of ferocious excesses. Although you are still very young, yet you have great potential for leadership. Why not do as Daniel O'Connel and fight for the cause you believe in through the honourable and legal process of political action.'

Con shook his head, but made no other reply, and for the first time Hardy frowned wearily.

'No, that method holds little appeal for the hot blood of youth, does it . . . You can see flags flying, hear drums beating, and are drawn by the lure of martial glory . . . But there is no glory to be found when you are choking in a noose, Shonley. And unless you act now to save yourself, that is your fate of a certainty.' He leaned nearer, and whispered urgently. 'For your own good, young man, tell me the truth. Tell me where the new arms are hidden? Tell me where I can find Tumelty?' Instantly Hardy realized his mistake, and watched with angry chagrin as the swollen lips before him parted in a mocking smile.

'Did you not tell me before, Mr Hardy, that Tumelty had already turned Queen's Evidence. Surely you must know where he is, if that is the case.'

Hardy shrugged, and admitted, 'I lied to you, Shonley, but the fact that I lied does not alter your predicament. I am sure that you know where modern arms are hidden in the Skibereen area. I am equally sure that although you did not aid John Tumelty to murder Jonas Clarke, you do know where he is hidden.

'The choice before you is simple. Give us the arms, and Tumelty, and you will go free. Do not give us what we want, and you will hang.' He fell silent, and kept his shadowed eyes fixed on the young man's troubled face. The seconds became minutes, and the minutes lengthened and multiplied. Finally Hardy ejected a loud gusting sigh.

'I am truly sorry that you see fit to persist in this course of self-destruction, Shonley.' He lifted the pewter jug and shook it. 'Here, there is still a little left.'

He poured it into Con's glass. 'Sip it slowly and savour it, young Shonley. I fear there will be little opportunity for you to savour more of the same. I must return to Skibereen now. Think hard on what I've told you, boy. Think very hard. If you should decide to save yourself, then send directly to me, and I will come post-haste.'

Con searched in his mind for some answer of ringing defiance. But could find no words, only a sense of gratitude for the man's undoubted kindness to him during this last hour.

Chapter Twenty-Three

Winter came upon the land once more, and famine reaped its grim harvest yet again. Landlords were murdered, and also gentlemen who were merely occupiers of land. Workhouses were besieged by desperate hordes seeking admittance to the comfortless havens, and to provide further accommodation for the homeless, starving masses, disused buildings of every sort were hired by the Poor Law Guardians. Derelict warehouses, old breweries, even barns, without water, without sanitation, without heating were filled with the children, women, invalids and aged who had been ejected from the normal workhouses to make room for the destitute able-bodied men previously refused outdoor relief.

Lord Bessborough's successor as Lord Lieutenant of Ireland was the tactful and charming George William Frederick Villiers, Earl of Clarendon. An aristocratic liberal with much sympathy for the suffering people, he had accepted the post reluctantly and came to Ireland expecting to fail . . . He did so!

By November 1847, he was convinced that rebellion was imminent. He asked for, and was granted by the Government, fresh penal powers to deal with the threat. Strict control of arms among the populace was one of these new powers. Fifteen thousand extra troops, drawn from the cavalry, infantry, artillery and Marines were drafted into the country, but still the killings of landlords and gentry continued, and a trembling fear spread through the middle and upper classes.

By the beginning of 1848, Lord Clarendon was driven to

declare with utter conviction, 'That the condition of Ireland is that of a servile war . . . A slave rebellion!'

The iron-shod hooves pounded against the iron-hard ground like blacksmiths' hammers striking anvils. By sheer bodily strength Augustus Hardy brought his galloping mount to a sliding halt, and fighting to control its excited buckings bellowed, 'Take the rear, Macarthy.'

The green-clad troopers split into well-drilled sections dismounting with every fourth man holding the reins of his comrades' plunging horses, as unslinging their carbines they ran to surround the tiny chapel with its adjoining cabin and outhouses. With his long-barrelled Lovell percussion pistol in his hand, Hardy ran to the front door of the priest's cabin, and kicked its panels with his boot. 'Open in the Queen's Name!' he shouted.

All was silent within. Hardy tried the door and found it locked. He ordered the men with him to break it open, and stood aside while meaty shoulders sent heavy hammers thudding in unison until the rotting wood surrounds of the rusted lock sagged and gave way. Before the Inspector could follow his men inside a shout came from the chapel entrance.

'The priest is here, Sir.'

Hardy lifted his pistol in acknowledgement. 'Search well, men. Lift the hearth stones, try the chimney, check the floors,' he instructed briefly, then hurried across to the chapel. In the entrance he halted. Father Boyce was at the far end of the narrow building, kneeling bare-headed before the ornate altar, apparently deep in prayer. Hardy removed his peaked forage cap and entered the chapel alone. His spurred boots made a jingling clatter on the stone-slabbed floor and before he had covered half the distance to the altar steps the little priest genuflected and rose to face him. Boyce's dewdrop quivered as he saw the pistol in Hardy's hand.

'Arrah now, man dear, it's not seemly to carry loaded guns when ye enter the Lord's house,' he remonstrated, but a twinkle of laughter lurked in his deep-set eyes.

The Inspector ignored the sally. Instead from his black-leather waist-pouch he produced a sheet of thick paper. 'I have a Warrant issued by the Resident Magistrate at Skibereen, empowering me to search the chapel and all its adjoining buildings and environs, Father Boyce.'

The priest took this coolly enough. Shrugging his narrow shoulders he held out both frost-chapped hands in invitation. 'Didn't the Saviour say, "render unto Caesar that which is Caesar's," Inspector Hardy. Please, make as free a search as you wish, but have the courtesy to respect the sanctity of this chapel. Tell your men to search gently and with care and reverence.' Again humour twinkled in his eyes, despite the gravity of his expression. 'After all, the days of Cromwell are long gone. It's not the done thing now to stable horses in God's House, and use the sacred relics for target practice.'

Hardy inclined his head in curt acknowledgement. 'My men are not Ironsides, Father. They will, of course, take great care to avoid committing any damage or sacrilege.'

The troopers came in at a signal from Hardy, removing their caps and leaning their carbines against the entrance porch. Then they commenced the search.

The priest watched them in silence for a time, then his small, spike-haired head tilted upwards to the Inspector's face.

'Exactly what is it ye're looking for? Perhaps I could help ye?'

Hardy remained intent on a large constable who was tapping at the sides of the altar. 'I think you know well enough what it is we seek here, Father Boyce,' he answered evenly.

The little man chuckled softly, and the thin shoulders shrugged once more beneath the rusty cloth of the over-large cassock. 'In these times, it could be anything, Inspector. Perhaps even joints of roast beef to feed the hungry. Arrah yes now, that would indeed be a fine thing to seek and find, wouldn't it just.'

It was Hardy's turn to have humour lurking in his eyes, as he replied, 'Indeed it would, Father Boyce, and to speak from experience, what better places to seek and find such viands, than in the houses of some of your parish priests.'

Boyce chortled with real delight. 'I like that one, Inspector. And by all that's Holy, ye speak truly.'

The search was long, thorough and fruitless, and the policemen carrying it out grumbled beneath their breath, and thought resentfully of all the other fruitless searches for arms they had engaged in these last months. The big trooper that Hardy had been watching seemed fascinated by the marble altar. Time and again he returned to it. Examining each joint and pillar with care, and tapping its sides with his knuckles.

The Inspector moved up to him, and asked, 'What is it, Clancy?'

The man's doubt was plain to see on his stolid weather-beaten features. ''Tis this altar, Sor. I can't make up me mind iffen it's hollow or not.'

Hardy glanced quickly behind him to where the priest was standing, apparently engrossed in admiring the pattern formed by the early wintry sunlight lancing through the chapel's only stained glass window. With his pistol butt Hardy tapped the sides and ends of the stone panels, moving the light blows in patterned sequences. There was a definite suggestion of hollowness at various points.

'Father Boyce?'

The priest looked across at the call. 'What is it, Inspector?'

'I'm going to have my men lift the top off the altar.' Watching closely, Hardy thought he discerned a hint of fear cross the priest's eyes.

'I think that would count as a sacrilege, Inspector. A trick of your man, Cromwell's.'

'I'm sorry you should think that, Father. I can only assure you that it is not intended as such. Nevertheless, the altar top will be lifted.'

'I shall write direct to the Bishop, and tell him of this, Inspector. He'll undoubtedly have strong words with your superiors about it. You cannot commit such outrages with

173

impunity, even in this oppressed and unhappy country. It is a mortal sin to desecrate an altar.'

The Englishman saw the effect these words were having on his listening men. Stalwart and loyal though they were, they were still for the most part Irish countrymen, brought up to revere and fear the trappings of Catholic faith. A doubt wavered in his mind. His career in the RIC had not been a shining one up to this point, and if he fell foul of the Church, then it would hamper his uncertain prospects of promotion considerably. For a moment or two he was undecided, then suspected that the little priest was gloating in triumph.

'I'm sorry, Father, but my duty impels me,' he snapped, and ordered his men to lift the top slab.

With evident reluctance they cleared the altar furnishings and obeyed. There was a space inside. Quite a large space. Sufficiently large to hold a crouching man. But it was empty. Hardy swung on his heels and stalked outside. He drew in long draughts of icy, frost-laden air, and tried to dismiss the nagging thoughts of possible unhappy repercussions for what he had ordered done.

Sergeant Macarthy came from the cabin, and after saluting, shook his head. 'Nothing, Sir. It's as clean as a whistle.'

'Dammit!' Hardy hissed softly. 'Very well, Sergeant, call back the men. We'll go into Kincaid's farm and try our luck there.'

Father Boyce stood in the small entrance porch of the chapel and watched the police troopers remount and reform, preparatory to leaving. 'Inspector?' he called.

Hardy swung in his saddle to look back at him. Boyce smiled sweetly. 'You were only doing what your uniform forces you to do, Inspector. I'll not be making any complaint to the Bishop.'

The Englishman flushed redly, his feelings an unsettling mingling of embarrassment, resentment, anger and thankfulness. He saluted with a flick of one hand, and led his men away.

Once the echo of their progress had faded Boyce returned

inside the chapel, closing and bolting its door behind him. He went to the altar, its top now replaced, and with a strength belying his stature tugged the heavy slab so that it pivoted to open the cavity once more. The priest's long bony fingers tapped three times on the red-brick inner flooring, paused, tapped twice, paused, then tapped three times again.

A section of the flooring abruptly slid to one side, disclosing beneath it the upturned face of Phelim Rourke. He was standing on a wooden ladder leading down into a narrow shaft. That shaft was the entrance to an ancient, long forgotten crypt. Which Boyce had only discovered by accidentally finding a ventilation hole leading into it from the outer walls of the chapel. It was in the large dry chamber that the guns, and the fugitive, Tumelty, were hidden . . .

'All right, ye can all come up now, Phelim. By all the Saints, but I thought the Peelers had us that time for sure.' Boyce's relief made him talk excitedly.

Men began to rise up from the dark shaft, until there were twelve of them ranged around the little priest.

'Now boys, as I was saying before we were so rudely interrupted. Young Shonley is still at Bandon barracks. They haven't yet moved him to the prison. It's up to us to get the poor fella out of it.'

The men listened intently. Each one present had been carefully chosen. They were the pick of the little priest's grenadiers, his elite shock-troops, varying in age from a veteran of fifty, to a youth of nineteen years. It was Peter O'Shea, the grizzled fifty-year-old, who questioned, 'How do we get him out, Father? There must be nigh on a hundred soldiers in the barracks, not to mention Peelers.'

Boyce grinned. 'Arrah yes, there'll be that many without a doubt. To be perfectly honest with ye, I haven't yet decided on a plan. But I wanted to give ye the choice of joining with me to do this thing, or not joining with me. If anyone of ye doesn't want to help, then you're at liberty to leave now. There'll be no hard words from me if you choose to leave, and ye'll still be a part of our movement.

But for meself, I think we owe it to young Shonley to try and set him free. He's a good comrade, and he's proved his worth and his loyalty to us. If he had chosen to inform, the Peelers would have lifted the lot of us by now, guns and all.'

John Tumelty lifted his hand. 'With respect, Father. I'm not a man to leave others suffering for something I've done. Wouldn't it be best if I was to go to Bandon and give meself up to the Peelers. They'd have to let Shonley go then.'

The priest frowned angrily. 'Haven't we already talked enough about that, you and I. Quite apart from the question of having been granted sanctuary, there is no guarantee that the Peelers would set Shonley free, and also they might break you by torture and find out about the guns. So ye'll forget all thought of surrendering yourself, and be silent!' His authority derived not from physical stature, but from his impassioned sincerity, and the man obeyed him without further argument.

'Now, is there anyone of you who wishes to leave?' The priest's long nose quested at each man in turn. No one moved. Boyce grinned happily. 'I'm proud to know ye. Go now, I've much thinking and planning to do, and little time to do it in. I want the lad free in days if possible . . . Phelim,' he signalled Rourke to remain, and when the rest had gone, asked him, 'how is Callaghan taking it? Have you seen him this week?'

'He's taking it, Father, although unwillingly, and I've seen him twice.'

'Good! Will he continue to keep his mouth shut, d'ye think?'

The ex-soldier pondered for a moment, his hard face intent on his questioner. Then he said briefly, 'I'm sure he will, Father.'

'Good!' The little priest rubbed his nose pensively. 'I'm thinking that Shonley's sweetheart would be useful to us. I'll away and see her. I've a couple of notions in my mind . . .'

*   *   *

176

Denis Callaghan was a changed man. His laughter, once so free and easy, had dried within him. The winter had brought death in abundance and unceasing work for the burial men. But now Denis Callaghan made no jokes to lighten the mood of his fellow workers. Instead he performed his gruesome tasks in dour silence, his round pink face set and grin. His woman, Maggie Nolan, had tried to rouse him from his depression in every way she knew, but had failed utterly.

Now she sat at the fire in Mulrooney's and poured out her troubles to Grainne MacDermott . . .

'I reckon Denis would welcome dying himself these days, and that's the truth of it.' She drew on the broken-stemmed clay pipe held in her hand, and let the acrid-smelling smoke dribble from her mouth. 'The trouble is, d'ye see, that he loves your Con like he was his own brother, and there's nothing he can do to save him from the hangman.' She glanced about her, and satisfied they were alone, leaned forward to whisper conspiratorially, 'D'ye know what he told me last night when he was half-mad wi' the drink?'

Her bleared eyes stared with such a burning intensity into Grainne's for so long a time, that the young girl was impelled to beg her to go on without further pause. Maggie Nolan shook back her wild tangle of hair, and whispered, 'Denny went to see the little priest that day youse all come back from Bandon, and he's never breathed the word about it to anyone until last night. Anyway, he saw this Father Boyce, d'ye call him. Denny told your man that he'd inform on all the bloody Croppies in the district to get Con freed . . . ' Again the tangled mess of hair was tossed back as Maggie re-checked that no one was in the room with them, before leaning again towards Grainne.

'Boyce told Denny that if he informed he'd be a dead man, and that I'd be slaughtered as well, and you also . . . Denny was going to hit your man a belt in the chops, black crow or no black crow that he is, when in comes that hard-chaw, Rourke, d'ye call him. With a bloody big gun in his hands, and didn't he up with the gun and shove it into Denny's throat and beg the priest to give him the word to pull the trigger so that he could blow Denny's poor head from his shoulders!'

The woman's dramatic gestures, and impassioned manner of speech held Grainne enthralled. 'Well now, Denny told me that it wasn't his own life he gave a hell's damn for, but 'twas you and me he had to think about, and so he couldn't inform . . . So now the poor bowsy drinks himself bloody unconscious every night, and never the bit o' crack or the smile splits his lips, he's so sick in his soul about poor Con . . . '

Grainne's delicate features were patterned by her own sickness of soul over Con Shonley. Night after night in her attic room she lay racking her brains for some way of rescuing her lover, and night after night ended with her weeping tears of helpless despair.

The older woman's whispers penetrated Grainne's consciousness once again, bringing her welcome respite from her own thoughts. 'The wee priest told Denny that himself and his Croppies were going to set Con free. They'd burn the bloody barracks down to do it. Denny told your man it was all wind and piss, but your man said, no. They'd do it all right.'

'Dear God, let them,' Grainne begged silently. 'Let them get Con free, and let me help them do it . . . '

Her prayer was answered within minutes, as Father Boyce came scurrying up Old Chapel Lane, and knocked on Mulrooney's door.

Chapter Twenty-Four

Sergeant Timothy Slattery stood before the mottled full-length mirror in the guardroom at Bandon barracks and stared at the man reflected in it. Almost six feet in height, broad-shouldered, narrow-waisted, lean-hipped. His reckless sun-tanned face with its faded scars, its light eyes and luxuriant blond-brown mustachios drew women's glances and created a certain disturbing warmth in their bodies. His well-cut, tight fitting blue uniform with its plentiful gold braiding and high-polished brass buttons, and the dashing pill-box hat tilted at a rakish angle upon his bushy hair had helped him conquer not a few susceptible females. He smiled complacently and white teeth gleamed. 'By the left, Slattery, but I think you'll do,' he told himself, and after a final check he tucked his swagger cane under his arm and sauntered out in search of excitement.

Behind him in the guardroom a private muttered to a corporal, 'Did you see the way he smiled at himself? Like a bloody lover . . . Fucking big ponce!'

The corporal scowled savagely. 'Shut your mouth, Jenkins, afore I put ye in the Hole to learn respect for your superior officers.'

The private glowered sullenly, and the corporal winked . . .

Saturday afternoon in Bandon meant that the alehouses, inns and shebeens were full, even in a famine. If a man's wages were not sufficient to buy food enough for his family, at least they were sufficient to buy him a few hours' relaxation and happy oblivion to his troubles.

In the main street running parallel to the river, the

winter sunlight had tempted people to stroll and meet each other. Young girls walked like queens despite their poverty of dress and shawl, and young men swaggered and cat-called and horse-played to draw young girls' eyes. Old women stood gossiping, their cracked voices imparting tales of birth and death, and old men talked gravely of days gone by.

Here and there blue-jacketed cavalrymen staggered from shebeen to alehouse, and back to shebeen. Since the Eighth was a native Irish regiment there was little hostility displayed towards them by the civilians. There were no drunkenly staggering policemen, however. These sober men patrolled in pairs, carbines slung on shoulders, bayonets slung from hips, eyes constantly moving from side to side, evaluating passing jaunting-cars, carts, horsemen, pedestrians and the ever-present swarms of beggars of all types and descriptions. The Royal Irish Constabulary were feared rather than respected, but this very fear ensured that only a covert hostility met their presence.

Several priests could be seen along the main street. Their black flapping cassocks and cloaks and their broad-brimmed low-crowned hats bringing respectful salutations from visiting countryfolk, and friendly greetings from the townsfolk. Even the Protestant citizens were polite with their passing nods.

Under the courtyard archway of a small inn a priest and a young woman stood together, watching the passing parade.

'There he is now, across there.' The priest touched the girl's arm and indicated the tall Hussar sergeant approaching on the opposite side of the street. 'That's the one who took Con prisoner. His name is Slattery, he's the ideal man for us to use.'

Grainne MacDermott swallowed nervously. 'All right, Father Boyce, you'd best leave me now.'

The priest slipped from her side and Grainne let her shawl fall back from her head, and used both hands to pull her long shining hair free of the cloth's encumbrance.

Slattery noticed the girl immediately she walked out

180

from the archway and across the street. He vented a silent whistle of admiration. She was by far the most strikingly attractive female he had yet seen in Bandon. She reached the footpath and turned to walk in the same direction as himself. The sergeant lengthened his stride to draw alongside the girl and spoke. 'Well now, if it isn't young Maureen! Maureen Houlihan!'

Grainne's head turned and Slattery experienced a surge of visual pleasure. This girl was more than merely pretty, she was beautiful. She regarded him in silence, but Slattery was too experienced a hunter to allow her lack of response to disconcert him. He drew himself smartly to his full height and saluted her, then smiled.

'I do apologize, Ma'am, I see now that 'twas a mistake in identity. Maureen Houlihan has not one half of your good looks.'

Grainne allowed a brief smile to curve her lips, then demurely dropped her eyes and walked on. Timothy Slattery felt his customary confidence as he saw her smile. The girl found him attractive, that much was clear. He hastened to catch up with her again.

'I've said I'm sorry for the mistake,' he told her. 'Please won't you tell me that you accept my apology. I'd hate to think that I'd offended such a pretty girl.'

Again the green eyes met his, and the fleeting smile curved the full moist lips.

'Ahhh, come on now, at least say I'm forgiven,' the man cajoled, happy to play out the age-old game.

Grainne nodded. 'You're forgiven.'

He smiled with a dazzle of white teeth. 'Sure now, haven't you the lovely voice. It falls on the ear like a summer's breeze.'

'Dear God, ye'll have me thinking I'm part of the weather,' the girl giggled, and Slattery's confidence came to full flower.

'This is going to be easy,' he told himself, 'but don't rush your fences, Timmy me boy. Take them slow and easy.'

Exercising all his considerable charm he continued to

flatter and banter Grainne as they walked on down the street, and she played up to him, her wits sharp and agile. By the time they had come to a section of the ruined walls, the sergeant was ready to advance his campaign a little further.

'Tell me, pretty girl, what is it they call ye?'

'Theresa . . . Theresa Donleavy.'

'Theresa.' He seemed to taste the name and savour it. 'Sure, it's fit for a queen, and as far as looks go, you're a queen of hearts, pretty girl.'

'Ye're not so ill-looking yourself, Sergeant,' she flirted girlishly, 'but I shouldn't be talking with you. Me Da doesn't like me talking to strange men, least of all soldiers.'

'I'm no stranger. I'm Sergeant Timothy Slattery of the Eighth Hussars, the Royal Irish.'

'Sure, ye're a Queen's man then.' Grainne turned full-face to him, and Slattery found her increasingly delicious.

'By Jasus, I'll have to watch me step,' he warned himself. 'She could take the heart from me, could this one.' Aloud, he asked, 'Why doesn't your father like soldiers?'

Her long lashes veiled her downcast eyes. 'He thinks that they only want girls for sport. In fact, I think that meself. That's why I'll leave you now.'

A shock of actual alarm galvanized Slattery. 'No, Theresa, don't go. Talk a little more with me.'

She shook her long raven-black hair, and Slattery caught a scent of warm heather blossoms. 'Oh no, please don't go . . . Or at least, say you'll meet me again.'

For a moment or two Grainne pretended to consider his plea.

He gently urged her once more, and then she nodded. 'All right, I'll meet you, but we'll have to be secret and careful, I don't want my Da to know about it, and people round here have awful long tongues.'

'That's great!' He felt an acute pleasure, and was surprised at the depth of attraction he was feeling towards this girl. They arranged a trysting place, then parted.

The sergeant was buoyant as he retraced his steps and entered an alehouse. 'By Jesus, but she's the rare lovely girl,' he told himself, and winked at his reflection in the bar-mirror. 'Congratulations, Slattery, my boy, you've caught the sweetest little fish in a week's march from here.' He lifted his glass of porter, and toasted his own image in the gold-lettered glass.

Chapter Twenty-Five

At Leap, the meeting took place on a moonless night. One by one the men slipped through the gloom and softly tapped on the chapel door. In the surrounding area other men lay concealed and vigilant. Ready to raise the alarm should police or soldiers come raiding. Inside the chapel Father Boyce sat before the altar, perched on the top of its mounting steps with Grainne to his right hand, and Phelim Rourke to his left. The altar top was pivoted open, so that in need those present could quickly hide in the vault below. No one spoke or moved, only muffled coughs and hoarse-sounding breathing betrayed their positions.

'Arrah yes, we're all here now, boys, thanks be to God.' Boyce used a penetrating whisper. 'So Grainne here will tell ye what she has learned these past weeks.'

The girl took her cue and began to speak. 'Con is to be moved next week to Spike Island, and kept there until his trial.'

There was a sharp exhalation from some of her listeners. The grim island fortress-prison opposite the Cobh township in Cork Harbour was a place of evil renown.

'He'll be taken with two or three other poor devils from the Bandon barracks. There'll be a guard of soldiers and police, and they're to set out early on the Wednesday morning.'

'That's a good twenty miles or more to travel from Bandon to the harbour, no matter which point they're aiming for,' Peter O'Shea, the grizzled veteran observed quietly.

Boyce nodded unseen in the almost pitch blackness, then realized he was practically invisible and spoke up. 'The question is, boys, at what point on their journey do we attack the van and get Con out of it . . . And what's more important, keep him out . . . So let's get to business, and discuss what's to be done . . .'

At his side Grainne sat in silent gratitude. These were the men who would set her lovely Con free, and at that moment she loved each and every one of them.

During the next few days fortune smiled on the plotters. Through friends in the priesthood Boyce knew that on the Wednesday in question a demonstration had been organized to take place in Bandon to protest about the application of the recent Poor Law Extension Act. Boyce was jubilant, knowing that from the early hours of the morning the streets of the town would be swarming with people.

'That's where we'll make our attack,' he told his men. 'In the streets of the town itself. They'll never expect us to strike there.'

'But it's too near the barracks,' one man objected.

Boyce's dewdrop quivered as he pointed his long nose at the objector and declared witheringly, 'Don't be so damned stupid, Mulligan. That's the whole point of it. There'll be so many desperate-looking characters floating about the town, that the Peelers and soldiers won't know where to start looking.'

Boyce went to Bandon himself, and through a fellow Young Irelander, managed to arrange a secure hiding-place in the town itself for the rescued Con Shonley.

Phelim Rourke also went to Bandon, and spent a long time wandering the streets, his shrewd gaze absorbing what he needed to know.

Grainne herself continued to keep assignations with Timothy Slattery, and he was increasingly casual about disclosing the plans to move the prisoners. The plotters learned through Grainne that a closed van drawn by two horses was to be used for the prisoners' transport. One armed constable would be locked inside the van, the prisoners would be chained together, and secured to stout rings embedded in the van's flooring.

'We'll need blacksmiths' hammers and cold chisels,' Boyce instructed.

The escort was to consist of ten Hussar privates and NCOs commanded by Lieutenant O'Donoghue plus a civilian van driver, and another armed constable and sergeant on the top of the van with him.

'We'll use twelve men,' Phelim Rourke decided. 'We'll have those three pistols available, the rest will have to use shillelaghs. It'll be all close-quarter stuff anyway, and we can't really hope to get the muskets through the streets without someone noticing we're armed.'

He himself knew the location of the house in which Con was to be hidden. He imparted this information only to Patrick O'Shea and the youth, Dillon, his two most trusted and capable aides.

Grainne and Father Boyce would be at the cabin outside the town where Grainne was already staying with another family of Young Ireland sympathizers.

The rescue group spent long hours poring over the rough maps Phelim Rourke had drawn of the ambush site and the surrounding streets. Several of the men had been to Bandon and knew the town. They aided Phelim Rourke to implant a mental picture of the site firmly into their comrades' heads.

Finally, on Monday and Tuesday, the rescue group made their way by ones and twos to Bandon, where they mingled unnoticed with the hordes already pouring into the town for the big meeting and demonstration.

'Can you think of anything that we've left undone, Phelim?' Father Boyce asked before the big man left Leap on Tuesday morning. Phelim Rourke considered for a moment or two, then gave an emphatic, 'No!'

The tiny priest grinned like a mischievous schoolboy. 'Arrah yes, Phelim, I can think of something we've missed.'

The other's hard face frowned. 'What?'

'We haven't yet asked the Good Lord for help and His blessing on our plans.' Boyce caught the big man's hand and pulled him down to his knees, then knelt himself and prayed long and fervently.

Chapter Twenty-Six

Con Shonley was losing count of time. Each passing day merged into the next unvaried by change. The beatings had stopped, and he had been released from his fetters. Rough grey clothing replaced his own stinking garments, and he was allowed to clean out his cell each morning. Twice a day he was fed a chunk of hard stale bread and a bowl of weak and watery skilly.

Once he had been escorted from his cell and brought to the barrack office, where a genteely mannered magistrate remanded him into further custody. None of the soldiers or constables guarding Con spoke to him beyond imparting necessary instructions, and he was content that this should be so. For his secret pride had been badly humbled, for he knew only too well, how close he had come to breaking and turning informer.

'One more kicking session and I'd have poured out my soul to that big bastard, MacMahon.' Con was pacing up and down his cell, his thoughts sombre and morose. 'No word from Grainne, no word from Denis or Maggie, or Bridget Mulrooney . . . No word from Boyce or Rourke, dear God, do they not know where I am? They must surely know . . . Why could not one of them at least have come to see me?'

The vision of Grainne's loveliness rose before his eyes, and he felt a gnawing empty pain in his belly. 'I love her, and already she's forgotten me,' he told himself miserably. 'If I'd informed, at least I'd be free, and could go and see her and talk to her.' He pushed the thought from him. 'No. If I inform now, then I've endured this for naught. I'd be less than a man. I'll not inform even if I'm abandoned by those I believed my friends.' He grinned sardonically to himself. 'By Jesus, but aren't you the noble, saintly knight, Con Shonley. You're enjoying playing the martyr, I swear.'

He heard footsteps and the jingling of spurs in the corridor, but paid little heed to them. Then they halted outside his door, and the key and bolts were turned and drawn.

'What in hell do they want with me now, I've already had breakfast.' There was only time to wonder briefly before the door opened, and Sergeant Slattery walked into the cell. He was dressed in full riding order, his brown busby topping his bushy hair, and his accoutrements a shimmer of brass, silver and polished leather. His white teeth gleamed wolfishly as he asked, 'Tell me, Shonley, what is Theresa Donleavy to you?'

Con stared in blank amazement. 'Who?' he queried.

'Theresa Donleavy, what is she to you?' the NCO repeated.

Con shook his head. 'I know no woman of that name.'

Hot anger lurked in the depths of Slattery's light eyes. 'Oh yes, Shonley, I think ye do. She's young and pretty, with black hair and green eyes.'

Con could not prevent a quick flash of recognition to show on his face, and quick though he was to smother it, the other man had seen and understood. Slattery's burning anger momentarily burst out. 'By Jasus, the little cow has been codding me right enough!'

He stamped out of the cell, slamming the door thunderously behind him. Con's thoughts raced.

It had to be Grainne that the soldier had talked of, but what in God's name was happening out there beyond the walls of his prison? What was Grainne doing passing herself under another name? And what damage had he done to her by allowing his recognition to show? He resumed his pacings, his mind feverish with fearful anxieties . . .

Sergeant Timothy Slattery was a first-class soldier.

Brave, tough, disciplined. He was also highly intelligent. For some weeks now he had been meeting with the green-eyed girl. She had repulsed his more pressing sexual overtures, while permitting him sufficient liberties to keep his desire for her aflame. All that time also she had chattered artlessly about his duties in Bandon, and had asked innocent questions about the barrack routines, and its inmates, military, police and prisoners. A worm of doubt had begun to wriggle in Slattery's acute mind. He had allowed her to extract information from him, all the while trying to perceive where her particular interest lay. Then he had finally come to the conclusion that she was trying to find out more about the prisoner, Con Shonley.

The brief passage with the young man had settled any remaining doubts in the sergeant's mind. From the cell he went directly to the barrack office. He found his squadron commander, Captain Sinclair there, together with District Inspector MacMahon. Slattery saluted, his upraised arm quivering with the energy expended.

'With your permission, Sir, may I have a few words with yourself and the District Inspector. It's about the prisoner, Conrad Shonley . . . '

The long-bodied, high-sided black van with its two black horses and black-cloaked driver resembled a huge hearse; and the dull dark-green of the police uniforms only enhanced its funereal appearance. It was drawn up close to the door which opened onto the inner courtyard of the barracks. Armed soldiers in the great courtyard archway to the outer street pushed the avidly curious onlookers back with irascible shouts, as one by one the fettered prisoners were hustled down the barrack steps and into the van's interior.

A small urchin dropped the round ball of tightly wadded rags he held in his hands, and it rolled between the nearest sentry's legs and into the courtyard itself. The barefooted child ducked under the soldier's arm and ran after his ball. He picked it up and for a few moments stood staring with wide eyes at the squad of mounted Hussars drawn up

189

before the van. Two officers, resplendent in shoulder-slung, scarlet-lined, lambswool pelisses and high-plumed busbies stood directly before the urchin. He listened intently as Captain Sinclair loudly instructed.

'Now hear me well, Mr O'Donoghue, I require your closest attention. There is a strong possibility that a rescue attempt will be made. Keep a good watch at all times, and have a three man point for the entire journey. If there is to be such an attempt, I would think it highly likely that it will take place in the neighbourhood of Ballinhassig; it's a nest of rebel scum, and the Owenboy river offers a rapid means of transport by small boat. So be on your guard.'

'Very well, Sir.' The junior officer saluted and went to where his horse was being held by a canvas-jacketed fatigue-man.

'Sarn't Slattery?' The lieutenant's tone was languid.

'Sir?'

'Are the prisoners secured?'

'I'll see, Sir.' Slattery walked his horse to the rear entrance door of the van. He exchanged some muttered words with the policemen inside, and called, 'Not quite, Sir, it'll be a few moments yet.'

Lieutenant O'Donoghue's glum languidity appeared to weigh even more depressingly on his ornate shoulders as he heard that news.

The urchin scampered away. Wriggling like a small agile animal through the forest of legs clustering around the outer gates, he ran through the people-crowded streets, his tow hair streaming behind him, and came to a place where four streets converged.

Phelim Rourke reached out with one big hand and halted the urchin's head-long gallop. 'Here, sonny-boy. I'm here.' He pulled the small figure to him. 'Now whisper to me.' He bent his caubeened head low, and the child breathlessly whispered all he had seen and heard into the large hairy ear next to his lips.

'Good boy, so ye are.' The man pushed some coins into the child's hand. 'There now, that'll buy ye plenty sweeties, won't it . . . Away ye go, good boy.' For once the man's tough features wore a tenderness as he watched the child skip gleefully along the street, whooping his joy at possessing such wealth.

Rourke looked about him. The houses were old and decrepit, the converging streets narrow and twisting. In one street were three men wearing the black swallow-tailed coats of burial men. They were standing around a handcart on which were piled the reason for their being. Four roughly fashioned coffins, two of which held deceased occupants. Rourke lifted his hand in a brief signal, and the nearest of the burial men nodded.

Among the passersby, the housewives, the beggars, the artisans, the shopkeepers and the labourers were men lounging aimlessly against walls, and in doors and entryways, carrying shillelaghs tucked under their arms. They were in no way noticeable. Any countryman who ever walked through Bandon's streets carried his shillelagh as a matter of course.

A little distance down that street along which the prisoners would be carried, was a vendor of baked potatoes and roasted chestnuts. His wares held on a fourlegged metal chest, under which was a broad iron tray heaped with a mass of glowing charcoal. He did a brisk trade among the passersby, and kindly allowed the half-naked beggar children to warm themselves at his fire. He too momentarily met Phelim Rourke's eyes, and nodded briefly.

Mentally Rourke acknowledged the invaluable aid given to his group by certain of the local Young Ireland sympathizers. Without their help the ambush would of necessity have been a much cruder and more makeshift affair. Satisfied that all was well, the big man drew his short blue cloak tighter about his broad chest, and with his hand caressed the curved butt of the pistol concealed under his arm beneath the cloak. He drew a deep breath and steeled himself for what lay only minutes ahead.

Sergeant Slattery rode point with two privates directly behind him. Some twenty yards back were Lieutenant O'Donoghue and one private, then the great lurching van, with the six remaining hussars bringing up the rear. The Sergeant's light eyes were wary. He didn't think that a rescue attempt would be necessarily made in the Ballinhassig area, as his officers appeared to assume. It could come at any point on their journey, and sooner rather than later.

As he rode, Slattery's thoughts kept returning to the green-eyed girl he knew as Theresa Donleavy. He was still strongly attracted to her, despite his near-certainty that she had only been using him to gain information. Slattery fluctuated between anger and desire. He was unused to being the supplicant for love, and it was a new and disturbing experience for him to endure the knowledge of rejection by a woman. His nose caught the richly appetising scent of baking potatoes, and his mouth salivated. Breakfast that morning had consisted of a mug of gritty coffee and a hunk of stale bread.

Behind him the rumble of iron-rimmed wheels across the cobbles told him that the van was drawing nearer to him, and mindful of his orders he put his mount into a trot to widen the gap once more. The people in the streets paused to watch the van's progress, and some spat ostentatiously upon the ground.

Phelim Rourke stood against the wall of the corner house where the four streets crossed and waited his moment. He glanced at the passing sergeant and two privates, and noted the wary look on the NCO's features. Some instinct warned Rourke that the man's obvious tension was due to some prior knowledge of a rescue attempt and momentary doubt assailed him. Had an informer been at work? Rourke forced the doubt from his mind. It was an impossibility! The men privy to the plot could all be trusted.

The great black van loomed nearer, and Rourke moved his hand. The burial men lifted the handles of their hand-cart and pushed its morbid load towards the crossing. The cotter-pin had been previously removed from the off-side wheel and with a jerk the axle was slid free and the hand-cart collapsed on its side directly in front of the oncoming van, forcing the driver to haul his team to a halt. The coffins slid and tumbled and the lid of one came off, disclosing the naked cold flesh of the corpse inside it.

Even as the coffins fell Rourke was running forwards. The chestnut vendor snatched up a small hand-shovel and used it to hurl showers of burning charcoal at the horses of the hussars behind the van. The glowing lumps stung the beasts into terrified buckings and two men were immediately hurled from their saddles. The rest of the rescue party went into action with flailing shillelaghs. Lieutenant O'Donoghue snatched for his pistol then screamed aloud as a shillelagh shattered his wrist. His horse reared and plunged, its hooves striking into the private's horse next to it, and causing that in its turn to plunge and buck and unseat its rider. The shouts of the men and the squealing neighs of the animals created a deafening uproar.

The sergeant and constable on the van's top lifted their carbines, seeking desperately for a target. Rourke aimed his long-barrelled pistol as he ran, and snapped off a shot. A round hole appeared beneath the sergeant's left eye and gouted blood as he plunged headlong from his high perch. At the rear of the van two men with blacksmiths' hammers smashed the lock and tore the door open.

'Make way, boys.' Patrick O'Shea shouldered them aside and shouted to the constable inside, 'Throw down your gun!' As he went to enter the van a carbine exploded and O'Shea was punched backwards as the heavy lead ball smashed into his chest. Young Dillon, armed with a pistol, cocked and fired into the van in one fluid motion. Then other carbines roared in the van's shadowed interior and Dillon went down choking, his mouth and throat torn to bloody shreds by the bullets.

A shillelagh-wielding rescuer tried to clamber up onto the driver's seat, and the constable there fired at point-blank range into his skull. The hussars around the van fought as best they could, but the shock of ambush had worked against them, and one by one they were beaten into bloody senselessness. Again carbines volleyed from inside the van and another of the rescuers dropped screaming and kicking his legs wildly.

Rourke cursed horribly, and bellowed, 'It's a trap, get away!' Then ran for his life along the street, knocking over a man and woman who stood in his way. Timothy Slattery had drawn his sabre and its silver sheen flashed as he cut at one of the fleeing burial men. The steel bit deep into the side of the man's neck, and his head fell over at a grotesque angle as blood jetted from the terrible gash.

Then, abruptly, it was all done with, and the only attackers left were the dead and dying as their comrades fled. Ashen-faced with the agony of his shattered wrist, O'Donoghue ordered Slattery to ride to the barracks and raise a general alarm. The sergeant galloped through the streets, his light eyes gleaming with a fierce pleasure. 'That'll teach ye to try and cod me, Theresa Donleavy,' he exulted inwardly. 'That'll teach ye, ye green-eyed besom bitch!'

Chapter Twenty-Seven

The young son of the family with whom Grainne and Father Boyce were staying brought the news of the blood-soaked failure to them later that morning.

'Sure, it was a trap.' The youthful face was pale and drawn with angry grief. 'They wasn't really prisoners in the van, they was bloody Peelers, and they'd got lots o' guns hidden in there all loaded and ready to use.'

Father Boyce's deep-sunk eyes were tragic, and Grainne felt physically nauseated as she heard the story.

'Five of the boys are killed. One was still living when they took him into the barracks, but he died in a half-hour. Two Peelers are dead, and a couple of the soldiers are so sore hurt that they say they might die.'

The tiny priest's cheeks had lost all colour, and his face was skull-like in his wretchedness. 'Oh dear God, why did you forsake us?' he muttered again and again.

Grainne gave way to hopeless despair, and felt that her own death would be a sweet release from her mental torment.

'The thing is, Father, ye'll have to go from here and quick,' the young man went on. 'The Peelers and the soldiers are searching through the town. They'll be here later on without a doubt. Ye'll have to get away.'

With immense effort Boyce forced his mind to work. 'They'll be looking particularly for you, Grainne, I feel sure of it. That sergeant knows your face so well, he'll be able to give a good description of you.'

She nodded absently, unable to bring herself to care what happened to her. 'I've five deaths on my soul now, and that's only counting my friends who were trying to help me, never mind the police and soldiers,' she thought with a bitter remorse. 'How will I ever be able to look the families of those men in the face again, knowing that it was through me their men went to their deaths?'

As if he read her thoughts, the tiny priest patted the girl's slender shoulder. 'There now, girl dear, don't be blaming yourself for what has happened. Sure it was God's will that this should turn out this way. He'll have some good reason for it, which He'll reveal to us in His own good time . . . Though what good reason, I'm damned if I can think right now,' he added angrily.

The young man urged them again: 'Father, I'm not meaning to be rude and inhospitable, but ye'd best get on your way before the Peelers get here. I can help you. I'll borrow me uncle's jaunting-car. I think ye'd best head for Kilbrittain, from there ye can make your own way to Timouleague and through Clonakilty to your home. The soldiers won't have blocked the lanes that way yet.'

In a mental daze Grainne let herself be directed by Boyce and the young man, and within the hour the three of them were perched on a jaunting-car being drawn by a fast-trotting donkey towards the town of Kilbrittain.

Con Shonley was told of the ambush that afternoon by Sergeant Slattery. To his credit the soldier did not boast or gloat about the success of the trap, but merely related quietly what had happened.

'That wee girl must be powerful fond of ye, Shonley, and so must your friends. Five of them have died for ye to prove it.'

The news affected Con like a physical blow and he felt a terrible sickness in the pit of his stomach as he listened. The sergeant left him, and he slumped down onto his pallet, his mind a confused jumble.

Later, District Inspector MacMahon came to the cell with two constables and took Con out through the court-yard and into a stable. The dead ambushers were lying in a row, hands crossed on their chests, sightless eyes open and staring.

'There are your friends, Shonley. You needn't bother trying to deny that you know them. Sub-Inspector Hardy will be here to identify them for us tomorrow. But you might as well give us their names now,' MacMahon said.

Con looked at each face in turn, and the flickering shadows cast by the swinging oil lamp made it seem that the dead men were winking and grimacing at him. He shuddered uncontrollably.

'Well, will ye give us their names?' the policeman questioned impatiently.

Con shook his head, and swallowed the sour bile that had suddenly soured his mouth. 'I don't know them,' he muttered.

'Ye're a bloody liar, but no matter, we'll know them all by tomorrow.' MacMahon jerked his head at the constables. 'Take him back to his cell.'

As Con was led away the Inspector added, 'Ye'll be leaving for Spike Island tomorrow, Shonley. Ye'll stay there until ye come up for trial and hanging.'

Back in his cell Con welcomed the darkness, for in its concealment he could cast aside the forced mask of control, and allow his grief and despair to flood over him. He had now lost hope, and knew that his own life would shortly be brought to an end on the gallows. His thoughts were a tumultuous anguish of regrets. Regrets for his cutting of all family ties and his cruelty to his sweet mother. Regrets that he would never more hold his beloved Grainne close-locked in his arms and see her smile of love. Regrets that he would never again laugh at Denis Callaghan's droll quips. Regrets for the five fine men who had died because of him.

A guttural moan tore loose from his throat, and he felt the scalding of tears in his eyes. Con abandoned his last vestiges of control, and wept . . .

Con Shonley travelled to his new prison in an ordinary closed coach, his escort a police sergeant and two constables all wearing plain clothes. Con was free of his fetters and felt light-bodied without their familiar weight. The day was fine and clear, but Con was unnoticing of the bleak beauty of the countryside. He sat staring blankly through the coach windows, and paid no heed to the casual talk between his escorts.

Hours later at Ringaskiddy village he stepped from the coach and was led towards a landing stage which jutted out into Cork Harbour.

A rowing boat manned by four men waited there. The harbour water was a grey-green and so calm that an oily sheen covered its surface. Far in the distance, faint and blue, were the summits of Knockmealdown, but Con had no eyes for their mysterious loveliness. Instead he gazed with foreboding at the island, its hill crowned with the long walls and grim buildings of the fortress-prison. Sitting between two of his escorts in the stern of the boat as it moved across the water, Con's spirits unaccountably began to lift from the deep depression that had dominated him. The sea was freedom incarnate, and perhaps escape was possible upon it even from this secure cage he was being taken into.

The boat swung into the small island harbour, and Con stared up at the battery of great guns which commanded the entrance. Blue-uniformed, shako-wearing Royal Marine Artillerymen peered out from the embrasures at this fresh arrival, and one freckle-faced youngster among them waved in a friendly manner. The rowers shipped their oars alongside a landing jetty, and Con was led from the gently-rocking boat and up to where an elderly grave-faced civilian wearing a top-hat and caped greatcoat was waiting for them. He spoke with the police sergeant out of Con's earshot and then the three policemen left their prisoner alone and re-embarked in the boat.

'Follow me, Shonley.' The elderly man led Con up the hill and over the fortress drawbridge, past several Marine sentries armed with long-bayoneted muskets, their posture unmoving, their faces expressionless. With a great ring of keys the elderly man unlocked and locked a series of grated doors and the pair passed deeper into the fortress, finally emerging into a small square courtyard. Doors were set into its windowless walls, and the elderly man unlocked one and beckoned for Con to enter.

He stepped into a large vaulted room. A box-bed, small scrubbed table and chair, and a wash-basin and water jug on a stand comprised its furnishings. Con's surprise showed on his face, and the elderly man's gravity was lightened by a thin-lipped smile. 'All the comforts of home, are there not, Shonley?'

The young man nodded. 'So it would seem.'

The elderly man left without another word, and a turnkey dressed in a blue uniform frockcoat and soft-topped peaked forage cap came into the courtyard. 'All right, Shonley, make yourself at home. Ye'll not be leaving here for a while.' The man had a rosy, cheerful plump face, and when he grinned a mass of brown-stubbed teeth filled his large mouth. 'Me name is Turk . . . But when there's anyone else around but we two, then it's Mr Turk, or Sir.' He winked broadly. 'So don't forget, I'm your turnkey and ye have to do what I tell ye to . . . Now, have yez any money?'

Con shook his head.

Turk's brown teeth clicked in disappointment. 'Pity that! Ne'er mind it though. A man like you will have friends enough outside wi' money to spare, that I don't doubt.' He winked again. 'And Old Turk here is just the boyo to know how to use it for your best advantage, Shonley . . . Everything can be made sweet and easy iffen ye've got some money coming in . . . Even Spike Island.'

Con Shonley began to wonder just what sort of a prison he had come to . . .

Augustus Hardy moved along the line of corpses. 'O'Shea, Dillon, Clarke, O'Mahoney, Mulligan,' he identified each one in turn, and felt a grim satisfaction as he did so. Each name had been on his list of top suspects. Those men who had dropped out of the normal drill sessions attended by his informers.

'What arms were taken, Sir?'

199

'Two pistols only,' MacMahon told him. 'And a few shillelaghs.'

Disappointment creased the Englishman's thin features. 'Pity they hadn't a musket or two with them, it would have been timely confirmation for us.'

'Aye, true enough, still, let's be thankful for small mercies. That's five rebels less to deal with when the time comes.'

The two men left the stable and crossed the courtyard, chatting easily together. When they reached the barrack office MacMahon lifted a broadsheet that lay on his desk and passed it to his companion. 'Here, read this.'

Hardy scanned the flaunting capitals at the top of the page. 'The United Irishman,' he read aloud, and then his eyes absorbed the rebellious and inflammatory paragraphs beneath. When he had finished he stared bleakly at his superior officer. 'This man, John Mitchel, what in Hell's name are the Government about to allow him to publish this treasonous garbage with apparent impunity.'

The District Inspector grinned mirthlessly. 'There's always been a deal of verbal license allowed in Ireland, Hardy. It's better that men should rant and rave in the open, than plan quietly in secret.' He rummaged among the papers that littered his desk and lifted one up. 'This is the latest report from Dublin Castle. Your man, Mitchel, has broken with the Young Irelanders, and he with Fintan Lalor have formed their own party. They're openly stating that they are dedicated to armed rebellion.

'Lalor wants the countryfolk to refuse to pay their rents, and Mitchel says that no one should pay the Poor Rates. According to the report the pair of them think that this'll bring about a revolution in short order. They think it'll be the spark to ignite the gunpowder.' The florid face grinned mirthlessly again. 'Anyway, that's neither here nor there at the moment . . . I'm more concerned with the cannonading I'm getting meself from Phoenix Park.'

Hardy experienced a sudden apprehension. The Headquarters of the Royal Irish Constabulary at Phoenix Park, Dublin, were not given to issuing meaningless reprimands. He listened as MacMahon went on.

'Phoenix Park want to know why we haven't found any arms in this area. We know from our agents in France that arms have been shipped to Cork and Cobh, so they're here somewhere, and we haven't found a single one. Phoenix Park appear to think that we are not trying hard enough.'

'Dear God above, that is grossly unjust!' Hardy interjected indignantly. 'My men have been searching nonstop, raiding night and day. It's not through a lack of zeal that we have failed up to now.'

MacMahon frowned. 'That's as maybe, Hardy, but Phoenix Park is convinced that there is an abundance of arms hidden in this area, and they are adamant that those arms be found, and quickly. I've had the County Inspector snapping at my heels for weeks now, and his temper is worsening by the day. I don't care how you do it, Hardy, but I am telling you now, that you will find arms for me, or start seeking other areas of employment for yourself.' He paused to allow time for his threat to sink home, before continuing. 'We know that those ambushers came from your district. I want the ones who escaped brought in, and I want arms found. If you fail, then you may well find yourself rag-picking for your daily bread among the other beggars who fail in life . . . Is that clearly understood?'

The Englishman's temper burned hotly, and for a split-second he was tempted to challenge the other man. To call him out and face him with pistols or swords. But he literally bit hard on his own tongue, and finally replied, 'It is clearly understood, Sir.'

MacMahon frowned. 'Then be about it, Sub-Inspector, be about it now . . . '

Morose and half-drunk, Denis Callaghan listened to Grainne's harrowing story in a silence broken only by the gurgling of his throat as he gulped the fiery poteen down its capacious depths. When she had finished and sat in despondent silence, he bent and spat sizzlingly into the burning peat on Mulrooney's filthy hearth.

'So, pretty girl, what's to be done now, hey?'

201

'I don't know, Denis.' Her green eyes shone with unshed tears. 'Con will hang for sure now, and five men died for naught.'

'What did the wee black crow have to say afore he left ye?' Callaghan questioned.

The girl's lustrous hair swung gently as she shook her head. 'Not much, Denis. He just said that we'd have to keep quiet, and pray God for help, and hope for the best. Rourke's gone on the run and so have the other men who were at Bandon.'

'God blast my eyes!' the man swore in sudden fury. 'Isn't that just the stamp o' that bastard black crow . . . Con can hang, and the other lads have their heads shot away, and the rest being hunted like hares by the Peelers, and all that wee bastard can say, is keep quiet and pray to his bloody useless God to help ye.'

'Father Boyce means well, Denis,' Grainne tried to calm him.

'Means well, d'ye tell me?' Callaghan's bloodshot eyes glared madly at her. 'O' course he means well, but only to his bloody self! He's sitting safe and comfortable, isn't he just. He took good care that he wasn't fighting wi' the others. No one can point the finger at him and say that he was one o' them who tried to rescue Con.' The man's shaggy head rocked from side to side, and he swayed on his three-legged stool as he swigged from the bottle in his hand.

'Father Boyce takes risks like we all do,' Grainne persisted, in her defence of the priest. 'Hasn't he still got Tumelty hidden in his chapel, and those guns as well.'

For a few moments Callaghan made no reply, only blinked owlishly at her. Then a sly gleam entered his eyes. 'Sure now, so he has, and your man, Rourke, and the other bully-boys are on the run!' He breathed the words with immense satisfaction, then whispered hoarsely, as if to himself. 'And if a man, or a woman was to go to the Peelers with such information, wouldn't the Peelers give that man or that woman pretty well anything they could ask for?'

Grainne stared hard at the man before her. Comprehension of the possible import of his words becoming clearer in her mind.

A sense of dread assailed her as Callaghan added, again in a hoarse whisper, 'Wouldn't the Peelers give an innocent man his freedom, in exchange for a guilty man, and some guns?'

Grainne's breath caught in her throat, and her heart pounded frantically. She was swept by waves of giddy nausea. 'Oh no, we couldn't! We couldn't do such a thing,' she ejaculated softly, and now came the flooding temptation that appalled and horrified her, even as she let it enfold her.

Denis Callaghan scowled fiercely, and lifted his bottle high in the air. 'Then let's drink a toast to the hangman who'll stretch Con's neck!' he shouted like a madman . . .

Chapter Twenty-Eight

As one day succeeded another Con Shonley began to feel that he was living in a dream. His clothing was now the rough homespun brown jacket and trousers of a convict, but his treatment was that of a captive guest, rather than an accused murderer. He ate the same boiled beef and whole-meal bread, and drank the ration coffee of the Marine garrison and turnkeys. He did no labour such as oakum picking in his cell, and was allowed to exercise in the small courtyard whenever he wished. He had no contact with the other convicts on Spike Island, who were awaiting transport to penal colonies such as Van Diemens Land.

From his cell window, he could by peering out at an acute angle see the buildings of Cobh rising up their hillside across the harbour, and occasionally catch glimpses of convicts and their guards crossing the open space of the parade ground. Mr Turk was his only companion, and he was always pleasant and jovial-mannered. At times Con would question the turnkey, asking why he, Con, was being given such favourable treatment. The man would laugh heartily, but refuse to be drawn, only replying, 'Arrah, ye're a man that the big-wigs has their eyes on. They're expecting great things o' ye.'

After ten days a faultlessly dressed civilian came to Con's cell in the early morning.

'Stand to attention for the Governor!' Turk shouted officiously. Con rose from his chair and stood erect.

'Good morning to you, Shonley. My name is Grace.' The man was of Con's height, and had exceptionally clear blue-grey eyes, which examined the prisoner with great thoroughness. Con looked at the pearl-grey frockcoat, the diamond stick-pin in the silken cravat, the slender braided trousers and highly-polished soft leather boots, and inwardly acknowledged the aptness of the Governor's name. He did indeed present an appearance of grace.

'Are you comfortable here, Shonley, is your treatment satisfactory?' Grace asked with a seemingly genuine interest.

'Yes, as comfortable and satisfactory as captivity allows,' Con answered.

'Call the Governor, Sir, when you speak,' Turk barked.

Grace lifted his well-shaped hand. 'No matter, Mr Turk. No matter . . . I'll have the schoolteacher call in to see you, Shonley. He has access to books and perhaps may find you something to your taste to read, and so pass the time more easily.'

'Sir?' Con's puzzlement had deepened unbearably. 'Tell me, Sir, why am I being accorded such favourable treatment?'

The Governor was momentarily taken aback. 'I am following instructions, Shonley, that is all. Besides, we are not barbarians, all our prisoners are treated with as much humanity as is possible. I'll bid you good day.' With that, he left Con to his puzzlement.

That afternoon a tall cadaverous, shabbily-dressed man came to the cell and introduced himself. 'I'm Thomas Delaney, the schoolmaster.' Then he went on to explain; 'We maintain a small school here for the child convicts. I do my best to teach the poor souls their letters before they are sent abroad. The Governor informs me that you need reading matter. I've a wee store of books here on the island. Some might be to your taste . . . Do you enjoy Disraeli, or Kingslake, or Prescot?' His speech was staccato and jerky.

'Anything will suit, Mr Delaney,' Con gestured, 'but what I would appreciate above all else are pen and paper. I'd like to send a letter.'

The cadaverous features flinched, and the man's nervous mannerisms became more pronounced. 'Oh, I don't know about that, Shonley. I've naught to do with the mails.' He shook his head violently, and his lank, thinning hair fell across his forehead. 'Oh no! I couldn't bring you such things. No! It's out of the question.' He departed, still muttering, 'No! It's out of the question.'

Turk, who had been standing nearby to listen, laughed at Con's bemused expression. 'He's the quare one, isn't he just. The boys call him the "Wandering Skull". Sure, he's half-mad like all the rest of us here.'

The young man could only wonder how much truth there was in that statement by the turnkey.

Some time later the schoolmaster came back, carrying some books in his arms. 'Here you are, Shonley. I've brought you some of Charles Dickens' works, Carlyle's *French Revolution* and the Marryat novels. They're light-weight stuff I fear. But they may afford you some entertainment.'

'My thanks to you, Mr Delaney.'

The man's lank head twitched sharply, then he whispered, 'Are you still loyal to the Cause, Con Shonley?'

'What "Cause"?' Con asked, his voice deliberately neutral.

A rictus-like grimace twisted Delaney's pale lips, in what was intended to be a smile. 'Our poor country's freedom from tyranny, Shonley. What other Cause is there?'

'None other for a true Irishman,' Con said firmly, 'and I count myself a true one.'

The other man's head twitched again. 'Well said, my friend, well said. Then listen to me carefully. Do not be beguiled by the good treatment they're affording you. It is only to serve their own ends. They know how important you are in the rebel movement. They want you to betray your friends and their plans.'

'But I'm of no importance,' Con protested, 'I couldn't betray any plans . . . I know nothing.'

The rictus smile twisted the pale lips. 'Now don't be taking me for a fool, Mr Shonley. Five men do not give their lives in a rescue attempt for someone of no importance. It's widely accepted that you are one of the leaders of

206

the forthcoming rebellion. So be on your guard at all times . . . God bless you, for a true patriot!' Delaney grabbed Con's hand and pressed it fervently.

As Turk came into the cell Delaney left with a final warning stare at Con Shonley.

It took some time for the young man to collect his disordered thoughts. Then he smiled sardonically. 'Dear God, another rescue attempt and poor misguided fools like Delaney will be proclaiming me the true King of Ireland,' he told himself with a bitter amusement . . .

Chapter Twenty-Nine

The idea implanted in her mind by Denis Callaghan's drunken maunderings gave Grainne no rest. By day she would fight to reject it, and for brief periods succeed. But at night it would relentlessly invade her thoughts, and she would toss and turn on her narrow pallet for long long hours as it reverberated through her consciousness . . . 'Turn informer. Inform on the priest and on Tumelty. Show the Peelers where the guns are hidden. Set Con free! Set Con free! Set Con free! Inform, and set Con free!'

She would drift into exhausted slumber and even there find no peace. Her dreams were terrifying visions of high gallows, trees with hooded men dangling from their thick, tarred beams, and she would wake with sobs of terror from her nightmare to lie sick and spent, weeping helplessly.

After Con Shonley's removal to Spike Island the hunt for his would-be rescuers scoured over the whole of County Cork, but although many men were taken in for questioning, all were later released. Grainne kept to the Mulrooney house, hardly ever venturing from its malodorous rooms. Once soldiers had come there searching for men and arms, and had taken three lodgers with them when they left. But Grainne herself was never suspected, or even questioned. Unknown to her, she owed this to Sergeant Timothy Slattery. The man possessed his own sense of chivalry. Because he felt that the girl he knew as Theresa Donleavy had acted as she had to save a man she truly loved, he decided to accept with good grace the fact that for once he had been the exploited in romance, instead of the exploiter. The description he gave to his superior officers of Theresa

Donleavy differed in almost every physical aspect to Grainne MacDermott.

'To tell the truth,' Timothy Slattery admitted to himself, 'I've still a powerful fancy for that wee girl. I'd hate to see her looks became raddled in some stinking Bridewell . . . And who knows what the future might bring? Mayhap we'll meet again on some happy day, and she'll be suitably grateful for my knightly action.' He grinned in wry recognition of his own vanities . . .

Two days became three, then four, then six, twelve, eighteen and soon it was three weeks since Con Shonley's transfer to the island prison. Three weeks nearer to his trial and inevitable hanging.

Grainne tortured herself with the swift passage of time. Then, after one night of endless horrific dreams in which she saw her lover's face blacken and swell until he became unrecognizable, Grainne rose from her bed determined that she would do whatever she had to do, to save Con from the gallows. She would try to bargain information for his life and freedom . . .

The twice-folded, wax-sealed scrap of paper was on Augustus Hardy's desk the following morning, placed there by a constable who had been handed it by a heavily-veiled woman as he patrolled a country road. Hardy stared at the grubby, flimsy sheet, and listened to the constable report that he could not recognize the veiled woman who had implored secrecy, and that none other than Inspector Hardy himself should read what was written.

Hardy dismissed the man and breaking the seals unfolded the paper. The message was short; 'Come to the Calvary on the Baltimore road at dusk. Come alone. I have information for you about John Tumelty and the guns.'

The policeman studied the handwriting. It was neat and small, and appeared feminine. He pondered for a while about what he should do. It could be a trick. A bait to lure him to a lonely spot where an assassin would be waiting with a loaded gun. Other policemen had been decoyed and murdered by such means. Yet the Englishman's instinct told him that this was no trickery. That the note was genuine.

He steepled his fingers in his habitual gesture, and touched their tips to his lips. 'I'll go,' he decided, 'but cautiously, and armed.'

Though it was only still mid-February the weather was mild and calm. Hardy loaded and capped his pistol, and strapped a cutlass to his waistbelt. He decided against wearing his riding cloak, its voluminous folds would badly hinder him if a fight should take place.

He left the police barracks in Skibereen while it was still light enough to see some considerable distance cross-country, intending to be close to the Calvary when dusk fell, so as to ensure that no one had gone before to lie in waiting for him. When he reached the Baltimore road the inspector slowed his horse to a walk and stared keenly about him. All was peaceful, no human or animal moved in the deserted-appearing fields around him. He halted and dismounted, then tethered the horse in a thicket of thorn bushes and moved across the muddy bare-earthed farm-land on foot, utilizing the cover of the scrubby hedgerows and drystone walls which dissected the mean fields. He came to within fifty yards of the wayside shrine, and squatted for concealment behind a hedgerow. Dusk slowly fell and deepened, and stars began to glimmer faintly in the night sky. Hardy waited patiently, knowing that with informers, no hard and fast time could ever be set for a rendezvous.

It seemed that hours had passed when he sensed, rather than saw movement at the shrine and peered hard, trying to clarify an outline. Drawing his pistol from its stiff leather holster he cocked the hammer and moved slowly and stealthily towards the dimly pale shaft of the shrine. As he neared it he thought he could distinguish a darker mass in the obscure shadows. He halted and waited until he was sure that someone stood there, and then crept up to within ten yards of the motionless figure, and called softly, 'This is Inspector Hardy. I've a loaded pistol, ready-cocked and aiming at your head. So do not make any rapid move, stand perfectly still.'

A frightened ejaculation came from the figure, and a female voice faltered, 'There's no treachery intended here. You've no need to point pistols.'

The Englishman relaxed, and walked quickly up to the young girl's side. Even in the darkness he recognized Grainne MacDermott, and his hopes rose high. She was Con Shonley's sweetheart, and undoubtedly knew much about what rebellious preparations were taking place in the area.

'Well, young woman, what information do you have for me?' he questioned, his manner gentle.

Twice the girl tried to speak, and twice coughed nervously and fell silent. Grainne was fighting a gruelling mental battle. All her life she had been conditioned by the contempt and hatred any informer was viewed with in the west of Ireland, and she was now to join their despised ranks. She forced herself to think of Con Shonley, and envisaged his face in her mind's eye, then tried to speak again. 'I've knowledge that would be valuable to you, but there's a price for it,' she said haltingly.

'There always is,' Hardy thought with a flash of grim humour, but aloud said only, 'What is that price, girl?'

'Con Shonley's freedom,' Grainne blurted out, and now felt stronger and more able to do what she was doing.

'I see.' The policeman stood in ruminative silence for some moments, before asking, 'How can I be sure that your information is worth the price that you ask?'

'You can be sure,' Grainne told him positively, her whole being now intent on saving her lover, no matter what the cost. 'For it's well known how hard you Peelers have been searching for the guns, and for John Tumelty, and now for those men who attacked the police van at Bandon.'

The Englishman experienced a warm glow of pleasure. If what this girl said was the truth, and if she could indeed deliver all these things into his hands, the effect on his career would be dramatically beneficial. He could rise to the very heights of the Constabulary service. But innate caution, implanted by years of police experience, prevented him from becoming openly effusive. 'You are asking a high price, nonetheless,' he remarked. 'For inevitably, sooner or later we shall find what we are seeking for.'

The tension Grainne was under sharpened her natural acuteness of mind, and without hesitation, she replied, 'I don't think you will catch the men, or find the guns, until the actual day of rebellion, Mr Hardy. They're too well-hidden for that . . . Besides, you know yourself full well, that Con is innocent of any murder. If you Peelers had hard proof of his guilt you would have hung him before now.'

'Can you guarantee to deliver what you promise?' Hardy pressed.

'Can you guarantee to deliver Con from jail,' the girl riposted.

'I personally, no,' the policeman stated frankly, and for a split second Grainne again sensed the black pit of failure yawning before her, but Hardy continued, 'However, my superior officers can guarantee Shonley's release; and if they agree to your terms, then you may be sure that they will keep to their part of the bargain.'

'How can I be sure?' Grainne's rekindled doubts tormented her.

'I accept how difficult it is for you to be completely sure in your own mind, my dear,' the man's voice was kindly, 'but let me assure you, that the authorities can be trusted to keep their word in matters of this kind. To speak openly, that is how we are able to continually find informers that we can rely on. What we promise them as reward, is always given in full.' He paused to let his words sink in, then added, 'I will report this meeting to my superiors. Do not be alarmed about your own identity being disclosed. That will remain a close secret between you and I, which only we shall share. If my superiors are agreeable to your terms, then, when I have taken Tumelty and the other men, and have the guns in my hands, Conrad Shonley will be released.'

'The men from Bandon are on the run, I can't guarantee

that you'll capture them,' Grainne sounded distressed.

'No matter,' Hardy reassured her, 'we'll settle for Tumelty and the guns, and the identities of those other men . . . Can you meet me here at this hour, four nights from now?'

'I will,' the girl murmured, her voice catching in her throat.

'Good, I trust I shall have an answer for you by then . . . Go now, and I will follow.'

As the girl's slim figure melted into the night, Hardy heard the wrenching sobs that were tearing from her, and he pitied her with all his heart for what she had been driven to become . . .

Chapter Thirty

Four nights later Augustus Hardy was able to give Grainne MacDermott the guarantee of Con Shonley's freedom; and in return she gave the policeman all the information she possessed. Hardy returned to the police barracks elated and exultant. All his suspicions of the priest, Father Boyce, confirmed beyond his hopes.

As soon as he reached his headquarters, Hardy sent for Sergeant Macarthy and issued a series of detailed orders . . .

Leap village was shuttered and sleeping as the squadron of mounted policemen moved towards the chapel and its cabin. By hand signals Hardy directed his men into a rough circle around the buildings, keeping six constables with him as an assault group. The rainclouds were scudding in from the coast and when dawn came it was wet and dreary . . . But Hardy was unaware of the day's gloom. His excited expectancy overlaid any such mundane matters.

He and his assault group left their horses some forty yards from their target, discarded their riding capes and checked their weapons.

'Now hear me,' Hardy instructed in a low-pitched voice. 'We take whoever is in there alive, if possible, but should they attempt to resist, then shoot to kill.'

The men nodded in silent acquiescence, their faces wet with rain and strained with anticipation of what was to come.

'You have your orders, Sergeant, I trust you fully understand them?' Hardy looked up at the big man sitting easily in the saddle of his bit-champing horse.

'I understand them, Sir.'

'Very well.' The inspector took a last long look about him at the sleeping cabins and empty fields, then drew his pistol. 'Cavan Murphy, cover the chapel, the rest of you follow me,' he ordered, and ran at the head of his assault group.

The cabin door smashed open and before Father Boyce had roused from sleep he was dragged from his bed by strong arms and bundled outside wearing only his knee-length night shirt. At the same instant two constables burst into the chapel, carbines at the ready. It was empty. Hardy had Boyce brought with him to the altar.

'We know all about your hiding place, Father Boyce,' the inspector's tone was heavy with surety.

The priest's spiky hair and bedraggled, ragged-edged night shirt made him a grotesquely amusing sight, but the anguish that carved deep furrows into his mobile features prohibited laughter.

The altar top was tipped and heaved clear, the stone slab impacting across the steps and splitting into two pieces.

'Do not you think it better to call up those who are below, Father?' Hardy advised. 'It might well save their lives.'

The tiny priest glared at the tall, burly green-uniformed men surrounding him, and his eyes glistened with tears of chagrin. But without verbal protest he bent over the open-topped altar and tapped out the signal.

'John, it's me, Father Boyce. Will ye come up, it's all over with us. The Peelers are here,' he called, and now the tears were in his voice.

The redbricks slid to one side and the be-whiskered, frightened face of John Tumelty showed itself. He clambered out of the shaft, and was seized by two constables.

'Is anyone else down there?' Hardy wanted to know.

The priest shook his head.

'Fetch that lantern here.' The inspector pointed to one of the hanging lamps. It was brought and lit, and Hardy disappeared into the shaft. Holding the lantern high he

215

gazed at what the vaulted crypt contained, and his heart sang within him. Muskets were racked around the walls, and kegs of gunpowder, boxes of percussion caps, chests of cartridges, sheet lead and moulds for making musket balls. Hardy remounted the ladder, and could not help smiling in victory as he faced the two miserable captives.

'There'll be no rebellion in my district now, I'm thinking, will there, Father Boyce?' he challenged happily.

Boyce made a valiant attempt at defiance. 'Don't be too sure of that, Inspector. 'Tis men that make rebellion, not guns alone.'

'Bring them along.' Hardy strode to the door and the small procession of captives and captors followed. Once outside Hardy shouted to the circle of men . . . 'Close in on me . . . Sergeant Macarthy, post guards on these buildings. No one is to enter or come within twenty yards of them on any pretext whatsoever.'

The small area around the chapel porch filled with men and horses. Macarthy dismounted and with his reins loosely held in his hand, asked his superior, 'Are the guns there, Sir?'

Hardy nodded emphatically. 'They are indeed, Sergeant. There must be near three score of them, and enough powder and caps to supply a regiment.'

The constables standing at each side of the priest had relaxed their grips and were intent on the exchange between the officers. Suddenly Boyce tore free and hurled himself into the saddle of the sergeant's horse. The priest clung with both hands to the high pommel and frantically kicked his bare heels into the beast's ribs, screaming, 'Get up! Get up!'

The horse squealed in fright and bolted, careening into the surrounding horsemen and sending them reeling.

'Stop him,' Hardy bawled, 'Stop him, blast you!'

A young inexperienced constable automatically lifted his carbine and fired. The ball struck the horse in the side of its head. At full gallop its forelegs buckled and it thudded down, catapulting Boyce over its head. His scrawny body somersaulted and thumped soggily headfirst into the

216

muddy ground. Men ran to him, but he made no move, his legs and arms sprawling like pale wind-blown twigs in the black mud. The first constable to reach the spot bent and lifted the thin narrow shoulders upright. The white face was becoming masked by scarlet as the hammering rain washed and diluted the streaming blood, and the spiky-haired head fell back at an impossible angle. The constable lowered the shoulders gently down once more, and stood up to shout, 'He's dead, Sir. His neck's broke to pieces . . .'

Chapter Thirty-One

On the morning of March 10 1848, Con Shonley was set free. He found his method of release as strange as all else that had come his way on Spike Island. The elderly man who had first met Con on his arrival at the prison came to the cell after breakfast of coffee and bread had been brought to Con by the turnkey. In his hands he carried the clothes, now washed and clean, that the young man had been wearing when first arrested by the Hussars.

'Here you are, Mr Shonley. As soon as you have breakfasted, and changed, you may go. A boat is waiting for you.'

Con stared in blank amazement. 'Go?' he echoed, 'go where?'

'Wherever you may please, Mr Shonley. You have regained your liberty.'

'But how?' Con could still not fully comprehend what was happening.

The elderly man placed the clothing on the bed. 'It's no use your questioning me further, young man. I know only that you are to be immediately released.'

Turk the turnkey, who was lounging against the door-post, laughed at Con's bewilderment. 'If I was ye, Shonley my jewel, I'd skedaddle afore they change their mind and decide to keep ye here.'

Con quickly changed his clothes, pulling his old garments over his lean torso. The elderly man handed him some coins.

'Here, Mr Shonley. Five shillings to enable you to buy sustenance on your way home.'

He led the way through the grated doors of the passages

and past the motionless Marine sentinels. The four-oared boat headed away from the island and within a short time Con was landed at Cork, still unable to believe in what had happened.

The main streets of the city were filled with excited mobs, and across the width of the roadways were slung long streamers of gaily-coloured buntings. Con gazed at a lighted transparency and read the words upon it, 'France is free, an example to the world.'

'What has happened in France?' he asked a stout ruddy-faced man standing next to him.

The man grinned waggishly. 'Sure now, are ye coddin' me? What sort of a question is that? How can ye not know, have ye been locked up in jail, or something?'

Con chuckled wryly, 'I think you could term it, "or something".'

'The French had a revolution,' the man told him. 'Their king has been kicked offa his throne, and he's come to England. France is a republic again . . . By Christ, they're the great example to us, aren't they just?'

Con nodded and walked on, his mind churning with the news. 'If France could become a republic, and its people cast off the chains of monarchy so easily, then what was to stop Ireland doing the same? I must get back home straight away,' he told himself, 'Father Boyce will know what we should do now.'

It took him two days to walk from Cork to Skibereen, and on his journey he saw ample evidence of the endless sufferings of the Irish poor. Famine still gripped the land, and Death's riders, starvation, disease and cold reaped their grim harvest.

'Rebellion must come soon,' Con continually reiterated to himself. 'It must come soon if it is to save our people.'

He reached Skibereen in the early afternoon, and went through the streets searching for a friendly face among the hordes of homeless, wretched people who had come into the town in a vain search for food and shelter. He saw one man he knew, a crony of Michael Kearney. The man stared at him with open surprise, then deliberately spat on the ground and turned his back. Con was shocked, not understanding why he had been so insulted. For a moment he hesitated, debating crossing the street and asking the man for an explanation. Then he shrugged. That could wait, what was more important was to find his beloved Grainne.

Mulrooney's appeared deserted. There was no one in the long room or in the kitchen or wash house behind.

Con called out, 'Grainne, Denis, Maggie, Bridget, is anyone here?'

Only the plaintive miaowing of a skinny rip-eared cat answered him.

He went upstairs and climbed the ladder to his attic bedroom. Grainne was there, lying on his pallet asleep. He stood, gazing down at her. She lay like a child on her back, her head with its thick wreaths of raven-hued hair slightly turned to one side, her lips parted as though she smiled in dreams showing the gleam of her white teeth.

For long moments Con was content to stand silently and visually drink in the beauty of this young woman whom he loved with such consuming passion. She stirred and breathed in deeply, and her full, firm breasts rose and fell. Con felt desire stir him and a passionate need for her coursed through his being. He knelt by her side and tenderly touched his lips to hers, tasting the sweetness of her mouth.

Grainne opened her eyes and joy surged through her. She lay passively as with an infinite delicacy he drew her clothing from her and her own desire mounted as she saw the smooth muscularity of his lean body. For brief seconds he let his eyes travel down her body and she gloried in the knowledge that he found her beautiful to look upon, her breasts pale globes crowned by dark jutting nipples, her belly rounded and firm, and her womanhood a warm black invitation between her smooth white thighs. She reached up for him, hungering for his manhood to fill the aching, needing void within her, and she heard his breath sobbing in his throat as their flesh gently merged and mingled. She gasped as his throbbing maleness entered her and her arms and legs enfolded him with a joyous welcoming passion. No word was spoken because no word was necessary for their communion. Only the delirious, delicious, fiercely tender knowledge of each other's pulsing bodies.

It was many hours later and night had come before the lovers went down to the long room where Callaghan, Maggie Nolan and the blind fiddler were waiting. When Con and Grainne had not been physically loving they had talked. But each time Con asked for news of Father Boyce, Grainne could not bring herself to tell him of the priest's death. Instead, in an effort to divert him from this dangerous topic she would smother him with kisses and tease him with caresses, inflaming his desires until all thought was submerged by physical delight.

But once they had come down to the long room, Denis Callaghan, half-drunk, blurted out the news almost in the instant of reunion with his friend.

'No!' Con exclaimed in horror, his dark eyes wide and unbelieving. 'But how did the Peelers find out?'

Denis Callaghan had long since guessed that Grainne had told them, and felt a terrible guilt because it was he who had implanted the idea in her head. Lacking the courage to inform himself, he had in all truth forced her to assume the dreadful burden. Neither of them ever spoke of it to the other, but it lay between them, and both shrank back from it in bitter self-disgust and remorse. Now Callaghan averted his red-rimmed eyes, and covered his guilty reactions by swigging poteen and singing a broken snatch of song instead of answering Con directly.

'It had to be an informer, didn't it?' Con stated definitely, so upset with the news that he had failed to notice Callaghan's prevarication.

'Of course it had to be an informer. Bad cess to the evil bastard, may he rot in Hell!' the blind fiddler spoke out angrily from his seat at the hearth.

'Is there any notion about who it was?' By now Con's initial shock was rapidly metamorphozing into a coldly savage lust for revenge.

The blind man spat expressively into the fire, his

aesthetic features displaying hatred like a banner. 'No one knows, bad cess to them!'

Grainne sat silent, all the joy draining from her and the terrible guilt she bore tearing at her heart like some ferocious beast.

Con went on badgering his friends with a stream of questions but they could add nothing which would give him any clue as to the informer's identity.

'Well, there's one good thing come out of it anyway,' Denis Callaghan remarked with satisfaction. 'There'll be no bloody rebellion in these parts now. What with all the guns being took, and those hotheads who arn't killed being on the run. There's no one left to lead the idjits who want to fight.'

'You're wrong there, Denis,' Con Shonley stated with grim calmness. 'There'll be men from these parts to join the rebellion if I have to lead them myself into the fight.'

'Oh God, no!' Grainne gasped softly, a sickening despair engulfing her as she heard his words. Was it all for nothing? Had she betrayed a good man and been the cause of his death for nothing? Had she taken a mortal sin upon her soul for nothing? She stared piteously at Con, and he felt a guilt-inspired resentment as he saw the mute appeal in her frightened eyes.

'Now why do you look at me so?' he asked her, tenderness and irritation mingled in his tone.

With desperation in her voice and heart she burst out, 'Oh Con, I thought we'd get married now, and go to America. I've money enough. Look!' With a feverish eagerness she pulled the small leather bag from her skirt pocket and showed him the gold coins it contained. 'There's enough, and more than enough to get us away from here, Con.' Her voice was tremulous and pleading, and she could do nothing to steady it, so great was her distress. 'Please Con, let's marry and go! Please! If you don't want to wed me, then it doesn't matter, we can still go together to America. Please, say yes, Con.'

Her green eyes were huge with tears and they imparted to her face a beauty so poignant as to be heartbreaking.

Con felt the love he bore her tighten his chest and constrict his throat. How could he ever bring himself to hurt this girl-woman whom he adored above all else in life. He swallowed hard, and blurted out, 'Let's talk no more of it now, my lovely girl. I've had too much distressing news already this night. My head is aching with it. Let's go to our sleep, and we'll talk in the morning.'

Grainne was too upset to argue further, and with a heavy sadness weighing upon her quietly acquiesced.

Although bone-tired from the effects of his long journey and the shared passions of reunion with Grainne, Con could not sleep, but instead lay awake through the hours of darkness, his mind in turmoil and the memory of Father Boyce a grieving despair. At dawn he rose leaving Grainne dozing fitfully, and went downstairs.

Denis Callaghan was sat on a bench, his upper body sprawled across a trestle table, and a half-empty stone jug of poteen within reach of his mouth. He was snoring loudly and muttering in unquiet sleep.

The peat fire was still smouldering and Con rebuilt it with fresh blocks of fuel before going out to the wash house pump and gouting jets of icy water over his head and bare torso. He dried himself on his shirt and replaced it before going back into the long room. Shivering with cold he took a mouthful of the poteen and was grateful for its fire biting and spreading through his chilled tissues.

Callaghan snorted horribly, and came awake with a jerk, his hands trembling from the effects of too much raw alcohol in his system. Without a word Con handed him the stone jug and Callaghan snatched at it and sucked greedily at the narrow mouth. He put it from him and groaned aloud, rubbing with both hands at his red-rimmed, sleep-bleared eyes, and frowsty shaggy hair.

After a while the refurbished fire glowed redly and gave off a comforting heat. The two friends chatted quietly. There was work in plenty once more for the burial men and Con decided to go and ask Doctor Donovan to let him join them again.

'I need to earn money, Denis. Grainne and I can't eat

223

air, and I'll not take that money she earned working for Kearney from her. It wouldn't be right.'

Denis Callaghan glared at him angrily, and snarled, 'By Jasus, boy! But your head must be as thick as a plank. Why don't ye get wise, ye young idjit. Marry yon wee girl and get off with her to America as soon as ye can. Use the money she has. That's what she wants. She's a jewel of a girl, and she loves ye more than she loves her own life. What badness in ye is making ye torment her so?'

Con felt an initial flash of angry resentment at the other's words, but realized the justice in them, and cooled down. 'Denis, I can't help myself,' he pleaded for understanding as he searched for words with which to explain his motives. 'I love Grainne, and I'd gladly die for her, but I can't go now to America with her. Not until I've struck my blow for Ireland. I don't know myself what drives me, but it's something so strong and demanding within me, that I'm powerless to struggle against it. I only know that I've got to stay here and be part of the fight for my nation. If we fail, so be it! But the attempt must be made, and until I've been a part of that attempt, I'll never be at peace in my heart, and I'll never be free of what is holding me here . . . I cannot help it, Denis!' He gripped his friend's shoulder and squeezed hard, so distraught were his emotions. 'I cannot help being like I am; and God knows, it is a torment that rends my heart in two every time I look at my sweet Grainne!'

With that last outburst of despondent acceptance, he got to his feet. 'I'm away to see the Doctor.'

Callaghan belched resoundingly, and took another swig of poteen, then spat into the fire. 'Ye're one o' the damned, Conrad Shonley, my poor young friend,' he muttered bitterly, 'ye're one o' the damned!'

Doctor Donovan was an exhausted man, and the physical effects of his strength-sapping fight against the ravages of the famine were witnessed to by the tremor of his hands, his grey complexion, and the tired, deep-sunk eyes which now regarded the young man in front of him with ambiguity.

'So, you wish to rejoin your friend Callaghan in my employ, do you?'

'I do, Sir,' Con replied firmly.

The elder man sighed wearily. 'In all truth, Shonley, I've a use for your strength of body, but your political disloyalty makes me reluctant to employ you.'

His sojourn in prison had hardened Con's attitudes towards those who were counted his worldly superiors. 'Indeed, Sir, I cannot think that any corpse cares what loyalty the man who buries it holds to.' His tone took any suggestion of insolence from the words.

'Truly said,' Donovan acknowledged gravely. 'Tell me, are you even yet prepared to fight under the rebel flag should an uprising break out?'

Con didn't try to hedge his words. 'Yes Sir, I am . . . But until that time should come I am also prepared to work and earn my way in the world.'

The other man turned from him, and from a cubbyhole in his desk took a broadsheet. When he faced his companion again, a light of anger burned in Donovan's sunken eyes. 'All my life, Shonley, I have been dedicated to preserving the lives of my fellow human beings. I have been witness to such agonies of mind and body suffered by human beings, that I have come to loathe all forms of violence and mindless destruction.

'The men you are ready to follow, and blindly follow apparently, are dedicated to bringing yet more agonies and sufferings upon our poor wretched people. This rag calls itself, *The United Irishman*. Hark to what it contains . . . '

He went on to read in a voice, strained by anger, ferocious directions for street-fighting. Blood-curdling descriptions of how to manufacture hand-grenades from empty bottles and vitriol acids. Of how to tempt soldiers into narrow streets and alleyways where heavy objects and boiling water could be poured down upon them from the rooftops, to smash and scald flesh and bone. Of how to construct barricades to guard against infantry attacks, and how to use broken glass strewn in roadways to prevent cavalry charges . . .

Before he had finished the paper Donovan cast it aside in patent disgust. 'There, Shonley!' he burst out, 'there are the words published only this week of these self-styled patriots. They are an obscenity in the eyes of men like myself, who have spent our lives trying to ease pain and hold back death.'

The gentle doctor's virulence took Con by surprise. Never before had he seen Donovan in such a mood.

'I still have the money left by Mr Mahoney for your use, Shonley. Why do you not use it to leave this land? You are young, your life stretches before you. Why waste it in this arid hatred for those whom God has seen fit to make your rulers?'

Con's own mood had hardened as he had listened. 'Do not attribute foreign tyranny to divine intention, Doctor Donovan,' he answered levelly. 'I came here only to ask for work. Work of a type which few men even now are prepared to undertake. They would sooner risk starving. I did not come here to be taken to task for my personal beliefs. If you wish to refuse me work, then tell me straightly. Do not subject me to lectures and personal attacks which good manners preclude me from replying to in kind. All I wish to hear from you, Sir, is a plain, yes, or a plain, no.'

For a moment the two men glared hard at each other, then again Donovan's weary sigh gusted from him, and he turned his back to stare through the window. Rubbing his fingers across his temples and without looking at Con, he said, 'Very well, Shonley, my answer is yes. You may again become one of my burial men . . . But I will tell you frankly, that I have no longer any sympathy with you. You need expect no favours or kind words from me in the future. I shall continue to keep Mr Mahoney's money here; and if at some future date you should change your mind about taking it, then come to me at that instant, and I will have it ready for you.'

He did not turn from the window until the young man had gone from the room.

Con walked back towards Skibereen feeling a sensation

226

of hurt and loss, that his relationship with the doctor, once one of mutual liking and esteem, should have become so eroded in both respects.

Grainne came awake with a start. For a few moments she lay half-dazed by sleep and then the memories of the night crowded in on her and she felt a simultaneous urge to laugh with joy and weep with sadness. The faint warmth left by Con's body still lingered in the bed beside her and she turned, burying her face in the coarse linen, breathing in the scents left imprinted by her lover's flesh. Remembering her distress of the previous night she grimaced ruefully.

'Love has weakened me,' she decided. 'It's sapped my courage, when instead it should be an added source of strength to me.' Her full lips firmed. 'It shall be a strength to me from now on.' Her determination steeled. 'I'll get Con and me away to America somehow or other. I'll get us away.'

She rose, dressed and went downstairs to wash. Afterwards, skin clean and tingling from the cold water of the pump she went into the long room where Denis Callaghan was nursing his hangover before the peat fire. What he told her brought fresh anxieties flooding into her, and she hurried out to go in search of her man.

She met him on the edge of the town. 'Is it true what Denis tells me, Con?' she questioned, the moment they came face to face. 'Are you becoming a burial man again?'

He nodded, and her face became crestfallen. Con essayed a tentative smile. 'Come now, honey, the work is well paid. We'll be able to eat good food and clothe ourselves warmly.'

'And what use will good food and warm clothes be to us, when you're lying in a coffin through taking fever from those you bury?' she protested sullenly.

'I'll take no fever,' Con spoke with an absolute certainty which had abruptly burgeoned in his mind. 'Grainne, my love, I'm sure that there is a destiny that I'm meant to fulfil . . . I'm sure of it . . . And I'm also sure that some day you and I will go to all those places that we only dream of now. We'll go to America, to France, to Germany, perhaps to China and the Indies even; and we'll go as citizens of a free nation. As subjects of the Irish Republic, able to hold our heads high, and be proud of that liberty.' His spirits soared as he talked, and a wave of happiness filled him, flushing his face and bringing a hint of laughter into his voice. His infectious optimism touched Grainne, and she was sufficiently influenced by it to smile and clasp his arm tightly with her own as side by side they walked through the streets of Skibereen.

A shadow might have fallen across their mutual happiness if they had noticed the two men watching them through a window of a shebeen at the bottom of Old Chapel Lane.

'There now, Michael, there he goes now.' It was the man who had turned his back on Con Shonley who spoke.

Michael Kearney's heavy-jowled features were a mask of hatred as he saw the young couple pass by, and noted the loving clasp and shared smiles. Almost to himself the Gombeen Man growled, 'Look at that wee whore, how she clings to the young scut. I owe those two whelps. They've both done me down . . . And Michael Kearney's not the man to sit easy and let them away with that.' He moved his ponderous head in slow arcs. 'No, indeed, he's not . . . I know how to fix that Shoneen bastard, and his thievin' whore . . .'

Chapter Thirty-Two

During the early spring of 1848 it seemed that Europe had exploded, and cast off the chains of the existing ruling establishments forever.

The Sicilians had revolted in January, forcing their king to concede a constitution. In February the French had taken to the barricades and their king, Louis Phillipe, had fled to England. The King of Prussia was forced to hide like a fugitive in Potsdam when his oppressed subjects took to arms. In Vienna the Emperor of Austria trembled, and his reactionary minister, Metternich, flew for his life as the Viennese put the government troops to terror-stricken rout. On the plains of Lombardy the Milanese drove out their Austrian rulers, and in ancient Venice La Serenissima, a provisional government was declared and the armouries and powder magazines seized by triumphant insurgents.

Even in rich, secure and mighty England mass unemployment had increased the numbers of the working class Chartist Movement to millions, and revolution was openly threatened by the hotheads among them.

The leaders of Young Ireland were ecstatic!

'Ireland's opportunity, thank God and France, has come at last! Its challenge rings in our ears like a call to battle, and warms our blood like wine,' Gavin Duffy proclaimed for the world to hear. 'We must answer, if we would not be slaves for ever. We must resist, we must act, we must leap all barriers and if needs be we must die, rather than let this providential hour pass over us unliberated!'

His comrades thundered in concert with him. 'If the Government of Ireland insists upon being a government of dragoons and bombardiers, of detectives and light infantry, then up with the barricades and invoke the God of Battles!' wrote Meagher of the Sword in the *Nation* newspaper.

Fintan Lalor was no less eloquent in his call to arms. 'Will Ireland perish like a lamb?' he demanded to be told, 'or will she turn? . . . As turns the baited lion!'

Con Shonley thrilled to their words, and himself longed for the day of reckoning to dawn. 'By God, but it's grand stuff, this. Grand stuff!' His face was alight with his enthusiasm. 'Listen to this, Grainne . . . ' He went on to read aloud the latest diatribe from John Mitchel in *The United Irishman*, and finished by hammering his own knee in applause. Abruptly he became aware that Grainne was not sharing his delight. He couldn't help frowning in annoyance.

'Why must you be so glum all the time?' he complained, and the girl's heart went out to him, he so much resembled a boy rather than a man at that moment. But even though her heart was touched, Grainne refused to soften her manner towards him.

'Sure, you've been nearly a month from prison, and all I've heard from you is talk of war and revolution,' she told him petulantly.

'I've also told you often enough that I love you, have I not?' he answered indignantly. 'But I can't be talking of love every hour of the day and night, Grainne. There are great events taking place in the world, which are also worth talking about.'

Her face retained its sulky pout, and in exasperation Con flung the paper to one side. 'I'm going out,' he told her. 'You've been sulking for days now, and I'm tired of seeing your face so miserable.'

She ignored him, and snatching up his jacket he stormed down the attic ladder and made his way into the street.

He walked aimlessly, thinking back over the happiness of the past weeks. His gruesome work filled nearly all the daylight hours, but he had found it easier to face this time, having learned to detach his mind from what his body was being forced to do.

What had not been so easy to face, however, had been the attitudes of those men he had once drilled with in the valley under the guidance of Phelim Rourke. Con thought that their obvious reluctance even to acknowledge him was understandable if the police were keeping watch on him, which they undoubtedly were. But what was so disconcerting and upsetting was the undercurrent of hostility he sensed in all his old acquaintances who held rebel sympathies. Con wondered if they held him responsible for the deaths of the men involved in the ambush, even though it was no fault of his that they had occurred as they had.

He put his unhappy thoughts from his mind when he came to a street corner where a knot of countrymen, dressed in ragged cloaks and breeches were standing talking together. Con recognized two of the Murphy brothers from Leap village among the men. He greeted them gladly, knowing them as generous, light-hearted youths who had shared many a joke and much laughter with him. They both glanced at him briefly, and did not return his greeting. Con halted in mid-stride and faced the small group.

'Why won't you speak, Tom, or you, Andy?' he asked the brothers in turn.

Each man stared at him for a long moment, and he was taken aback by the naked hatred in their eyes. Then, in sequence, they spat at his feet and turned their backs on him. Con reached forward to take hold of Tom Murphy's arm, determined to have an explanation for their behaviour. A shillelagh touched his hand, blocking its forward motion, and one of the brothers' companions warned, 'Just get on about your business, Con Shonley, and leave the company be.'

Con looked hard at the man. 'What have I done to them, or to any of you, that you should act this way towards me?' He made a conscious effort to speak calmly and reasonably.

'You heard what he said, Shonley. Get away out of it, or it'll be the worse for ye,' another man put in, waving his shillelagh in threat.

'I'll not get away until one of you tells me what is

wrong.' Con spat the words through clenched teeth as his own temper rose.

'Then stay here, blast ye eyes!' the first man yelled, and swung his heavy stick. The blow took Con squarely on the forehead, knocking him to his knees. His senses reeling, he tried to come to his feet and fight back, but more shillelaghs flew and he was battered onto the dirt.

Slowly he came to his senses, and pushed himself upright, clutching at the rough surface of the wall to steady his swaying body. His attackers had disappeared, and only two thumb-sucking children gazed at him with large-eyed curiosity.

Con put his hand to his head and his fingers stickied with blood. One of his eyes had swollen and was rapidly closing, and already the bruises on his upper body were making their painfully throbbing presence known whenever he moved. Con could bear the bodily pains with a stoic fortitude, but his heart was sick within him, and his mental torment almost unendurable.

'Why?' he kept asking himself, 'why should they do this?'

'I'll tell ye why.' In Mulrooney's kitchen, Maggie Nolan put her hands on her hips, and tossed her shaggy mop of hair back from her red-mottled face. 'It's because they think that you informed agin Father Boyce, so that ye could get outta Spike Island!'

Con's single open eye widened incredulously.

'Shut your big mouth, woman!' Denis Callaghan shouted at her, and she turned on him like a virago.

'I'll not shut my mouth, and neither you nor any other man will make me,' she stormed, and pointed one grimy hand at the seated Con. 'The poor bowsy has near been bate to death, and him not knowing what for . . . Well, he's got to know, and it's me that'll tell him, because ye haven't the guts for it.'

Con had collected his thoughts. 'Maggie,' he said gently, 'now calm yourself, and tell me what you know.'

The woman's angry eyes softened as she looked at his

battered head. 'It's like this, Con dear, I was down in Clancy's shebeen . . . '

She saw Callaghan scowl and again turned on him. 'No need for you to lose your rag about that, Callaghan. Ye're not me husband, and I was only down there for the wee drink . . . ' Her man subsided, partly cowed, and she went on to Con, 'Anyways, like I was saying, I was down at Clancy's having me wee drink in the corner, and who should come in but yon Gombeen bastard, Kearney, with some of his scum friends.

'Well, didn't I sit like a bloody statue, and they not noticing me there, went on shouting their mouths off, saying that it was you who had told the Peelers about the guns under the chapel, and about Father Boyce hiding Tumelty. They said that was why ye'd been let out from Spike Island to reward ye for it, for shopping Boyce. Kearney said he's seen ye talking with the Peelers since ye'd been back here in Skibereen, and didn't he say that ye'd been arm in arm laughing with Sergeant Macarthy, and the Limey, Hardy, like ye was a band o' brothers . . . '

A terrible fury burned in Con's mind. 'I've been like a blind man!' he castigated himself aloud with disgust. 'I thought that the people here blamed me for the deaths of those men in the ambush. Because five was too high a price to pay to try and get a nobody like me out of jail . . . I never dreamed that they were thinking that I'd informed against the Father.' His voice rose, 'By God, I swear that I'll kill that animal Kearney!'

Grainne had been bathing his swollen eye while the talk was going on around her and each word of it had been like a physical blow directed at her. It was only by exerting every atom of her will-power that she had been able to go on with what she was doing. But now, hearing Con's wild threat, fear clutched her like a nightmare, and she burst out, 'Don't say that, Con. Let's just take what we have and leave here.'

'Why should we leave?' Con questioned angrily. 'I was beaten worse than a dog in Bandon barracks, and I never told the Peelers anything. I was offered bribes in Spike

Island, and I never spoke a word. They were threatening to hang me for something I hadn't done, and I would have gone to the gallows with my lips closed. I've proven my loyalty to the Cause. So, should I now leave because an animal like Kearney tells lies about me which some idiots appear to believe in? No!' he finished adamantly. 'No! I'll not leave! I'll call Kearney out in front of the whole town, and I'll force him to speak the truth, if I have to near kill him to get it from him.'

Grainne's heart was palpitating with terror. She had not told Con about Kearney's attempt to rape her, and her subsequent blackmailing of the Gombeen Man. Now she was terrified of her lover finding that she had withheld this from him, and then doubting her in all other things. 'Holy Mary, save me,' she begged silently. 'Don't let Con find out what I've done. I've sinned, that I know, and I beg forgiveness for it, but I only did it for the best.'

'Hey, go steady, girl. That's damned sore.'

Con's groaned protest brought her out of her thoughts. In her agitation she had been pressing at his wounded eye as if she were scrubbing stained clothing. 'I'm sorry, love,' she apologized. 'I'm upset at what you say, that's all.'

'Listen to me, boy.' For once Denis Callaghan was sober, and he had guessed at the reason for Grainne's agitation, and sensed her fears. 'There's nothing to be gained by you calling out Kearney. Even if you bate him half to death and he tells the world he was lying, then the world will only say that he changed his tune because of the beating he was taking . . . Why don't you be sensible, and do what Grainne wants. Leave here now, today, and go to America. What use is it for you to stay here, when every man's hand is agin ye. Just go away and forget all about what's happened. It's done now, and can't be undone. Leave these bloody Young Irelanders to stew in their own juice, and build a new life for Grainne and yourself in America.'

Maggie Nolan added her urgings. 'Denis is right, Con. Go to America. Get out and leave these scum behind ye . . . Besides, look at the state ye're in. Ye'll stand no chance agin Kearney and his blaggards like that, half-blind afore the fight starts even.'

'Then I'll just have to wait until I'm healed before I call him out, won't I,' Con stated with a determined finality, which caused his friends to fall silent, knowing that nothing they could say would move him from his intentions . . .

'God help me now,' Grainne begged silently. 'Give me the courage to cope with whatever is coming . . . '

Chapter Thirty-Three

Grainne was aware of the new life forming itself in her body. The morning sickness had only confirmed what she had already sensed. She was bearing Con's child. Her reactions were mixed. One part of her was clamorous with joy, the other part afraid, and doubtful of her hold on her lover, doubtful that she could ever really win him from that other love that so consumed him.

'Before I tell Con, I'll make sure of it being true,' she decided, and went in search of Doctor Donovan. The medical man listened to her without making any comment, then after a careful examination, told her, 'Yes, young woman, you are pregnant, and also unchurched, I see.' Grainne flushed with embarrassment as the man went on, 'I take it that Con Shonley is the father?'

Grainne nodded.

'Does he know that you are expecting his child?'

Grainne shook her head, her eyes downcast.

'Will he marry you?'

Grainne nodded. 'I think so,' she whispered.

The doctor smiled sympathetically. 'Then he'd best make an honest woman of you as soon as possible, my dear . . . But why you young fools bring more mouths into this cruel world to be fed in time of famine, I cannot for the life of me understand.'

Grainne walked back to Mulrooney's nursing her knowledge, and silently begging Mary the Mother of God to help her, and to protect her unborn baby.

*　　*　　*

Con and Denis Callaghan were digging a grave in the ruins of Abbey Strowry when the doctor rode up on his horse and called, 'Shonley, a word with you, if you please.' With a sombre expression he watched the tall young man make his way across the hummocky ground, and saw the attraction that the swarthy handsome features and powerful physique would exert on females.

'Yes, Doctor Donovan, what is it?' Con's bruises were clearing, and only a rim of discolouration remained around his eye.

'Your sweetheart, Grainne MacDermott, has been to see me.'

Sudden concern showed in Con's face. 'She's not ill, is she?' he questioned anxiously.

'No, she is not ill, but she is pregnant with your child. I suggest you go to a priest with her as soon as possible . . . Good day to you, young man.' He touched the brim of his black top hat in farewell, and rode away leaving Con staring dazedly after him.

'What did he want?' Denis Callaghan came to stand at Con's side.

'To tell me that Grainne is carrying my child.' Con's lips suddenly curved in a smile of pure joy. 'Isn't that great news, Denis, Grainne and me are going to have a baby!' He threw back his head and the cords of his muscular throat stood out as he crowed aloud in sheer delight, 'By God, I must go to her straight away,' and set off at a run towards Skibereen. When he reached Mulrooney's he burst through the door shouting, 'Grainne? Where are you? Grainne?'

She was sitting on the pallet in the attic room they shared, her fingers nervously twisting and twining on her lap. She heard Con's shouts and the clatter of his boots on the stairs, and her breath became shallow and rapid. 'Holy Mary, help me!' she prayed. 'Don't let him be angry with me when I tell him about the baby. Don't let him turn from me!'

His tousled black curls came into view, and she saw his delighted smile. 'What are we going to call our son?' he

237

demanded excitedly, and Grainne's eyes filled with tears of happy relief . . .

Con went to see Father Barry at the chapel in Skibereen within the hour, and the priest agreed to perform the wedding ceremony in two days' time. Whistling happily the young man hurried back to Grainne. Strangely she did not appear overjoyed at his news. He looked at her with a growing perplexity.

'What's troubling you, honey?'

She rose from the pallet and went to stand by the window overlooking the thatch and tiles of the roofs of Old Chapel Lane. Her face was drawn, and faint lines of strain etched her smooth brow. She summoned all her courage. 'You must do it now!' a voice that would not be gainsaid urged in her mind, and inwardly she answered that voice, 'I will. I'll do it now.'

'There's something I must tell you before we wed, Con.' She spoke tremulously, and her hands kneaded together in agitation. 'It's about the money I have.'

Con's perplexity increased, and he experienced a surge of nervous dread. 'Well tell me then, don't be afraid,' he urged quietly.

She looked at him and her eyes were dark and shadowed as she told him the story of Kearney's attack on her, and her blackmail of him in return. As Con listened his fists clenched spasmodically and a lust to kill the Gombeen Man throbbed through his being.

When Grainne finished she stared at him with an expression full of doubt and asked hesitantly, 'Do you still want to marry me, now that you know how sinful I really am?' And in her mind she thought, 'Dear Jesus, what will I do if he turns from me now? What will I do?'

The fear in the luminous green eyes touched Con's heart, and calmed him. He went to her, and with great tenderness lifted her chin with his fingers, and softly kissed her lips. 'I would want to marry you, my honey, even if your soul was as black as peat with sin,' he whispered.

Tears filled her eyes and spilled upon her pale cheeks.

Con's lips sought and tasted the salt moistness, and he held her close until the sobs ceased to shake her body.

'Someday I'll make Kearney pay for what he has done to you and to me, my love,' Con promised. 'But for now, forget the dirty animal, and think only of our wedding, and the life we are bringing into the world.'

Grainne clung to him with all her strength, and her love was a fierce flame burning away all doubts. 'I love you, Con Shonley! I love you more than I love life itself!' she told him over and over again.

The ceremony in the chapel made little impression on Grainne. For her, Con was already her husband, with or without the blessing of the church. Denis Callaghan and Maggie Nolan were the only witnesses, and Grainne could hear the loud weeping and sniffing of Maggie all through the short service. Grainne looked at the serious face of her husband and felt weak with love.

'By God, I'll never do aught to harm this man of mine,' she vowed silently. 'I'll spend my life trying to make him happy.'

The four walked back towards Old Chapel Lane, and Grainne carried herself like a queen. Con feasted his eyes on her loveliness and thought that never had a man been so blessed as he in his choice of wife.

Grainne's happiness was total. She glimpsed her reflection in a house window and marvelled at how elegant she appeared in her new dark green dress and shawl, and slippers on her feet. Then she glanced up at her husband, and a thrill of pride went through her body, at how handsome and manly he was.

As the wedding party passed through Mulrooney's door, a roar of welcoming cheers greeted them, and Grainne stared in surprise at the transformation that had taken place in the house during the short time they had been absent from it. The long room had never been so clean. Even the stone flags of the floor glowed as if polished, and the walls were bright with fresh whitewash.

The inhabitants of the lodging house had all washed their

hands and faces in honour of the occasion, and Bridget Mulrooney herself was resplendent with flounces and petticoats and a brand new white mobcap atop her frizz of hair. On the trestle tables were ranged stone jugs of porter and poteen, and despite the famine there were dishes of baked potatoes, new bread, oatcakes and meat.

The guests crowded about the newly-weds and Con's hand was pumped and his back slapped by the men, and Grainne's lips reddened by the congratulatory kisses of the women. Grainne felt near to tears, so moved was she by the kindliness of these poor wretches, who despite their poverty had put together all their meagre resources to make her wedding day a time of festivity.

Denis Callaghan got up onto a table, displaying his own finery, a pair of bright blue socks which covered his grimy feet and ankles. His pink face glowed as he shouted, 'Now ladies and gentlemen, and any lords who might be present. We'll have no bloody speeches, except to wish Con and Grainne long life and happiness . . . ' For the first time in weeks Denis was his old self again, and his toothless mouth gaped with his laughter. 'So, let's all drink, eat and be merry, especially drink . . . And where's that bloody old bowsy of a fiddler . . . Let's have some music.'

The blind fiddler struck up with the Black Nag jig, and even before the poteen and porter began their potent flow, heels were beating the rhythm and fingers were snapping in concert. Tin whistles fluted in to join the fiddle's wild music and a bodrhan drum pounded the hypnotic beat. Couples took to the floor and the jigs, hornpipes and country dances filled the hours, while tunes like the Chanter's Rant, The Hag with the Money, Old Molly Hare, Four and Twenty Virgins and the Rakes of Mallow entered the blood like a madness, causing legs, bodies, arms and heads to explode into frenzied flowing motion.

Con and Grainne danced and drank and ate and laughed and loved, while the old house shook around them, and the distant stars slowly faded from view in the dawning sky . . .

After their wedding night, Con took Grainne to live in a

small cabin some distance from the town, which he had rented from Mr Macarthy Downing. For both young people it was an idyllic period. The spring, although cold, had now brought a degree of warmth to the earth and leafy green buds to the trees and hedgerows where birds sang to welcome the advent of summer.

After his day's work was done, Con would hurry back to his new bride and bathe in the stream and change all his clothes before entering the cabin, so afraid was he of bringing infection with him.

Their nights were by turn passionate and tender, and although both of them had come as virgins to the other, still their lovemaking had from the first been a mutual joy and a complete and fulfilling satisfaction.

The only cloud on Con's happiness was the continued hostility that he met with from those of rebel sympathies in the district. But he bore the hard looks, and occasional shouted taunt stoically, knowing that Grainne would become distressed if he resorted to physical violence in retaliation. Several times they had awoken to find the outside walls of their neat cabin smeared with human and animal excreta. For Grainne's sake, Con would smother his hot rage, and simply clean and wash the walls, knowing that no matter what insults might be directed at him, his happiness was only dependent on Grainne's well-being.

The only matter on which they differed was Con's continued refusal to emigrate to America. Grainne constantly reiterated her pleas that they should go, but Con equally constantly refused to consider leaving Ireland. It was an overwhelming compulsion for him to remain in this unhappy land, and he was powerless to resist it.

Michael Kearney's hatred of the young couple smouldered ever more fiercely. He was torn by jealousy and lusted for revenge. He continually urged on his cronies to find means of harassing Con Shonley. Since the young man kept himself from town life during his free hours, opportunities to do him harm were few, but Kearney watched, and waited, and hoped . . .

*   *   *

Grainne and Con had been visiting Mulrooney's and had spent most of Saturday in company with their friends there. Arm in arm the young couple walked from the lodging house, and laughed together at some parting quip of Denis Callaghan's, who these days had recovered his old light-heartedness.

Michael Kearney was drinking with some of his friends in Clancy's shebeen, and one of the men with him pointed through the window at the lane.

'See who's coming, Michael!'

The Gombeen Man's brutish features twisted in hatred. 'Will ye look at them!' he spat out. 'Lord bloody Muck and his mott . . . Come on, boys, let's have a bit o' sport with the Shoneen bastard.'

Grainne saw the men emerge from the low doorway of the shebeen, and recognized Kearney. Her hand involuntarily tightened on Con's arm, and she drew in a sharp nervous breath. Con noticed her apprehension, and frowned when he saw who had caused it.

'Just ignore them, Con, if they say anything,' she begged in a whisper.

He nodded grimly. 'I will, honey. I don't want to put you at risk by getting into a fight. We've the baby to think of.'

Kearney's mood was ugly with drink, and now he shouted, 'See who's here, boys, the fuckin' Shoneen Milord himself . . . Informer Shonley in person.'

The Gombeen Man's cronies jeered raucously, egging their leader on.

'Will ye look at his mott?' Kearney bellowed, enjoying the sensation he was causing among the passersby and loungers. 'Grainne MacDermott as used to be. Isn't she the fine-dressed lady now, with shoes on her feet and all. But then, all whores dress well. They earn good money on their backs . . . Easy work it is too, just laying there with their legs open . . .'

Inside Con's head a sharp pain was throbbing, so intense was his rage. The width of the lane divided him from Kearney, and Con desired above all things to cross that narrow width and smash his fist into the foul mouth that spewed such filth from its liver-lips. Grainne's grip on his arm was so tight that her fingers dug deep into the hard muscles beneath the jacket sleeve.

'Please Con, ignore him! Please!' she pleaded frantically.

And Con, loving her as he did, made a supreme effort of will and forced himself to walk on with his head held high and his eyes fixed straight ahead.

'Arrah, he's a yellow-gutted bastard, is the Shoneen!' Kearney sneered loudly. 'Hasn't got the guts to stand up like a man and resent an insult. He'd sooner go sneaking to his friends, the Peelers, late at night, and do his informing in secret. He's like his fuckin' father. He was another yellow-gutted, English-loving bastard, and he was married to a whore as well.'

Con's teeth gritted together with such force that they seemed in danger of breaking, and he felt the hot flush of angry shame that turned his face a fiery red.

'Come on, Con. Please don't stop, keep walking and ignore them,' Grainne's frightened pleas dinned into his ears, and he tried to concentrate solely on them, and shut out the voices of Kearney and his hangers-on. Slowly the shouted insults and abuse fell behind, finishing with a hurled barrage of rubbish picked up from the alley's rutted surface. The missiles fell short, and at last Con and Grainne were free of their tormentors. Con's body shock with tension, and he drew breath in great shuddering gasps.

'I'll kill that filthy animal some day,' he jerked out. 'I swear on my dear father's grave, that I'll kill him.'

Grainne's green eyes were fearful as she saw and sensed the tumultuous emotions raging through her husband.

'Don't do anything that will take you from me again, Con. Please don't! It would be the death of me to lose you.'

It seemed as though he could no longer hear her voice. He walked as if in a dream, only the redness in his eyes showing the bloodlust in his soul, for having been made to look the coward, that above all other things, he was not, nor ever would be . . .

Chapter Thirty-Four

April became May, May became June. The leaders of
Young Ireland addressed massed meetings all across the
country; and those thousands of desperate people at the
meetings called for arms, food, and leadership. The leaders
of Young Ireland promised them that all these things would
be theirs, and in the very near future.

In Dublin Castle the leaders of the Government adminis-
tration sat in the middle of their webs of detectives and
informers, and in concert with their masters, the Government at Westminster, made their own promises, and
preparations . . .

William Smith O'Brian and Meagher of the Sword were
arrested and put on trial for sedition. Both juries refused to
convict, and the two Young Irelanders were released to a
triumphant welcome from their supporters. John Mitchel,
the fiery editor of *The United Irishman* was next to be taken
and tried on May 25 on charges under the new Treason
Felony Act. He was convicted, and sentenced to fourteen
years' transportation.

Another triumph for the Government was the alienation
of the Irish clergy, both Catholic and Protestant, from the
rebel cause. Whereas in the rising of '98 the rebel priests
could be counted in tens of hundreds, support for the
Young Irelanders among the priesthood could barely be
numbered in tens.

More and more troops were poured into Ireland,
because the politicians in London took the wild claims of
the Young Ireland leadership to have an army of hundreds
of thousands, at face value. Dublin took on the appearance
of a city under siege. Its streets swarming with scarlet, blue

and green uniforms, and its great public buildings such as Linen Hall, Trinity College, the Custom House and others requisitioned as barracks and strongpoints for the newly arrived garrison.

With no money, few arms, few trained officers, but an abundance of dreams, the Young Ireland movement commenced formal preparation for rebellion; and such was their naïvety that those preparations were completely unconcealed. The police knew of them in detail, and the newspapers entertained their readers with full descriptions of the rebel Confederate Clubs, now rapidly training and increasing in numbers throughout the country.

Never had a rebellion been so openly proclaimed in advance, by those who sought to lead it . . .

They came from the slopes of the Sheehy and the Boggreragh and the Derrynasaggart mountains. They came from the shores of Bantry Bay, Dunmanus Bay, and Kenmare. They came from the banks of the Sullane, and the Lee, and the Bandon, and the Roughty. They came from the villages and the towns, the bogs, the valleys, and the hills of the counties of Cork and Kerry. They came in their thousands, young men and old, rich and poor, sick and healthy, to the great meeting at Ballymakeera, where Smith O'Brian, Meagher of the Sword and Fintan Lalor were waiting for them.

Near to the ruined medieval church known as Tempall Ghobnatan was a flat, high-wheeled cart, and the three leaders of Young Ireland stood upon its rough planking and looked out over the heads of the vast crowd, ever-increasing in numbers as more contingents arrived. Some marching in grimly intent military-style array, others coming casually as if for a day of pleasure-seeking.

Stationed around the edges of the crowd were squads of mounted policemen and Hussars, and away to one side two companies of the feared Scottish Highlanders of Her Majesty's army were drawn up in dark-kilted, red-jacketed blocks of steel-tipped menace.

Con and Grainne had also come to the meeting, the

presence of the legendary Meagher of the Sword acting as a magnet for the steel in the young man's soul. With them were Denis Callaghan and Maggie Nolan.

Grainne stared with avid interest at the trio standing on the flat cart. Smith O'Brian was tall, soberly-dressed, with a long nose and chin and his hair cut in the style of a medieval knight. By his side Fintan Lalor looked a weakly, broken-bodied squat creature, and his dress of blue cloak, black breeches and floppy caubeen did nothing to enhance his stature. It was Meagher of the Sword who visually most impressed Grainne. A handsome man with dark hair and shining blue eyes, his dress was elegant and his cravat and braiding dandified. Even at a distance he exuded personal charisma and emitted an aura of power.

Augustus Hardy, now promoted to District Inspector Hardy, shared Grainne Shonley's assessment of Thomas Francis Meagher, and thought it a great pity that the man's obvious gifts could not be used in the service of the Queen, rather than against her Government.

With a small patrol of mounted constables Hardy was moving slowly from one squad to another of his policemen, monitoring the mood of the crowd as he rode about its edges. Here and there in the mass of people Hardy recognized individual features and noted some of those present for future reference. One small party to take his attention was that of Con Shonley's. Hardy reflected wryly, ''Pon my soul, Shonley, I would have wagered you had learned your lesson by now. Especially after the persecution your own people have been subjecting you to . . . It seems I was wrong . . . ' He deliberately caught the young man's eye as he led his patrol past him, and saluted in greeting. Con Shonley politely inclined his own head in reply, but his facial expression betrayed no hint of his feelings at having been singled out for notice.

The leader of another group some distance from Con Shonley's had been watching the police progress, and he saw the Inspector's salutation, and who it was directed at. Michael Kearney grinned malignantly, and told his companions, 'Well now, if it isn't the Shoneen himself, and

246

he's got the gall to come here among real patriots . . . We'll have some fun with him by and by, that we will.'

Unsuspecting of the Gombeen Man's presence, Con Shonley and his party waited patiently for the speeches to begin.

Only Meagher spoke. His accent was that of an upper-class Englishman, and surprise showed plainly on the faces of many of his audience when they first heard him. But when he had warmed to his theme his eloquence and sentiments gripped his listeners so strongly that all covert resentment at his anglicized voice disappeared, and their enthusiasm increased by the moment.

' . . . You must be ready!' he finally exhorted them. 'You must form your Confederate Clubs. You must learn to drill and to march . . . You must learn to use your weapons and become an army . . . An Irish army who fights only for Ireland! I say that a deputation of eminent Irishmen shall go to London and tell those gentlemen in the Houses of Parliament that they are being presented with an ultimatum . . . Either we get an Irish constitution, and an Irish Parliament, as we had in 1782, or we throw up the barricades, AND INVOKE THE GOD OF BATTLES!'

A mighty storm of cheering greeted his closing sentence, and from all over the vast multitude voices took up the cry of, 'PIKES! PIKES! PIKES! PIKES!'

Con Shonley's face shone with pleasure and excitement. 'By God, what a man!' he told those with him. 'And what a speaker! I'd follow him to the cannon's mouth, be damned if I'd not!'

Grainne's heart sank as she heard him, but loving him as she did, she could not bring herself to spoil his pleasure by arguing against him, and so remained silent.

The sections of the crowd nearest to the flat cart lifted the Young Ireland leaders aloft and bore them shoulder-high to where their carriage was waiting. Once his three passengers were inside the coachman whipped up his horses and the vehicles rolled swiftly away through the cheering, hat and stick waving mobs. A troop of Hussars went clattering after the carriage and then the masses began slowly to disperse.

Only a slight rounding of her belly and a fuller curve to her firm breasts betrayed Grainne's pregnancy, and she had made little of the long walk to Ballymakeera. Con was concerned about her, however, and said that if the others would wait by the ruined church he would go to the village and try to hire a jaunting-car for the return journey.

Within half-an-hour he was back with a car and a driver.

'Should we call and have a drink before we start the trip? I've a powerful thirst and the dust on the road will choke us near to death,' Denis suggested.

'Do you know of an inn hereabouts?' Con asked the elderly driver, who rubbed his white-bristled chin reflectively, and closed his eyes to concentrate on the question. At last, as the four were exchanging smiles invoked by the oddness of his manner, the answer came.

'Sure now, isn't there an alehouse in the village, or hereabouts?' His tone made the reply into a question.

'Isn't that what we've just asked you, good man?' Denis Callaghan laughed.

Again the rheumy eyes closed and the liver-flecked hand rubbed the bristled chin. Then the balding head nodded. 'To be sure, ye did ask me, and aren't I telling ye that there's an alehouse in the village.'

'Well take us there first, and we'll have a couple of drams to set us up for the road,' Callaghan instructed.

The car was drawn by a strong-backed, raw-boned mule and made good speed, passing the Highland soldiers, and the mounted police who were forming into their different detachments prior to moving off. On the outskirts of the village a familiar voice bawled, 'There goes the informer! He's running to get some poor bowsy hung or transported . . . Shonley's his name, we know him well in Skibereen.'

Grainne's heart thudded painfully, and desperately she hoped Con had not heard. But it was a forlorn hope, and dread gripped her as Con made the driver stop the car, and then stood up and looked about him for Michael Kearney. The Gombeen Man was walking along the road towards the alehouse in company with a bunch of roughs, all of them showing signs of drink and carrying cudgels. Grainne also stood up on the back of the car to hold Con from jumping down.

'Leave it, Con,' she begged, 'for pity's sake, leave it, and let's get away from here.'

Con's face was hard and his eyes cold as he looked at her. 'I'll leave it no longer,' he said angrily. 'I'm sick of trying to avoid trouble with that animal, it just makes him bolder every time we happen to see him.'

'Look at your man standing so bold!' Kearney jeered. 'He got poor sainted Father Boyce killed, and John Tumelty is to hang, and five good men were slaughtered because of that Shoneen bastard. He informed on all o' them to save his own miserable neck.'

The people thronging the village were standing to hear and watch, and many of them were glowering at this young man who was being called an informer. The roughs with Kearney were increasingly aggressive and threatening.

Con jumped down from the jaunting-car. 'I've taken all I can stand from your lying mouth, Kearney, you Gombeen scum, and now I'm going to ram your lies down your fat throat. So let's you and I settle this here and now, or haven't you got courage enough to face me man to man?'

Augustus Hardy was at the head of a large squad of police, and as he rode into the village approaches, his experienced eyes took in and understood the possible repercussions of the scene before him. The meeting had gone peacefully, but the policeman knew that these people were in a highly volatile state, and any incident could trigger off a riot. He would have to stop this present confrontration between these two men becoming that trigger.

With a shouted command he brought his men to a stop, surrounding the jaunting-car and forming a screen of men and horses between the two antagonists.

'Get back onto that car, young Shonley,' Hardy ordered, 'and leave the village. I want no riots here. And you, Kearney, be on your way also!'

When Con still stood, Hardy warned him, 'If you don't do as I say, young man, then I'll have my men take you into custody.'

'Arrah, his friends have come along to save him again.'
Kearney moved slowly away as he shouted, 'You can see
for yourselves that I spoke the truth about the informing
bastard.'

Many of the onlookers growled their hatred at Con, now
convinced that he was indeed one of the despised and
reviled informers.

Con, sick at heart, knew that he must obey the policeman, and reluctantly he turned towards the car on which
Grainne was still standing, her face pale and drawn with
worry. As Con went to step up beside her a thrown cudgel
came twisting over the heads of the policemen and struck
the mule on its hind-quarters. The beast squealed and
jumped, jerking the car violently. Grainne lost her balance
on the narrow footing and was pitched from the boards,
falling heavily face downwards on the stony ground.
Instantly Con was kneeling beside her, his hands gently
turning and lifting her body.

'Are you hurt, honey?' His heart was pounding with
fright.

Her face was white, except for the dirt plastered on one
cheek from the roadway. Her hands clutched her stomach,
and pain lanced through her body like a red-hot blade.

'I hit hard on here, Con,' she jerked out, and her green
eyes were fearful. 'It's hurting badly, I think it's the baby!'

The crowd were jeering and hostile, and Hardy
brusquely ordered his troopers to drive them back into a
larger circle and break up the most threatening mobs. Then
he dismounted and helped Con, Denis and Maggie Nolan
to lift Grainne onto the car.

'You'd best get your wife back to her own home,' the
policeman told Con. 'We'll escort you. This crowd will
turn on you otherwise.'

Con cradled Grainne in his arms and tried to comfort
her. During the long journey she began to lose blood, and
she fainted. By the time Skibereen was reached it was
necessary for Doctor Donovan to be sent for. He could do
nothing . . . Grainne had by then lost her baby . . .

Chapter Thirty-Five

As the days of July passed Con became increasingly worried about his beloved Grainne. She seemed to have lost all interest in life, now that she had lost her baby. Whenever he tried to console her, she would stare at him with tortured eyes, and say only, 'It's God's will, Con. I'm being punished for my sins.' She was racked by this conviction, that the loss of her baby was part of the payment she must make for her blood-guilt for the death of Father Boyce, and the coming death of John Tumelty. But even now she dared not confess to Con that she had informed to save him; and this necessity to bottle her awful self-guilt up inside her was an ever-increasing torment as time went by.

The cabin, once as clean and neat as human hands could make it, was now dirty and odorous, and her own appearance deteriorated as she neglected herself. She would sit for long hours gazing into the fire, and many many times Con would come back from his work to find her sitting by the dead ashes of the fire, no food prepared, no housework done, nothing to welcome him home.

The incident at Ballymakeera had also led to further unpleasant repercussions. The action of the police in escorting Con and his friends out of danger, had come to the ears of the people in Skibereen district in a maliciously garbled form. Now, it seemed that every man's hand was against Con Shonley and he was regarded as a proven informer. Clods of earth and filth were almost nightly hurled against the cabin walls and Con was frequently hooted and verbally abused on the streets of Skibereen and its neighbouring villages.

For himself, he could have faced up to all the lies and abuses, and refused to turn tail, but Grainne was suffering also, and now, when she talked longingly of going to America, Con was increasingly inclined to defer to her wishes and take her across the ocean in search of a new life in a new land. Yet he still could not bring himself to make that final break from his country. Always, when he would listen to Grainne's pleas and be on the verge of saying yes, something within his mind would hold him back, and his lips could not form the word.

In the darkness before the dawn Grainne lay by the side of her sleeping husband. Tentatively she mentally explored her own emotions, and hardly dared to let herself believe in what she found among them. But, slowly at first, and then with an ever-increasing rapidity she accepted the joyous realization that the black cloud of depression that had enveloped her since she had lost her baby seemed to have lifted, and while ecstatic happiness had not replaced it, yet the knowledge that happiness could be hers once more had driven away the demons that had so tortured her for seemingly endless days and nights.

She breathed in deeply, drawing the cold air into her lungs, and her relief was such that she wanted to shout aloud in thanksgiving. Unable to contain herself any longer she turned to her husband and shook him into wakefulness.

'Con! Con, I feel well again,' she repeated constantly, and his eyes filled with tears of thankfulness, and he held her close and stroked her hair, and kissed her tenderly.

He went to his work whistling happily, and equally happily Grainne brushed her long hair until it shone, and carefully dressed herself in her green gown, then singing to herself walked towards the town of Skibereen to shop at the market there, intending to buy beefsteaks to prepare for Con's evening meal, feeling that such an expense could be justified as a celebration of her return to normality.

She was in sight of the market stalls in the centre of the town when a hurled stone struck her agonizingly on the side of her chest and a raucous shout resounded in her ears.

'Dirty mott! Dirty informer's mott!'

It had been a gruelling day for the burial men. Five corpses to be interred, and long distances to be walked between each interment.

Con came up the narrow track towards the cabin, and saw with pleasure that smoke was pluming from its chimney. Grainne must be preparing a meal, he thought happily, remembering how when he had left her that morning she had seemed almost like her old self, and smiled and kissed him, and said that she was going to the market at Skibereen. Con had worked with a light heart this day, feeling that at last the turning point had come, and Grainne was on the road to recovery.

The cabin door was ajar and the late afternoon sunlight was a golden shaft into the dark interior.

'Grainne, I'm home, love.' Con stepped into the room, and saw that the fire was blazing high, then ejaculated in horrified shock. Grainne was crouching naked before the blaze, using a piece of wood to stir her new green dress and shawl so that the flames could consume them quickly. But Con's horror was caused by the sight of his wife's hair. It had been hacked off close to the roots, and even as he watched she laid aside the wood, took up a knife and chopped the last long tresses from her head and pitched them into the fire, where the lustrous raven-black exploded into yellow-red smoke and flame.

'What in God's name are you doing?' his fear made him shout angrily, and he ran across and pulled her up and round to face him. A thick weal of bruised flesh ran down the side of her cheek from eyebrow to chin.

'I had to burn the clothes and my hair, Con,' her voice was level, her manner calm, 'the women in the town threw pitch at me. It wouldn't be possible to clean it off.' She ran a slender finger down the livid weal. 'One of them hit me with a stick. They shouted at me to go from the town and never return. They said I was a dirty informer's mott!'

'Oh dear God!' Con groaned softly, and held her in his

arms, his hands stroking her shorn, defenceless-looking scalp. 'Did you say it was women who did this?' he asked gently, and felt her nodding against his chest.

'Some of the men stopped them, or they might have killed me,' her muffled voice trembled with need, 'Con, let's leave here. Please let's go to America!'

He sighed deeply and harshly, and then in his turn replied, 'Very well, honey. We'll go. I'll collect what money is owed me by Doctor Donovan tomorrow, and we'll leave here.'

She clung to him with a desperate gratitude that was more eloquent of her feelings than words could ever be . . .

'You are taking a wise course, young man,' the doctor said gravely. 'There is naught in this country for you.'

Con made no reply, he was too heartsick at the prospect of leaving Ireland for any words to soothe his feelings. The two men were in the doctor's dispensary, and now the older man rummaged in a cupboard and took from its jumbled contents a dusty brandy bottle, and two glasses. He filled both glasses with the golden fluid, and taking one himself, handed the other to his companion.

'I fear I have not been kind to you, Shonley.' The care-worn features were gentle, and the deep-sunk eyes studied the younger man with concern. 'But, I have watched you closely these last months, and I feel that I have been unduly harsh in my appraisal of you. After all, you are still but a young man, and in their ignorance of life the young can appear unwittingly cruel and unfeeling in the eyes of their elders. So let us part as friends, Shonley.' The doctor lifted his glass. 'And I give the toast of a happy and successful future across the seas for you and your bride.'

The gesture moved Con, who responded gratefully, before they drank.

'Do you not think that you should visit your mother in England, before going to America?' Donovan went on to ask. 'It would be only fitting.'

Con nodded. 'I intend to, Sir. I want to beg her forgiveness, and to attempt to heal the breach between us.'

'Good!' The doctor smiled warmly. 'I'm most happy to hear those sentiments.' He poured more brandy for them both, and then said casually, 'Your friend, Callaghan, will sorely miss you. He was almost in tears when he heard of your imminent departure. He loves you as a brother, and would dearly like to go with you to America.'

To Con it was an additional sadness. 'His feelings are fully reciprocated by myself, Sir. But he has no money for the voyage, nor has Maggie Nolan; and Grainne and myself have barely enough to take us to England and then across the Atlantic. As it is we shall arrive all but penniless in New York. If I had the money I would gladly take Denis and Maggie with us . . . Tragically, I have not.'

'Just so,' the doctor nodded, then increased Con's sense of guilt by adding, 'The poor fellow has suffered much abuse because he refused to abandon his friendship with you. I fear that he will have a hard time of it when you are gone, and he will be left here alone to face his enemies.'

'But what else can I do, but go?' Con questioned in real distress. 'My wife is in a parlous mental condition. To save her health, and perhaps even her sanity, I must take her far away from here.'

'Of course you must, my boy,' Donovan was quick to reassure him, 'but there is a way that you can take your friends with you also.' He paused. 'And to speak frankly, Shonley, I think that you owe it to Maggie Nolan and Denis Callaghan to repay the loyalty that they have so freely shown towards yourself.'

Con sensed what was to come, and began to open his mouth in refusal. But Donovan allowed him no time to voice any protest.

'Take Mr Mahoney's money, Shonley, and use it to save your friends from grief, and to give them a chance to build a new and a better life for themselves. That would be a fine thing to do . . . a truly Christian act!' He continued pouring our arguments against which Con could find no reasonable reply, and at last the young man swallowed his stubborn pride and agreed to the doctor's suggestion.

Donovan smiled happily, and pumped the young man's

hand with great enthusiasm. 'Capital, Shonley! Capital! I am proud to know you.'

Con grinned ruefully, remembering his own stubbornness. 'On reflection, Sir, I think rather that it is I who should be proud to say that I have known you . . . '

To prepare for their journey took only a day or two. The farewells took only minutes. Apart from Bridget Mulrooney and her lodgers there was no one else to wish the four a safe journey. They took the Night Mail coach from Skibereen, each carrying their personal possessions in a canvas sack. The few articles of cabin furniture Con gave to Bridget Mulrooney.

They stayed at Cork only long enough to book rides on a Bianconi Company long-car to Wexford, where they intended to take a ferry-boat to England. The long open car drawn by relays of four horses went through Midleton, Killeagh and Youghal, up and over the Drum Hills and skirted the Monavultagh Mountains on their southern edges heading for Waterford.

Con Shonley was melancholy as he watched the green and lovely landscapes of his homeland pass by, but for the sake of his wife and friends, he tried to maintain an outward show of cheerfulness. At times he closed his eyes and conjured up the voice of his father, who had loved to recite the verses of the bard, Amergin. In his mind Con could clearly hear the mellow accents of Daniel Shonley . . .

> 'I speak for Erin,
> Sailed and fertile sea.
> Fertile fruitful mountains,
> Fruitful moist woods.
> Moist overflowing lochs,
> Flowing hillside springs . . . '

Con would open his eyes and see that same loveliness of vision all about him, and his heart felt as if it were being torn from his body in its lust to remain here in its own land, and among its own people.

Then he would catch Grainne's anxious eyes upon him, and he would force a reassuring smile.

As the car approached the outskirts of the small town of Kilmacthomas, Con saw ahead of them in the road a rough barricade of farm-carts and tree stumps. Soldiers wearing back and fore-peaked Albert shakoes, and scarlet jackets with blue facings and white cross-belts manned the make-shift barrier, and as the driver brought his horses to a standstill, other soldiers carrying short-barrelled Brunswick rifles with fixed sword-bayonets, surrounded the car. The brass badge-plates on the fronts of the tall shakoes were fashioned like flaming grenades, and Con recognized the men's regiment as the Seventh Fusiliers.

Although it was an English regiment the lanky corporal who ordered the passengers out of the car spoke in the lilting accents of the Wicklow mountains. Con stepped down and turned to help Grainne and Maggie follow him. The corporal and two of the privates made a check of the luggage remaining in the car, opening boxes and bags, testing for concealed hiding places in the car's floor and sides.

A long side-whiskered, English sergeant marched up, his silvery-white chevrons glinting in the sunlight. His piercing eyes quickly dismissed the other passengers, who were two nuns and three elderly gentlemen, and selected Con.

'Where are you heading for?' he demanded with scant courtesy, since he saw that the young man wore only the rough-cut clothing of a peasant.

'To England,' Con told him quietly. 'We've come from Cork, and before that, Skibereen.'

The sergeant shook his head. 'You will not be going to England this day, Paddy, and maybe not for quite a while . . . ' He called to the men searching the car, 'Is everything in order?'

'Yes, Sarn't, nothing amiss here. They're not Croppies by the look on it.'

'You can't go by looks in this country,' the sergeant murmured, then said louder, 'You said you came from

Cork, and before that Skibereen on this journey? Any sign of armed men or anything amiss on the road?'

'We did, and have come from those places,' Denis Callaghan interjected, 'and no, we saw nothing amiss on the road, and we'd like to be getting on our way, if it pleases ye. There's a horse change in the next town, and I've a raging thirst to be quenched while they're doing it.'

'Then mayhap you'll be able to quench it at Dungarvan,' the Englishman suggested.

'But we're only after coming from there!' Denis exclaimed indignantly.

The sergeant stepped back so that he could see and be heard by all the passengers, then explained in a loud voice, 'The roads to Waterford are closed to all civilian traffic by orders of the Garrison Commander. This part of the country has been placed under Martial Law; the rebels have come out at last!'

There was a concerted gasp of astonishment and fear from the passengers, and Grainne closed her eyes as if by doing so she could blot out what she had heard.

The sergeant continued; 'All travellers must return to their point of departure, and remain there until this present emergency has been dealt with. Those are the orders of the General Officer Commanding the Waterford Garrison. Failure to comply with those orders will be punished under Martial Law. So I'd advise you kindly to do as you are told.' The man's shako tilted as he squinted up at the sun, and its rays tinted his fair whiskers with bright gold. 'You've a good many hours of daylight still before you. You'd best get on your way back to Cork, and try and find a secure place to stay in by nightfall. Those rebels might catch you, and have some fun. Especially with you ladies.'

'The first bowsy as tries to have fun wi' me, will lose his bollocks in short order,' Maggie Nolan growled, and the two nuns blushed and giggled, their faces rosy in their white whimples.

'Turn these horses, driver,' the sergeant instructed, ignoring the protests and entreaties to be allowed to continue the journey onwards from the passengers.

The driver began to manoeuvre his team, and the sergeant marched back to the barricade.

Con had heard the news with a thrill of wild excitement. The rebels were out at last! The Young Irelanders had struck their blow for liberty!

Hardly able to contain himself he went to the Irish corporal and demanded eagerly, 'What exactly has been happening, friend? We've been on the road for a good while and have heard no news.'

The corporal shrugged his white-epauletted shoulders. 'There's not much news to tell, good man. It came over the telegraph to Dublin that the Government in London had passed a Bill doing away with the Habeas Corpus for Ireland, and begod, didn't your men, them Young Irelanders, jump up like scalded cats and say they was going to fight it out then and there! And since then we heard on Sunday and Monday that Smith O'Brian and his crew were out across the country calling out all them Confederate Clubs to fight.'

'But where are the rebel forces?' Con pressed quickly.

The corporal shrugged again. 'Jasus might know, but I don't. We was told at muster parade this morning that they was a few miles north of here, over the mountains. Up around Callan and Garrick way. But it doesn't really matter a pin where they're at. The bowsies have no chance anyway. We've thousands of troops round this part o' the country, and a lot of organized moveable colums, wi' enough artillery to blow a mountain away, and enough cavalry to hunt down every hare in the land.' The man grinned with something akin to sympathy, 'and that's all them rebels will be for us Queen's men, a load o' running hares. The poor bastards have no chance . . . No chance at all!'

By now Con was the only dismounted passenger and the car was turned and ready to go. Thanking the man for his information, and with his mind whirling, Con went to the others who were shouting for him to hurry.

The tired horses moved slowly and Con sat staring at the blue outlines of the mountains to the north. What was it the corporal had said . . . That the rebels were reported as being only a few miles distant across the high rounded shoulders of earth and rock. The yearning to join those rebels and strike his own blow for liberty twisted Con's innards sickeningly, and he cursed the fate that was taking him away from this land, at the very moment that he, and others like him, were most needed.

Grainne's huge green eyes were intent on her husband's troubled face, and she sensed what was happening inside him. A struggle was raging in her own mind also. She knew that Con would not abandon her and go off to fight. She also knew that by forcing him to run from that fight she was destroying his pride and his sense of manhood.

The faces of Father Boyce, and the dead men from the Bandon ambush rose up in her mind's eye to torment her. Father Boyce had died because of what she had done, and her baby had been part of the blood-guilt she had to pay. But if she forced Con to go with her now, how could he ever feel free of the blood-debt he owed those who had died trying to save him at Bandon?

Even before they had reached Dungarvan, Grainne had reached her decision. She clasped Con's hands with her slender fingers and said softly in his ear, 'When we reach the next town, Con, hire a horse and go north!'

His eyes were incredulous, and he went to speak, but she placed her fingers across his lips. 'We can wait for you in Cork, and if need be take ship from there.' Her features were set and determined. 'If you run from this fight now, Con, you'll never forgive yourself, and some day you will begin to hate me for having caused you to run.'

Denis Callaghan and Maggie Nolan exchanged glances of pure astonishment, but were wise enough to keep their own counsel. This was a matter between man and wife only, and no other person had the right to interfere.

Conflicting emotions pulsed through Con Shonley. With all his heart and soul he wanted to go north. Yet, when he looked at his love's thin delicate face, he knew that he loved her above all else in this world. On a deeper level, however, he accepted what she had said concerning the future, knowing it to be the truth. If he did turn away from this fight for freedom, he would only despise himself, and eventually come to blame his wife for the emotional chains she had bound him with at this time.

Grainne smiled at him. 'Go north, honey,' she whispered, 'for both our sakes.'

His heart pounded wildly and he had never loved her so deeply as at this moment. Unable to trust himself to speak, he could only hug her to him, and cover her face with kisses.

Chapter Thirty-Six

In the central square of Dungarvan Con left the car.

'We'll find a lodging in Cork, and leave an address at the Postal Office for ye to find us.' Denis Callaghan's bright blue eyes were reddening with distress, and Maggie Nolan wept noisily and pressed a sloppy kiss upon Con's cheek.

Grainne clung to her man with all her strength, and though it seemed that her heart was breaking within her, yet she kept the smile on her lips, and fought to contain and master the raging maelstrom within her mind. 'I curse you, Dark Lady of Erin!' she silently raged, 'I curse the evil thing you are doing to me. I curse you for the heartbreak you will bring on so many, many women before this rebellion is over and done with. And I swear by all that I hold sacred that you will only ever take my man from me this one time. I'll never let you take him from me again. I swear to that. I swear to that.' A torrent of grief burst over her, but with a courage that she had never known she possessed, she kept the smile upon her lips and sent her man from her without any words of reproach, telling him only; 'I love you, Con Shonley. With all my heart and soul, I love you. And I'll be waiting for you to come back to me. I'll be waiting, my love . . .'

Knowing that to linger would only increase the mutual pain of parting, Con went quickly away, and could not risk unmanning himself by watching the Bianconi car travel on with his loved ones aboard it.

At a livery stable he hired a strong bay mare, and within minutes was galloping northwards. He followed the road through the pass that bisected the Knockmealdown and

Monavultagh mountains. Within scant hours he had crossed into the County of Tipperary, and at Clonmel Town he stopped to rest his horse. While he waited he drank the cider made from the apples of the great orchards in the surrounding area, and listened to the talk of his fellow drinkers in the inn.

What he heard at first dismayed him. The Young Ireland leaders had been through Kilkenny, Callan, Carrick on Suir and the mighty Rock of Cashel, and in all those places wildly cheering crowds had poured into the streets to greet them. But cheers were all that they received. In each place the local Confederate Clubs had refused to rise in rebellion. They gave a lack of arms as their excuse, or the nearby presence of British soldiers, or the sheer bodily weakness of their half-starved members; and all asked for more time to prepare for the Day of Rising.

'It's all one big cod!' a scarlet-complexioned apple-farmer declared roundly. 'Them Young Irelanders is not different from any other gang of hooligans. In the heel of the hunt they're only fit to talk big, and act small.'

His listeners, with one exception, agreed vociferously, and mocking gibes were directed against the rebels, each gibe greeted by laughter and applause.

Con, standing alone and unobserved by the wooden bar-counter, had noticed the exception. A youngish, be-spectacled man clad in shabby frockcoat and trousers. Pale-faced and slender-bodied he looked what he was, a counting-house clerk. Unobtrusively Con moved to sit next to him, and remarked casually, 'These people here-abouts do not seem over-fond of the Young Irelanders.'

Behind the square-lensed spectacles the man's watery hazel eyes blinked hard. He regarded Con closely, then said, 'If Smith O'Brian, or Meagher of the Sword was to walk in here this minute at the head of their men, those who are now shouting the loudest against them, would be the first to offer them drinks and hurrahs! They hunt with the hounds and run with the hare, these people here.'

'And you?' Con queried.

The man studied Con for almost a minute, then blinked

hard once, twice, three times, before finally replying firmly, 'I say God bless Young Ireland, and what it stands for.' He tapped his knee, and for the first time Con noticed the heavy wood and metal brace that supported the wasted leg. 'If I wasn't a useless cripple, I'd be shouldering a pike for liberty this very minute.' He grinned knowingly at Con, showing a glittering array of porcelain false teeth. 'Arrah yes, my friend, I'd be off in the direction of Mullinahone, for I have it on good authority that there's a gathering of pikes there, and the men that's not afraid to use them.'

'Many thanks.' Con shook the proffered hand, and collecting his horse headed north-west through the flowering furze, lilacs, broom and whitethorn of the Golden Vale, before swinging directly north along the low winding valleys that led up to the Devilsbit mountains.

By keeping to the cross-country lanes Con avoided traffic. At times he saw people in the distance, and once a troop of brass-helmeted, red-coated dragoons appeared on the ridge of a hill and rode parallel with him for some time before disappearing from view. Darkness fell, and still Con rode, his horse frothing and sweating and trembling with fatigue. Then, borne on the wind, he heard the ringing of chapel bells. He slowed his mount to a walk and stared about him through the darkness. He saw a mass of flickering reddish lights in the distance, and the bells sounded louder and nearer as the wind gusted . . . It was Mullinahone!

He dismounted to ease the aching muscles in his hips and thighs and his horse's breath was like a furnace bellows, as it stood swaying, its head hung low and strings of thick mucus dangling from its dilated nostrils. Pity for the poor beast impelled Con to loosen its girth, and leave it where it stood so that it might recover.

He went on foot towards the lights and the crazed ringing of the bells. In the lanes and alleys and the open spaces around the tiny village, men marched and drilled beneath the flaring, smoking pitch-torches, their movements a frieze of red-tinged shadows in the gloom. There seemed thousands of them. Men in rags, men well-clad, old men and youths, tall and strong, thin and weak. They carried long-shafted pikes, and pitchforks and cudgels and shillelaghs, some few had fowling pieces. Their drill was clumsy and unsynchronized and their marching pathetically out of step. But their expressions were grimly earnest, and the sweat shone on their skins as token of the whole-hearted efforts they were making.

Con Shonley's spirit was exultant. This was what he had always longed to witness and be part of; Irishmen come together with the stern intent to free their country, or die trying!

At the local smithy mighty-muscled men in leather aprons and with bare soot-streaked, sweat-shining torsoes, hammered out pikes on the anvil without pause for rest or refreshment; and as each hatcheted-hooked steel head came glowing from the hammer it was tempered and cooled, fitted to its long shaft and eagerly clamoured for by the masses waiting around the smithy.

Con knew that he must find a section to join up with, and he thought it best to seek out the leaders and ask them to place him. At the smithy he enquired of a man where the leaders could be found.

'I don't have the notion, man dear. Ye'd do best to stay with your own Club, until we get the full orders given us. I should think our generals are far too busy to bother with one man alone at this moment.'

The young man experienced an increasing frustration. He had come expecting to be welcomed and enfolded into the ranks of rebellion, and was instead wandering without direction like a homeless waif. He set off through the village once more, and again was struck by the grim determination on the faces he encountered. 'This is the real thing, this time,' he thought with glad satisfaction. 'These men really mean to conquer, or die!'

He came to an open space on which a group of men were standing in two lines, each man armed with a musket or fowling piece. In front and facing them was a rigid, burly, cloaked and caubeened figure, and Con heard this man's voice, and stopped in astonishment.

' . . . It takes months to teach a man his drills, and more months to teach him how to make best use of his weapons . . . And then it takes a battle to make him a soldier!'

There was no mistaking that distinct voice with its sing-song inflexions of speech. It was Phelim Rourke who stood there . . .

For a full hour Con stood to one side watching the men being instructed how to load, aim and fire in unison on the word of command. His initial surprise at seeing Rourke here soon disappeared. After all, for a man on the run what better place to be than among those whose victory would lift the shadow of the gallows from his neck.

Rourke told the men to dismiss for fifteen minutes' rest, and they broke ranks, but there was little laughter or talk among them as they clustered in the pools of light cast by the torches. The large head in its floppy caubeen turned towards where Con was standing.

'Well, Con Shonley, have you no greeting for an old comrade?'

Con walked up to the ex-soldier, and when he reached him said, 'In Skibereen, and Schull, and Leap and Baltimore, people call me the Shoneen Informer. They say that I informed on Father Boyce and John Tumelty to save my own neck.'

The other man's strong brown teeth bared, and he asked, 'Tell me, young Shonley, these people who call you informer, have ye seen any of them hereabouts this night?'

Con shook his head, and Rourke chuckled. 'No, and ye won't see them either. Ye never do see them where the bullets are seeking men's lives.' He held out one vast hand. 'Shake that, boy, I know ye better than those who becall ye!'

A flood of gratitude threatened to bring tears to Con's eyes, and gladly he took the proffered hand in his own strong clasp.

'I've a musket ye can have,' Rourke told him. 'Ye'll be my sergeant. I'm an officer d'ye see, in the army of the

Republic of Ireland . . . Despite what I said to ye in the past, I've always been one o' these bloody silly Young Irelanders at heart . . . Ye've remembered your drills, I hope?'

Con nodded smilingly. 'Indeed I have. I had a good instructor.'

Rourke laughed hoarsely, and hugged the younger man in a rough embrace. 'Good man yourself, Con! I'm real happy that ye've come!'

Con was happy he had come also. He felt in some strange way that he had finally completed a long, arduous, lonely journey, and at last, had come home . . .

Chapter Thirty-Seven

Through the remaining hours of darkness Con drilled with the other men of Rourke's section, and gloried in his ability to perform the complicated evolutions with ease and confidence. When dawn came Rourke called a halt to the work, and the tired and hungry men sat or squatted where they were.

'When will the rations be given out?' one man wanted to know, and his question triggered off a volley of demands for food.

'I'll go now, and find out,' Rourke calmed them, and in company with Con went through the village towards the smithy. All around them the drills had stopped and the men were gathered in expectant groups.

'They're all waiting for food,' Rourke told his young friend, 'and to speak frankly, I think that's what brought a good many of the poor bowsies here in the first place. This part of the country has been hit really hard by the famine. It's worse than in a lot of other places I could name, and they're bad enough, God knows!'

Outside the smithy, Con saw William Smith O'Brian standing in heated argument with a small, white-coated man.

'That wee fella is James Stephens,' Rourke explained. 'He's a quare one for arguing, but a brave wee scut for the cause all the same.'

The ex-soldier saluted the Young Ireland leader. 'It's about the ration issue, Sir. My men are sore hungry.'

Smith O'Brian's eyes were glazed and he seemed to have difficulty in understanding Rourke's words. The little white-coated man gesticulated excitedly. 'There now,

William, what did I tell you. We must have food! The men are starving!'

The tall, long-nosed O'Brian nodded absently, his whole manner suggesting a man existing in a dreamy inner world of his own. 'I've some money . . . Enough to buy a little bread for a few of the men. The rest will have to find their own supplies.'

The drawn, wan faces of those onlookers who had heard him registered dismay. One man threw down his pike in a fit of disgusted temper and walked off. Like ever-widening ripples upon water the news that there was little or no food available spread through the village. Loud grumbling erupted into even louder dissent, and first in ones and twos, and then in tens and hundreds, the men threw down their makeshift weapons, and the trickle leaving the village became a flood.

'There goes our army!' Stephens declaimed dramatically. 'That's the last we'll see of them!'

O'Brian's look was still absent, and his manner dream-like. 'They'll come back,' he murmured. 'They've merely gone to find food. In the meantime we have more important things to do than to worry about filling our bellies. We must take the police barracks here, and make its garrison our prisoners.'

Con Shonley had watched and listened with an amazed disbelief at what was happening before his eyes. Rourke pulled him back, away from the crowd surrounding the leaders, his hard face angry.

'Take the bloody garrison prisoners,' he spat out. 'There's not more than five bloody Peelers there! God blast my eyes, I don't know whether to laugh or cry!' he finished in disgust.

O'Brian and Stephens were now joined by another man, and the trio primed and loaded pistols and with a few pike-armed men walked towards the small police barracks in the village.

Rourke jerked his head. 'Come on, Con. We might as well see what happens.' The two of them followed in the rear of the party.

At the barracks there were no sentinels posted, and the three leaders went through the front door, while their followers clustered together some distance away. After a while the three emerged, and Con saw the mystified expression on James Stephens' features. He felt an increasing mystification himself. For him personally, this revolt was rapidly beginning to resemble some theatrical farce.

After fifteen minutes had elapsed O'Brian formed up his pikemen and again advanced towards the police-station. As he entered the front door, there was a sudden commotion at the rear of the building, and Con saw four or five green-uniformed figures carrying carbines, running from the rear of the barracks towards open country.

By now many other curious spectators had gathered, and when the white coat of Stephens appeared in the front entrance of the barracks, his arms lifted in triumph, a great roar of cheering burst out.

'THEY'VE TAKEN THE BARRACKS! THE BLOODY PEELERS ARE ON THE RUN! THEY'VE TAKEN THE BARRACKS! WE'VE WON! WE'VE WON!'

At Con's side Rourke cursed bitterly. 'Hark to the stupid bastards! Ye'd think we'd won a great bloody victory. Instead of which it looks as if that fool O'Brian let the Peelers cod him so that they could get away with their weapons and ammunition . . . They're all fuckin' mad!' He walked away, still fuming, and Con went with him.

'All our bloody leaders are mad, Con! And by Jasus, so are we mad to be following the fuckin' clowns!'

At this particular moment, Con, with a sinking heart, could only agree with his friend's sentiments.

By midday, of the thousands who had gathered the previous night, only some five hundred remained. Smith O'Brian placed himself at their head and led them north towards the village of Ballingarry. Only a few of Rourke's section marched, and he and Con formed them as a rearguard for the tiny army. In the various hamlets they passed through on their march, people gathered to watch them go by. They stood in gaunt family groups, blue-cloaked caubeened men, shawled women and half-naked, barefoot children. Smith O'Brian exhorted them to join him, but their faces, made seamed and haggard by want and hardship, remained impassive, and none stepped out in reply to his stirring addresses.

At Ballingarry itself another large crowd had gathered, and Con felt optimistic that recruits would join them here. Many men in the watching crowd already carried pitch-forks, mattocks and other improvised weapons. They halted by the Catholic chapel and O'Brian stood on the chapel wall to speak to the crowd. His first announcement was that he could not supply any food. Con's tentative optimism evaporated in only seconds as he heard and saw the bitter reactions of those about him. They were ready to rebel to fill their empty bellies, and the empty bellies of their loved ones, but how could they fight on empty bellies?

O'Brian went on to instruct all volunteers to go home and provide themselves with at least four days' rations of food. Oatmeal, bread and hard eggs, he told them, were the ideal supplies.

Here and there in the crowd jeering laughter could be heard. Most of those present had been, and were, existing on the Government Relief of a pound of Indian maize meal per day . . .

'You are rushing on to your ruin if you heed this man!' The interruption came from a party of black-cassocked priests, who had stood in the chapel yard listening to O'Brian. Their spokesman, a powerful-voiced, hard-featured man, now went into the crowd, calling on men by their names.

'You, Peter Gallagher, and you Tim Tiley, and you Tim Muldoon, go back to your wives and families, you born idjits! This man is trying to lead you on the road to ruin! D'ye want your wives to be widows, and your bairns to be left fatherless? Go home, before ye put yourselves in a state of mortal sin. Ye know well that the Holy Father himself has warned against joining these wicked men who wish to

271

rebel against all lawful and God-given authority. Go home to your families!'

The priest's exhortations took effect with what was for the rebels a heart-breaking rapidity. Men left the crowd and even from their own ranks others laid down their pikes and pitchforks and declared that they were done with such a hopeless cause.

Con saw O'Brian's sallow features crease in anguish, and tears run down each side of the long nose. Within the hour only half of the five hundred who had marched into Ballingarry were still standing in their ranks before the chapel yard.

Phelim Rourke turned to Con and asked, 'Well boy, what about it?'

Con glanced across to where Smith O'Brian walked alone, hands clasped behind his back, his shoulders bowed as if in defeat. The young man experienced an angry stubbornness burgeoning in his own mind.

'I'm not done with it yet, Phelim,' he said from between clenched teeth. 'I'll stay with O'Brian and the cause.'

The elder man grimaced and sighed, then nodded. 'I may as well keep you company. There's precious little other entertainment to be found hereabouts today, anyway.' His brown-stained grin came, and they both chuckled at the irony of his words . . .

Throughout the night men slipped away, and by morning there were only fifty followers left to William O'Brian. He received one recruit during that night, however. Terence McManus, a prosperous young merchant from Liverpool who had crossed to Ireland as soon as he had heard about the revolt. His arrival was a tonic for jaded spirits, and his rollicking laughter cheered the hearts of those who heard it. He was also in a position to cheer their empty bellies for he had come with considerable personal funds and so was able to buy food for the men.

The leaders held a Council of War on Thursday morning. Once it was finished the chapel bells were set ringing and the lanes and buildings of the district scoured for laggard recruits. About a hundred and fifty were finally mustered, and the Council's decision was to march back through Mullinahone and attempt to raise the country around Slievenamon, which was thought to be ripe for rebellion.

Con Shonley and Phelim Rourke were not to march with the others. They were ordered to stay in Ballingarry and train some of the younger and fitter recruits as shock-troops. A meal was made ready before the march began, and while the men were eating, the priest who had talked to them the previous day again passed among them, imploring them to quit the rebel cause. When the order to march was given almost a third of those present obeyed the priest's injunctions, and went home.

Con watched the diminished band march gallantly away, and felt a spirit-draining loss of hope. But steeled himself to go on with the work at hand.

On Friday night the men who had marched for Slievenamon with such gallant high hopes returned to Ballingarry, dispirited and despairing. Years of starvation had taken a heavy toll of physical strength and courage, and it was now becoming obvious to all that there were few men in the country who had the will to fight. Only a handful, instead of the hoped-for thousands of recruits had come forward, and to make matters worse the Government had begun to take its counter-measures. Fintan Lalor and many other leading Young Irelanders across the country had been arrested, and thousands of troops and police were being concentrated at key points preparatory to moving in force against the rebels.

With his section of young trainees, Con Shonley stood guard at the public house near Boulagh Common, Ballingarry, while upstairs the remaining leaders of the Confederate Clubs gathered for yet another disheartening Council of War.

Con watched them arrive, Meagher of the Sword, still dandified and seemingly undaunted. A despondent Smith O'Brian. The diminutive and fiery James Stephens, wearing his now notorious white coat. Terence McManus, Dillon, Doheny, O'Mahoney, O'Donoghue and the rest entered the building and mounted the creaking stairs. Con heard voices raised in anger, and a babbling of vehement disputes, and in his own heart knew that this hare-brained venture he was part of was doomed to utter failure. Paradoxically this inner certainty only reinforced his own determination to see it through to the end, no matter how bitter that end might be.

Just over an hour later the Council broke up, and the leaders went their different ways, some to try and raise other parts of the country for the cause, some to seek arms, some to seek food, and some to make their own escapes . . .

Con dismissed his men, and made his way back to the small hut that he was sharing with Phelim Rourke. The ex-soldier was sitting reading a book by the light of a solitary candle. The pale glow reflected on his bronzed bald scalp and etched shadows in the grooves of his features so that he appeared elderly and somewhat frail. He smiled at his young friend, and said, 'I expect they were loud enough at their talk.'

Con nodded. 'Indeed they were. If loud talk were deeds, then Ireland would be free this very hour.'

'Ireland will be free one day, Con,' Rourke said with conviction. 'But it won't be in my day, or yours I think. After this is all over, you do what I told you to do months ago. Get away to America.'

The young man experienced a sudden aching need to see Grainne and hold her close, and in his mind's eye he saw her beloved face so vividly that she could have been there with him in this very room. He sighed longingly, and then another curious vision filled his mind. An old woman, bent by toil, ragged-shawled, her seamed face haggard with hunger and hardship . . . 'That woman is my real mistress,' the young man suddenly realized with a frightening and foreboding clarity, 'and nothing will ever be strong enough to break the chains that bind me to her . . . She is the Shan Van Vocht . . . She will always draw me back to her breasts, withered dugs and sour-milked though they might be. She will never let me be free of her . . . ' Con Shonley's body shivered with something that was neither cold, nor fear, but precognition . . .

Chapter Thirty-Eight

At dawn they paraded in a field at the hamlet of Farrenrory some distance from Ballingarry. The air was fresh and cool and Con Shonley filled his lungs with its sweetness. There were over a hundred of them standing in three ranks, but less than half of them were armed and only twenty had muskets, or fowling pieces and a few with pistols; and for these guns hardly more than a single charge of powder each. Women were also in the ranks, and they and those men without arms were designated as stone-throwers.

The tall straight-backed figure of Terence McManus moved slowly inspecting the motionless lines. For once he was without laughter, and he looked searchingly into each face as he passed, as if seeking reassurance that they would stand with him.

All around the edges of the field crowds of men, women and children had come as spectators. They were silent and still, and a sense of foreboding crept over Con Shonley. It seemed to his depressed imagination that this day held in store an as yet unperceived tragedy.

After the inspection McManus moved to the front to join Smith O'Brian and James Stephens, and then addressed his minute army.

'Soldiers of the army of the Irish Republic, we will march across the Kilkenny border and link up with our comrades who are awaiting us at Urlingford. Together we will have sufficient forces to attack the police post there. Make ready to move off!' He shouted a series of orders, and the armed men shouldered their pikes and pitchforks and guns, then turned into column of march. McManus

275

was about to place himself at their head when a furiously galloping horseman burst onto the field, scattering the spectators in his path.

'Stay put! Stay put!' he yelled as he neared the ranked rebels. 'The Peelers are coming from Ballingarry way. There's a strong force of them.'

His news created an instant panicky uproar. Men broke free from their lines and clustered about their leaders, shouting and jostling. Con remained at Phelim Rourke's side, and between them they managed to hold their section of musket men steady.

'Mr Rourke, get these people clear of us!' Smith O'Brian bawled, and led by Con and Phelim their section pushed back the excited clusters and managed to clear a space for McManus, Stephens and O'Brian to confer with the newly arrived messenger, John Cavanagh, a leader of a Dublin Confederate Club. After a brief discussion Cavanagh galloped away on a fresh reconnaissance, and the three leaders issued new orders.

Baulks of timber and carts were fetched and a crude barricade was hastily thrown up on the road along which the police must come. Pike and pitchfork men ran out a hundred yards in advance of the barricade and hid themselves in a hollow on the left of the road. McManus took the male and female stone-throwers to the front as well, and they lay concealed with their missiles also on the left of the road.

Some musket men took up positions behind the barricade under the command of Phelim Rourke; and James Stephens brought Con and the other musket men into some nearby houses which commanded the barricade. In a surprisingly short time all preparations for the ambush were completed, and a tense silence ensued, broken only by a devout rebel reciting his rosary in a frantic whispered gabble.

The country surrounding the hamlet was low rolling hills, and from his vantage point up in the window of the house Con had a clear view of their green slopes. He saw a swarm of minute figures coming over the brows of the hills and descending towards the road, and even as he watched them the red-haired man next to him exclaimed excitedly, 'Look there, boys. We've friends on the way, a whole bloody army of them!'

Far down the winding road a column of dark-green uniformed men marching four abreast, carbines sloped on their shoulders and led by a mounted officer came slowly into view. Now Con heard faintly the shrill whistles emitted by the hillside hordes as they also sighted the police.

'Keep steady, boys, and wait for my word of command before you fire,' Con instructed, and peered at the approaching column, estimating its strength at about fifty men. He swallowed hard, nervous at the prospect of fighting, yet at the same time elated that at last he was going to strike his blow against the oppressors of his nation.

On the road behind the police more masses of people were coming and Con's excited window-mate hooted with glee.

'By Jesus, isn't this just the ticket! Look at them there. Must be the whole of Tipperary coming to help us fight.'

Con shook his head, smiling wryly at the red-haired man. 'It's more likely they're coming to watch us fight, not help us . . .'

Sub-Inspector Trant, the mounted officer, did not share Con Shonley's views on the masses of countryfolk advancing against his small column. An elderly man who had grown grey in the police service, what was now happening was alien to his experience. The piercing whistles shrilling out from the hillsides were eerily unnerving, and every few seconds he rose in his stirrups and looked back across the peaked forage caps of his men. To his rear, left flank and front, thousands of men and women were apparently hurrying to surround his force. To his right he saw a road winding up a long shallow-sloping hill.

'Corporal Donleavy, where does that road lead to?'

'Towards the Kilkenny border, Sir.'

'Very well.' The inspector pondered briefly, and then ordered the column to wheel to the right along this new road. As the police veered the whistling intensified, and faint shouting sounded from Trant's old front of advance. Peering towards the shouting he noticed for the first time the uneven outlines of the barricade, and heaved a sigh of thankfulness that he had had such a narrow escape from what looked to be the focal point of the rebel ambush. Again he rose in his stirrups and stared wildly about him. The masses of men and women were running now and paralleling his line of march on both flanks and the rear.

'Quicken the step, men,' he ordered, 'quicken the step!'

The sweating constables behind him were becoming infected by the officer's obvious nervousness, and they increased the pace until it became almost a run.

The shouting from the barricade was being done by the Young Ireland leaders, who saw the police swing away from their line of advance, and assumed that their own ambush had been discovered. Smith O'Brian, a military style green and gold kepi covering his medieval haircut, ran to the house where the musket men were positioned. 'Come boys,' he shouted, 'we must give chase, else the Peelers will escape us.'

'By Jasus, we've got them on the run all right. Isn't this just the ticket!' Con Shonley's window-mate was ecstatic, and the entire rebel party took up the pursuit, yelling and hallooing in triumphant excitement.

Con ran fast and easily, his musket at the trail, and was soon among the foremost of the pursuers. A large stone farmhouse stood in its own cabbage garden on the hillside, and now Con saw the police column suddenly dissolve into a disordered mob scurrying towards the building, and a tremendous howl went up from the thousands of people chasing them. His red-haired window-mate halted and fired at the police, and Con's anger surged at the man's disobedience of orders.

'Don't waste powder and ball, you fool. You're too far away to hit anything,' he shouted.

Inspector Trant was the last policeman to reach shelter, and his panic was such that he jumped from his horse and left it by the stables at the rear of the house with his brace of pistols still in its saddle-holsters. The police stormed through the rooms with Trant bellowing at them.

'Barricade the windows front and rear, upstairs and down.' His mind was working more efficiently now, his panic calmed by the protection the thick stone walls offered against the fury swarming outside. Using mattresses, tables, chairs, tearing doors from hinges and mantel-shelves from grates, his men quickly blocked the windows. Strongly at the front of the house, less strongly to its rear where the stables offered additional protection. The men heaved and strained, snarling curses when they impeded each other. From the kitchen came the tinkling smash of crockery as the great dresser was manhandled from its wall and slammed against the window.

A constable came thumping down the stairs from the upper storey. 'Mr Trant, Sir, there's five wee children up here. They say their Ma went out earlier on an errand.'

Trant realized immediately that there might be an advantage to be gained from holding these hapless hostages to fortune. 'Then be very kind and gentle to them, man,' he instructed, 'and above all else make sure that they are in a safe place.'

Outside the crowds had swirled and halted in a vast seething circle around the house, and the rebel leaders were trying to extricate their own handful of people from these myriads of onlookers. Terence McManus, mindful of the threatening barrels of police carbines jutting through the barricaded windows, crept cautiously nearer to the house on hands and knees, and circuited it.

Con Shonley was standing by Smith O'Brian, James Stephens and the Dublin Confederate, John Cavanagh, when McManus returned from his reconnaissance.

'We'll need cannon to take that place, its walls are so thick,' he reported.

Smith O'Brian rubbed his long nose between his finger and thumb. 'We must still attack, gentlemen, even though we lack artillery.' His face was pale, and a sheen of nervous sweat oozed from his forehead, but his manner exuded a grim determination.

'Then the only way open to us is to smoke them out,' McManus declared. 'There's a stackyard full of hay bales round by the stables, we can break through the stable walls to get at the rear of the house. James' musket men can cover us, and we'll use the hay to set fire to the place.'

Con, for perhaps the first time since his initial entry into Mullinahone, began to think that perhaps the rebellion might begin to generate a slim chance of success after all. At last the leaders seemed to know exactly what they were about, and be equally determined to carry it through.

Leaving the front of the house to be covered by Cavanagh's pikemen, Stephens and McManus led the twenty musket men and a further twenty men armed with hatchets, pikes and pitchforks to the rear of the buildings. They smashed great holes through the stables' crumbling walls, and the musket men trained their weapons on the weakly barricaded back windows of the house, forcing the few police stationed there to draw back into the rooms' depths.

'Come now, lads, fetch up the hay,' McManus ordered, but no one moved. McManus raised clenched fists and shouted furiously, 'Did you not hear what I said . . . Fetch up the hay!'

The hatchet and pikemen were falling back to hide behind the strong outer garden walls. One man, older than the rest, shuffled his broken shoes upon the dirt in shamed embarrassment, and mumbled, 'We'll be sitting ducks for the Peelers inside there if we try to cross the yard. Ye'll have us getting our heads blown off for nothing gained.' He joined his companions crouched behind the walls.

'Be damned to ye for a pack of cowards!' McManus stormed. 'I'll do it myself.'

Working like a demon he dragged up bale after bale to the stables, and Con Shonley and Phelim Rourke ran out from their cover to help him pile the hay against the rear door of the house. Every second he was so exposed Con expected to feel the slamming impact of carbine bullets tearing through his flesh and bone. But he fought and mastered his fear, and felt proud when McManus praised him and Rourke for their courage.

Once the pile was high, McManus crouched low and went forward with his pistol. He fired into the hay several times in an attempt to ignite it, but no sparks took hold. James Stephens called for lucifer matches, and his small face was a caricature of incredulity when it transpired that not one man among them possessed a single match. Con could not restrain a shout of laughter, the irony of the situation struck him so forcibly. Taking up his musket he ran forward and fired into the hay, and from behind him other shots rang out as men followed his example.

Then thin whirls of smoke started to writhe upwards, and flames licked across the loose-packed bales. At that very moment, as if conjured by magic, an hysterically screaming woman, long hair tumbling about her face and neck erupted into the stables. All eyes turned as Smith O'Brian appeared behind her.

'Quick, put that fire out!' he shouted excitedly. 'This poor woman's children are inside the house there.'

'We've seen nothing of them; and heard nothing either!' McManus protested.

The woman tore at her hair with both hands, and shrieked, 'My children will burn to death, and you'll be their murderers!'

Her frantic howls sent a horrified shiver down Con Shonley's spine, and each man's face reflected a similar reaction to her terrible anguish.

'Put the blaze out, man,' O'Brian reiterated, 'she's the Widow MaCormack, she says the police have agreed to make terms. She was shouting to them at the front before she came to me.'

There was no further hesitation, and Con helped Stephens and McManus to drag the burning hay away from the house, and leave it to flame harmlessly on clear ground.

Con was torn between tears and angry laughter. From its very beginnings the rebellion had resembled a black and bitter farce, and this latest happening plunged him again into despair. It seemed that God Himself was mocking the Young Irelanders . . .

With the musket men, the leaders made their way to the front of the house. O'Brian approached alone to a window and climbing on its sill thrust his hand through the barricade to shake the hands of the policemen behind its shelter. His followers waited tensely some fifteen yards behind, and they could hear the agitated arguing between O'Brian and the Sub-Inspector inside. Then, at the rear of the house, those men still hiding behind the garden walls, who had been afraid to bring up the hay, suddenly decided to launch their own attack. They jumped up and volleyed stones against the back windows, smashing glass and hitting policemen. Carbines instantly roared out their reply from both sides of the building. Next to Con Shonley, his red-haired window-mate spun round on his heels, his gun falling to the ground and his hands clutching his chest. Con went to the man, but already the blood from his shattered rib-cage was soaking through his threadbare clothing, and his eyes rolled upwards in death.

O'Brian stepped back from the window as more carbines spewed out their deadly slugs. McManus lifted his pistol and returned the police fire, and at Phelim Rourke's bellowed command the musket men loosed off an ill-aimed volley. Then McManus went down, and the men near him retreated, one or two crashing to the earth screaming their agonies to the uncaring sky. O'Brian still stood defiantly facing the police guns, refusing to turn away or fall back from the danger he was in. Phelim Rourke shouted to Con, 'Keep your section closed up, and fall back.'

Con was hard-pressed to prevent them from bolting, and he was forced to threaten one or two of them with instant execution if they refused to return fire. The stone-throwers fled in a body, and many of the pike and pitchfork men joined them in their headlong flight.

The vast crowds of spectators eddied backwards creating an ever-widening circle, afraid but held by the dreadful fascination of the violent scenes being enacted before them.

More men fell dying, and within scant minutes the rebels had shot off their ammunition. Con and Phelim Rourke tried desperately to lead their sections forwards to storm the house by hand, but none would follow.

The carbine fire slackened and a priest who had run out from the spectators to tend the wounded and dying, now with waving arms went up to a window of the house and tried to parley. The firing became a scatter of individual shots, then ceased, and to Con's relief he saw that McManus was not seriously wounded, but erect and walking, albeit with a severe limp. He watched Stephens and McManus go to O'Brian's side, the tall O'Brian still standing rooted in the same place, as if inviting death to take him. After some gesticulating argument the two men took O'Brian by his arms and by sheer force dragged him out of range of the carbine fire.

Phelim Rourke rallied the remaining musket men, and some of the pike and pitchfork men, and withdrew them to a sunken, narrow lane where others from the rebel force had already taken shelter.

Here they dressed their wounds and took stock of what weapons they had left to them. After a time a man ran into the lane and shouted breathlessly, 'It's all up with us, boys! There's more Peelers come, foot and horse! Hundreds o' the buggers! And Smith O'Brian has just rode away on a horse someone brought for him . . . We're all that's left. The rest are running like the clappers o' Hell!'

'Be damned to this!' a raw-boned Kerryman shouted, and hurled away his gun as he ran. His example swept through the rest of the men, and they scattered, even the injured hobbling frantically after the others. Within seconds only Phelim Rourke and Con Shonley were left standing amid a scattering of pikes, pitchforks and guns on the sunken track . . .

Phelim Rourke sighed, then gently laid his own musket down upon the ground, and said to Con, 'Come on, boy, we'd best be gone from here, before the Peelers find us keeping company with these tools.'

The young man was sitting on the earth with his head

averted, and Rourke had the delicacy to leave him alone and walk a few yards up the lane.

When Con joined him, the young eyes were reddened as if he had been weeping tears of bitter shame and disappointment.

'Is this it then, Phelim? Is this the end of the rebellion?' His voice trembled faintly.

The old soldier put his arm around the young muscular shoulders. 'Arrah yes, I reckon for sure that this is the end of our glorious rebellion,' he spoke resignedly.

The young man drew in a long shuddering breath, and then asked in a firmer voice, 'Where will you go, Phelim. I've money enough waiting in Cork if you want to come to America.'

Rourke expressed his gratitude, but finished, 'No, boy, many thanks, but no. I've no wish to see America yet, and I've money of my own stowed away with a good woman I know in Dublin. But come now, let's get clear of here.'

Carefully they climbed from the sunken track and studied the area. The vast amorphous masses of men, women and children swirled like a human sea around Widow MaCormack's house and cabbage patch, but mounted and foot police kept them from intruding physically on the widow's property.

Small patrols of police were moving towards the east, from where the occasional distant pop of a carbine shot indicated some fugitive rebel was being chased. Other small groups of police hovered around the crowd, but were merely talking together and moved with a lethargic aimlessness.

'What we'll do, boy, is take a gentle stroll down and join the crowd,' Phelim Rourke said. 'That's the last place in the world anyone will expect to find a pair of bloody rebels. We'll just mingle easy and slow, and then drift away in the heel of the hunt.'

Sick at heart Con allowed himself to be led, and found that it was as easy as Rourke had said. Easy to mingle, and then drift away with the family groups and the sight-seers who had tired of the entertainment. The danger of being stopped and questioned by the police was practically non-existent unless a man actually carried a weapon or wounds of combat on his body. The police numbers were too limited, and the crowds too numerous. The two friends walked sedately southwards, until at a crossroads Phelim Rourke halted and held out one mighty hand.

'This is where we go our separate ways, Con Shonley. May God go with you, my friend, on all your journeys.'

The younger man was forced to swallow hard to dispel the lump in his throat, before he was able to reply, 'And may He walk with you, Phelim . . . Tell me one thing before we part? Were we right to do it? To try and fight back? Or were we just stupid, mad idiots?'

The man's strong brown teeth bared in a grin. 'We were all stupid, mad idiots, my friend, but by God above, we were right to do it! Yes! We were right to try and fight back!' He winked one hard grey eye hugely. 'And we'll do it again someday, you'll see.'

Tears blurred Con's eyes as the tall soldierly figure disappeared from view.

In the young man's mind a vision appeared of an old woman's careworn, seamed face, and Con said aloud, 'I'm leaving you now, Shan Van Voght. There's someone else needs me more than you do.' Another face, young with huge green eyes and framed by lustrous raven-hued hair arose in his vision, and all else disappeared as he turned his footsteps southwards to where Grainne, his love, was waiting for him . . .